George MacDonald (10 December 1824 – 18 September 1905) was a Scottish author, poet and Christian minister. He was a pioneering figure in the field of fantasy literature and the mentor of fellow writer Lewis Carroll. In addition to his fairy tales, MacDonald wrote several works on Christian apologetics. His writings have been cited as a major literary influence by many notable authors including W. H. Auden, J. M. Barrie, Lord Dunsany, Hope Mirrlees, Robert E. Howard, L. Frank Baum, T.H. White, Lloyd Alexander, C. S. Lewis, J. R. R. Tolkien, Walter de la Mare, E. Nesbit, Peter S. Beagle, Neil Gaiman and Madeleine L'Engle. C. S. Lewis wrote that he regarded MacDonald as his "master": "Picking up a copy of Phantastes one day at a train-station bookstall, I began to read. A few hours later", said Lewis, "I knew that I had crossed a great frontier." G. K. Chesterton cited The Princess and the Goblin as a book that had "made a difference to my whole existence". (Source: Wikipedia)

Literary works:
Phantastes: A Fairie Romance for
Men and Women (1858)
"Cross Purposes" (1862)
"The Second Sight" (1864)
Dealings with the Fairies (1867)
At the Back of the North Wind (1871)
Works of Fancy and Imagination (1871)
The Princess and the Goblin (1872)
The Wise Woman: A Parable (1875)
The Gifts of the Child Christ and Other Tales
The Day Boy and the Night Girl (1882)
The Princess and Curdie (1883)

Home Again
&
The Elect Lady

George MacDonald

PRINCE CLASSICS

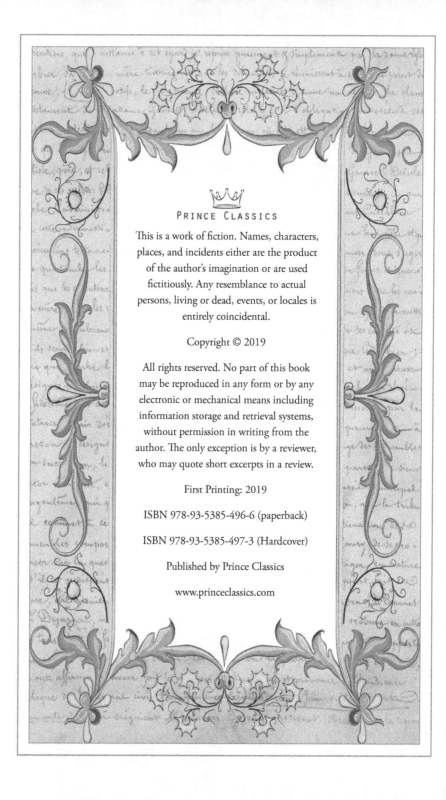

PRINCE CLASSICS

First Printing: 2019

ISBN 978-93-5385-496-6 (paperback)

ISBN 978-93-5385-497-3 (Hardcover)

Published by Prince Classics

www.princeclassics.com

Contents

HOME AGAIN   **11**

CHAPTER I. THE PARLOR.   11

CHAPTER II. THE ARBOR.   15

CHAPTER III. A PENNYWORTH OF THINKING.   18

CHAPTER IV. A LIVING FORCE.   23

CHAPTER V. FLUTTERBIES.   25

CHAPTER VI. FROM HOME.   31

CHAPTER VII. A CHANGE.   35

CHAPTER VIII. AT WORK.   38

CHAPTER IX. FLATTERY.   41

CHAPTER X. THE ROUND OF THE WORLD.   47

CHAPTER XI. THE SONG.   50

CHAPTER XII. LOVE.   54

CHAPTER XIII. "HOME IS WHERE THE HEART IS."   58

CHAPTER XIV. A MIDNIGHT REVIEW.   62

CHAPTER XV. REFLECTION.   66

CHAPTER XVI. THE RIDE TOGETHER.   70

CHAPTER XVII. HIS BOOK.   74

CHAPTER XVIII. A WINTER AFTERNOON.   77

CHAPTER XIX. THE BODILESS.   82

CHAPTER XX. THE SOULLESS.   85

CHAPTER XXI. THE LAST RIDE.   92

CHAPTER XXII. THE SUMMER-HOUSE.   96

CHAPTER XXIII. THE PARK.   102

CHAPTER XXIV. THE DRAWING-ROOM.   104

CHAPTER XXV. A MIDNIGHT INTERVIEW.   110

CHAPTER XXVI. A PERIOD.   117

CHAPTER XXVII. A FRUITLESS JOURNEY.   129

CHAPTER XXVIII. DOING AND DREAMING.   134

CHAPTER XXIX. DREAM-MOLLY.   140

CHAPTER XXX. WORKADAY MOLLY.   145

CHAPTER XXXI. THIS PICTURE AND THIS.   150

CHAPTER XXXII. THE LAST, BUT NOT THE END.   158

THE ELECT LADY   **163**
CHAPTER I. LANDLORD'S DAUGHTER AND TENANT'S SON.   163
CHAPTER II. AN ACCIDENT.   167
CHAPTER III. HELP.   169
CHAPTER IV. THE LAIRD.   172
CHAPTER V. AFTER SUPPER.   175
CHAPTER VI. ABOUT THE LAIRD.   180
CHAPTER VII. THE COUSINS.   184
CHAPTER VIII. GEORGE AND THE LAIRD.   186
CHAPTER IX. IN THE GARDEN.   189
CHAPTER X. ANDREW INGRAM.   193
CHAPTER XI. GEORGE AND ANDREW.   208
CHAPTER XII. THE CRAWFORDS.   217
CHAPTER XIII. DAWTIE.   221
CHAPTER XIV. SANDY AND GEORGE.   226
CHAPTER XV. MOTHER AND DAUGHTER.   229
CHAPTER XVI. ANDREW AND DAWTIE.   233
CHAPTER XVII. DAWTIE AND THE CUP.   240
CHAPTER XVIII. DAWTIE AND THE LAIRD.   247
CHAPTER XIX. ANDREW AND ALEXA.   257
CHAPTER XX. GEORGE AND ANDREW.   261
CHAPTER XXI. WHAT IS IT WORTH?   266
CHAPTER XXII. THE GAMBLER AND THE COLLECTOR.   270
CHAPTER XXIII. ON THE MOOR.   277
CHAPTER XXIV. THE WOOER.   286
CHAPTER XXV. THE HEART OF THE HEART.   292
CHAPTER XXVI. GEORGE CRAWFORD AND DAWTIE.   298
CHAPTER XXVII. THE WATCH.   300
CHAPTER XXVIII. THE WILL.   302
CHAPTER XXIX. THE SANGREAL.   305
CHAPTER XXX. GEORGE AND THE GOLDEN GOBLET.   310
CHAPTER XXXI. THE PROSECUTION.   320
CHAPTER XXXII. A TALK AT POTLURG.   324
CHAPTER XXXIII. A GREAT OFFERING.   328
CHAPTER XXXIV. ANOTHER OFFERING.   331
CHAPTER XXXV. AFTER THE VERDICT.   335
CHAPTER XXXVI. AGAIN THE GOBLET.   340
CHAPTER XXXVII. THE HOUR BEFORE DAWN.   343
About Author   347

Home Again
&
The Elect Lady

HOME AGAIN

CHAPTER I. THE PARLOR.

In the dusk of the old-fashioned best room of a farm-house, in the faint glow of the buried sun through the sods of his July grave, sat two elderly persons, dimly visible, breathing the odor which roses unseen sent through the twilight and open window. One of the two was scarcely conscious of the odor, for she did not believe in roses; she believed mainly in mahogany, linen, and hams; to the other it brought too much sadness to be welcomed, for it seemed, like the sunlight, to issue from the grave of his vanished youth. He was not by nature a sad man; he was only one that had found the past more delightful than the present, and had not left his first loves.

The twilight of his years had crept upon him and was deepening; and he felt his youth slowly withering under their fallen leaves. With more education, and perhaps more receptivity than most farmers, he had married a woman he fervently loved, whose rarely truthful nature, to which she had striven to keep true, had developed the delicate flower of moral and social refinement; and her influence upon him had been of the eternal sort. While many of their neighbors were vying with each other in the effort to dress, and dwell, and live up to their notion of gentility, Richard Colman and his wife had never troubled themselves about fashion, but had sought to please each the taste of the other, and cultivate their own. Perhaps now as he sat thus silent in the dimmits, he was holding closer converse than he knew, or any of us can know, with one who seemed to have vanished from all this side of things, except the heart of her husband. That clung to what people would call her memory; I prefer to call it her.

The rose-scented hush was torn by the strident, cicala-like shrilling of a self-confident, self-satisfied female voice—

"Richard, that son of yours will come to no good! You may take my word for it!"

Mr. Colman made no answer; the dusky, sweet-smelling waves of the silence closed over its laceration.

"I am well aware my opinion is of no value in your eyes, Richard; but that does not absolve me from the duty of stating it: if you allow him to go on as he is doing now, Walter will never eat bread of his own earning!"

"There are many who do, and yet don't come to much!" half thought, but nowise said the father.

"What do you mean to make of him?" persisted Miss Hancock, the half-sister of his wife, the a in whose name Walter said ought to have been an e.

"Whatever he is able to make himself. He must have the main hand in it, whatever it be," answered Mr. Colman.

"It is time twice over he had set about something! You let him go on dawdling and dawdling without even making up his mind whether or not he ought to do anything! Take my word for it, Richard, you'll have him on your hands till the day of your death!"

The father did not reply that he could wish nothing better, that the threat was more than he could hope for. He did not want to provoke his sister-in-law, and he knew there was a shadow of reason in what she said, though even perfect reason could not have sweetened the mode in which she said it. Nothing could make up for the total absence of sympathy in her utterance of any modicum of truth she was capable of uttering. She was a very dusty woman, and never more dusty than when she fought against dust as in a warfare worthy of all a woman's energies—one who, because she had not a spark of Mary in her, imagined herself a Martha. She was true as steel to the interests of those in whose life hers was involved, but only their dusty interests, not those which make man worth God's trouble. She was a vessel of clay in an outhouse of the temple, and took on her the airs—not of gold, for gold has no airs—but the airs of clay imagining itself gold, and all the golden vessels nothing but clay.

"I put it to you, Richard Colman," she went on, "whether good ever came of reading poetry, and falling asleep under hay-stacks! He actually writes poetry!—and we all know what that leads to!"

"Do we?" ventured her brother-in-law. "King David wrote poetry!"

"Richard, don't garble! I will not have you garble! You know what I mean as well as I do myself! And you know as well as I do what comes of writing poetry! That friend of Walter's who borrowed ten pounds of you— did he ever pay you?"

"He did, Ann."

"You didn't tell me!"

"I did not want to disappoint you!" replied Richard, with a sarcasm she did not feel.

"It was worth telling!" she returned.

"I did not think so. Everybody does not stick to a bank-note like a snail to the wall! I returned him the money."

"Returned him the money!"

"Yes."

"Made him a present of ten pounds!"

"Why not?"

"Why then?"

"I had more reasons than one."

"And no call to explain them! It was just like you to throw away your hard earnings upon a fellow that would never earn anything for himself! As if one such wasn't enough to take all you'd got!"

"How could he send back the money if that had been the case! He proved himself what I believed him, ready and willing to work! The money went for a fellow's bread and cheese, and what better money's worth would you have?"

"You may some day want the bread and cheese for yourself!"

"One stomach is as good as another!"

"It never was and never will be any use talking to some people!" concluded sister Ann, in the same tone she began with, for she seldom lost her temper—though no one would have much minded her losing it, it was so little worth keeping. Rarely angry, she was always disagreeable. The good that was in her had no flower, but bore its fruits, in the shape of good food, clean linen, mended socks, and such like, without any blossom of sweet intercourse to make life pleasant.

Aunt Ann would have been quite justified in looking on poetry with contempt had it been what she imagined it. Like many others, she had decided opinions concerning things of which her idea nowise corresponded with the things themselves.

CHAPTER II. THE ARBOR.

While the elders thus conversed in the dusky drawing-room, where the smell of the old roses almost overpowered that of the new, another couple sat in a little homely bower in the garden. It was Walter and his rather distant cousin, Molly Wentworth, who for fifteen years had been as brother and sister. Their fathers had been great friends, and when Molly's died in India, and her mother speedily followed him, Richard Colman took the little orphan, who was at the time with a nurse in England, home to his house, much to the joy of his wife, who had often longed for a daughter to perfect the family idea. The more motherly a woman is, the nearer will the child of another satisfy the necessities of her motherhood. Mrs. Colman could not have said which child she loved best.

Over the still summer garden rested a weight of peace. It was a night to the very mind of the fastidious, twilight-loving bat, flitting about, coming and going, like a thought we can not help. Most of Walter's thoughts came and went thus. He had not yet learned to think; he was hardly more than a medium in which thought came and went. Yet when a thought seemed worth anything, he always gave himself the credit of it!—as if a man were author of his own thoughts any more than of his own existence! A man can but live so with the life given him, that this or that kind of thoughts shall call on him, and to this or that kind he shall not be at home. Walter was only at that early stage of development where a man is in love with what he calls his own thoughts.

Even in the dark of the summer-house one might have seen that he was pale, and might have suspected him handsome. In the daylight his gray eyes might almost seem the source of his paleness. His features were well marked though delicate, and had a notable look of distinction. He was above the middle height, and slenderly built; had a wide forehead, and a small, pale mustache on an otherwise smooth face. His mouth was the least interesting feature; it had great mobility, but when at rest, little shape and no attraction.

For this, however, his smile made considerable amends.

The girl was dark, almost swarthy, with the clear, pure complexion, and fine-grained skin, which more commonly accompany the hue. If at first she gave the impression of delicacy, it soon changed into one of compressed life, of latent power. Through the night, where she now sat, her eyes were too dark to appear; they sank into it, and were as the unseen soul of the dark; while her mouth, rather large and exquisitely shaped, with the curve of a strong bow, seemed as often as she smiled to make a pale window in the blackness. Her hair came rather low down the steep of her forehead, and, with the strength of her chin, made her face look rounder than seemed fitting.

They sat for a time as silent as the night that infolded them. They were not lovers, though they loved each other, perhaps, more than either knew. They were watching to see the moon rise at the head of the valley on one of whose high sloping sides they sat.

The moon kept her tryst, and revealed a loveliness beyond what the day had to show. She looked upon a wide valley, that gleamed with the windings of a river. She brightened the river, and dimmed in the houses and cottages the lights with which the opposite hill sparkled like a celestial map. Lovelily she did her work in the heavens, her poor mirror-work—all she was fit for now, affording fit room, atmosphere, and medium to young imaginations, unable yet to spread their wings in the sunlight, and believe what lies hid in the light of the workaday world. Nor was what she showed the less true for what lay unshown in shrouded antagonism. The vulgar cry for the real would bury in deepest grave every eternal fact. It is the cry, "Not this man, but Barabbas!" The day would reveal a river stained with loathsome refuse, and rich gardens on hill-sides mantled in sooty smoke and evil-smelling vapors, sent up from a valley where men, like gnomes, toiled and caused to toil too eagerly. What would one think of a housekeeper so intent upon saving that she could waste no time on beauty or cleanliness? How many who would storm if they came home to an untidy house, feel no shadow of uneasiness that they have all day been defiling the house of the Father, nor at night lifted hand to cleanse it! Such men regard him as a fool, whose joy a foul river can poison; yet, as soon as they have by pollution gathered and saved their god,

16

they make haste to depart from the spot they have ruined! Oh, for an invasion of indignant ghosts, to drive from the old places the generation that dishonors the ancient Earth! The sun shows all their disfiguring, but the friendly night comes at length to hide her disgrace; and that well hidden, slowly descends the brooding moon to unveil her beauty.

For there was a thriving town full of awful chimneys in the valley, and the clouds that rose from it ascended above the Colmans' farm to the great moor which stretched miles and miles beyond it. In the autumn sun its low forest of heather burned purple; in the pale winter it lay white under snow and frost; but through all the year winds would blow across it the dull smell of the smoke from below. Had such a fume risen to the earthly paradise, Dante would have imagined his purgatory sinking into hell. On all this inferno the night had sunk like a foretaste of cleansing death. The fires lay smoldering like poor, hopeless devils, fain to sleep. The world was merged in a tidal wave from the ocean of hope, and seemed to heave a restful sigh under its cooling renovation.

CHAPTER III. A PENNYWORTH OF THINKING.

"A penny for your thought, Walter!" said the girl, after a long silence, in which the night seemed at length to clasp her too close.

"Your penny, then! I was thinking how wild and sweet the dark wind would be blowing up there among the ringing bells of the heather."

"You shall have the penny. I will pay you with your own coin. I keep all the pennies I win of you. What do you do with those you win of me?"

"Oh, I don't know! I take them because you insist on paying your bets, but—"

"Debts, you mean, Walter! You know I never bet, even in fun! I hate taking things for nothing! I wouldn't do it!"

"Then what are you making me do now?"

"Take a penny for the thought I bought of you for a penny. That's fair trade, not gambling. And your thought to-night is well worth a penny. I felt the very wind on the moor for a moment!"

"I'm afraid I sha'n't get a penny a thought in London!"

"Then you are going to London, Walter?"

"Yes, indeed! What else! What is a man to do here?"

"What is a man to do there?"

"Make his way in the world."

"But, Walter, please let me understand! indeed I don't want to be disagreeable! What do you wish to make your way to?"

"To such a position as—"

Here he stopped unsure.

"You mean to fame, and honor, and riches, don't you, Walter?" ventured Molly.

"No—not riches. Did you ever hear of a poet and riches in the same breath?"

"Oh, yes, I have!—though somehow they don't seem to go together comfortably. If a poet is rich, he ought to show he couldn't help it."

"Suppose he was made a lord, where would he then be without money?"

"If to be a lord one must be rich, he ought never to wish to be a lord. But you do not want to be either lord or millionaire, Walter, do you?"

"I hope I know better!"

"Where does the way you speak of lead then, Walter? To fame?"

"If it did, what would you have to say against it? Even Milton calls it 'That last infirmity of noble mind!'"

"But he calls it an infirmity, and such a bad infirmity, apparently, that it is the hardest of all to get rid of!"

The fact was that Walter wanted to be—thought he was a poet, but was far from certain—feared indeed it might not be so, therefore desired greatly the verdict of men in his favor, if but for his own satisfaction. Fame was precious to him as determining, he thought, his position in the world of letters—his kingdom of heaven. Well read, he had not used his reading practically enough to perceive that the praise of one generation may be the contempt of another, perhaps of the very next, so that the repute of his time could assure him of nothing. He did not know the worthlessness of the opinion that either grants or withholds fame.

He looked through the dark at his cousin, thinking, "What sets her talking of such things? How can a girl understand a man with his career before him!"

She read him through the night and his silence.

"I know what you are thinking, Walter!" she said. "You are thinking

19

women can't think. But I should be ashamed not to have common sense, and I can not see the sense of doing anything for a praise that can help nothing and settle nothing."

"Why then should all men have the desire for it?"

"That they may get rid of it Why have all men vanity? Where would the world be on the way to now, if Jesus Christ had sought the praise of men?"

"But He has it!"

"Not much of it yet, I suspect. He does not care for the praise that comes before obedience!—that's what I have heard your father say."

"I never heard him!"

"I have heard him say it often. What could Jesus care for the praise of one whose object in life was the praise of men!"

Walter had not lived so as to destroy the reverence of his childhood. He believed himself to have high ideals. He felt that a man must be upright, or lose his life. So strongly did he feel it, that he imagined himself therefore upright, incapable of a dishonest or mean thing. He had never done, never could, he thought, do anything unfair. But to what Molly said, he had no answer. What he half thought in his silence, was something like this: that Jesus Christ was not the type of manhood, but a man by himself, who came to do a certain work; that it was both absurd and irreverent to talk as if other men had to do as He did, to think and feel like Him; that He was so high above the world He could not care for its fame, while to mere man its praises must be dear. Nor did Walter make any right distinction between the approbation of understanding men, who know the thing they praise, and the empty voice of the unwise many.

In a word, Walter thought, without knowing he did, that Jesus Christ was not a man.

"I think, Molly," he said, "we had better avoid the danger of irreverence."

For the sake of his poor reverence he would frustrate the mission of the

Son of God; by its wretched mockery justify himself in refusing the judgment of Jesus!

"I know you think kindly of me, Molly," he went on, "and I should be sorry to have you misunderstand me; but surely a man should not require religion to make him honest! I scorn the notion. A man must be just and true because he is a man! Surely a man may keep clear of the thing he loathes! For my own honor," he added, with a curl of his lip, "I shall at least do nothing disgraceful, however I may fall short of the angelic."

"I doubt," murmured Molly, "whether a man is a man until he knows God."

But Walter, if he heard the words, neither heeded nor answered them. He was far from understanding the absurdity of doing right from love of self.

He was no hypocrite. He did turn from what seemed to him degrading. But there were things degrading which he did not see to be such, things on which some men to whom he did not yet look up, would have looked down. Also there was that in his effort to sustain his self-respect which was far from pure: he despised such as had failed; and to despise the human because it has fallen, is to fall from the human. He had done many little things he ought to be, and one day must be, but as yet felt no occasion to be—ashamed of. So long as they did not trouble him they seemed nowhere. Many a youth starts in life like him, possessed with the idea, not exactly formulated, that he is a most precious specimen of pure and honorable humanity. It comes of self-ignorance, and a low ideal taken for a high one. Such are mainly among the well-behaved, and never doubt themselves a prize for any woman. They color their notion of themselves with their ideal, and then mistake the one for the other. The mass of weaknesses and conceits that compose their being they compress into their ideal mold of man, and then regard the shape as their own. What composes it they do not heed.

No man, however, could look in the refined face of Walter Colman and imagine him cherishing sordid views of life. Asked what of all things he most admired, he might truly answer, "The imaginative intellect." He was a fledgling poet. He worshiped what he called thoughts, would rave about

21

a thought in the abstract, apostrophize an uncaught idea. When a concrete thinkable one fell to him, he was jubilant over the isolate thing, and with his joy value had nothing to do. He would stand wrapped in the delight of what he counted its beauty, and yet more in the delight that his was the mind that had generated such a meteor! To be able to think pretty things was to him a gigantic distinction! A thought that could never be soul to any action, would be more valuable to him than the perception of some vitality of relation demanding the activity of the whole being. He would call thoughts the stars that glorify the firmament of humanity, but the stars of his firmament were merely atmospheric—pretty fancies, external likenesses. That the grandest thing in the world is to be an accepted poet, is the despotic craze of a vast number of the weak-minded and half-made of both sexes. It feeds poetic fountains of plentiful yield, but insipid and enfeebling flow, the mere sweat of weakness under the stimulus of self-admiration.

CHAPTER IV. A LIVING FORCE.

Walter was the very antipode of the Molly he counted commonplace, one outside the region of poetry; she had a passion for turning a think into a thing. She had a strong instinctive feeling that she was in the world to do something, and she saw that if nobody tried to keep things right, they would go terribly wrong: what then could she be there for but to set or keep things right! and if she could do nothing with the big things, she must be the busier with the little things! Besides, who could tell how much the little might have to do with the big things! The whole machine depended on every tiny wheel! She could not order the clouds, but she could keep some weeds from growing, and then when the rain came, they would not take away the good of it!

The world might be divided into those who let things go, and those who do not; into the forces and facts, the slaves and fancies; those who are always doing something on God's creative lines, and those that are always grumbling and striving against them.

"Another penny for your thought, Walter!" said Molly.

"I am not going to deal with you. This time you would not think it worth a penny! Why are you so inquisitive about my thoughts?"

"I want to know what you meant when you said the other day that thoughts were better than things."

Walter hesitated. The question was an inclined plane leading to unknown depths of argument!

"See, Walter," said Molly, "here is a narcissus—a pheasant's eye: tell me the thought that is better than this thing!"

How troublesome girls were when they asked questions!

"Well," he said, not very logically, "that narcissus has nothing but air around it; my thought of the narcissus has mind around it."

"Then a thought is better than a thing because it has thought round about it?"

"Well, yes."

"Did the thing come there of itself, or did it come of God's thinking?"

"Of God's thinking."

"And God is always the same?"

"Yes."

"Then God's thought is about the narcissus still—and the narcissus is better than your thought of it!"

Walter was silent.

"I should so like to understand!" said Molly. "If you have a thought more beautiful than the narcissus, Walter, I should like to see it! Only if I could see it, it would be a thing, would it not? A thing must be a think before it be a thing. A thing is a ripe think, and must be better than a think—except it lose something in ripening—which may very well be with man's thoughts, but hardly with God's! I will keep in front of the things, and look through them to the thoughts behind them. I want to understand! If a thing were not a thought first, it would not be worth anything! And everything has to be thought about, else we don't see what it is! I haven't got it quite!"

Instead of replying, Walter rose, and they walked to the house side by side in silence.

"Could a thought be worth anything that God had never cared to think?" said Molly to herself as they went.

CHAPTER V. FLUTTERBIES.

Mr. Colman and his adopted daughter were fast friends—so fast and so near that they could talk together about Walter, though but the adoptive brother of the one, and the real son of the other. Richard had inherited, apparently, his wife's love to Molly, and added to it his own; but their union had its root in the perfect truthfulness of the two. Real approximation, real union must ever be in proportion to mutual truthfulness. It was quite after the usual fashion, therefore, between them, when Molly began, to tell her father about the conversation she had had with Walter.

"What first made you think, Molly, of such a difference between thoughts and things?" asked Mr. Colman.

"I know quite well," answered Molly. "You remember our visit to your old school-friend, Mr. Dobson?"

"Of course; perfectly."

Mr. Dobson was a worthy clergyman, doing his weary best in a rural parish.

"And you remember Mrs. Evermore?"

"Yes."

"You thought her name a funny one; but you said it ought to have been 'Nevermore," because she seemed never to get any further!"

"Come, come, Molly! that won't do! It was you, not I, that said such a spiteful thing!" "It was true any way!" answered Molly; "and you agreed with me; so if I said it first, you said it last! Well, I had to study this Mrs. Evermore. From morning to night she was evermore on the hunt after new fancies. She watched for them, stalked them, followed them like a boy with a butterfly-net She caught them too, of the sort she wanted, plentifully. But none ever came to anything, so far as I could see. She never did anything with one of them. Whatever she caught had a cage to itself, where it sat on 'the all-alone-stone.' Every other moment, while you and Mr. Dobson were talking, she would cry 'oh! oh! o—o—oh!' and pull out her note-book, which was the cork-box in which she pinned her butterflies. She must have had a whole museum of ideas! The most accidental resemblance between words would suffice to start one: after it she would go, catch it, pin it down, and call it a correspondence. Now and then a very pretty notion would fall to her net, and often a silly one; but all were equally game to her. I found her amusing and interesting for two days, but then began to see she only led nothing nowhere. She was touchy, and jealous, and said things that disgusted me; never did anything for anybody; and though she hunted religious ideas most, never seemed to imagine they could have anything to do with her life. It was only the fineness of a good thought even that she seemed to prize. She would startle you any moment by an exclamation of delight at some religious fancy or sentimentality, and down it most go in her book, but it went no further than her book: she was just as common as before, vulgar even, in her judgments of motives and actions. She seemed made for a refined and delicate woman, but not to take the trouble to be what she was made for. You told me, you know, that God makes us, but we have to be. She talked about afflictions as one might of manure: by these afflictions, of which she would complain bitterly, she was being fashioned for life eternal! It was all the most dreary, noisome rubbish I had ever come across. I used to lie awake thinking what could ever rouse such a woman to see that she had to do something; that man nor woman can become anything without having a hand in the matter. She seemed to expect the spirit of God to work in her like yeast in flour, although there was not a sign of the dough rising. That is how I came to see that one may have any number of fine thoughts and fancies and be nothing the better, any more than the poor woman in the gospel with her doctors! And when Walter, the next time he came home, talked as he did about thoughts, and quoted Keats to the same effect, as if the finest thing in the universe were a fine thought, I could not bear it, and that made me speak to him as I did."

"You have made it very clear, Molly; and I quite agree with you: thinks are of no use except they be turned into things."

"But perhaps, after all, I may have been unfair to her!" said Molly.

"People are so queer! They seem sometimes to be altogether made up of odd bits of different people. There's Aunt Ann now! she would not do a tradesman out of a ha'penny, but she will cheat at backgammon!"

"I know she will, and that is why I never play with her. It is so seldom she will give herself any recreation, that it makes me sorry to refuse her."

"There is one thing that troubles me," said Molly, after a little pause.

"What is it, my child? I always like to hear something troubles you, for then I know you are going to have something. To miss is the preparation for receiving."

"I can't care—much—about poetry—and Walter says such fine things about it! Walter is no fool!"

"Far from one, I am glad to think!" said Richard, laughing. Molly's straightforward, humble confidence, he found as delightful as amusing.

"It seems to me so silly to scoff at things because you can't go in for them! I sometimes hear people make insulting remarks about music, and music I know to be a good and precious and lovely thing. Then I think with myself, they must be in the same condition with regard to music, that I am in with regard to poetry. So I take care not to be a fool in talking about what I don't know. That I am stupid is no reason for being a fool. Any one whom God has made stupid, has a right to be stupid, but no right to call others fool because they are not stupid."

"I thought you liked poetry, Molly!"

"So I do when you read it, or talk about it. It seems as if you made your way of it grow my way of it. I hear the poetry and feel your feeling of it. But when I try to read it myself, then I don't care for it. Sometimes I turn it into prose, and then I get a hold of it."

"That is about the best and hardest test you could put it to, Molly! But perhaps you have been trying to like what ought not, because it does not deserve to be liked. There is much in the shape of poetry that set in gold and diamonds would be worth nothing."

"I think the difficulty is in myself. Sometimes I am in the fit mood, and other times not. A single line will now and then set something churning, churning in me, so that I can not understand myself. It will make me think of music, and sunrise, and the wind, and the song of the lark, and all lovely things. But sometimes prose will serve me the same. And the next minute, perhaps, either of them will be boring me more than I can bear! I know it is my own fault, but—"

"Stop there, Molly! It may sometimes be your own fault, but certainly not always! You are fastidious, little one; and in exquisite things how can one be too fastidious! When Walter is gone, suppose we read a little more poetry together?"

Richard Colman had made some money in one of the good farming times, but of late had not been increasing his store. But he was a man too genuinely practical to set his mind upon making money.

There are parents who, notwithstanding they have found possession powerless for their own peace, not the less heap up for the sons coming after, in the weak but unquestioned fancy that possession will do for them what it could not do for their fathers and mothers. Richard was above such stupidity. He had early come to see that the best thing money could do for his son, was to help in preparing him for some work fit to employ what faculty had been given him, in accordance with the tastes also given him. He saw, the last thing a foolish father will see, that the best a father can do, is to enable his son to earn his livelihood in the exercise of a genial and righteous labor. He saw that possession generates artificial and enfeebling wants, overlaying and smothering the God-given necessities of our nature, whence alone issue golden hopes and manly endeavors.

He had therefore been in no haste to draw from his son a declaration of choice as to profession. When every man shall feel in himself a call to this or that, and scarce needs make a choice, the generations will be well served; but that is not yet, and what Walter was fit for was not yet quite manifest. It was only clear to the father that his son must labor for others with a labor, if possible, whose reflex action should be life to himself. Agriculture seemed inadequate to the full employment of the gifts which, whether from paternal partiality or genuine insight, he believed his son to possess; neither had Walter shown inclination or aptitude for any department of it. All Richard could do, therefore, was to give him such preparation as would be fundamentally available for any superstructure: he might, he hoped, turn to medicine or the law. Partly for financial reasons, he sent him to Edinburgh.

There Walter neither distinguished nor disgraced himself, and developed no inclination to one more than another of the careers open to a young man of education. He read a good deal, however, and showed taste in literature—was indeed regarded by his companions as an authority in its more imaginative ranges, and specially in matters belonging to verse, having an exceptionally fine ear for its vocal delicacies. This is one of the rarest of gifts; but rarity does not determine value, and Walter greatly overestimated its relative importance. The consciousness of its presence had far more than a reasonable share in turning his thoughts to literature as a profession.

When his bent became apparent, it troubled his father a little. He knew that to gain the level of excellence at which labor in that calling insured the merest livelihood, required in most cases a severe struggle; and for such effort he doubted his son's capacity, perceiving in him none of the stoic strength that comes of a high ideal, and can encounter disappointment, even privation, without injury. Other and deeper dangers the good parent did not see. He comforted himself that, even if things went no better than now, he could at least give his son a fair chance of discovering whether the career would suit him, until he should attain the material end of it. Long before Miss Hancock's attack upon his supposed indifference to his son's idleness, he had made up his mind to let him try how far he could go in the way to which he was drawn; and the next day told his son, to his unspeakable delight, that he was ready to do what lay in his power to further his desire; that his own earthly life was precious to him only for the sake of the children he must by and by leave; and that when he saw him busy, contented, and useful, he would gladly yield his hold upon it.

Walter's imagination took fire at the prospect of realizing all he had longed for but feared to subject to paternal scrutiny, and he was at once eager to go out into the great unhomely world, in the hope of being soon regarded by his peers as the possessor of certain gifts and faculties which had not yet handed in their vouchers to himself. For, as the conscience of many a man seems never to trouble him until the look of his neighbors bring their consciences to bear upon his, so the mind of many a man seems never to satisfy him that he has a gift until other men grant his possession of it. Around Walter, nevertheless, the world broke at once into rare bloom. He became like a windy day in the house, vexing his aunt with his loud, foolish gladness, and causing the wise heart of Molly many a sudden, chilly foreboding. She knew him better than his father knew him. His father had not played whole days with him, and day after day! She knew that happiness made him feel strong for anything, but that his happiness was easily dashed, and he was then a rain-wet, wind-beaten butterfly. He had no soul for bad weather. He could not therefore be kept in wadding, however! He must have his trial; must, in one way or another, encounter life, and disclose what amount of the real might be in him—what little, but enlargeable claim he might have to manhood!

CHAPTER VI. FROM HOME.

Every morning, a man may say,

Calls him up with a new birth-day;

Every day is a little life,

Sunny with love, stormy with strife;

Every life is a little death,

From which too soon he awakeneth—

—as Walter himself wrote, not then knowing half that the words meant. As with the skirt of her mantle the dark wipes out the day, so with her sleep the night makes a man fresh for the new day's journey. If it were not for sleep, the world could not go on. To feel the mystery of day and night, to gaze into the far receding spaces of their marvel, is more than to know all the combinations of chemistry. A little wonder is worth tons of knowledge. But to Walter the new day did not come as a call to new life in the world of will and action, but only as the harbinger of a bliss borne hitherward on the wind of the world. Was he not going forth as a Titanic child to become a great man among great men! Who would be strong among the weak! who would be great among the small! He did not suspect in himself what Molly saw, or at least suspected in him. When a man is hopeful, he feels strong, and can work. The thoughts come and the pen runs. Were he always at his best, what might not a man do! But not many can determine their moods; and none, be they poets or economists, can any more secure the conditions of faculty than they can create the faculty. When the mood changes and hope departs, and the inward atmosphere is grown damp and dismal, there may be whose imagination will yet respond to their call; but let some certain kind of illness come, and every one must lose his power; his creature-condition will assert itself; he is compelled to discover that we did not create ourselves, neither live by ourselves.

Walter loved his father, but did not mind leaving him; he loved Molly, but did not mind leaving her; and we can not blame him if he was glad to escape from his aunt. If people are not lovable, it takes a saint to love them, or at least one who is not afraid of them. Yet it was with a sense of somewhat dreary though welcome liberty, that Walter found himself, but for the young man his father had befriended, alone in London. With his help he found an humble lodging not far from the British Museum, to the neighborhood of which his love of books led him; and for a time, feeling no necessity for immediate effort, he gave himself to the study of certain departments of our literature not hitherto within his easy reach. In the evening he would write, or accompany his new friend to some lecture or amusement; and so the weeks passed. To earn something seemed but a slowly approaching necessity, and the weeks grew to months. He was never idle, for his tastes were strong, and he had delight in his pen; but so sensitive was his social skin, partly from the licking of his aunt's dry, feline tongue, that he shrunk from submitting anything he wrote to Harold Sullivan, who, a man of firmer and more world-capable stuff than he, would at least have shown him how things which the author saw and judged from the inner side of the web, must appear on the other side. There are few weavers of thought capable of turning round the web and contemplating with unprejudiced regard the side of it about to be offered to the world, so as to perceive how it will look to eyes alien to its genesis.

It would be to repeat a story often told, to relate how he sent poem after poem, now to this now to that periodical, with the same result—that he never heard of them again. The verses over which he had labored with delight, in the crimson glory they reflected on the heart whence they issued, were nothing in any eyes to which he submitted them. In truth, except for a good line here and there, they were by no means on the outer side what they looked to him on the inner. He read them in the light of the feeling in which he had written them; whoever else read them had not this light to interpret them by, had no correspondent mood ready to receive them. It was the business of the verse itself, by witchery of sound and magic of phrase, to rouse receptive mood: of this it was incapable. A course of reading in the first attempts of such as rose after to well-merited distinction, might reveal not a few things—among the rest, their frequent poverty. Much mere babbling often issues before worthy speech begins. There was nothing in Walter's mind to be put in form except a few of the vague lovely sensations belonging to a poetic temperament. And as he grew more and more of a reader, his inspiration came more and more from what he read, less and less from knowledge of his own heart or the hearts of others. He had no revelation to give. He had, like most of our preachers, set out to run before he could walk, begun to cry aloud before he had any truth to utter; to teach, or at least to interest others, before he was himself interested in others. Now and then, indeed, especially when some fading joy of childhood gleamed up, words would come unbidden, and he would throw off a song destitute neither of feeling nor music; but this kind of thing he scarcely valued, for it seemed to cost him nothing.

He comforted himself by concluding that his work was of a kind too original to be at once recognized by dulled and sated editors; that he must labor on and keep sending.

"Why do you not write something?" his friend would say; and he would answer that his time was not come.

The friends he made were not many. Instinctively he shrunk from what was coarse, feeling it destructive to every finer element. How could he write of beauty, if, false to beauty, he had but for a moment turned to the unclean? But he was not satisfied with himself: he had done nothing, even in his own eyes, while the recognition of the world was lacking!

He was in no anxiety, for he did not imagine it of consequence to his father whether he began a little sooner or a little later to earn. The governor knew, he said to himself, that to earn ought not to be a man's first object in life, even when necessity compelled him to make it first in order of time, which was not the case with him! But he did not ask himself whether he had substituted a better object. A greater man than himself, he reflected—no less a man, indeed, than Milton—had never earned a dinner till after he was thirty years of age! He did not consider how and to what ends Milton had all the time been diligent. He was no student yet of men's lives; he was interested almost only in their imaginations, and not half fastidious enough as to whether those imaginations ran upon the rails of truth or not. He was rapidly filling his mind with the good and bad of the literature of his country, but he had not yet gone far in distinguishing between the bad and the good in it. Books were to him the geological deposits of the literary forces. He pursued his acquaintance with them to nourish the literary faculty in himself. They afforded him atmosphere and stimulant and store of matter. He was in full training for the profession that cultivates literature for and upon literature, and neither for nor upon truth.

CHAPTER VII. A CHANGE.

A big stone fell suddenly into the smooth pool of Walter's conditions. A letter from his father brought the news that the bank where he had deposited his savings had proved but a swollen mushroom. He had lost all.

"Indeed, my son," wrote the sorrowful Richard, "I do not see how with honesty to send you a shilling more! If you have exhausted the proceeds of my last check, and can not earn a sufficiency, come home. Thank God, the land yet remains!—so long as I can pay the rent."

In the heart of Walter woke a new impulse. He drew himself up for combat and endurance. I am afraid he did not feel much trouble for his father's trouble, but he would have scorned adding to it. He wrote at once that he must not think of him in the affair; he would do very well. It was not a comforting letter exactly, but it showed courage, and his father was glad.

He set himself to find employment in some one of the mechanical departments of literature—the only region in which he could think to do anything. When the architect comes to necessity, it is well if stones are near, and the mason's hammer: if he be not the better mason that he is an architect, alas for his architecture! Walter was nothing yet, however, neither architect nor mason, when the stern hand of necessity laid hold of him. But it is a fine thing for any man to be compelled to work. It is the first divine decree, issuing from love and help. How would it have been with Adam and Eve had they been left to plenty and idleness, the voice of God no more heard in the cool of the day?

But the search for work was a difficult and disheartening task. He who has encountered it, however, has had an experience whose value far more than equals its unpleasantness. A man out of work needs the God that cares for the sparrows, as much as the man whose heart is torn with ingratitude, or crushed under a secret crime. Walter went hither and thither, communicated his quest to each of his few acquaintances, procured introductions, and even without any applied to some who might have employment to bestow, putting so much pride in his pockets that, had it been a solid, they must have bulged in unsightly fashion, and walked till worn with weariness, giving good proof that he was no fool, but had the right stuff in him. He neither yielded to false fastidiousness, nor relaxed effort because of disappointment—not even when disappointment became the very atmosphere of his consciousness. To the father it would have been the worst of his loss to see his son wiping the sweat and dust from the forehead his mother had been so motherly proud of, and hear the heavy sigh with which he would sink in the not too easy chair that was all his haven after the tossing of the day's weary groundswell. He did not rise quite above self-pity; he thought he was hardly dealt with; but so long as he did not respond to the foolish and weakening sentiment by relaxation of effort, it could not do him much harm; he would soon grow out of it, and learn to despise it. What one man has borne, why should not another bear? Why should it be unfit for him any more than the other? Certainly he who has never borne has yet to bear. The new experience is awaiting every member of the Dives clan. Walter wore out his shoes, and could not buy another pair; his clothes grew shabby, and he must wear them: it was no small part of his suffering, to have to show himself in a guise which made him so unlike the Walter he felt. But he did not let his father know even a small part of what he confronted.

He had never drawn close to his father; they had come to no spiritual contact. Walter, the gentleman, saw in Richard the farmer. He knew him an honorable man, and in a way honored him; but he would have been dissatisfied with him in such society to which he considered himself belonging. It is a sore thing for a father, when he has shoved his son up a craggy steep, to see him walk away without looking behind. Walter felt a difference between them.

He had to give up his lodgings. Sullivan took him into his, and shared his bed with him—doing all he could in return for his father's kindness.

Where now was Walter's poetry? Naturally, vanished. He was man enough to work, but not man enough to continue a poet. His poetry!—how could such a jade stand the spur!

But to bestir himself was better than to make verses; and indeed of all the labors for a livelihood in which a man may cultivate verse, that of literature is the last he should choose. Compare the literary efforts of Burns with the songs he wrote when home from his plow!

Walter's hope had begun to faint outright, when Sullivan came in one evening as he lay on the floor, and told him that the editor of a new periodical, whom he had met at a friend's house, would make a place for him. The remuneration could suffice only to a grinding economy, but it was bread!—more, it was work, and an opening to possibilities! Walter felt himself equal to any endurance short of incapacitating hunger, and gladly accepted the offer. His duty was the merest agglomeration; but even in that he might show faculty, and who could tell what might follow! It was wearisome but not arduous, and above all, it left him time!

CHAPTER VIII. AT WORK.

Walter found that compulsory employment, while taking from, his time for genial labor, quickened his desire after it, increased his faculty for it, and made him more careful of his precious hours of leisure. Life, too, had now an interest greater than before; and almost as soon as anxiety gave place, the impulse to utterance began again to urge him. What this impulse is, who can define, or who can trace its origin? The result of it in Walter's case was ordered words, or, conventionally, poetry. Seldom is such a result of any value, but the process is for the man invaluable: it remained to be seen whether in Walter it was for others as well as himself.

He became rapidly capable of better work. His duty was drudgery, but drudgery well encountered will reveal itself as of potent and precious reaction, both intellectual and moral. One incapable of drudgery can not be capable of the finest work. Many a man may do many things well, and be far from reception into the most ancient guild of workers.

Walter labored with conscience and diligence, and brought his good taste to tell on the quality of his drudgery. He is a contemptible workman who thinks of his claims before his duties, of his poor wages instead of his undertaken work. There was a strong sense of fairness in Walter; he saw the meanness of pocketing the poorest without giving good work in return; he saw that its own badness, and nothing else, makes any work mean—and the workman with it. That he believed himself capable of higher work was the worst of reasons for not giving money's worth for his money. That a thing is of little value is a poor excuse for giving bad measure of it. Walter carried his hod full, and was a man.

Sullivan was mainly employed in writing the reviews of "current literature." One evening he brought Walter a book of some pretension, told him he was hard pressed, and begged him to write a notice of it. Walter, glad of the opportunity of both serving his friend and trying his own hand, set himself at once to read the book. The moment he thus took the attitude of a reviewer, he found the paragraphs begin, like potatoes, to sprout, and generate other paragraphs. Between agreeing and disagreeing he had soon far more than enough to say, and sought his table, as a workman his bench.

To many people who think, writing is the greatest of bores; but Walter enjoyed it, even to the mechanical part of the operation. Heedless of the length of his article, he wrote until long after midnight, and next morning handed the result to his friend. He burst out laughing.

"Here's a paper for a quarterly!" he cried. "Man, it is almost as long as the book itself! This will never do! The world has neither time, space, money, nor brains for so much! But I will take it, and see what can be done with it."

About a sixth part of it was printed. In that sixth Walter could not recognize his hand; neither could he have gathered from it any idea of the book.

A few days after, Harold brought him a batch of books to review, taking care, however, to limit him to an average length for each. Walter entered thus upon a short apprenticeship, the end of which was that, a vacancy happening to occur, he was placed on "the staff" of the journal, to aid in reviewing the books sent by their publishers. His income was considerably augmented, but the work was harder, and required more of his time.

From the first he was troubled to find how much more honesty demanded than pay made possible. He had not learned this while merely supplementing the labor of his friend, and taking his time. But now he became aware that to make acquaintance with a book, and pass upon it a justifiable judgment, required at least four times the attention he could afford it and live. Many, however, he could knock off without compunction, regarding them as too slight to deserve attention: "indifferent honest," he was not so sensitive in justice as to reflect that the poorest thing has a right to fair play; that, free to say nothing, you must, if you speak, say the truth of the meanest. But Walter had not yet sunk to believe there can be necessity for doing wrong. The world is divided, very unequally, into those that think a man can not avoid, and those who believe he must avoid doing wrong. Those live in fear of death; these set death in one eye and right in the other.

His first important review, Walter was compelled to print without having finished it. The next he worked at hardest, and finished, but with less deliberation. He grew more and more careless toward the books he counted of little consequence, while he imagined himself growing more and more capable of getting at the heart of a book by skimming its pages. If to skim be ever a true faculty, it must come of long experience in the art of reading, and is not possible to a beginner. To skim and judge, is to wake from a doze and give the charge to a jury.

Writing more and more smartly, he found the usual difficulty in abstaining from a smartness which was unjust because irrelevant.

So far as his employers were concerned, Walter did his duty, but forgot that, apart from his obligation to the mere and paramount truth, it was from the books he reviewed—good, bad, or indifferent, whichever they were—that he drew the food he eat and the clothes that covered him.

His talent was increasingly recognized by the editors of the newspaper, and they began to put other, and what they counted more important work in his way, intrusting him with the discussion of certain social questions of the day, in regard to which, like many another youth of small experience, he found it the easier to give a confident opinion that his experience was so small. In general he wrote logically, and, which is rarer, was even capable of being made to see where his logic was wrong. But his premises were much too scanty. What he took for granted was very often by no means granted. It mattered, little to editors or owners, however, so long as he wrote lucidly, sparklingly, "crisply," leaving those who read, willing to read more from the same pen.

CHAPTER IX. FLATTERY.

Within a year Walter began to be known—to the profession, at least—as a promising writer; and was already, to more than a few, personally known as a very agreeable, gentlemanly fellow, so that in the following season he had a good many invitations. It was by nothing beyond the ephemeral that he was known; but may not the man who has invented a good umbrella one day build a good palace? His acquaintance was considerably varied, but of the social terraces above the professional, he knew for a time nothing.

One evening, however, he happened to meet, and was presented to Lady Tremaine: she had asked to have the refined-looking young man, of whom she had just heard as one of the principal writers in the "Field Battery," introduced to her. She was a matronly, handsome woman, with cordial manners and a cold eye; frank, easy, confident, unassuming. Under the shield of her position, she would walk straight up to any subject, and speak her mind of it plainly. It was more than easy to become acquainted with her when she chose.

The company was not a large one, and they soon found themselves alone in a quiet corner.

"You are a celebrated literary man, Mr. Colman, they tell me!" said Lady Tremaine.

"Not in the least," answered Walter. "I am but a poor hack."

"It is well to be modest; but I am not bound to take your description of yourself. Your class at least is in a fair way to take the lead!"

"In what, pray?"

"In politics, in society, in everything."

"You ladyship can not think it desirable."

"I do not pretend to desire it. I am not false to my own people. But the fact remains that you are coming to the front, and we are falling behind. And the sooner you get to the front, the better it will be for the world, and for us too."

"I can not say I understand you."

"I will tell you why. There are now no fewer than three aristocracies. There is one of rank, and one of brains. I belong to the one, you to the other. But there is a third."

"If you recognize the rich as an aristocracy, you must allow me to differ from you—very much!"

"Naturally. I quite agree with you. But what can your opinion and mine avail against the rising popular tide! All the old families are melting away, swallowed by the nouveaux riches. I should not mind, or at least I should feel it in me to submit with a good grace, if we were pushed from our stools by a new aristocracy of literature and science, but I do rebel against the social régime which is every day more strongly asserting itself. All the gradations are fast disappearing; the palisades of good manners, dignity, and respect, are vanishing with the hedges; the country is positively inundated with slang and vulgarity—all from the ill-breeding, presumption, and self-satisfaction of new people."

Walter felt tempted to ask whether it was not the fault of the existent aristocracy in receiving and flattering them; whether it could not protect society if it would; whether in truth the aristocracy did not love, even honor money as much as they; but he was silent.

As if she read his thought, Lady Tremaine resumed:

"The plague of it is that younger sons must live! Money they must have!—and there's the gate off the hinges! The best, and indeed the only thing to help is, that the two other aristocracies make common cause to keep the rich in their proper place."

It was not a very subtle flattery, but Walter was pleased. The lady saw she had so far gained her end, for she had an end in view, and changed the subject.

"You go out of an evening, I see!" she said at length. "I am glad. Some authors will not."

"I do when I can. The evening, however, to one who—who—"

"—Has an eye on posterity! Of course! It is gold and diamonds! How silly all our pursuits must appear in your eyes! But I hope you will make an exception in my favor!"

"I shall be most happy," responded Walter, cordially.

"I will not ask you to come and be absorbed in a crowd—not the first time at least! Gould you not manage to come and see me in the morning?"

"I am at your ladyship's service," replied Walter.

"Then come—let me see!—the day after to-morrow—about five o'clock. 17, Goodrich Square."

Walter could not but be flattered that Lady Tremaine was so evidently pleased with him. She called his profession an aristocracy too! therefore she was not patronizing him, but receiving him on the same social level! We can not blame him for the inexperience which allowed him to hold his head a little higher as he walked home.

There was little danger of his forgetting the appointment. Lady Tremaine received him in what she called her growlery, with cordiality. By and by she led the way toward literature, and after they had talked of several new books—

"We are not in this house altogether strange," she said, "to your profession. My daughter Lufa is an authoress in her way. You, of course, never heard of her, but it is twelve months since her volume of verse came out."

Surely Walter had, somewhere about that time, when helping his friend Sullivan, seen a small ornate volume of verses, with a strange name like that on the title-page! Whether he had written a notice of it he could not remember.

"It was exceedingly well received—for a first, of course! Lufa hardly thought so herself, but I told her what could she expect, altogether unknown as she was. Tell me honestly, Mr. Colman, is there not quite as much jealousy in your profession as in any other?"

Walter allowed it was not immaculate in respect of envy and evil speaking.

"You have so much opportunity for revenge, you see!" said Lady Tremaine; "and such a coat of darkness for protection! With a few strokes of the pen a man may ruin his rival!"

"Scarcely that!" returned Walter. "If a book be a good book, the worst of us can not do it much harm; nor do I believe there are more than a few in the profession who would condescend to give a false opinion upon the work of a rival; though doubtless personal feeling may pervert the judgment."

"That, of course," returned the lady, "is but human! You can not deny, however, that authors occasionally make furious assaults on each other!"

"Authors ought not to be reviewers," replied Walter. "I fancy most reviewers avoid the work of an acquaintance even, not to say a friend or enemy."

The door opened, and what seemed to Walter as lovely a face as could ever have dawned on the world, peeped in, and would have withdrawn.

"Lufa," said Lady Tremaine, "you need not go away. Mr. Colman and I have no secrets. Come and be introduced to him."

She entered—a small, pale creature, below the middle height, with the daintiest figure, and child-like eyes of dark blue, very clear, and—must I say it?—for the occasion "worn" wide. Her hair was brown, on the side of black, divided in the middle, and gathered behind in a great mass. Her dress was something white, with a shimmer of red about it, and a blush-rose in the front. She greeted Walter in the simplest, friendliest way, holding out her tiny hand very frankly. Her features were no smaller than for her size they ought to be, in themselves perfect, \Walter thought, and in harmony with her whole being and carriage. Her manner was a gentle, unassuming assurance—almost as if they knew each other, but had not met for some time. Walter felt some ancient primeval bond between them—dim, but indubitable.

The mother withdrew to her writing-table, and began to write, now and then throwing in a word as they talked. Lady Lufa seemed pleased with her new acquaintance; Walter was bewitched. Bewitchment I take to be the approach of the real to our ideal. Perhaps upon that, however, depends even the comforting or the restful. In the heart of every one lies the necessity for homeliest intercourse with the perfectly lovely; we are made for it. Yet so far are we in ourselves from the ideal, which no man can come near until absolutely devoted to its quest, that we continually take that for sufficing which is a little beyond.

"I think, Mr. Colman, I have seen something of yours! You do put your name to what you write?" said Lady Lufa.

"Not always," replied Walter.

"I think the song must have been yours!"

Walter had, just then, for the first time published a thing of his own. That it should have arrested the eye of this lovely creature! He acknowledged that he had printed a trifle in "The Observatory."

"I was charmed with it!" said the girl, the word charmingly drawled.

"The merest trifle!" remarked Walter. "It cost me nothing."

He meant what he said, unwilling to be judged by such a slight thing.

"That is the beauty of it!" she answered. "Your song left your soul as the thrush's leaves his throat. Should we prize the thrush's more if we came upon him practicing it?"

Walter laughed.

"But we are not meant to sing like the birds!"

"That you could write such a song without effort, shows you to possess the bird-gift of spontaneity."

Walter was surprised at her talk, and willing to believe it profound.

"The will and the deed in one may be the highest art!" he said. "I hardly

45

know."

"May I write music to it?" asked Lady Lufa, with upward glance, sweet smile, and gently apologetic look.

"I am delighted you should think of doing so. It is more than it deserves!" answered Walter. "My only condition is, that you will let me hear it."

"That you have a right to. Besides, I dared not publish it without knowing you liked it."

"Thank you so much! To hear you sing it will let me know at once whether the song itself be genuine."

"No, no! I may fail in my part, and yours be all I take it to be. But I shall not fail. It holds me too fast for that!"

"Then I may hope for a summons?" said Walter, rising.

"Before long. One can not order the mood, you know!"

CHAPTER X. THE ROUND OF THE WORLD.

Birds when they leave the nest carry, I presume, their hearts with them; not a few humans leave their hearts behind them—too often, alas! to be sent for afterward. The whole round of the world, many a cloud-rack on the ridge of it, and many a mist on the top of that, rises between them and the eyes and hearts which gave their very life that they might live. Some as they approach middle age, some only when they are old, wake up to understand that they have parents. To some the perception comes with their children; to others with the pang of seeing them walk away light-hearted out into the world, as they themselves turned their backs on their parents: they had been all their own, and now they have done with them! Less or more, have we not all thus taken our journey into a far country? But many a man of sixty is more of a son to the father gone from the earth, than he was while under his roof. What a disintegrated mass were the world, what a lump of half-baked brick, if death were indeed the end of affection! if there were no chance more of setting right what was so wrong in the loveliest relations! How gladly would many a son who once thought it a weariness to serve his parents, minister now to their lightest need! and in the boundless eternity is there no help?

Walter was not a prodigal; he was a well-behaved youth. He was only proud, only thought much of himself; was only pharisaical, not hypocritical; was only neglectful of those nearest him, always polite to those comparatively nothing to him! Compassionate and generous to necessity, he let his father and his sister-cousin starve for the only real food a man can give, that is, himself. As to him who thought his very thoughts into him, he heeded him not at all, or mocked him by merest ceremony. There are who refuse God the draught of water He desires, on the ground that their vessel is not fit for Him to drink from: Walter thought his too good to fill with the water fit for God to drink.

He had the feeling, far from worded, not even formed, but certainly in him, that he was a superior man to his father. But it is a fundamental necessity of the kingdom of heaven, impossible as it must seem to all outside it, that each shall count other better than himself; it is the natural condition of the man God made, in relation to the other men God has made. Man is made, not to contemplate himself, but to behold in others the beauty of the Father. A man who lives to meditate upon and worship himself, is in the slime of hell. Walter knew his father a reading man, but because he had not been to a university, placed no value on his reading. Yet this father was a man who had intercourse with high countries, intercourse in which his son would not have perceived the presence of an idea.

In like manner, Richard's carriage of mind, and the expression of the same in his modes and behavior, must have been far other than objectionable to the ushers of those high countries; his was a certain quiet, simply, direct way, reminding one of Nathanael, in whom was no guile. In another man Walter would have called it bucolic; in his father he shut his eyes to it as well as he could, and was ashamed of it. He would scarcely, in his circle, be regarded as a gentleman! he would look odd! He therefore had not encouraged the idea of his coming to see him. He was not satisfied with the father by whom the Father of fathers had sent him into the world! But Richard was the truest of gentlemen even in his outward carriage, for he was not only courteous and humble, but that rare thing—natural; and the natural, be it old as the Greek, must be beautiful. The natural dwells deep, and is not the careless, any more than the studied or assumed.

Walter loved his father, but the root of his love did not go deep enough to send aloft a fine flower: deep in is high out. He seldom wrote, and wrote briefly. He did not make a confidant of his father. He did not even tell him what he was doing, or what he hoped to do. He might mention a success, but of hopes, fears, aspirations, or defeats, or thoughts or desires, he said nothing. As to his theories, he never imagined his father entering into such things as occupied his mind! The ordinary young man takes it for granted that he and the world are far ahead of "the governor;" the father may have left behind him, as nebulae sinking below the horizon of youth, questions the world is but just waking to put.

The blame, however, may lie in part at the parent's door. The hearts of the fathers need turning to the children, as much as the hearts of the children need turning to the fathers. Few men open up to their children; and where a man does not, the schism, the separation begins with him, for all his love be deep and true. That it is unmanly to show one's feelings, is a superstition prevalent with all English-speaking people. Now, wherever feeling means weakness, falsehood, or excitement, it ought not merely not be shown, but not to exist; but for a man to hide from his son his loving and his loathing, is to refuse him the divinest fashion of teaching. Richard read the best things, and loved best the best writers: never once had he read a poem with his son, or talked to him about any poet! If Walter had even suspected his father's insight into certain things, he would have loved him more. Closely bound as they were, neither knew the other. Each would have been astonished at what he might have found in the other. The father might have discovered many handles by which to lay hold of his son; the son might have seen the lamp bright in his father's chamber which he was but trimming in his.

CHAPTER XI. THE SONG.

AT length came the summons from Lady Lufa to hear her music to his verses.

It was not much of a song, neither did he think it was.

Mist and vapor and cloud
Filled the earth and the air!
My heart was wrapt in a shroud.
And death was everywhere.

The sun went silently down
To his rest in the unseen wave;
But my heart, in its purple and crown.
Lay already in its grave.

For a cloud had darkened the brow
Of the lady who is my queen;
I had been a monarch, but now
All things had only been!

I sprung from the couch of death:
Who called my soul? Who spake?
No sound! no answer! no breath!
Yet my soul was wide awake!

And my heart began to blunder

Into rhythmic pulse the while;

I turned—away was the wonder—

My queen had begun to smile!

Outbrake the sun in the west!

Outlaughed the crested sea!

And my heart was alive in my breast

With light, and love, and thee!

There was a little music in the verses, and they had a meaning—though not a very new or valuable one.

He went in the morning—the real, not the conventional—and was shown into the drawing-room, his heart beating with expectation. Lady Lufa was alone, and already at the piano. She was in a gray stuff with red rosebuds, and looked as simple as any country parson's daughter. She gave him no greeting beyond a little nod, at once struck a chord or two, and began to sing.

Walter was charmed. The singing, and the song through the singing, altogether exceeded his expectation. He had feared he should not be able to laud heartily, for he had not lost his desire to be truthful—but she was an artist! There was indeed nothing original in her music; it was mainly a reconstruction of common phrases afloat in the musical atmosphere; but she managed the slight dramatic element in the lyric with taste and skill, following tone and sentiment with chord and inflection; so that the music was worthy of the verses—which is not saying very much for either; while the expression the girl threw into the song went to the heart of the youth, and made him foolish.

She ceased; he was silent for a moment, then fervent in thanks and admiration.

"The verses are mine no more," he said. "I shall care for them now!"

"You won't mind if I publish them with the music?"

"I shall feel more honored than I dare tell you. But how am I to go to my work after this taste of paradise! It was too cruel of you, Lady Lufa, to make me come in the morning!"

"I am very sorry!"

"Will you grant me one favor to make up?"

"Yes."

"Never to sing the song to any one when I am present. I could not bear it."

"I promise," she answered, looking up in his face with a glance of sympathetic consciousness.

There was an acknowledged secret between them, and Walter hugged it.

"I gave you a frozen bird," he said, "and you have warmed it, and made it soar and sing."

"Thank you; a very pretty compliment!" she answered—and there was a moment's silence.

"I am so glad we know each other!" she resumed. "You could help me so much if you would! Next time you come, you must tell me something about those old French rhymes that have come into fashion of late! They say a pretty thing so much more prettily for their quaint, antique, courtly liberty! The triolet now—how deliriously impertinent it is! Is it not?"

Walter knew nothing about the old French modes of versifying; and, unwilling to place himself at a disadvantage, made an evasive reply, and went. But when at length he reached home, it was with several ancient volumes, among the rest "Clement Marot," in pockets and hands. Ere an hour was over, he was in delight with the variety of dainty modes in which, by shape and sound, a very pretty French something was carved out of nothing at all. Their fantastic surprises, the ring of their bell-like returns upon themselves, their music of triangle and cymbal, gave him quite a new pleasure. In some of them poetry seemed to approach the nearest possible to bird-song—to unconscious seeming through most conscious art, imitating the carelessness and impromptu of warblings as old as the existence of birds, and as new as every fresh individual joy; for each new generation grows its own feathers, and sings its own song, yet always the feathers of its kind, and the song of its kind.

The same night he sent her the following triolet

Oh, why is the moon

Awake when thou sleepest?

To the nightingale's tune,

Why is the moon

Making a noon,

When night is the deepest

Why is the moon

Awake when thou sleepest?

In the evening came a little note, with a coronet on the paper, but neither date nor signature:

"Perfectly delicious! How can such a little gem hold so much color? Thank you a thousand times!"

CHAPTER XII. LOVE.

By this Walter was in love with Lady Lufa. He said as much to himself, at least; and in truth he was almost possessed with her. Every thought that rose in his mind began at once to drift toward her. Every hour of the day had a rose-tinge from the dress in which he first saw her.

One might write a long essay on this they call love, and yet contribute little to the understanding of it in the individual case. Its kind is to be interpreted after the kind of person who loves. There are as many hues and shades, not to say forms and constructions of love, as there are human countenances, human hearts, human judgments and schemes of life. Walter had not been an impressionable youth, because he had an imagination which both made him fastidious, and stood him in stead of falling in love. When a man can give form to the things that move in him, he is less driven to fall in love. But now Walter saw everything through a window, and the window was the face of Lufa. His thinking was always done in the presence and light of that window. She seemed an intrinsic component of every one of his mental operations. In every beauty and attraction of life he saw her. He was possessed by her, almost as some are possessed by evil spirits. And to be possessed, even by a human being, may be to take refuge in the tombs, there to cry, and cut one's self with fierce thoughts.

But not yet was Walter troubled. He lived in love's eternal present, and did not look forward. Even jealousy had not yet begun to show itself in any shape. He was not in Lady Lufa's set, and therefore not much drawn to conjecture what might be going on. In the glamour of literary ambition, he took for granted that Lady Lufa allotted his world a higher orbit than that of her social life, and prized most the pleasures they had in common, which so few were capable of sharing.

She had indeed in her own circle never found one who knew more of the refinements of verse than a school-girl does of Beethoven; and it was a great satisfaction to her to know one who not merely recognized her proficiency, but could guide her further into the depths of an art which every one thinks he understands, and only one here and there does. It was therefore a real welcome she was able to give him when they met, as they did again and again during the season. How much she cared for him, how much she would have been glad to do for him, my reader shall judge for himself. I think she cared for him very nearly as much as for a dress made to her liking. An injustice from him would have brought the tears into her eyes. A poem he disapproved of she would have thrown, aside, perhaps into the fire.

She did not, however, submit much of her work to his judgment. She was afraid of what might put her out of heart with it. Before making his acquaintance, she had a fresh volume, a more ambitious one, well on its way, but fearing lack of his praise, had said nothing to him about it. And besides this diffidence, she did not wish to appear to solicit from him a good review. She might cast herself on his mercy, but it should not be confessedly. She had pride though not conscience in the matter. The mother was capable of begging, not the daughter. She might use fascination, but never entreaty; that would be to degrade herself!

Walter had, of course, taken a second look at her volume. It did not reveal that he had said of it what was not true; but he did see that, had he been anxious to praise, he might have found passages to commend, or in which, at least, he could have pointed out merit. But no allusion was made to the book, on the one hand because Lady Lufa was aware he had written the review, and on the other because Walter did not wish to give his opinion of it. He placed it in the category of first works; and, knowing how poor those of afterward distinguished writers may be, it did not annoy him that one who could talk so well should have written such rubbish.

Lady Lufa had indeed a craze for composition, and the indulgence of it was encouraged by her facility. There was no reason in heaven, earth, or the other place, why what she wrote should see the light, for it had little to do with light of any sort. "Autumn Leaves" had had no such reception as her mother would have Walter believe. Lady Tremaine was one of those good mothers who, like "good churchmen," will wrong any other to get for their own. She had paid her court to Walter that she might gain a reviewer who would yield her daughter what she called justice: for justice' sake she could curry favor! A half-merry, half-retaliative humor in Lufa, may have wrought for revenge by making Walter fall in love with her; at all events it was a consolation to her wounded vanity when she saw him, in love with her; but it was chiefly in the hope of a "good" review of her next book that she cultivated his acquaintance, and now she felt sure of her end.

Most people liked Walter, even when they laughed at his simplicity, for it was the simplicity of a generous nature; we can not therefore wonder if he was too confident, and from Lady Lufa's behavior presumed to think she looked upon him as worthy of a growing privilege. If she regarded literature as she professed to regard it, he had but to distinguish himself, he thought, to be more acceptable than wealth or nobility could have made him. As to material possibilities, the youth never thought of them; a worshiper does not meditate how to feed his goddess! Lady Lufa was his universe and everything in it—a small universe and scantily furnished for a human soul, had she been the prime of women! He scarcely thought of his home now, or of the father who made it home. As to God, it is hardly a question whether he had ever thought of Him. For can that be called thinking of another, which is the mere passing of a name through the mind, without one following thought of relation or duty? Many think it a horrible thing to say there is no God, who never think how much worse a thing it is not to heed Him. If God be not worth minding, what great ruin can it be to imagine His non-existence?

What, then, had Walter made of it by leaving home? He had almost forgotten his father; had learned to be at home in London; had passed many judgments, some of them more or less just, all of them more or less unjust; had printed enough for a volume of little better than truisms concerning life, society, fashion, dress, etc., etc.; had published two or three rather nice songs, and had a volume of poems almost ready; had kept himself the greater part of the time, and had fallen in love with an earl's daughter.

"Everybody is gone," said Lady Lufa, "and we are going to-morrow."

"To-day," he rejoined, "London is full; to-morrow it will be a desert!"

She looked up at him, and did not seem glad.

"I have enjoyed the season so much!" she said.

He thought her lip trembled.

"But you will come and see us at Comberidge, will you not?" she added.

"Do you think your mother will ask me?" he said.

"I think she will. I do so want to show you our library! And I have so many things to ask you!"

"I am your slave, the jin of your lamp."

"I would I had such a lamp as would call you!"

"It will need no lamp to make me come."

Lamps to call moths are plenty, and Lufa was herself one.

CHAPTER XIII. "HOME IS WHERE THE HEART IS."

London was very hot, very dusty, and as dreary as Walter had anticipated. When Lufa went, the moon went out of the heavens, the stars chose banishment with their mistress, and only the bright, labor-urging sun was left.

He might now take a holiday when he pleased, and he had money enough in hand. His father wanted him to pay them a visit; but what if an invitation to Comberidge should arrive! Home was a great way in the other direction! And then it would be so dull! He would of course be glad to see his father! He ought to go! He was owing there! What was he to do? He would not willingly even run the risk of losing his delight, for the sake of his first, best, truest earthly friend!

But he must take his holiday now, in the slack of the London year, and the heat was great! He need not be all day with his father, and the thought of Lufa would be entrancing in the wide solitudes of the moor! Molly he scarce thought of, and his aunt was to be forgotten. He would go for a few days, he said, thus keeping the door open for a speedy departure.

Just before he left, the invitation did arrive. He would have a week to dream about it under the old roof!

His heart warmed a little as he approached his home. Certain memories came to meet him. The thought of his mother was in the air. How long it was since she had spoken to him! He remembered her and his father watching by his bed while he tossed in a misery of which he could even now recall the prevailing delirious fancies. He remembered his mother's last rebuke; for insolence to a servant; remembered her last embrace, her last words; and his heart turned tenderly to his father. Yet when he entered the house and faced the old surroundings, an unexpected gloom overclouded him. Had he been heart-free and humble, they would have been full of delight for him; but pride had been busy in his soul. Its home was in higher planes! How many essential refinements, as he foolishly and vulgarly counted them, were lacking here! What would Lady Lufa think of his entourage? Did it well become one of the second aristocracy? He had been gradually filling with a sense of importance—which had no being except in his own brain; and the notion took the meanest of mean forms—that of looking down on his own history. He was too much of a gentleman still not to repress the show of the feeling, but its mere presence caused a sense of alienation between him and his. When the first greetings were over, nothing came readily to follow. The wave had broken on the shore, and there was not another behind it. Things did not, however, go badly; for the father when disappointed always tried to account for everything to the advantage of the other; and on his part, Walter did his best to respond to his father's love-courtesy. He was not of such as keep no rule over themselves; not willingly would he allow discomfort to wake temper; he did not brood over defect in those he loved; but it did comfort him that he was so soon to leave his uncongenial surroundings, and go where all would be as a gentleman desired to see it. No one needs find it hard to believe such snobbishness in a youth gifted like Walter Colman; for a sweet temper, fine sympathies, warmth of affection, can not be called a man's own, so long as he has felt and acted without co-operation of the will; and Walter had never yet fought a battle within himself. He had never set his will against his inclination. He had, indeed, bravely fronted the necessity of the world, but we can not regard it as assurance of a noble nature that one is ready to labor for the things that are needful. A man is indeed contemptible who is not ready to work; but not to be contemptible is hardly to be honorable. Walter had never actively chosen the right way, or put out any energy to walk in it. There are usurers and sinners nearer the kingdom of heaven than many a respectable, socially successful youth of education and ambition. Walter was not simple. He judged things not in themselves, but after an artificial and altogether foolish standard, for his aim was a false one—social distinction.

The ways of his father's house were nowise sordid, though so simple that his losses had made scarcely a difference in them; they were hardly even humble—only old-fashioned; but Walter was ashamed of them. He even thought it unlady-like of Molly to rise from the table to wait on her uncle or himself; and once, when she brought the tea-kettle in her own little brown hand, he actually reproved her.

The notion that success lies in reaching the modes of life in the next higher social stratum; the fancy that those ways are the standard of what is worthy, becoming, or proper; the idea that our standing is determined by our knowledge of what is or is not the thing, is one of the degrading influences of modern times. It is only the lack of dignity at once and courtesy that makes such points of any interest or consequence.

Fortunately for Walter's temper, his aunt was discreetly silent, too busy taking the youth's measure afresh to talk much; intent on material wherewith to make up her mind concerning him. She had had to alter her idea of him as incapable of providing his own bread and cheese; but as to what reflection of him was henceforth to inhabit the glass of her judgment, she had not yet determined, further than that it should be an unfavorable one.

It was a relief when bed-time came, and he was alone in what was always called his room, where he soon fell asleep, to dream of Lufa and the luxuries around her—facilities accumulated even to incumbrance, and grown antagonistic to comfort, as Helots to liberty. How different from his dreams were the things that stood around them! how different his thoughts from those of the father who knelt in the moonlight at the side of his bed, and said something to Him who never sleeps! When he woke, his first feeling was a pang: the things about him were as walls between him and Lufa!

From indifference, or preoccupation—from some cause—he avoided any tête-à-tête with Molly. He had no true idea of the girl, neither indeed was capable of one. She was a whole nature; he was of many parts, not yet begun to cohere. This unlikeness, probably, was at the root of his avoidance of her. Perhaps he had an undefined sense of rebuke, and feared her without being aware of it. Never going further than half-way into a thing, he had never relished Molly's questions; they went deeper than he saw difficulty; he was not even conscious of the darkness upon which Molly desired light cast. And now when, either from instinct, or sense of presence, he became aware that Molly was looking at him, he did not like it; he felt as if she saw some lack of harmony, between his consciousness and his history. He was annoyed, even irritated, with the olive-cheeked, black-eyed girl, who had been for so many years like his sister: she was making remarks upon him in that questioning laboratory of her brain!

Molly was indeed trying to understand what had gone different between them. She had never felt Walter come very near her, for he was not one who had learned, or would easily learn, to give himself; and no man who does not give at least something of himself, gives anything; but now she knew that he had gone further away, and she saw his father look disappointed. To Molly it was a sad relief when his departure came. They had not once disputed; she had not once offered him a penny for his thoughts, or asked him a single question, yet he did not even want her to go to the station with him.

CHAPTER XIV. A MIDNIGHT REVIEW.

From Comberidge a dog-cart had been sent to meet him at the railway. He drove up the avenue as the sun was setting behind the house, and its long, low, terraced front received him into a cold shadow. The servant who opened the door said her ladyship was on the lawn; and following him across the hall, Walter came out into the glory of a red sunset. Like a lovely carpet, or rather, like a green, silent river, the lawn appeared to flow from the house as from its fountain, issuing by the open doors and windows, and descending like a gentle rapid, to lose itself far away among trees and shrubs. Over it were scattered groups and couples and individuals, looking like the creatures of a half-angelic paradise. A little way off, under the boughs of a huge beech-tree, sat Lufa, reading, with a pencil in her hand as if she made notes. As he stepped from the house, she looked up and saw him. She laid her book on the grass, rose, and came toward him. He went to meet her, but the light of the low sun was directly in his eyes, and he could not see her shadowed face. But her voice of welcome came athwart the luminous darkness, and their hands found each other. He thought hers trembled, but it was his own. She led him to her mother.

"I am glad to see you," said Lady Tremaine. "You are just in time!"

"For what, may I ask?" returned Walter.

"It is out at last!"

"No, mamma," interrupted Lufa; "the book is not out! It is almost ready, but I have only had one or two early copies. I am so glad Mr. Colman will be the first to see it! He will prepare me for the operation!"

"What do you mean?" asked Walter, bewildered. It was the first word he had heard of her new book.

"Of course I shall be cut up! The weekly papers especially would lose half their readers did they not go in for vivisection! But mamma shouldn't have asked you now!"

"Why?"

"Well—you mightn't—I shouldn't like you to feel an atom less comfortable in speaking your mind."

"There is no fear of that sort in my thoughts," answered Walter, laughing.

But it troubled him a little that she had not let him know what she was doing.

"Besides," he went on, "you need never know what I think. There are other reviewers on the 'Battery!'"

"I should recognize your hand anywhere! And more than that, I should only have to pick out the most rigid and unbending criticism to know which must be yours. It is your way, and you know it! Are you not always showing me up to myself! That's why I was in such mortal terror of your finding out what I was doing. If you had said anything to make me hate my work," she went on, looking up at him with earnest eyes, "I should never have touched it again; and I did want to finish it! You have been my master now for—let me see—how many months? I do not know how I shall ever thank you!" Here she changed tone. "If I come off with a pound of flesh left, it will be owing entirely to the pains you have taken with me! I wonder whether you will like any of my triolets! But it is time to dress for dinner, so I will leave you in peace—but not all night, for when you go to bed you shall take your copy with you to help you asleep."

While dressing he was full of the dread of not liking the book well enough to praise it as he wished. A first book was nothing, he said to himself; it might be what it would; but the second—that was another matter! He recalled what first books he knew. "Poems by Two Brothers" gave not a foretaste of what was to come so soon after them! Shelley's prose attempts in his boyhood were below criticism! Byron's "Hours of Idleness" were as idle as he called them! He knew what followed these and others, but what had followed Lady Lufa's? That he was now to discover! What if it should be no better than what preceded! For his own part he did not, he would not much care. It was not for her poetry, it was for herself he loved her! What she wrote was not she, and could make no difference! It was not as if she had no genuine understanding of poetry, no admiration or feeling for it! A poet could do well enough with a wife who never wrote a verse, but hardly with one who had no natural relation to it, no perception what it was! A poet in love with one who laughed at his poetry!—that would want scanning! What or wherein could be their relation to each other?

He is a poor poet—and Walter was such a poet—who does not know there are better things than poetry. Keats began to discover it just ere he died.

Walter feared therefore the coming gift, as he might that of a doubted enchantress. It was not the less a delight, however, to remember that she said "your copy." But he must leave thinking and put on his neck-tie! There are other things than time and tide that wait for no man!

Lady Tremaine gave him Lufa, and she took his arm with old familiarity. The talk at table was but such as it could hardly help being—only for Walter it was talk with Lufa! The pleasure of talk often owes not much to the sense of it. There is more than the intellect concerned in talk; there is more at its root than fact or logic or lying.

When the scene changed to the drawing-room, Lufa played tolerably and sung well, delighting Walter. She asked and received his permission to sing "my song," as she called it, and pleased him with it more than ever. He managed to get her into the conservatory, which was large, and there he talked much, and she seemed to listen much. It was but the vague, twilight, allusive talk which, coming readily to all men in love, came the more readily to one always a poet, and not merely a poet by being in love. Every one in love sees a little further into things, but few see clearly, and hence love-talk has in general so little meaning. Ordinary men in love gain glimpses of truth more and other than they usually see, but from having so little dealing with the truth, they do not even try to get a hold of it, they do not know it for truth even when dallying with it. It is the true man's dreams that come true.

He raised her hand to his lips as at length she turned toward the drawing-room, and he thought she more than yielded it, but could not be sure. Anyhow she was not offended, for she smiled with her usual sweetness as she bade him good-night.

"One instant, Mr. Colman!" she added: "I promised you a sedative! I will run and get it. No, I won't keep you; I will send it to your room."

He had scarce shut his door when it opened again, and there was Lufa.

"I beg your pardon!" she said; "I thought you would not be come up, and I wanted to make my little offering with my own hand: it owes so much to you!"

She slipped past him, laid her book on his table, and went.

He lighted his candles with eager anxiety, and took it up. It was a dramatic poem of some length, daintily bound in white vellum, with gilt edges. On the title-page was written "The Master's Copy," with the date and Lufa's initials. He threw himself into a great soft chair that with open arms invited him, and began to read.

He had taken champagne pretty freely at dinner; his mind was yet in the commotion left by the summer-wind of their many words that might seem so much; he felt his kiss on her dainty hand, and her pressure of it to his lips; as he read, she seemed still and always in the door-way, entering with the book; its inscription was continually turning up with a shine: such was the mood in which he read the poem. Through he read it, every word, some of it many times; then rose and went to his writing-table, to set down his judgment of his lady's poem. He wrote and wrote, almost without pause. The dawn began to glimmer, the red blood of the morning came back to chase the swoon of the night, ere at last, throwing down his pen, he gave a sigh of weary joy, tore off his clothes, plunged into his bed, and there lay afloat on the soft waves of sleep. And as he slept, the sun came slowly up to shake the falsehood out of the earth.

CHAPTER XV. REFLECTION.

Walter slept until nearly noon, then rose, very weary, but with a gladness at his heart. On his table were spread such pages as must please Lufa! His thoughts went back to the poem, but, to his uneasy surprise, he found he did not recall it with any special pleasure. He had had great delight in reading it, and in giving shape to his delight, but he could not now think what kind of thing it was that had given him such satisfaction. He had worked too long, he said to himself, and this was the reaction; he was too tired to enjoy the memory of what he had so heartily admired. Aesthetic judgment was so dependent on mood! He would glance over what he had done, correct it a little, and inclose it for the afternoon post, that it might appear in the next issue!

He drank the cup of cold tea by his bedside, sat down, and took up his hurriedly written sheets. He found in them much that seemed good work— of his own; and the passages quoted gave ostensible grounds for the remarks made upon them; but somehow the whole affair seemed quite different. The review would incline any lover of verse to read the book; and the passages cited were preceded and followed by rich and praiseful epithets; but neither quotations nor remarks moved in him any echo of response. He gave the manuscript what correction it required, which was not much, for Walter was an accurate as well as ready writer, laid it aside, and took up the poem.

What could be the matter? There was nothing but embers where had been glow and flame! Something must be amiss with him! He recalled an occasion on which, feeling similarly with regard to certain poems till then favorites, he was sorely troubled, but a serious attack of illness very soon relieved his perplexity: something like it most surely be at hand to account for the contradiction between Walter last night and Walter this morning! Closer and closer he scanned what he read, peering if he might to its very roots, in agonized endeavor to see what he had seen as he wrote. But his critical consciousness neither acknowledged what he had felt, nor would grant him in a condition of poetic collapse. He read on and on; read the poem through; turned back, and read passage after passage again; but without one individual approach to the revival of former impression. "Commonplace! commonplace!" echoed in his inner ear, as if whispered by some mocking spirit. He argued that he had often found himself too fastidious. His demand for finish ruined many of his verses, rubbing and melting and wearing them away, like frost and wind and rain, till they were worthless! The predominance and overkeenness of the critical had turned in him to disease! His eye was sharpened to see the point of a needle, but a tree only as a blotted mass! A man's mind was meant to receive as a mirror, not to concentrate rays like a convex lens! Was it not then likely that the first reading gave the true impression of the ethereal, the vital, the flowing, the iridescent? Did not the solitary and silent night brood like a hen on the nest of the poet's imaginings? Was it not the night that waked the soul? Did not the commonplace vanish along with the "garish" day? How then could its light afford the mood fit for judging a poem—the cold sick morning, when life is but half worth living! Walter did not think how much champagne he had taken, nor how much that might have to do with one judgment at night and another in the morning. "Set one mood against another," he said, conscious all the time it was a piece of special pleading, "and the one weighs as much as the other!" For it was horrible to him to think that the morning was the clear-eyed, and that the praise he had lavished on the book was but a vapor of the night. How was he to carry himself to the lady of his love, who at most did not care half as much for him as for her book?

How poetry could be such a passion with her when her own was but mediocre, was a question Walter dared not shape—not, however, that he saw the same question might be put with regard to himself: his own poetry was neither strong nor fresh nor revealing. He had not noted that an unpoetic person will occasionally go into a mild ecstasy over phrase or passage or verse in which a poet may see little or nothing.

He came back to this:—his one hour had as good a claim to insight as his other; if he saw the thing so once, why not say what he had seen? Why should not the thing stand? His consciousness of the night before had certainly been nearer that of a complete, capable being, than that of to-day! He was in higher human condition then than now!

But there came another doubt: what was he to conclude concerning his other numerous judgments passed irrevocably? Was he called and appointed to influence the world's opinion of the labor of hundreds according to the mood he happened to be in, or the hour at which he read their volumes? But if he must write another judgment of that poem in vellum and gold, he must first pack his portmanteau! To write in her home as he felt now, would be treachery!

Not confessing it, he was persuading himself to send on the review. Of course, had he the writing of it now, he would not write a paper like that! But the thing being written, it could claim as good a chance of being right as another! Had it not been written as honestly as another of to-day would be? Might it not be just as true? The laws of art are so undefined!

Thus on and on went the windmill of heart and brain, until at last the devil, or the devil's shadow—that is, the bad part of the man himself—got the better, and Walter, not being true, did a lie—published the thing he would no longer have said. He thought he worshiped the truth, but he did not. He knew that the truth was everything, but a lie came that seemed better than the truth. In his soul he knew he was not acting truly; that had he honestly loved the truth, he would not have played hocus-pocus with metaphysics and logic, but would have made haste to a manly conclusion. He took the package, and on his way to the dining-room, dropped it into the post-box in the hall.

During lunch he was rather silent and abstracted; the package was not gone, and his conscience might yet command him to recall it! When the hour was passed, and the paper beyond recovery, he felt easier, saying to himself, what was done could not be undone; he would be more careful another time. One comfort was, that at least he had done no injustice to Lufa! He did not reflect that he had done her the greatest injustice in helping her to believe that worthy which was not worthy, herself worshipful who was not worshipful. He told her that he finished her drama before going to bed, and was perfectly charmed with it. That it as much exceeded his expectations then as it had fallen below them since, he did not say.

In the evening he was not so bright as before. Lufa saw it and was troubled. She feared he doubted the success of her poem. She led the way, and found he avoided talking about it. She feared he was not so well pleased with it as he had said. Walter asked if he might not read from it in the drawing-room. She would not consent.

"None there are of our sort!" she said. "They think literature foolishness. Even my mother, the best of mothers, doesn't care about poetry, can not tell one measure from another. Come and read a page or two of it in the summer-house in the wilderness instead. I want to know how it will sound in people's ears."

Walter was ready enough. He was fond of reading aloud, and believed he could so read the poem that he need not say anything. And certainly, if justice meant making the words express more than was in them, he did it justice. But in truth the situation was sometimes touching; and the more so to Walter that the hero was the lady's inferior in birth, means, and position— much more her inferior than Walter was Lufa's. The lady alone was on the side of the lowly born; father, mother, brothers, sisters, uncles, aunts, and cousins to the remotest degree, against him even to hatred. The general pathos of the idea disabled the criticism of the audience, composed of the authoress and the reader, blinding perhaps both to not a little that was neither brilliant nor poetic. The lady wept at the sound of her own verses from the lips of one who was to her in the position of the hero toward the heroine; and the lover, critic as he was, could not but be touched when he saw her weep at passages suggesting his relation to her; so that, when they found the hand of the one resting in that of the other, it did not seem strange to either. When suddenly the lady snatched hers away, it was only because a mischievous little bird spying them, and hurrying away to tell, made a great fluttering in the foliage. Then was Walter's conscience not a little consoled, for he was aware of a hearty love for the poem. Under such conditions he could have gone on reading it all the night!

CHAPTER XVI. THE RIDE TOGETHER.

Days passed, and things went on much the same, Walter not daring to tell the girl all he felt, but seizing every opportunity of a tête-à-tête, and missing none of the proximity she allowed him, and she never seeming other than pleased to be his companion. Her ways with him were always pretty, and sometimes playful. She was almost studious to please him; and if she never took a liberty with him, she never resented any he took with her, which certainly were neither numerous nor daring, for Walter was not presumptuous, least of all with women.

But Lufa was careful not to neglect their other guests. She was always ready to accompany any of the ladies riding out of a morning; and a Mr. Sefton, who was there when Walter arrived, generally rode with them. He was older than Walter, and had taken little notice of him, which Walter resented more than he would have cared to acknowledge. He was tall and lanky, with a look of not having been in the oven quite long enough, but handsome nevertheless. Without an atom of contempt, he cared nothing for what people might think; and when accused of anything, laughed, and never defended himself. Having no doubt he was in the right, he had no anxiety as to the impression he might make. In the hunting-field he was now reckless, now so cautious that the men would chaff him. But they knew well enough that whatever he did came either of pure whim or down-right good sense; no one ever questioned his pluck. I believe an intermittent laziness had something to do with his inconsistency.

It had been taken for granted by Lufa that Walter could not ride; whereas, not only had he had some experience, but he was one of the few possessed of an individual influence over the lower brotherhood of animals, and his was especially equine.

One morning, from an ailment in one of the horses, Lufa found that her mount required consideration. Sefton said the horse he had been riding would carry her perfectly.

"What will you do for a horse?"

"Go without."

"What shall we do for a gentleman?"

"Go without."

"I saw a groom this morning," suggested Walter, "on a lovely little roan!"

"Ah, Red Racket!" answered Lady Lufa, "He is no horse; he is a little fiend. Goes as gently as a lamb with my father, though, or any one that he knows can ride him. Try Red Racket, George."

They were cousins, though not in the next degree.

"I would if I could sit him. But I'm not a rough rider, and much disinclined to have my bones broken. It's not as if there was anything to be got by it, even a brush!"

"Two hours of your sister, your cousin, and their friend!" said Lufa.

"Much of you I should have with Red Racket under me—or over me as likely! at best jumping about, and taking all the attention I had! No, thank you!"

"Come, George," said his sister, "you will make them think you are no horseman!"

"Neither I am; I have not a good seat, and you know it! I am not going to make a fool of myself on compulsion! I know what I can do, and what I can't do."

"I wish I had the chance!" murmured Walter, as if to himself, but so that Lufa heard.

"You can ride?" said Lufa, with pleased surprise.

"Why not?" returned Walter. "Every Englishman should ride."

"Yes; every Englishman should swim; but Englishmen are drowned every day!"

"That is as often because they can swim, but have not Mr. Sefton's prudence."

"You mustn't think my cousin afraid of Red Racket!" she returned.

"I don't. He doesn't look like it!"

"Do you really wish to ride the roan?"

"Indeed I do!"

"I will order him round," she said, rising.

Walter did not quite enjoy her consenting so easily; had she no fear for him of the risk Mr. Sefton would not run?

"She wants me to cut a good figure!" he said to himself, and went to get ready.

I have no deed of prowess on Walter's part to record. The instant he was in the saddle, Red Racket recognized a master.

"You can't have ridden him before?" questioned Lufa.

"I never saw him till this morning."

"He likes you, I suppose!" she said.

As they returned, the other ladies being in front, and the groom some distance behind, Walter brought his roan side by side with Lufa's horse, and said—

"You know Browning's 'Last Ride Together'?"

"Yes," she answered, with a faint blush; "but this is not our last ride! It is our first! Why didn't you tell me? We might have had many rides together!"

"Promise me a last one," he said.

"How can I? How should I know it was the last?"

"Promise," he persisted, "that if ever you see just one last ride possible, you will let me know."

She hesitated a moment, then answered—

"I will."

"Thank you!" said Walter with fervor.

As by consent, they rode after the others.

Walter had not yet the courage to say anything definite. But he had said many things that must have compelled her to imagine what he had not said; therefore the promise she had given him seemed encouraging. They rode in silence the rest of the way.

When Sefton saw Red Racket as quiet as a lamb, he went up to him, stroked his neck, and said to Walter:

"With me he would have capered like an idiot till he had thrown me. It is always my luck with horses of his color! You must have a light hand!"

He stroked his neck once more, turned aside, and was too late to help the ladies dismount.

It was the last ride for the present, because of a change in the weather. In a few days came "The Field Battery" with Walter's review, bringing a revival of the self-reproach he had begun to forget. The paper felt in his hand like bad news or something nasty. He could not bear the thought of having to take his part in the talk it would occasion. It could not now be helped, however, and that was a great comfort! It was impossible, none the less, to keep it up! As he had foreseen, all this time came no revival of his first impression of the poem. He went to find his hostess, and told her he must go to London that same afternoon. As he took his leave, he put the paper In Lufa's hand, saying,

"You will find there what I have said about the poem."

CHAPTER XVII. HIS BOOK.

I need hardly say he found his first lonely evening dull. He was not yet capable of looking beneath the look of anything. He felt cabined, cribbed, confined. His world-clothing came too near him. From the flowing robes of a park, a great house, large rooms, wide staircases—with plenty of air and space, color, softness, fitness, completeness, he found himself in the worn, tight, shabby garment of a cheap London lodging! But Walter, far from being a wise man, was not therefore a fool; he was not one whom this world can not teach, and who has therefore to be sent to some idiot asylum in the next, before sense can be got into him, or, rather, out of him. No man is a fool, who, having work to do, sets himself to do it, and Walter did. He had begun a poem to lead the van of a volume, of which the rest was nearly ready: into it he now set himself to weave a sequel to her drama, from the point where she had left the story. Every hour he could spare from drudgery he devoted to it—urged by the delightful prospect of letting Lufa see what he could do. Gaining facility with his stanza as he went on, the pleasure of it grew, and more than comforted his loneliness. Sullivan could hardly get him from his room.

Finding a young publisher prepared to undertake half the risk, on the ground, unexpressed, of the author's proximity to the judgment-seat, Walter, too experienced to look for any gain, yet hoped to clear his expenses, and became liable for much more than he possessed.

He had one little note from Lufa, concerning a point in rhythm which perplexed her. She had a good ear, and was conscientious in her mechanics. There was not a cockney-rhyme from beginning to end of her poem, which is more than the uninitiated will give its weight to. But she understood nothing of the broken music which a master of verse will turn to such high service. There are lines in Milton which Walter, who knew far more than she, could not read until long after, when Dante taught him how.

In the month of December came another note from Lady Lufa, inviting him to spend a week with them after Christmas.

"Perhaps then we may have yet a ride together," added a postscript.

"What does she mean?" thought Walter, a pale fear at his heart. "She can not mean our last ride!"

One conclusion he came to—that he must tell her plainly he loved her. The thing was only right, though of course ridiculous in the eyes of worldly people, said the far from unworldly poet. True, she was the daughter of an earl, and he the son of a farmer; and those who called the land their own looked down upon those who tilled it! But a banker, or a brewer, or the son of a contractor who had wielded the spade, might marry an earl's daughter: why should not the son of a farmer—not to say one who, according to the lady's mother, himself belonged to an aristocracy? The farmer's son indeed was poor, and who would look at a poor banker, or a poor brewer, more than a poor farmer! it was all money! But was he going to give in to that? Was he to grant that possession made a man honorable, and the want of it despicable! To act as if she could think after such a silly fashion, would be to insult her! He would lay bare his heart to her! There were things in it which she knew what value to set upon—things as far before birth as birth was before money! He would accept the invitation, and if possible get his volume out before the day mentioned, so as, he hoped, to be a little in the mouth of the public when he went.

Walter, like many another youth, imagined the way to make a woman love him, was to humble himself before her, tell her how beautiful she was, and how much he loved her. I do not see why any woman should therefore love a man. If she loves him already, anything will do to make her love him more; if she does not, no entreaty will wake what is not there to be waked. Even wrong and cruelty and carelessness may increase love already rooted; but neither love, nor kindness, nor worship, will prevail to plant it.

In his formal acceptance of the invitation, he inclosed some verses destined for his volume, in which he poured out his boyish passion over his lady's hair, and eyes, and hands—a poem not without some of the merits made much of by the rising school of the day, and possessing qualities higher, perhaps, than those upon which that school chiefly prided itself. She made, and he expected, no acknowledgment, but she did not return the verses.

Lyric after lyric, with Lufa for its inspiration, he wrought, like damask flowers, into his poem. Every evening, and all the evening, sometimes late into the morning, he fashioned and filed, until at length it was finished.

When the toiling girl who waited on him appeared with the proof-sheets in her hand, she came like a winged ministrant laying a wondrous gift before him. And in truth, poor as he came to think it, was it not a gift greater than any angel could have brought him? Was not the seed of it sown in his being by Him that loved him before he was? These were the poor first flowers, come to make way for better—themselves a gift none but God could give.

The book was rapidly approaching its birth, as the day of Lufa's summons drew near. He had inscribed the volume to her, not by name, but in a dedication she could not but understand and no other would; founded on her promise of a last ride: it was so delightful to have a secret with her! He hoped to the last to take a copy with him, but was disappointed by some contretemps connected with the binding—about which he was as particular as if it had been itself a poem: he had to pack his portmanteau without it.

Continuously almost, on his way to the station, he kept repeating to himself: "Is it to be the last ride, or only another?"

CHAPTER XVIII. A WINTER AFTERNOON.

When Walter arrived, he found the paradise under snow. But the summer had only run in-doors, and there was blooming. Lufa was kinder than ever, but, he fancied, a little embarrassed, which he interpreted to his advantage. He was shown to the room he had before occupied.

It did not take him long to learn the winter ways of the house. Mr. and Miss Sefton were there; and all seemed glad of his help against consciousness; for there could be no riding so long as the frost lasted and the snow kept falling, and the ladies did not care to go out; and in, some country-houses Time has as many lives as a cat, and wants a great deal of killing—a butchery to be one day bitterly repented, perhaps; but as a savage can not be a citizen, so can not people of fashion belong to the kingdom of heaven.

The third morning came a thaw, with a storm of wind and rain; and after lunch they gathered in the glooming library, and began to tell ghost stories. Walter happened to know a few of the rarer sort, and found himself in his element. His art came to help him, and the eyes of the ladies, and he rose to his best. As he was working one of his tales to its climax, Mr. Sefton entered the room, where Walter had been the only gentleman, and took a chair beside Lufa. She rose, saying,

"I beg your pardon, Mr. Colman, but would you mind stopping a minute while I get a little more red silk for my imperial dragon? Mr. Sefton has already taken the sting out of the snake!"

"What snake?" asked Sefton.

"The snake of terror," she answered. "Did you not see him as you came in—erect on his coiled tail, drawing his head back for his darting spring?"

"I am very sorry," said Sefton. "I have injured everybody, and I hope everybody will pardon me!"

When Lufa had found her silk, she took a seat nearer to Walter, who resumed and finished his narrative.

"I wonder she lived to tell it!" said one of the ladies.

"For my part," rejoined their hostess, "I do not see why every one should be so terrified at the thought of meeting a ghost! It seems to me cowardly."

"I don't think it cowardly," said Sefton, "to be frightened at a ghost, or at anything else."

"Now don't say you would run away!" remonstrated his sister.

"I couldn't very well, don't you know, if I was in bed! But I might—I don't know—hide my head under the blankets!"

"I don't believe it a bit!"

"To be sure," continued Sefton, reflectively, "there does seem a difference! To hide is one thing, and to run is another—quite another thing! If you are frightened, you are frightened and you can't help it; but if you run away, then you are a coward. Yes; quite true! And yet there are things some men, whom other men would be afraid to call cowards, would run from fast enough! Your story, Mr. Colman," he went on, "reminds me of an adventure I had—if that be an adventure where was no danger—except, indeed, of losing my wits, which Lufa would say was no great loss. I don't often tell the story, for I have an odd weakness for being believed; and nobody ever does believe that story, though it is as true as I live; and when a thing is true, the blame lies with those that don't believe it. Ain't you of my mind, Mr. Colman?"

"You had better not appeal to him!" said Lufa. "Mr. Colman does not believe a word of the stories he has been telling. He regards them entirely from the artistic point of view, and cares only for their effect. He is writing a novel, and wants to study people under a ghost story."

"I don't indorse your judgment of me, Lady Lufa," said Walter, who did not quite like what she said. "I am ready to believe anything in which I can see reason. I should like much to hear Mr. Sefton's story. I never saw the man that saw a ghost, except Mr. Sefton be that man."

"You shall say what you will when you have heard. I shall offer no explanation, only tell you what I saw, or, if you prefer it, experienced; you must then fall back on your own metaphysics. I don't care what anybody thinks about it."

"You are not very polite!" said Lufa.

"Only truthful," replied Sefton.

"Please go on?"

"We are dying to hear!"

"A real ghost story!"

"Is it your best, George?"

"It is my only one," Sefton answered, and was silent a few moments, as if arranging his thoughts.

"Well, here goes!" he began. "I was staying at a country house—"

"Not here, I hope!" said Lufa.

"I have reasons for not saying where it was, or where it wasn't. It may have been in Ireland, it may have been in Scotland, it may have been in England; it was in one of the three—an old house, parts very old. One morning I happened to be late, and found the breakfast-table deserted. I was not the last, however; for presently another man appeared, whom I had met at dinner the day before for the first time. We both happened to be in the army, and had drawn a little together. The moment I saw him, I knew he had passed an uncomfortable night. His face was like dough, with livid spots under the eyes. He sat down and poured himself out a cup of tea. 'Game-pie?' I said, but he did not heed me. There was nobody in the room but ourselves, and I thought it best to leave him alone. 'Are you an old friend of the family?' he said at length. 'About the age of most friends,' I answered. He was silent again, for a bit, then said, 'I'm going to cut!' 'Ha, ha!' thought I, and something more. 'No, it's not that!' he said, reading my thought, which had been about a lady in the house with us. 'Pray don't imagine I want to know,' I replied. 'Neither do I want to tell,' he rejoined. 'I don't care to have fellows laugh at me!' 'That's just what I don't care to do. Nothing hurts me less than being laughed at, so I take no pleasure in it,' I said. 'What I do want,' said he, 'is to have you tell Mrs. ——' There! I was on the very edge of saying her name! and you would have known who she was, all of you! I am glad I caught myself in time!—'tell Mrs. Blank,' said he, 'why I went.' 'Very well! I will. Why are you going?' 'Can't you help a fellow to an excuse? I'm not going to give her the reason.' 'Tell me what you want me to say, and I will tell her you told me to say so.' 'I will tell you the truth.' 'Fire away, then.' 'I was in a beastly funk last night. I dare say you think as I did, that a man ought never to be a hair off the cool?' 'That depends,' I replied; 'there are some things, and there may be more, at which any but an idiot might well be scared; but some fools are such fools they can't shiver! What's the matter? I give you my word I'll not make game of it.' The fellow looked so seedy, don't you know, I couldn't but be brotherly, or, at least, cousinly to him!—that don't go for much, does it, Lufa? 'Well,' he said, 'I will tell you. Last night, I had been in bed about five minutes, and hadn't even had time to grow sleepy, when I heard a curious shuffling in the passage outside my door, and an indescribable terror came over me. To be perfectly open with you, however, I had heard that was the sign she was coming!' 'Who coming?' said I. 'The ghost, of course!' he answered. 'The ghost!' 'You don't mean to say you never heard of the ghost?' 'Never heard a word of it.' 'Well, they don't like to speak of it, but everybody knows it!' 'Go on,' said I; and he did, but plainly with a tearing effort. 'The shuffling was like feet in slippers much too big. As if I had been five instead of five-and-thirty, I dived under the blankets, and lay so for minutes after the shuffling had ceased. But at length I persuaded myself it was but a foolish fancy, and I had never really heard anything. What with fear and heat I was much in want of breath too, I can tell you! So I came to the surface, and looked out.' Here he paused a moment, and turned almost livid. 'There stood a horrible old woman, staring at me, as if she had been seeing me all the time, and the blankets made no difference!' 'Was she really ugly?' I asked. 'Well, I don't know what you call ugly,' he answered, 'but if you had seen her stare, you would have thought her ugly enough! Had she been as beautiful as a houri, though, I don't imagine I should have been less frightened!' 'Well,' said I, for he had come to a pause, 'and what came next?' 'I can not tell. I came to myself all trembling, and as cold and as wet as if I had been dipped in a well' 'You are sure you were not dreaming?' I said. 'I was not. But I do not expect you believe me!' 'You must not be offended,' I said, 'if I find the thing stiff to stow! I believe you all the same.' 'What?' he said, not quite understanding me. 'An honest man and a gentleman,' I answered. 'And a coward to boot!' 'God forbid!' I returned: 'what man can answer for himself at every moment! If I remember, Hector turned at last and ran from Achilles!' He said nothing, and I went on. 'I once heard a preaching fellow say, "When a wise man is always wise, then is the kingdom of heaven!" and I thought he knew something!' I talked, don't you know, to quiet him. 'I once saw,' I said, 'the best-tempered man I ever knew, in the worst rage I ever saw man in—though I must allow he had good reason!' He drank his cup of tea, got up, and said, 'I'm off. Good-bye—and thank you! A million of money wouldn't make me stay in the house another hour! There is that in it I fear ten times worse than the ghost?' 'Gracious! what is that?' I said. 'This horrible cowardice oozing from her like a mist. The house is full of it!' 'But what shall I say to Mrs. Blank?' 'Anything you like.' 'I will say then, that you are very sorry, but were compelled to go.' 'Say what you please, only let me go! Tell them to send my traps after me. Good-bye! I'm in a sepulcher! I shall have to throw up my commission!' So he went."

"And what became of him?"

"I've neither seen nor heard of him to this day!"

He ceased with the cadence of an ended story.

"Is that all?"

"You spoke of an adventure of your own!"

"I was flattering myself," said Lufa, "that in our house Mr. Colman was at last to hear a ghost story from the man's own lips!"

"The sun is coming out!" said Sefton. "I will have a cigar at the stables."

The company protested, but he turned a deaf ear to expostulation, and went.

CHAPTER XIX. THE BODILESS.

In the drawing-room after dinner, some of the ladies gathered about him, and begged the story of his own adventure. He smiled queerly.

"Very well, you shall have it!" he answered.

They seated themselves, and the company came from all parts of the room—among the rest, Lufa and Walter.

"It was three days, if I remember," began Sefton, "after my military friend left, when one night I found myself alone in the drawing-room, just waked from a brown study. No one had said good-night to me. I looked at my watch; it was half past eleven. I rose and went. My bedroom was on the first-floor.

"The stairs were peculiar—a construction later than much of the house, but by no means modern. When you reached the landing of the first-floor and looked up, you could see above you the second-floor, descended by a balustrade between arches. There were no carpets on stairs or landings, which were all of oak.

"I can not certainly say what made me look up; but I think, indeed I am almost sure, I had heard a noise like that the ghost was said to make, as of one walking in shoes too large: I saw a lady looking down over the balusters on the second-floor. I thought some one was playing me a trick, and imitating the ghost, for the ladies had been chaffing me a good deal that night; they often do. She wore an old-fashioned, browny, silky looking dress. I rushed up to see who was taking the rise out of me. I looked up at her as I ran, and she kept looking down, but apparently not at me. Her face was that of a middle-aged woman, beginning, indeed, to be old, and had an intent, rather troubled look, I should say; but I did not consider it closely.

"I was at the top in a moment, on the level where she stood leaning over the handrail. Turning, I approached her. Apparently, she neither saw nor heard me. 'Well acted!' I said to myself—but even then I was beginning to be afraid, without knowing why. Every man's impulse, I fancy, is to go right up to anything that frightens him—at least, I have always found it so. I walked close up to the woman. She moved her head and turned in my direction, but only as if about to go away. Whether she looked at me I can not tell, but I saw her eyes plain enough. By this time, I suppose, the idea of a ghost must have been uppermost, for, being now quite close to her, I put out my hand as if to touch her. My hand went through her—through her head and body! I am not joking in the least; I mean you to believe, if you can, exactly what I say. What then she did, or whether she took any notice of my movement, I can not tell; I only know what I did, or rather what I did not do. For, had I been capable, I should have uttered a shriek that would have filled the house with ghastliest terror; but there was a load of iron on my chest, and the hand of a giant at my throat. I could not help opening my mouth, for something drew all the muscles of my jaws and throat, but I could not utter a sound. The horror I was in, was entirely new to me, and no more under my control than a fever. I only wonder it did not paralyze me, that I was able to turn and run down the stair! I ran as if all the cardinal sins were at my heels. I flew, never seeming to touch the stairs as I went. I darted along the passage, burst into my room, shut and locked the door, lighted my candles, fell into a chair, shuddered, and began to breathe again."

He ceased, not without present signs of the agitation he described.

"But that's not all!"

"And what else?"

"Did anything happen?"

"Do tell us more."

"I have nothing more to tell," answered Sefton. "But I haven't done wondering what could have put me in such an awful funk! You can't have a notion what it was like!"

"I know I should have been in a worse!"

"Perhaps—but why? Why should any one have been terrified? The poor thing had lost her body, it is true, but there she was notwithstanding—all the same! It might be nicer or not so nice to her, but why should it so affect me? that's what I want to know! Am I not, as Hamlet says, 'a thing immortal as itself?' I don't see the sense of it! Sure I am that one meets constantly—sits down with, eats and drinks with, hears sing, and play, and remark on the weather, and the fate of the nation—"

He paused, his eyes fixed on Walter.

"What are you driving at?" said Lufa.

"I was thinking of a much more fearful kind of creature," he answered.

"What kind of a creature?" she asked.

"A creature," he said, slowly, "that has a body, but no soul to it. All body, with brain enough for its affairs, it has no soul. Such will never wander about after they are dead! there will be nothing to wander! Good-night, ladies! Were I to tell you the history of a woman whose acquaintance I made some years ago at Baden, you would understand the sort Good-night!"

There was silence for a moment or two. Had his sister not been present, something other than complimentary to Sefton might have crept about the drawing-room—to judge from the expression of two or three faces. Walter felt the man worth knowing, but felt also something about him that repelled him.

CHAPTER XX. THE SOULLESS.

In his room, Walter threw himself in a chair, and sat without thinking, for the mental presence of Lufa was hardly thought Gradually Sefton's story revived, and for a time displaced the image of Lufa. It was the first immediately authenticated ghost-narration he had ever heard. His fancy alone had hitherto been attracted by such tales; but this brought him close to things of import as profound as marvelous. He began to wonder how he was likely to carry himself in such an interview. Courage such as Mr. Sefton's he dared not claim—any more than hope for the distinction of ever putting his hand through a ghost! To be sure, the question philosophically considered, Sefton could have done no such thing; but where no relations existed, he reasoned, or rather assumed, the one could not be materially present to the other; a fortiori there could be no passing of the one through the other! Where the ghost was, the hand was; both existed in the same space at the same time; therefore the one did not penetrate the other! The ghost, he held, never saw Sefton, knew or thought of his presence, or was aware of any intrusive outrage from his hand! He shrunk none the less, however, from such phantasmic presence as Sefton had described; a man's philosophy made but a fool of him when it came to the pinch! He would indeed like to see a ghost, but not to be alone with one!

Here came back to him a certain look in Lufa's face, which he had not understood: was it possible she knew something about the thing? Could this be the house where it took place, where the ghost appeared? The room in which he sat was very old! the pictures in it none but for their age would hang up on any wall! And the bed was huger and gloomier than he had ever elsewhere seen! It was on the second-floor too! What if this was the very room the officer slept in!

He must run into port, find shelter from the terrors of the shoreless sea of the unknown! But all the harbor he could seek, was bed and closed eyes! The dark is a strange refuge from the darkness—yet that which most men seek. It is so dark! let us go further from the light! Thus deeper they go, and come upon greater terrors! He undressed hurriedly, blew out his candles, and by the light of the fire, glowing rather than blazing, plunged into the expanse which glimmered before him like a lake of sleep in the moonshine of dreams.

The moment he laid down his head, he became aware of what seemed unnatural stillness. Throughout the evening a strong wind had been blowing about the house; it had ceased, and without having noted the tumult, he was now aware of the calm. But what made him so cold? The surface of the linen was like a film of ice! He rolled himself round, and like a hedge-hog sought shelter within the circumference of his own person. But he could not get warm, lie close as he might to his own door; there was no admittance! Had the room turned suddenly cold? Could it be that the ghost was near, making the air like that of the sepulcher from which she had issued? for such ghosts as walk the world at night, what refuge so fit as their tombs in the day-time! The thought was a worse horror than he had known himself capable of feeling. He shivered with the cold. It seemed to pierce to his very bones. A strange and hideous constriction seized the muscles of his neck and throat; had not Sefton described the sensation? Was it not a sure sign of ghostly presence?

How much longer he could have endured, or what would have been the result of the prolongation of his suffering, I can not tell. Molly would have found immediate refuge with Him to whom belong all the ghosts wherever they roam or rest—with Him who can deliver from the terrors of the night as well as from the perplexities of the day; but Walter felt his lonely being exposed on all sides.

The handle of the door moved. I am not sure whether ghosts always enter and leave a room in silence, but the sound horribly shook Walter's nerves, and nearly made an end of him for a time. But a voice said, "May I come in?" What he answered or whether he answered, Walter could not have told, but his terror subsided. The door opened wider, some one entered, closed it softly, and approached the bed through the dull fire-light. "I did not think you would be in bed!" said the voice, which Walter now knew for Sefton's; "but at the risk of waking you, even of giving you a sleepless night, I must have a little talk with you!"

"I shall be glad," answered Walter.

Sefton little thought how welcome was his visit!

But he was come to do him a service for which he could hardly at once be grateful. The best things are done for any are generally those for which they are at the moment least grateful; it needs the result of the service to make them able to prize it.

Walter thought he had more of the story to tell—something he had not chosen to talk of to the ladies.

Sefton stood, and for a few moments there was silence. He seemed to be meditating, yet looked like one who wanted to light his cigar.

"Won't you take a seat?" said Walter.

"Thank you!" returned Sefton, and sat on the bed.

"I am twenty-seven," he said at length. "How old are you?"

"Twenty-three," answered Walter.

"When I was twenty-three, I knew ever so much more than I do now! I'm not half so sure about things as I was. I wonder if you will find it so!"

"I hope I shall—otherwise I sha'n't have got on."

"Well, now, couldn't you just—why not?—forestall your experience by making use of mine? I'm talking like a fool, I know, but never mind; it is the more genuine. Look here, Mr. Colman! I like you, and believe you will one day be something more than a gentleman. There, that won't do! What's my opinion, good or bad, to you? Listen to me anyhow: you're on the wrong tack here, old boy!"

"I'm sorry I don't understand you," said Walter.

"Naturally not; how could you? I will explain."

"Please. Don't mind me. I shall do my best not to be offended."

"That is more than I should have presumed to ask." Again a brief silence followed.

"You heard my story about the ghost?" said Sefton.

"I was on the point of asking you if I might tell it in print!"

"You may do what you like with it, except the other fellow's part."

"Thank you. But I wish you would tell me what you meant by that other more fearful—apparition—or what did you call it? Were you alluding to the vampire?"

"No. There are live women worse than vampires. Scared as I confess I was, I would rather meet ten such ghosts as I told you of, than another woman such as I mean. I know one, and she's enough. By the time you had seen ten ghosts you would have got used to them, and found there was no danger from them; but a woman without a soul will devour any number of men. You see she's all room inside! Look here! I must be open with you: tell me you are not in love with my cousin Lufa, and I will bid you good-night."

"I am so much in love with her, that I dare not think what may come of it," replied Walter.

"Then for God's sake tell her, and have done with it! Anything will be better than going on like this. I will not say what Lufa is; indeed I don't know what name would at all fit her! You think me a queer, dry, odd sort of a customer: I was different when I fell in love with Lufa. She is older than you think her, though not so old as I am. I kept saying to myself she was hardly a woman yet; I must give her time. I was better brought up than she; I thought things of consequence that she thought of none. I hadn't a stupid ordinary mother like hers. She's my second cousin. She took my love-making, never drew me on, never pushed me back; never refused my love, never returned it. Whatever I did or said, she seemed content. She was always writing poetry. 'But where's her own poetry?' I would say to myself. I was always trying to get nearer to what I admired; she never seemed to suspect the least relation between the ideal and life, between thought and action. To have an ideal implied no aspiration after it! She has not a thought of the smallest obligation to carry out one of the fine things she writes of, any more than people that go to church think they have anything to do with what they hear there. Most people's nature seems all in pieces. They wear and change their moods as they wear and change their dresses. Their moods make them, and not they their moods. They are different with every different mood. But Lufa seems never to change, and yet never to be in one and the same mood. She is always in two moods, and the one mood has nothing to do with the other. The one mood never influences, never modifies the other. They run side by side and do not mingle. The one mood is enthusiasm for what is not, the other indifference to what is. She has not the faintest desire to make what is not into what is. For love, I believe all she knows about it is, that it is a fine thing to be loved. She loves nobody but her mother, and her only after a fashion. I had my leg broken in the hunting-field once; my horse got up and galloped off; I lay still. She saw what had happened, and went after the hounds. She said she could do no good; Doctor Black was in the field, and she went to find him. She didn't find him, and he didn't come. I believe she forgot. But it's worth telling you, though it has nothing to do with her, that I wasn't forgot. Old Truefoot went straight home, and kept wheeling and tearing up and down before the windows, but, till his own groom came, would let no one touch him. Then when he would have led him to the stable, he set his forefeet out in front of him, and wouldn't budge. The groom got on his back, but was scarce in the saddle when Truefoot was oft in a bee-line over everything to where I was lying. There's a horse for you! And there's a woman! I'm telling you all this, mind, not to blame her, but to warn you. Whether she is to blame or not, I don't know; I don't understand her.

"I was free to come and go, and say what I pleased, for both families favored the match. She never objected; never said she would not have me; said she liked me as well as any other. In a word she would have married me, if I would have taken her. There are men, I believe, who would make the best of such a consent, saying they were so in love with the woman they would rejoice to take her on any terms: I don't understand that sort of love! I would as soon think of marrying a woman I hated as a woman that did not love me. I know no reason why any woman should love me, and if no woman can find any, I most go alone. Lufa has found none yet, and life and love too seem to have gone out of me waiting. If you ask me why I do not give it all up, I have no answer. You will say for Lufa, it is only that the right man is not come! It may be so; but I believe there is more than that in it. I fear she is all outside. It is true her poetry is even passionate sometimes; but I suspect all her inspiration comes of the poetry she reads, not of the nature or human nature around her; it comes of ambition, not of love. I don't know much about verse, but to me there is an air of artificiality about all hers. I can not understand how you could praise her long poem so much—if you were in love with her. She has grown to me like the ghost I told you of. I put out my hand to her, and it goes through her. It makes me feel dead myself to be with her. I wonder sometimes how it would be if suddenly she said she loved me. Should I love her, or should we have changed parts? She is very dainty—very lady-like—but womanly! At one time—and for this I am now punished—the ambition to wake love in her had no small part in my feeling toward her— ambition to be the first and only man so to move her: despair has long cured me of that; but not before I had come to love her in a way I can not now understand. Why I should love her I can not tell; and were it not that I scorn to marry her without love, I should despise my very love. You are thinking, 'Well then, the way is clear for me!' It is; I only want to prepare you for what I am confident will follow: you will have the heart taken out of you! That you are poor will be little obstacle if she loves you. She is the heiress, and can do much as she pleases. If she were in love, she would be obstinate. It must be in her somewhere, you will say, else how could she write as she does? But, I say again, look at the multitudes that go to church, and communicate, with whose being religion has no more to do than with that of Satan! I've said my say. Good-night!"

He rose, and stood.

He had not uttered the depth of what he feared concerning Lufa—that she was simply, unobtrusively, unconsciously, absolutely selfish.

Walter had listened with a beating heart, now full of hope that he was to be Hildebrand to this Undine, now sick with the conviction that he was destined to fare no better than Sefton.

"Let me have my say before you go," he protested. "It will sound as presumptuous in your ears as it does in mine—but what is to be done except put the thing to the question?"

"There is nothing else. That is all I want. You must not go on like this. It is sucking the life out of you. I can't bear to see it. Pray do not misunderstand me."

"That is impossible," returned Walter.

Not a wink did he sleep that night. But ever and again across his anxiety, throughout the dark hours, came the flattering thought that she had never loved man yet, and he was teaching her to love. He did not doubt Sefton, but Sefton might be right only for himself.

CHAPTER XXI. THE LAST RIDE.

In the morning, as Walter was dressing, he received a copy of his poems which he had taken in sheets to a book-binder to put in morocco for Lady Lufa. Pleased like a child, he handled it as if he might hurt it. Such a feeling he had never had before, would never have again. He was an author! One might think, after the way in which he had treated not a few books and not a few authors, he could scarcely consider it such a very fine thing to be an author; but there is always a difference between thine and mine, treated by the man of this world as essential. The book was Walter's book and not another's!—no common prose or poetry this, but the first-born of his deepest feeling! At length it had taken body and shape! From the unseen it had emerged in red morocco, the color of his heart, its edges golden with the light of his hopes!

As to the communication of the night, its pain had early vanished. Was not Sefton a disappointed lover? His honesty, however evident, could not alter that fact! Least of all could a man himself tell whether disguised jealousy and lingering hope might not be potently present, while he believed himself solely influenced by friendly anxiety!

"I will take his advice, however," said Walter to himself, "and put an end to my anxiety this very day!"

"Do you feel inclined for a gallop, Mr. Colman?" asked Lufa as they sat at the breakfast-table. "It feels just like a spring morning. The wind changed in the night. You won't mind a little mud—will you?"

In common phrase, but with a foolish look of adoring gratitude, Walter accepted the invitation. "How handsome he is!" thought Lufa; for Walter's countenance was not only handsome but expressive. Most women, however, found him attractive chiefly from his frank address and open look; for, though yet far from a true man, he was of a true nature. Every man's nature indeed is true, though the man be not true; but some have come into the world so much nearer the point where they may begin to be true, that, comparing them with the rest, we say their nature is true.

Lufa rose and went to get ready. Walter followed, and overtook her on the stair.

"I have something for you," he said; "may I bring it you?"

He could not postpone the effect his book might have. Authors young and old think so much of their books that they seldom conceive how little others care about them.

She was hardly in her room, when he followed her with the volume.

She took it, and opened it.

"Yours!" she cried. "And poetry! Why, Walter!"

She had once or twice called him by his name before.

He took it from her hand, and turning the title-page, gave it her again to read the dedication. A slight rose-tinge suffused her face. She said nothing, but shut the book, and gave it a tender little hug.

"She never did that to anything Sefton gave her!" thought Walter.

"Make haste," she said, and turning, went in, and closed her door.

He walked up and down the hall for half an hour before she appeared. When she came tripping down the wide, softly descending stair, in her tight-fitting habit and hat and feather, holding up her skirt, so that he saw her feet racing each other like a cataract across the steps, saying as she came near him, "I have kept you waiting, but I could not help it; my habit was torn!" he thought he had never seen her so lovely. Indeed she looked lovely, and had she loved, would have been lovely. As it was, her outer loveliness was but a promise whose fulfillment had been too long postponed. His heart swelled into his throat and eyes as he followed her and helped her to mount.

"Nobody puts me up so well as you!" she said.

He could hardly repress the triumph that filled him from head to foot. Anyhow, and whoever might object, she liked him! If she loved him and would confess it, he could live on the pride of it all the rest of his days!

They were unattended, but neither spoke until they were well beyond the lodge-gate. Winter though it was, a sweet air was all abroad, and the day was full of spring-prophecies: all winters have such days, even those of the heart! how could we get through without them? Their horses were in excellent spirits—it was their first gallop for more than a week; Walter's roan was like a flame under him. They gave them so much to do, that no such talk as Walter longed for, was possible. It consoled him, however, to think that he had never had such a chance of letting Lufa see he could ride.

At length, after a great gallop, they were quieter, seeming to remember they were horses and not colts, and must not overpass the limits of equine propriety.

"Is it our last ride, Lufa?" said Walter.

"Why should it be?" she answered, opening her eyes wide on him.

"There is no reason I know," he returned, "except—except you are tired of me."

"Nobody is tired of you—except perhaps George, and you need not mind him; he is odd. I have known him from childhood, and don't understand him yet."

"He is clever!" said Walter.

"I dare say he is—if he would take the trouble to show it."

"You hardly do him justice, I think!"

"How can I? he bores me! and when I am bored, I am horribly bored. I have been very patient with him."

"Why do you ask him so often then?"

"I don't ask him. Mamma is fond of him, and so—"

"You are the victim!"

"I can bear it; I have consolations!"

She laughed merrily.

"How do you like my binding?" he asked, when they had ridden awhile in silence.

She looked up with a question.

"The binding of my book, I mean," he explained.

"It is a good color."

He felt his hope rather damped.

"Will you let me read a little from it?"

"With pleasure. You shall have an audience in the drawing-room, after luncheon."

"Oh, Lufa! how could you think I would read my own poems to a lot of people!"

"I beg your pardon! Will the summer-house do?"

"Yes, indeed; nowhere better."

"Very well! The summer-house, after lunch!"

This was not encouraging! Did she suspect what was coming? and was she careful not to lead the way to it? She had never been like this before! Perhaps she did not like having the book dedicated to her! But there was no mention of her name, or anything to let "the heartless world" know to whom it was offered!

As they approached the house, Walter said,

"Would you mind coming at once to the summer-house?"

"Lunch will be ready."

"Then sit down in your habit, and come immediately after. Let me have my way for once, Lufa."

"Very well."

CHAPTER XXII. THE SUMMER-HOUSE.

The moment the meal was over, he left the room, and in five minutes they met at the place appointed—a building like a miniature Roman temple.

"Oh," said Lufa, as she entered, "I forgot the book. How stupid of me!"

"Never mind," returned Walter. "It was you, not the book I wanted."

A broad bench went round the circular wall; Lufa seated herself on it, and Walter placed himself beside her, as near as he dared. For some moments he did not speak. She looked up at him inquiringly. He sunk at her feet, bowed his head toward her, and but for lack of courage would have laid it on her knees.

"Oh, Lufa!" he said, "you can not think how I love you!"

"Poor, dear boy!" she returned, in the tone of a careless mother to whom a son has unburdened his sorrows, and laid her hand lightly on his curls.

The words were not repellent, but neither was the tone encouraging.

"You do not mind my saying it?" he resumed, feeling his way timidly.

"What could you do but tell me?" she answered.

"What could I do for you if you did not let me know! I'm so sorry, Walter!"

"Why should you be sorry? You can do with me as you please!"

"I don't know about such things. I don't quite know what you mean, or what you want. I will be as kind to you as I can—while you stay with us."

"But, Lufa—I may call you Lufa?"

"Yes, surely! if that is any comfort to you."

"Nothing but your love, Lufa, can be a comfort to me. That would make me one of the blessed!"

"I like you very much. If you were a girl, I should say I loved you."

"Why not say it as it is?"

"Would you be content with the love I should give a girl? Some of you want so much!"

"I will be glad of any love you can give me. But to say I should be content with any love you could give me, would be false. My love for you is such, I don't know how to bear it! It aches so! My heart is full of you, and longs for you till I can hardly endure the pain. You are so beautiful that your beauty burns me. Night nor day can I forget you!"

"You try to forget me then?"

"Never. Your eyes have so dazzled my soul that I can see nothing but your eyes. Do look at me—just for one moment, Lufa."

She turned her face and looked him straight in the eyes—looked into them as if they were windows through which she could peer into the convolutions of his brain. She held her eyes steady until his dropped, unable to sustain the nearness of her presence.

"You see," she said, "I am ready to do anything I can to please you!"

He felt strangely defeated, rose, and sat down beside her again, with the sickness of a hot summer noon in his soul.

But he must leave no room for mistake! He had been dreaming long enough! What had not Sefton told him!

"Is it possible you do not understand, Lufa, what a man means when he says, 'I love you'?"

"I think I do! I don't mind it!"

"That means you will love me again?"

"Yes; I will be good to you."

"You will love me as a woman loves a man?"

"I will let you love me as much as you please."

"To love you as much as I please, would be to call you my own; to marry you; to say wife to you; to have you altogether, with nobody to come between, or try to stop my worshiping of you—not father, not mother—nobody!"

"Now you are foolish, Walter! You know I never meant that! You must have known that never could be! I never imagined you could make such a fantastic blunder! But then how should you know how we think about things! I must remember that, and not be hard upon you!"

"You mean that your father and mother would not like it?"

"There it is! You do not understand! I thought so! I do not mean my father and mother in particular; I mean our people—people of our position—I would say rank, but that might hurt you! We are brought up so differently from you, that you can not understand how we think of such things. It grieves me to appear unkind, but really, Walter! There is not a man I love more than you—but marriage! Lady Lufa would be in everybody's mouth, the same as if I had run off with my groom! Our people are so blind that, believe me, they would hardly see the difference. The thing is simply impossible!"

"It would not be impossible if you loved me!"

"Then I don't, never did, never could love you. Don't imagine you can persuade me to anything unbecoming, anything treacherous to my people! You will find yourself awfully mistaken!"

"But I may make myself a name! If I were as famous as Lord Tennyson, would it be just as impossible?"

"To say it would not, would be to confess myself worldly, and that I never was! No, Walter; I admire you; if you could be trusted not to misunderstand, I might even say I loved you! I shall always be glad to see you, always enjoy hearing you read; but there is a line as impassable as the Persian river of death. Talk about something else, or I must go!"

Here Walter, who had been shivering with cold, began to grow warm again as he answered:

"How could you write that poem, Lady Lufa—full of such grand things about love, declaring love everything and rank nothing; and then, when it came to yourself, treat me like this! I could not have believed it possible! You can not know what love is, however much you write about it!"

"I hope I never shall, if it means any confusion between friendship and folly! It shall not make a fool of me! I will not be talked about! It is all very well and very right in poetry! The idea of letting all go for love is so splendid, it is the greatest pity it should be impossible. There may be some planet, whose social habits are different, where it might work well enough; but here it is not to be thought of—except in poetry, of course, or novels. Of all human relations, the idea of such love is certainly the fittest for verse, therefore we have no choice; we must use it. But because I think with pleasure of such lovers, why must I consent to be looked at with pleasure myself? What obligation does my heroine lay on me to do likewise? I don't see the thing. I don't want to pose as a lover. Why should I fall in love with you in real life, because I like you to read my poem about lovers? Can't you see the absurdity of the argument? Life and books are two different spheres. The one is the sphere of thoughts, the other of things, and they don't touch."

But for pride, Walter could have wept with shame: why should he care that one with such principles should grant or refuse him anything! Yet he did care!

"There is no reason at all," she resumed, "why we should not be friends. Mr. Colman, I am not a flirt. It is in my heart to be a sister to you! I would have you the first to congratulate me when the man appears whom I may choose to love as you mean! He need not be a poet to make you jealous! If he were, I should yet always regard you as my poet."

"And you would let me kiss your shoe, or perhaps your glove, if I was very good!" said Walter.

She took no notice of the outburst: it was but a bit of childish temper!

"You must learn," she went on, "to keep your life and your imaginations apart. You are always letting them mix, and that confuses everything. A poet of all men ought not to make the mistake. It is quite monstrous! as monstrous as if a painter joined the halves of two different animals! Poetry is so unlike life, that to carry the one into the other is to make the poet a ridiculous parody of a man! The moment that, instead of standing aloof and regarding, he plunges in, he becomes a traitor to his art, and is no longer able to represent things as they ought to be, but can not be. My mother and I will open to you the best doors in London because we like you; but pray do not dream of more. Do, please, Walter, leave it possible for me to say I like you—oh, so much!"

She had been staring out of the window as she spoke; now she turned her eyes upon him where he sat, crushed and broken, beside her. A breath of compassion seemed to ruffle the cold lake of her spirit, and she looked at him in silence for a moment. He did not raise his eyes, but her tone made her present to his whole being as she said,

"I don't want to break your heart, my poet! It was a lovely thought— why did you spoil it?—that we two understood and loved each other in a way nobody could have a right to interfere with!"

Walter lifted his head. The word loved wrought on him like a spell: he was sadly a creature of words! He looked at her with flushed face and flashing eyes. Often had Lufa thought him handsome, but she had never felt it as she did now.

"Let it be so!" he said. "Be my sister-friend, Lufa. Leave it only to me to remember how foolish I once made myself in your beautiful eyes—how miserable always in my own blind heart."

So little of a man was our poet, that out of pure disappointment and self-pity he burst into a passion of weeping. The world seemed lost to him, as it seemed at such a time to many a better man. But to the true the truth of things will sooner or later assert itself, and neither this world nor the next prove lost to him. A man's well-being does not depend on any woman. The woman did not create, and could not have contented him. No woman can ruin a man by refusing him, or even by accepting him, though she may go far toward it. There is one who has upon him a perfect claim, at the entrancing recognition of which he will one day cry out, "This, then, is what it all meant!" The lamp of poetry may for a time go out in the heart of the poet, and nature seem a blank; but where the truth is, the poetry must be; and truth is, however the untrue may fail to see it. Surely that man is a fool who, on the ground that there can not be such a God as other fools assert, or such a God as alone he is able to imagine, says there is no God!

Lufa's bosom heaved, and she gave a little sob; her sentiment, the skin of her heart, was touched, for the thing was pathetic! A mist came over her eyes, and might, had she ever wept, have turned to tears.

Walter sat with his head in his hands and wept. She had never before seen a man weep, yet never a tear left its heavenly spring to flow from her eyes! She rose, took his face between her hands, raised it, and kissed him on the forehead.

He rose also, suddenly calmed.

"Then it was our last ride, Lufa!" he said, and left the summer-house.

CHAPTER XXIII. THE PARK.

Walter did not know where he was going when he turned from Lufa. It was solitude he sought, without being aware that he sought anything. Must it not be a deep spiritual instinct that drives trouble into solitude? There are times when only the highest can comfort even the lowest, and solitude is the ante-chamber to his presence. With him is the only possibility of essential comfort, the comfort that turns an evil into a good. But it was certainly not knowledge of this that drove Walter into the wide, lonely park. "Away from men!" moans the wounded life. Away from the herd flies the wounded deer; away from the flock staggers the sickly sheep—to the solitary covert to die. The man too thinks it is to die; but it is in truth so to return to life—if indeed he be a man, and not an abortion that can console himself with vile consolations. "You can not soothe me, my friends! leave me to my misery," cries the man; and lo his misery is the wind of the waving garments of him that walks in the garden in the cool of the day! All misery is God unknown.

Hurt and bleeding Walter wandered away. His life was palled with a sudden hail-cloud which hung low, and blotted out color and light and loveliness. It was the afternoon; the sun was fast going down; the dreary north wind had begun again to blow, and the trees to moan in response; they seemed to say, "How sad thou art, wind of winter! see how sad thou makest us! we moan and shiver! each alone, we are sad!" The sorrow of nature was all about him; but the sighing of the wind-sifting trees around his head, and the hardening of the earth about the ancient roots under his feet, was better than the glow of the bright drawing-room, with its lamps and blazing fires, its warm colors and caressing softnesses. Who would take joy in paradise with hell in his heart! Let him stay out in the night with the suffering, groaning trees, with the clouds that have swallowed the moon and the stars, with the frost and the silent gathering of the companies, troops, and battalions of snow!

Every man understands something of what Walter felt. His soul was seared with cold. The ways of life were a dull sickness. There was no reason why things should be, why the world should ever have been made! The night was come: why should he keep awake! How cold the river looked in its low, wet channel! How listlessly the long grasses hung over its bank! And the boy on the other side was whistling!

It grew darker. He had made a long round, and unaware was approaching the house. He had not thought what he must do. Nothing so practical as going away had yet occurred to him. She had not been unkind! She had even pressed on him a sister's love! The moth had not yet burned away enough of its wings to prevent it from burning its whole body! it kept fluttering about the flame. Nor was absent the childish weakness, the unmanly but common impulse, to make the woman feel how miserable she had made him. For this poor satisfaction, not a few men have blown their brains out; not a few women drowned themselves or taken poison—and generally without success! Walter would stand before her the ruin she had made him, then vanish from her sight. To-morrow he would leave the house, but she must see him yet once, alone, before he went! Once more he must hang his shriveled pinions in the presence of the seraph whose radiance had scorched him! And still the most hideous thought of all would keep lifting its vague ugly head out of chaos—the thought that, lovely as she was, she was not worshipful.

The windows were dimly shining through their thick curtains. The house looked a great jewel of bliss, in which the spirits of paradise might come and go, while such as he could not enter! What should he do? Where should he go? To his room, and dress for dinner? It was impossible! How could he sit feeling her eyes, and facing Sefton! How endure the company, the talk, the horrible eating! All so lately full of refinement, of enchantment—the music, the pictures, the easy intercourse—all was stupid, wearisome, meaningless! He would go to his room and say he had a headache! But first he would peep into the drawing-room: she might be there—and looking sad!

CHAPTER XXIV. THE DRAWING-ROOM.

He opened a door into one of the smaller compartments of the drawing-room, looked, crept in, and closed the door behind him.

Lufa was there—alone! He durst not approach her, but if he seated himself in a certain corner, he could see her and she him! He did not, however, apprehend that the corner he had chosen was entirely in shadow, or reflect that the globe of a lamp was almost straight between them. He thought she saw him, but she did not.

The room seemed to fold him round with softness as he entered from the dreary night; and he could not help being pervaded by the warmth, and weakened by the bodily comfort. He sat and gazed at his goddess—a mere idol, seeming, not being, until he hardly knew whether she was actually before him, or only present to his thought. She was indeed a little pale—but that she always was when quiet; no sorrow, not a shadow was on her face. She seemed brooding, but over nothing painful. At length she smiled.

"She is pleased to think that I love her!" thought Walter. "She leans to me a little! When the gray hair comes and the wrinkles, it will be a gracious memory that she was so loved by one who had but his life to give her! 'He was poor,' she will say, 'but I have not found the riches he would have given me! I have been greatly loved!'"

I believe myself, she was ruminating a verse that had come to her in the summer-house, while Walter was weeping by her side.

A door opened, and Sefton came in.

"Have you seen the 'Onlooker'?" he said—a journal at the time in much favor with the more educated populace. "There is a review in it that would amuse you."

"Of what?" she asked, listlessly.

"I didn't notice the name of the book, but it is a poem, and just your sort, I should say. The article is in the 'Onlooker's' best style."

"Pray let me see it!" she answered, holding out her hand.

"I will read it to you, if I may."

She did not object. He sat down a little way from her, and read.

He had not gone far before Walter knew, although its name had not occurred as Sefton read, that the book was his own. The discovery enraged him: how had the reviewer got hold of it when he himself had seen no copy except Lufa's? It was a puzzle he never got at the root of. Probably some one he had offended had contrived to see as much of it, at the printer's or binder's, as had enabled him to forestall its appearance with the most stinging, mocking, playfully insolent paper that had ever rejoiced the readers of the "Onlooker." But he had more to complain of than rudeness, a thing of which I doubt if any reviewer is ever aware. For he soon found that, by the blunder of reviewer or printer, the best of the verses quoted were misquoted, and so rendered worthy of the epithet attached to them. This unpleasant discovery was presently followed by another—that the rudest and most contemptuous personal remark was founded on an ignorant misapprehension of the reviewer's own; while in ridicule of a mere misprint which happened to carry a comic suggestion on the face of it, the reviewer surpassed himself.

As Sefton read, Lufa laughed often and heartily: the thing was gamesomely, cleverly, almost brilliantly written. Annoyed as he was, Walter did not fail to note, however, that Sefton did not stop to let Lufa laugh, but read quietly on. Suddenly she caught the paper from his hand, for she was as quick as a kitten, saying:

"I must see who the author of the precious book is!"

Her cousin did not interfere, but sat watching her—almost solemnly.

"Ah, I thought so!" she cried, with a shriek of laughter. "I thought so! I could hardly be mistaken! What will the poor fellow say to it! It will kill him!" She laughed immoderately. "I hope it will give him a lesson, however!" she went on. "It is most amusing to see how much he thinks of his own verses!

He worships them! And then makes up for the idolatry by handling without mercy those of other people! It was he who so maltreated my poor first! I never saw anything so unfair in my life!"

Sefton said nothing, but looked grim.

"You should see—I will show it you—the gorgeous copy of this same comical stuff he gave me to-day! I am so glad he is going: he won't be able to ask me how I like it, and I sha'n't have to tell a story! I'm sorry for him, though—truly! He is a very nice sort of boy, though rather presuming. I must find out who the writer of that review is, and get mamma to invite him! He is a host in himself! I don't think I ever read anything so clever—or more just!"

"Oh, then, you have read the book?" spoke her cousin at length.

"No; but ain't those extracts enough? Don't they speak for themselves— for their silliness and sentimentality?"

"How would you like of a book of yours judged by scraps chopped off anywhere, Lufa!—or chosen for the look they would have in the humorous frame of the critic's remarks! It is less than fair! I do not feel that I know in the least what sort of book this is. I only know that again and again, having happened to come afterward upon the book itself, I have set down the reviewer as a knave, who for ends of his own did not scruple to make fools of his readers. I am ashamed, Lufa, that you should so accept everything as gospel against a man who believes you his friend!"

Walter's heart had been as water, now it had turned to ice, and with the coldness came strength: he could bear anything except this desert of a woman. The moment Sefton had thus spoken, he rose and came forward— not so much, I imagine, to Sefton's surprise as Lufa's and said,

"Thank you, Mr. Sefton, for undeceiving me. I owe you, Lady Lufa, the debt of a deep distrust hereafter of poetic ladies."

"They will hardly be annihilated by it, Mr. Colman!" returned Lufa. "But, indeed, I did not know you were in the room; and perhaps you did not know that in our circle it is counted bad manners to listen!"

"I was foolishly paralyzed for a moment," said Walter, "as well as unprepared for the part you would take."

"I am very glad, Mr. Colman," said Sefton, "that you have had the opportunity of discovering the truth! My cousin well deserves the pillory in which I know you will not place her!"

"Lady Lufa needs fear nothing from me. I have some regard left for the idea of her—the thing she is not! If you will be kind, come and help me out of the house."

"There is no train to-night."

"I will wait at the station for the slow train."

"I can not press you to stay an hour where you have been so treated, but—"

"It is high time I went!" said Walter—not without the dignity that endurance gives. "May I ask you to do one thing for me, Mr. Sefton?"

"Twenty things, if I can."

"Then please send my portmanteau after me."

With that he left the room, and went to his own, far on the way of cure, though not quite so far as he imagined. The blood, however, was surging healthily through his veins: he had been made a fool of, but he would be a wiser man for it!

He had hardly closed his door when Sefton appeared.

"Can I help you?" he said.

"To pack my portmanteau? Did you ever pack your own?"

"Oftener than you, I suspect! I never had but one orderly I could bear about me, and he's dead, poor fellow! I shall see him again, though, I do trust, let believers in dirt say what they will! Never till I myself think no more, will I cease hoping to see my old Archie again! Fellows must learn something through the Lufas, or they would make raving maniacs of us! God

107

be thanked, he has her in his great idiot-cage, and will do something with her yet! May you and I be there to see when she comes out in her right mind!"

"Amen!" said Walter.

"And now, my dear fellow," said Sefton, "if you will listen to me, you will not go till to-morrow morning. No, I don't want you to stay to breakfast! You shall go by the early train as any other visitor might. The least scrap of a note to Lady Tremaine, and all will go without remark."

He waited in silence. Walter went on putting up his things.

"I dare say you are right!" he said at length. "I will stay till the morning. But you will not ask me to go down again?"

"It would be a victory if you could."

"Very well, I will. I am a fool, but this much less of a fool, that I know I am one."

Somehow Walter had a sense of relief. He began to dress, and spent some pains on the process. He felt sure Sefton would take care the "Onlooker" should not be seen—before his departure anyhow. During dinner he talked almost brilliantly, making Lufa open her eyes without knowing she did.

He retired at length to his room with very mingled feelings. There was the closing paragraph of the most interesting chapter of his life yet constructed! What was to follow?

> *Into the gulf of an empty heart*
>
> *Something must always come.*
>
> *"What will it be?" I think with a start,*
>
> *And a fear that makes me dumb.*
>
> *I can not sit at my outer gate*
>
> *And call what shall soothe my grief;*
>
> *I can not unlock to a king in state,*

Can not bar a wind-swept leaf!

Hopeless were I if a loving Care
Sat not at the spring of my thought—
At the birth of my history, blank and bare.
Of the thing I have not wrought.

If God were not, this hollow need.
All that I now call me,
Might wallow with demons of hate and greed
In a lawless and shoreless sea!

Watch the door of this sepulcher,
Sit, my Lord, on the stone,
Till the life within it rise and stir.
And walk forth to claim its own.

This was how Walter felt and wrote some twelve months after, when he had come to understand a little of the process that had been conducted in him; when he knew that the life he had been living was a mere life in death, a being not worth being.

But the knowledge of this process had not yet begun. A thousand subtle influences, wrapped in the tattered cloak of dull old Time, had to come into secret, potent play, ere he would be able to write thus.

And even this paragraph was not yet quite at an end.

CHAPTER XXV. A MIDNIGHT INTERVIEW.

Walter drew his table near the fire, and sat down to concoct a brief note of thanks and farewell to his hostess, informing her that he was compelled to leave in haste. He found it rather difficult, though what Lufa might tell her mother he neither thought nor cared, if only he had his back to the house, and his soul out of it. It was now the one place on the earth which he would sink in the abyss of forgetfulness.

He could not get the note to his mind, falling constantly into thought that led nowhither, and at last threw himself back in his chair, wearied with the emotions of the day. Under the soothing influence of the heat and the lambent motions of the flames, he fell into a condition which was not sleep, and as little was waking. His childhood crept back to him, with all the delights of the sacred time when home was the universe, and father and mother the divinities that filled it. A something now vanished from his life, looked at him across a gulf of lapse, and said, "Am I likewise false? The present you desire to forget; you say, it were better it had never been: do you wish I too had never been? Why else have you left my soul in the grave of oblivion?" Thus talking with his past, he fell asleep.

It could have been but for a few minutes, though when he awoke it seemed a century had passed, he had dreamed of so much. But something had happened! What was it? The fire was blazing as before, but he was chilled to the marrow! A wind seemed blowing upon him, cold as if it issued from the jaws of the sepulcher! His imagination and memory together linked the time to the night of Sefton's warning: was the ghost now really come? Had Sefton's presence only saved him from her for the time? He sat bolt upright in his chair listening, the same horror upon him as then. It seemed minutes he thus sat motionless, but moments of fearful expectation are long drawn out; their nature is of centuries, not years. One thing was certain, and one only—that there was a wind, and a very cold one, blowing upon him. He stared at the door. It moved. It opened a little. A light tap followed. He could not speak.

Then came a louder, and the spell was broken. He started to his feet, and with the courage of terror extreme, opened the door—not opened it a little, as if he feared an unwelcome human presence, but pulled it, with a sudden wide yawn, open as the grave!

There stood no bodiless soul, but soulless Lufa!

He stood aside, and invited her to enter. Little as he desired to see her, it was a relief that it was she, and not an elderly lady in brown silk, through whose person you might thrust your hand without injury or offense.

As a reward of his promptitude in opening the door, he caught sight of Lady Tremaine disappearing in the corridor.

Lady Lufa walked in without a word, and Walter followed her, leaving the door wide. She seated herself in the chair he had just left, and turned to him with a quiet, magisterial air, as if she sat on the seat of judgment.

"You had better shut the door," she said.

"I thought Lady Tremaine might wish to hear," answered Walter.

"Not at all. She only lighted me to the door."

"As you please," said Walter, and having done as she requested, returned, and stood before her.

"Will you not take a seat?" she said, in the tone of—"You may sit down."

"Your ladyship will excuse me!" he answered.

She gave a condescending motion to her pretty neck, and said,

"I need hardly explain, Mr. Colman, why I have sought this interview. You must by this time be aware how peculiar, how unreasonable indeed, your behavior was!"

"Pardon me! I do not see the necessity for a word on the matter. I leave by the first train in the morning!"

"I will not dwell on the rudeness of listening—"

111

"—To a review of my own book read by a friend!" interrupted Walter, with indignation; "in a drawing-room where I sat right in front of you, and knew no reason why you should not see me! I did make a great mistake, but it was in trusting a lady who, an hour or two before, had offered to be my sister! How could I suspect she might speak of me in a way she would not like to hear!"

Lady Lufa was not quite prepared for the tone he took. She had expected to find him easy to cow. Her object was to bring him into humble acceptance of the treatment against which he had rebelled, lest he should afterward avenge himself! She sat a moment in silence.

"Such ignorance of the ways of the world," she said, "is excusable in a poet—especially—"

"Such a poet!" supplemented Walter, who found it difficult to keep his temper in face of her arrogance.

"But the world is made up of those that laugh and those that are laughed at."

"They change places, however, sometimes!" said Walter—which alarmed Lufa, though she did not show her anxiety.

"Certainly!" she replied. "Everybody laughs at everybody when he gets a chance! What is society but a club for mutual criticism! The business of its members is to pass judgment on each other! Why not take the accident, which seems so to annoy you, with the philosophy of a gentleman—like one of us! None of us think anything of what is said of us; we do not heed what we say of each other! Every one knows that all his friends pull him to pieces the moment he is out of sight—as heartily as they had just been assisting him to pull others to pieces. Every gathering is a temporary committee, composed of those who are present, and sitting upon those whose who are not present. Nobody dreams of courtesy extending beyond presence! when that is over, obligation is over. Any such imaginary restriction would render society impossible. It is only the most inexperienced person that could suppose things going on in his absence the same as in his presence! It is I who ought

112

to be pitied, not you! I am the loser, not you!"

Walter bowed and was silent. He did not yet see her drift. If his regard had been worth anything, she certainly had lost a good deal, but, as it was, he did not understand how the loss could be of importance to her.

With sudden change of tone and expression, she broke out—

"Be generous, Walter! Forgive me. I will make any atonement you please, and never again speak of you as if you were not my own brother!"

"It is not of the least consequence how you speak of me now, Lady Lufa: I have had the good though painful fortune to learn your real feelings, and prefer the truth to the most agreeable deception. Your worst opinion of me I could have borne and loved you still; but there is nothing of you, no appearance of anything even, left to love! I know now that a woman may be sweet as Hybla honey, and false as an apple of Sodom!"

"Well, you are ungenerous! I hope there are not many in the world to whom one might confess a fault and not be forgiven. This is indeed humiliating!"

"I beg your pardon; I heard no confession!"

"I asked you to forgive me."

"For what?"

"For talking of you as I did.'

"Which you justified as the custom of society!"

"I confess, then, that in your case I ought not to have done so."

"Then I forgive you; and we part in peace."

"Is that what you call forgiveness?"

"Is it not all that is required? Knowing now your true feeling toward me, I know that in this house I am a mistake. Nothing like a true relation exists, nothing more than the merest acquaintance can exist between us!"

"It is terrible to have such an enemy!"

"I do not understand you!"

"The match is not fair! Here stands poor me undefended, chained to the rock! There you lurk, behind the hedge, invisible, and taking every advantage! Do you think it fair?"

"I begin to understand! The objection did not seem to strike you while I was the person shot at! But still I fail to see your object. Please explain."

"You must know perfectly what I mean, Walter! and I can not but believe you too just to allow a personal misunderstanding to influence your public judgment! You gave your real unbiased opinion of my last book, and you are bound by that!"

"Is it possible," cried Walter, "that at last I understand you! That you should come to me on such an errand, Lady Lufa, reveals yet more your opinion of me! Could you believe me capable of such vileness as to take my revenge by abusing your work?"

"Ah, no! Promise me you will not."

"If such a promise were necessary, how could it set you at your ease? The man who could do such a thing would break any promise!"

"Then whatever rudeness is offered me in your journal, I shall take as springing from your resentment."

"If you do you will wrong me far worse than you have yet done. I shall not merely never review work of yours, I will never utter an opinion of it to any man."

"Thank you. So we part friends!"

"Conventionally."

She rose. He turned to the door and opened it. She passed him, her head thrown back, her eyes looking poisonous, and let a gaze of contemptuous doubt rest on him for a moment. His eyes did not quail before hers.

She had left a taper burning on a slab outside the door. Walter had but half closed it behind her when she reappeared with the taper in one hand and the volume he had given her in the other. He took the book without a word, and again she went; but he had hardly thrown it on the hot coals when once more she appeared. I believe she had herself blown her taper out.

"Let me have a light, please," she said.

He took the taper from her hand, and turned to light it. She followed him into the room, and laid her hand on his arm.

"Walter," she said, "it was all because of Sefton! He does not like you, and can't bear me to like you! I am engaged to him. I ought to have told you!"

"I will congratulate him next time I see him!" said Walter.

"No, no!" she cried, looking at once angry and scared.

"I will not, then," answered Walter; "but allow me to say I do not believe Sefton dislikes me. Anyhow, keep your mind at ease, pray. I shall certainly not in any way revenge myself."

She looked up in his eyes with a momentary glimmer of her old sweetness, said "Thank you!" gently, and left the room. Her last glance left a faint, sad sting in Walter's heart, and he began to think whether he had not been too hard upon her. In any case, the sooner he was out of the house the better! He must no more trifle with the girl than a dipsomaniac with the brandy bottle!

All the time of this last scene, the gorgeous book was frizzling and curling and cracking on the embers. Whether she saw it or not I can not say, but she was followed all along the corridor by the smell of the burning leather, which got on to some sleeping noses, and made their owners dream the house was on fire.

In the morning, Sefton woke him, helped him to dress, got him away in time, and went with him to the station. Not a word passed between them about Lufa. All the way to London, Walter pondered whether there could be any reality in what she had said about Sefton. Was it not possible that she might have imagined him jealous? Sefton's dislike of her treatment of him might to her have seemed displeasure at her familiarity with him! "And indeed," thought Walter, "there are few friends who care so much for any author, I suspect, as to be indignant with his reviewers!"

CHAPTER XXVI. A PERIOD.

If London was dreary when Lufa left it, it was worse than dreary to Walter now that she was gone from his world; gone from the universe past and future both—for the Lufa he had dreamed of was not, and had never been! He had no longer any one to dream about, waking or asleep. The space she had occupied was a blank spot, black and cold, charred with the fire of passion, cracked with the frost of disappointment and scorn. It had its intellectual trouble too—the impossibility of bringing together the long-cherished idea of Lufa, and the reality of Lufa revealed by herself; the two stared at each other in mortal irreconcilement. Now also he had no book to occupy him with pleasant labor. It had passed from him into the dark; the thought of it was painful, almost loathesome to him. No one, however, he was glad to find, referred to it. His friends pitied him, and his foes were silent. Three copies of it were sold. The sneaking review had had influence enough with the courted public to annihilate it.

But the expenses of printing it remained; he had yet to pay his share of them; and, alas, he did not know how! The publisher would give him time, no doubt, but, work his hardest, it would be a slow clearance! There was the shame too of having undertaken what he was unable at once to fulfill! He set himself to grind and starve.

At times the clouds would close in upon him, and there would seem nothing in life worth living for; though in truth his life was so much the more valuable that Lufa was out of it. Occasionally his heart would grow very gentle toward her, and he would burrow for a possible way to her excuse. But his conclusion was ever the same: how could he forget that laugh of utter merriment and delight when she found it was indeed himself under the castigation of such a mighty beadle of literature! In his most melting mood, therefore, he could only pity her. But what would have become of him had she not thus unmasked herself! He would now be believing her the truest, best of women, with no fault but a coldness of which he had no right to complain, a coldness comforted by the extent of its freezing!

But there was far more to make London miserable to him: he was now at last disgusted with his trade: this continuous feeding on the labor of others was no work for a gentleman! he began to descry in it certain analogies which grew more and more unpleasant as he regarded them. For his poetizing he was sick of that also. True, the quality or value of what he had written was nowise in itself affected by its failure to meet acceptance. It had certainly not had fair play; it had been represented as it was not; its character had been lied away! But now that the blinding influence of their chief subject was removed, he saw the verses themselves to be little worth. The soul of them was not the grand all-informing love, but his own private self-seeking little passion for a poor show of the lovable. No one could care for such verses, except indeed it were some dumb soul in love with a woman like, or imaginably like the woman of their thin worship! Not a few were pretty, he allowed, and some were quaint—that is, had curious old-flavored phrases and fantastic turns of thought; but throughout there was no revelation! They sparkled too with the names of things in themselves beautiful, but whether these things were in general wisely or fairly used in his figures and tropes and comparisons, he was now more than doubtful. He had put on his singing robes to whisper his secret love into the two great red ears of the public!—desiring, not sympathy from love and truth, but recognition from fame and report! That he had not received it was better than he deserved! Then what a life was it thus to lie wallowing among the mushrooms of the press! To spend gifts which, whatever they were, were divine, in publishing the tidings that this man had done ill, that other had done well, that he was amusing, and she was dull! Was it worth calling work, only because it was hard and dreary? His conscience, his taste, his impulses, all declined to back him in it any longer. What was he doing for the world? they asked him. How many books had he guided men to read, by whose help they might steer their way through the shoals of life? He could count on the fingers of one hand such as he had heartily recommended. If he had but pointed out what was good in books otherwise poor, it would have been something! He had not found it easy to be at once clever, honest, and serviceable to his race: the press was but for the utterance of opinion, true or false, not for the education of thought! And why should such as he write

118

books, who had nothing to tell men that could make them braver, stronger, purer, more loving, less selfish!

What next was to be done? His calling had vanished! It was not work worthy of a man! It was contemptible as that of the parson to whom the church is a profession! He owed his landlady money: how was he to pay her? He must eat, or how was he to work? There must be something honest for him to do! Was a man to do the wrong in order to do the right?

The true Walter was waking—beginning to see things as they were, and not as men regarded them. He was tormented with doubts and fears of all kinds, high and low. But for the change in his father's circumstances, he would have asked his help, cleared off everything, and gone home at once; and had he been truer to his father, he would have known that such a decision would even now have rejoiced his heart.

He had no longer confidence enough to write on any social question. Of the books sent him, he chose such as seemed worthiest of notice, but could not do much. He felt not merely a growing disinclination, but a growing incapacity for the work. How much the feeling may have been increased by the fact that his health was giving way, I can not tell; but certainly the root of it was moral.

His funds began to fail his immediate necessities, and he had just come from pawning the watch which he would have sold but that it had been his mother's, and was the gift of his father, when he met Harold Sullivan, who persuaded him to go with him to a certain theater in which the stalls had not yet entirely usurped upon the enjoyable portion of the pit. Between the first and second acts, he caught sight of Lady Lufa in a box, with Sefton standing behind her. There was hardly a chance of their seeing him, and he regarded them at his ease, glad to see Sefton, and not sorry to see Lufa, for it was an opportunity of testing himself. He soon perceived that they held almost no communication with each other, but was not surprised, knowing in how peculiar a relation they stood. Lufa was not looking unhappy—far from it; her countenance expressed absolute self-contentment: in all parts of the house she was attracting attention, especially from the young men. Sefton's look was certainly not one of content; but neither, as certainly, was it one of discontent; it suggested power waiting opportunity, strength quietly attendant upon, hardly expectant of the moment of activity. Walter imagined one watching a beloved cataleptic: till she came alive, what was to be done but wait! God has had more waiting than any one else! Lufa was an iceberg that would not melt even in the warm southward sea, watched by a still volcano, whose fires were of no avail, for they could not reach her. Sparklingly pretty, not radiantly beautiful, she sat, glancing, coruscating, glittering, anything except glowing: glow she could not even put on! She did not know what it was. Now and then a soft sadness would for a moment settle on Sefton's face—like the gray of a cloudy summer evening about to gather into a warm rain; but this was never when he looked at her; it was only when, without seeing, he thought about her. Hitherto Walter had not been capable of understanding the devotion, the quiet strength, the persistent purpose of the man; now he began to see into it and wonder. While a spark of hope lay alive in those ashes of disappointment that had often seemed as if they would make but a dust-heap of his bosom, there he must remain, by the clean, cold hearth, swept and garnished, of the woman he loved—loved strangely, mysteriously, inexplicably even to himself!

Walter sat gazing; and as he gazed, simultaneously the two became aware of his presence. A friendly smile spread over Sefton's face, but, with quick perception, he abstained from any movement that might seem to claim recognition. To Walter's wonder, Lufa, so perfectly self-contained, so unchangingly self-obedient, colored—faintly indeed, but plainly enough to the eyes of one so well used to the white rose of her countenance. She moved neither head nor person, only turned her eyes away, and seemed, like the dove for its foot, to seek some resting-place for her vision—and with the sight awoke in Walter the first unselfish resolve of his life. Would he not do anything—could he not do something to bring those two together? The thought seemed even to himself almost a foolish one; but spiritual relations and potencies go far beyond intellectual ones, and a man must become a fool to be wise. Many a foolish thought, many a most improbable idea, has proved itself seed-bearing fruit of the kingdom of heaven. A man may fail to effect, or be unable to set hand to work he would fain do—and be judged, as Browning says in his "Saul," by what he would have done if he could. Only the would must be as true as a deed; then it is a deed. The kingdom of heaven is for the dreamers of true dreams only!

Was there then anything Walter could do to help the man to gain the woman he had so faithfully helped Walter to lose? It was no plain task. The thing was not to enable him to marry her—that Sefton could have done long ago—might do any day without help from him! As she then was, she was no gain for any true man! But if he could help to open the eyes of the cold-hearted, conceited, foolish girl, either to her own valuelessness as she was, or her worth as she might be, or again to the value, the eternal treasure of the heart she was turning from, she would then be a gift that in the giving grew worthy even of such a man!

Here, however, came a different thought, bearing nevertheless in the same direction. It was very well to think of Lufa's behavior to Sefton, but what had Walter's been to Lufa? It may seem strange that the reflection had not come to him before; but in nothing are we slower than in discovering our own blame—and the slower that we are so quick to perceive or imagine we perceive the blame of others. For, the very fact that we see and heartily condemn the faults of others, we use, unconsciously perhaps, as an argument that we must be right ourselves. We must take heed not to judge with the idea that so we shall escape judgment—that by condemning evil we clear ourselves. Walter's eyes were opened to see that he had done Lufa a great wrong; that he had helped immensely to buttress and exalt her self-esteem. Had he not in his whole behavior toward her, been far more anxious that he should please her than that she should be worthy? Had he not known that she was far more anxious to be accepted as a poet than to be admired as a woman?—more anxious indeed to be accepted than, even in the matter of her art, to be worthy of acceptance—to be the thing she wished to be thought? In that review which, in spite of his own soul, he had persuaded himself to publish, knowing it to be false, had he not actively, most unconscientiously, and altogether selfishly, done her serious intellectual wrong, and heavy moral injury? Was he not bound to make what poor reparation might be possible? It mattered nothing that she did not desire any such reparation; that she would look upon the attempt as the first wrong in the affair—possibly as a pretense for the sake of insult, and the revenge of giving her the deepest possible pain: having told her the lies, he must confess they were lies! having given her the poison of falsehood, he must at least follow it with the only antidote, the truth! It was not his part to judge of consequences so long as a duty remained to be done! and what could be more a duty than to undeceive where he had deceived, especially where the deception was aggravating that worst of diseases, self-conceit, self-satisfaction, self-worship? It was doubtful whether she would read what he might write; but the fact that she did not trust him, that, notwithstanding his assurance, she would still be in fear of how he might depreciate her work in the eyes of the public, would, he thought, secure for him a reading. She might, when she got far enough to see his drift, destroy the letter in disgust; that would be the loss of his labor; but he would have done what he could! He had begun to turn a new leaf, and here was a thing the new leaf required written upon it!

As to Sefton, what better thing could he do for him, than make her think less of herself! or, if that were impossible, at least make her understand that other people did not think so much of her as she had been willingly led to believe! In wronging her he had wronged his friend as well, throwing obstacles in the way of his reception! He had wronged the truth itself!

When the play was over, and the crowd was dispersing, he found himself close to them on the pavement as they waited for their carriage. So near to Lufa was he that he could not help touching her dress. But what a change had passed on him! Not once did he wish her to look round and brighten when she saw him! Sefton, moved perhaps by that unknown power of presence, operating in bodily proximity but savoring of the spiritual, looked suddenly round and saw him. He smiled and did not speak, but, stretching out a quiet hand, sought his. Walter grasped it as if it was come to lift him from some evil doom. Neither spoke, and Lufa did not know that hands had clasped in the swaying human flood. No physical influence passed between Walter and her.

Having made up his mind on the way, he set to work as soon as he reached home. He wrote and destroyed and rewrote, erased and substituted, until, as near as he could, he had said what he intended, so at least as it should not be mistaken for what he did not intend, which is the main problem in writing. Then he copied all out fair and plain, so that she could read it easily—and here is his letter, word for word:

"MY DEAR LADY LUFA,—In part by means of the severe lesson I received through you, a great change has passed upon me. I am no longer able to think of myself as the important person I used to take myself for. It is startling to have one's eyes opened to see one's self as one is, but it very soon begins to make one glad, and the gladness, I find, goes on growing. One's nature is so elevated by being delivered from the honoring and valuing of that which is neither honorable nor valuable, that the seeming loss is annihilated by the essential gain; the being better makes up—infinitely makes up for showing to myself worse. I would millions of times rather know myself a fool than imagine myself a great poet. For to know one's self a fool is to begin to be wise; and I would be loyal among the sane, not royal among lunatics. Who would be the highest, in virtue of the largest mistake, of the profoundest self-idolatry!

"But it was not to tell you this I began to write; it was to confess a great wrong which once I did you; for I can not rest, I can not make it up with my conscience until I have told you the truth. It may be you will dislike me more for confessing the wrong than for committing it—I can not tell; but it is my part to let you know it—and none the less my part that I must therein confess myself more weak and foolish than already I appear.

"You will remember that you gave me a copy of your drama while I was at your house: the review of it which appeared in the 'Battery' I wrote that same night. I am ashamed to have to confess the fact, but I had taken more champagne than, I hope, I ever shall again; and, irreverent as it must seem to mention the fact in such a connection, I was possessed almost to insanity with your beauty, and the graciousness of your behavior to me. Everything around me was pervaded with rose-color and rose-odor, when, my head and heart, my imagination and senses, my memory and hope full of yourself, I sat down to read your poem. I was like one in an opium-dream. I saw everything in the glory of an everlasting sunset, for every word I read, I heard in the tones of your voice; through the radiant consciousness of your present beauty, received every thought that awoke. If ever one being was possessed by

123

another, I was that night possessed by you. In this mood, like that, I say again, of an opium-dream, I wrote the criticism of your book.

"But on the morning after the writing of it, I found, when I began to read it, I could so little enter into the feeling of it, that I could hardly believe I had actually written what lay before me in my own hand. I took the poem again, and scanned it most carefully, reading it with deep, anxious desire to justify the things I had set down. But I failed altogether. Even my love could not blind me enough to persuade me that what I had said was true, or that I should be other than false to print it. I had to put myself through a succession of special pleadings before I could quiet my conscience enough to let the thing go, and tell its lies in the ears of the disciples of the 'Battery.' I will show you how falsely I dealt. I said to myself that, in the first place, one mood had, in itself, as good a claim, with regard to the worth of what it produced, as another; but that the opinion of the night, when the imagination was awake, was more likely to be just with regard to a poem than that of the cold, hard, unpoetic day. I was wrong in taking it for granted that my moods had equal claims; and the worse wrong, that all the time I knew I was not behaving honestly, for I persisted in leaving out, as factor in one of the moods, the champagne I had drunk, not to mention the time of the night, and the glamour of your influence. The latter was still present, but could no longer blind me to believe what I would, most of all things, have gladly believed. With the mood the judgment was altered, and a true judgment is the same in all moods, inhabiting a region above mood.

"In confession, a man must use plain words: I was a coward, a false friend, a false man. Having tried my hardest to keep myself from seeing the fact as plainly as I might have seen it, had I looked it in the face with the intent of meeting what the truth might render necessary, yet knowing that I was acting falsely, I sent off, regardless of duty, and in the sole desire of pleasing you, and had printed, as my opinion concerning your book, what was not my opinion, had never been my opinion, except during that one night of hallucination—a hallucination recognized as such, for the oftener I read, the more I was convinced that I had given such an opinion as must stamp me the most incompetent, or the falsest of critics. Lady Lufa, there is

124

nothing remarkable in your poem. It is nicely, correctly written, and in parts skillfully contrived; but had it been sent me among other books, and without indication of the author, I should certainly have thrown it aside as the attempt of a school-girl, who, having more pocket money than was good for her, had been able to print it without asking her parents or guardians. You may say this judgment is the outcome of my jealous disappointment; I say the former was the outcome of my loving fascination; and I can not but think something in yourself will speak for me, and tell you that I am speaking honestly. Mr. Sefton considers me worthy of belief; and I know myself worthier of belief than ever before—how much worthier than when I wrote that review! Then I loved you—selfishly; now I love the truth, and would serve you, though I do not love you the same way as before. Through the disappointment you caused me, my eyes have been opened to see the way in which I was going, and to turn from it, for I was on the way of falsehood. Oh, Lady Lufa, let me speak; forget my presumption; you bore with my folly—bear now with what is true though it come from a foolish heart! What would it be to us, if we gained the praises of the whole world, and found afterward they were for what was counted of no value in the great universe into which we had passed! Let us be true, whatever come of it, and look the facts of things in the face! If I am a poor creature, let me be content to know it! for have I not the joy that God can make me great! And is not the first step toward greatness to refuse to call that great which is not great, or to think myself great when I am small? Is it not an essential and impassable bar to greatness for a man to imagine himself great when there is not in him one single element of greatness? Let us confess ourselves that which we can not consent to remain! The confession of not being, is the sole foundation for becoming. Self is a quicksand; God is the only rock. I have been learning a little.

"Having thus far dared, why should I not go further, and say one thing more which is burning within me! There was a time when I might have said it better in verse, but that time has gone by—to come again, I trust, when I have that to say which is worth saying; when I shall be true enough to help my fellows to be true. The calling of a poet, if it be a calling, must come from heaven. To be bred to a thing is to have the ears closed to any call.

"There is a man I know who forever sits watching, as one might watch at evening for the first star to come creeping out of the infinite heaven; but it is for a higher and lovelier star this man watches; he is waiting for a woman, for the first dawn of her soul. He knows well the spot where the star of his hope must appear, the spot where, out of the vast unknown, she must open her shining eyes that he may love her. But alas, she will not arise and shine. He believes or at least hopes his star is on the way, and what can he do but wait, for he is laden with the burden of a wealth given him to give—the love of a true heart—the rarest, as the most precious thing on the face of his half-baked brick of a world. It was easy for me to love you, Lady Lufa, while I took that for granted in you which did not yet exist in myself! But he knows the truth of you, and yet loves. Lady Lufa, you are not true! If you do not know it, it is because you will not know it, lest the sight of what you are should unendurably urge you toward that you will not choose to be. God is my witness I speak in no poor anger, no mean jealousy! Not a word I say is for myself. I am but begging you to be that which God, making you, intended you to be. I would have the star shine through the cloud—shine on the heart of the watcher! the real Lufa lies hidden under a dusky garment of untruth; none but the eye of God can see through to the lovely thing He made, out of which the false Lufa is smothering the life. When the beautiful child, the real Lufa, the thing you now know you are not, but ought to be, walks out like an angel from a sepulcher, then will the heart of God, and the heart of George Sefton, rejoice with a great joy. Think what the love of such a man is. It is your very self he loves; he loves like God, even before the real self has begun to exist. It is not the beauty you show, but the beauty showing you, that he loves—the hidden self of your perfect idea. Outward beauty alone is not for the divine lover; it is a mere show. Until the woman makes it real, it is but a show; and until she makes it true, she is herself a lie. With you, Lady Lufa, it rests to make your beauty a truth, that is, a divine fact.

"For myself, I have been but a false poet—a mask among poets, a builder with hay and stubble, babbling before I had words, singing before I had a song, without a ray of revelation from the world unseen, carving at clay instead of shaping it in the hope of marble. I am humbler now, and trust the divine humility has begun to work out mine. Of all things I would be true, and pretend nothing.

"Lady Lufa, if a woman's shadow came out of her mirror, and went about the world pretending to be herself and deceiving the eyes of men, that figure thus walking the world and stealing hearts, would be you. Would to God I were such an exorcist as could lay that ghost of you! as could say, 'Go back, forsake your seeming, false image of the true, the lovely Lufa that God made! You are but her unmaking! Get back into the mirror; live but in the land of shows; leave the true Lufa to wake from the swoon into which you have cast her; she must live and grow, and become, till she is perfect in loveliness.'

"I shall know nothing of the fate of my words. I shall see you no more in this world—except it be as I saw you to-night, standing close to you in a crowd. The touch of your garment sent no thrill through me; you were to me as a walking shadow. But the man who loves you sees the sleeping beauty within you! His lips are silent, but by the very silence of his lips his love speaks. I shall soon—but what matters it! If we are true, we shall meet, and have much to say. If we are not true, all we know is that falsehood must perish. For me, I will arise and go to my father, and lie no more. I will be a man, and live in the truth—try at least so to live, in the hope of one day being true.

"WALTER COLMAN."

Walter sent the letter—posted it the next morning as he went to the office. It is many years since, and he has not heard of it yet. But there is nothing hidden that shall not be revealed.

The writing of this letter was a great strain to him, but he felt much relieved when it was gone. How differently did he feel after that other lying, flattering utterance, with his half-sleeping conscience muttering and grumbling as it lay. He walked then full of pride and hope, in the mid-most of his dream of lore and ambition; now he was poor and sad, and bowed down, but the earth was a place that might be lived in notwithstanding! If only he could find some thoroughly honest work! He would rather have his weakness and dejection with his humility, than ten times the false pride with which he paced the street before. It was better to be thus than so!

But as he came home that night, he found himself far from well, and altogether incapable of work. He was indeed ill, for he could neither eat nor sleep, nor take interest in anything. His friend Sullivan was shocked to see him look so pale and wild, and insisted he must go home. Walter said it might be but a passing attack, and it would be a pity to alarm them; he would wait a day or two. At length he felt so ill that one morning he did not get up. There was no one in the house who cared to nurse him; his landlady did little or nothing for him beyond getting him the cup of tea he occasionally wanted; Sullivan was himself ill, and for some days neither saw nor heard of him; and Walter had such an experience of loneliness and desertion as he had never had before. But it was a purgatorial suffering. He began to learn how insufficient he was for himself; how little self-sustaining power there was in him. Not there was the fountain of life! Words that had been mere platitudes of theological commonplace began to show a golden root through their ancient mold. The time came back to him when father and mother bent anxiously over their child. He remembered how their love took from him all fear; how even the pain seemed to melt in their presence; all was right when they knew all about it! they would see that the suffering went at the proper time! All gentle ministrations to his comfort, the moving of his pillows, the things cooked by his mother's own hands, her watch to play with—all came back, as if the tide of life had set in the other direction, and he was fast drifting back into childhood. What sleep he had was filled with alternate dreams of suffering and home-deliverance. He recalled how different his aunt had been when he was ill: in this isolation her face looking in at his door would have been as that of an angel! And he knew that all the time his debts were increasing, and when would he begin to pay them off! His mind wandered; and when Sullivan came at length, he was talking wildly, imagining himself the prodigal son in the parable.

Sullivan wrote at once to Mr. Colman.

CHAPTER XXVII. A FRUITLESS JOURNEY.

It was the afternoon when Sullivan's letter, on the lower left hand corner of which he had written Har., Sul., arrived. Mr. Colman had gone to a town at some distance, whence he would not return till the last train. Not many letters came to him, and this, with the London postmark, naturally drew the attention of Aunt Ann and Molly. The moment the eyes of the former fell on the contracted name in the corner, they blazed.

"The shameless fellow!" she cried; "writing to beg another ten-pound note from my poor foolish brother!"

"I don't think that is it, aunt," returned Molly.

"And why not, pray? How should you know?"

"Mr. Sullivan has had plenty of work, and can not need to borrow money. Why are you so suspicious, auntie?"

"I am not. I never was suspicious. You are a rude girl to say so! If it is not money, you may depend upon it, it is something worse!"

"What worse can you mean?"

"That Walter has got into some scrape."

"Why should he not write himself if it were so?"

"He is too much ashamed, and gets his friend to do it for him. I know the ways of young men!"

"Perhaps he is ill!" said Molly.

"Perhaps. It is long since I saw a letter from him! I am never allowed to read or hear one!"

"Can you wonder at that, when you are always abusing him? If he were my son, I should take care you never saw a scrap of his writing! It makes me wild to hear those I love talked of as you talk of him—always with a sniff!"

"Love, indeed! Do you suppose no one loves him but you?"

"His father loves him dearly!"

"How dare you hint that I do not love him!"

"If yours is love, auntie, I wish I may never meet it where I've no chance of defending myself!"

Molly had a hot temper where her friends were concerned, though she would bear a good deal without retorting.

"There!" said Aunt Ann, giving her the letter; "put that on the mantelpiece till he comes."

Molly took it, and gazed wistfully at it, as if fain to read it through the envelope. She had had that morning a strange and painful dream about Walter—that he lay in his coffin, with a white cat across his face.

"What if he should be ill, auntie?" she said.

"Who ill?"

"Walter, of course!"

"What then? We must wait to know!"

"Father wouldn't mind if we just opened it to make sure it was not about Walter!"

"Open my brother's letter! Goodness gracious, what next! Well, you are a girl! I should just like to see him after you had opened one of his letters!"

Miss Hancock had herself once done so—out of pure curiosity, though on another pretense—a letter, as it happened, which he would rather not have read himself than have had her read, for it contained thanks for a favor secretly done; and he was more angry than any one had ever seen him. Molly remembered the occurrence, though she had been too young to have it explained to her; but Molly's idea of a father, and of Richard Colman as that father, was much grander than that of most children concerning fathers. There is indeed a much closer relation between some good men and any good child than there is between far the greater number of parents and their children.

She put the letter on the chimney-piece, and went to the dairy; but it was to think about the letter. Her mind kept hovering about it where it stood on the chimney-piece, leaning against the vase with the bunch of silvery honesty in it. What if Walter was ill! Her father would not be home till the last train, and there would be none to town before the slow train in the morning! He might be very ill!—and longing for some one to come to him—his father of course—longing all day long! Her father was reasonable as he was loving: she was sure he would never be angry without reason! He was a man with whom one who loved him, and was not presuming, might take any honest liberty! He could hardly be a good man with whom one must never take a liberty! A good man was not the man to stand on his dignity! To treat him as if he were, was to treat him as those who can not trust in God behave to Him! They call Him the Supreme Euler! the Almighty! the Disposer of events! the Judge of the whole earth!—and would not "presume" to say "Father, help thy little child!" She would not wrong her father by not trusting him! she would open the letter! she would not read one word more than was needful to know whether it came to say that Walter was ill! Why should Mr. Sullivan have put his name outside, except to make sure of its being attended to immediately!

She went hack to the room where lay the letter. Her aunt was there still. Molly was glad of it: the easiest way of letting her know, for she would not have done it without, was to let her see her do what she did! She went straight to the chimney, reached up, and took the letter.

"Leave that alone!" cried Miss Hancock. "I know what you are after! You want to give it to my brother, and be the first to know what is in it! Put it back this moment!"

Molly stood with the letter in her hand.

"You are mistaken, auntie," she said. "I am going to open it."

"You shall do nothing of the sort—not if I live!" returned Aunt Ann, and flew to take the letter from her. But Molly was prepared for the attack, and was on the other side of the door before she could pounce.

She sped to her room, locked the door, and read the letter, then went instantly to her bonnet and cloak. There was time to catch the last train! She inclosed the letter, addressed it to her father, and wrote inside the envelope that she had opened it against the wish of her aunt, and was gone to nurse Walter. Then taking money from her drawer, she returned to Aunt Ann.

"It is about Walter. He is very ill," she said. "I have inclosed the letter, and told him it was I that opened it."

"Why such a fuss?" cried Aunt Ann. "You can tell him your impertinence just as well as write it! Oh, you've got your bonnet on!—going to run away in a fright at what you've done! Well, perhaps you'd better!"

"I am going to Walter."

"Where?"

"To London to Walter."

"You!"

"Yes; who else?"

"You shall not. I will go myself!"

Molly knew too well how Walter felt toward his aunt to consent to this. She would doubtless behave kindly if she found him really ill, but she would hardly be a comfort to him!

"I shall be ready in one moment!" continued Miss Hancock. "There is plenty of time, and you can drive me to the station if you like. Richard shall not say I left the care of his son to a chit of a girl!"

Molly said nothing, but rushed to the stable. Nobody was there! She harnessed the horse, and put him to the dog-cart with her own hands, in terror lest her aunt should be ready before her.

She was driving from the yard when her aunt appeared, in her Sunday best.

"That's right!" she said, expecting her to pull up and take her in.

But Molly touched up her horse, and he, having done nothing for some time, was fresh, and started at speed. Aunt Ann was left standing, but it was some time before she understood that the horse had not run away.

Ere Molly reached the station, she left the dog-cart at a neighboring inn, then told one of the porters, to whom her father was well known, to look out for him by the last train, and let him know where the trap was.

As the train was approaching London, it stopped at a station where already stood another train, bound in the opposite direction, which began to move while hers stood. Molly was looking out of her window, as it went past her with the slow beginnings of speed, watching the faces that drifted by, in a kind of phantasmagoric show, never more to be repeated, when, in the further corner of a third-class carriage near the end of the train, she caught sight of a huddled figure that reminded her of Walter; a pale face was staring as if it saw nothing, but dreamed of something it could not see. She jumped up and put her head out of the window, but her own train also was now moving, and if it were Walter, there was no possibility of overtaking him. She was by no means sure, however, that it was he. The only way was to go on to her journey's end!

CHAPTER XXVIII. DOING AND DREAMING.

Walter had passed a very troubled night, and was worse, though he thought himself better. His friend looked in to see him before going to the office, and told him that he would come again in the evening. He did not tell him that he had written to his father.

Walter slept and woke and slept again. All the afternoon he was restless, as one who dreams without sleeping. The things presented to his mind, and seeming with him, were not those about him. Late in the afternoon, the fever abated a little, and he felt as one who wakes out of a dream. For a few minutes he lay staring into the room, then rose and with difficulty dressed himself, one moment shivering, the next burning. He knew perfectly what he was doing; his mind was possessed with an unappeasable longing and absolute determination to go home. The longing had been there all the night and all the day, except when it was quieted by the shadowy assuagement of his visions; and now with the first return of his consciousness to present conditions, came resolve. Better die at home, he said to himself, than recover in such a horrible place! On he went with his preparations, mechanical but methodical, till at last he put on his great-coat, took his rug, searched his purse, found enough to pay a cab to the railway station, went softly down the stair, and was in the street, a man lonely and feeble, but with a great joy of escape. Happily a cab was just passing, and he was borne in safety, half asleep again after his exertions, to the station. There he sought the station-master, and telling him his condition, prevailed upon him to take his watch as a pledge that he would send him the price of his ticket.

It was a wet night, but not very cold, and he did not suffer at first—was in fact more comfortable than he had been in bed. He seemed to himself perfectly sane when he started, but of the latter half of his journey he remembered nothing connectedly. What fragments of it returned to his recollection appeared as the remnants of a feverish dream.

The train arrived late in the dark night, at an hour when a conveyance was rarely to be had. He remembered nothing, however, of setting out to walk home, and nothing clearly as to how he fared on the way. His dreaming memory gave him but a sense of climbing, climbing, with a cold wind buffeting him back, and bits of paper, which must have been snow-flakes, beating in his face: he thought they were the shreds of the unsold copies of his book, torn to pieces by the angry publisher, and sent swirling about his face in clouds to annoy him. After that came a great blank.

The same train had taken up Mr. Colman at a junction. The moment he got out of it, the porter to whom Molly had spoken in the morning, addressed him, with the message Molly had left for him. Surprised and uneasy, he was putting some anxious questions to the man, when his son passed him. The night was still dark, and cloudy with snow, the wind was coming in gusts, now and then fiercely, and the lamps were wildly struggling against being blown out: neither saw the other. Walter staggered away, and Richard set out for the inn, to drive home as fast as possible: there only could he get light on Molly's sudden departure for London! In her haste she had not left message enough. But he knew his son must be ill; nothing else could have caused it! He met with some delay at the inn, but at length was driving home as fast as he dared through the thick darkness of the rough ascent.

He had not driven far, before one of those little accidents occurred to his harness which, small in themselves, have so often serious results: the strap of the hames gave way, and the traces dropped by the horse's sides. Mr. Colman never went unprovided for accidents, but in a dark night, in the middle of the road, with a horse fresh and eager to get home, it takes time to rectify anything.

At length he arrived in safety, and having roused the man, hastened into the house. There he speedily learned the truth of his conjecture, and it was a great comfort to him that Molly had acted so promptly. But he bethought himself that, by driving to another station some miles further off, at which a luggage train stopped in the night, he could reach town a few hours earlier. He went again to the stable, and gave orders to have the horse well fed and ready in an hour. Then he tried to eat the supper his sister-in-law had prepared for him, but with small success. Every few minutes he rose, opened the door, and looked out. It was a very dark morning, full of wind and snow.

By and by he could bear it no longer, and though he knew there was much time to spare, got up to go to the stable. The wind met him with an angry blast as he opened the door, and sharp pellets of keen snow stung him in the face. He had taken a lantern in his hand, but, going with his head bent against the wind, he all but stumbled over a stone seat, where they would sit by the door of a summer evening. As he recovered himself, the light of his lantern fell upon a figure huddled crouching upon the seat, but in the very act of tumbling forward from off it. He caught it with one arm, set down the light, raised its head, and in the wild, worn, death-pale features and wandering eyes, knew the face of his son. He uttered one wailing groan, which seemed to spend his life, gathered him to his bosom, and taking him up like a child, almost ran to the house with him. As he went he heard at his ear the murmured word,

"Father, I have sinned—not worthy—"

His heart gave a great heave, but he uttered no second cry.

Aunt Ann, however, had heard the first. She ran, and, opening the door, met him with the youth in his arms.

"I'm afraid he's dead!" gasped Richard. "He is cold as a stone!"

Aunt Ann darted to the kitchen, made a blazing fire, set the kettle on it and bricks around it, then ran to see if she could help.

Richard had got his boy into his own bed, had put off his own clothes, and was lying with him in his arms to warm him. Aunt Ann went about like a steam-engine, but noiseless. She got the hot bricks, then hot bottles, and more blankets. The father thought he would die before the heat got to him. As soon as he was a little warm, he mounted his horse, and rode to fetch the doctor. It was terrible to him to think that he must have passed his boy on the way, and left him to struggle home without help.

Ere he returned, Walter had begun to show a little more life. He moaned, and murmured, and seemed going through a succession of painful events.

136

Now he would utter a cry of disgust, now call for his father; then he would be fighting the storm with a wild despair of ever reaching his father.

The doctor came, examined him, said they were doing quite right, but looked solemn over him.

Had it not been for that glimpse she had at the station where last the train stopped, Molly would have been in misery indeed when, on arriving at Walter's lodging, and being told that he was ill in bed, she went up to his room, and could find him nowhere. It was like a bad dream. She almost doubted whether she might not be asleep. The landlady had never heard him go out, and until she had searched the whole house, would not believe he was not somewhere in it. Rather unwillingly, she allowed Molly to occupy his room for the night; and Molly, that she might start by the first train, stretched herself in her clothes on the miserable little horse-hair sofa. She could not sleep, and was not a little anxious about Walter's traveling in such a condition; but for all that, she could not help laughing more than once or twice to think how Aunt Ann would be crowing over her: basely deserted, left standing in the yard in her Sunday clothes, it was to her care after all that Walter was given, not Molly's! But Molly could well enough afford to join in her aunt's laugh: she had done her duty, and did not need to be told that we have nothing to do with consequences, only with what is right. So she waited patiently for the morning.

But how was she to do when she got home? Aunt Ann would have installed herself as nurse! It would not matter much while Walter was really ill; so long Aunt Ann would be good to him! but when he began to be himself again—for that time Molly must look out and be ready!

When she reached home, she was received at the door by her father who had been watching for her, and learned all he had to tell her. Aunt Ann spoke to her as if she had but the minute before left the room, vouchsafing not a single remark concerning Walter, and yielding her a position of service as narrow as she could contrive to make it. Molly did everything she desired without complaint, fetching and carrying for her as usual. She received no recognition from the half-unconscious Walter.

If it had not been that Aunt Ann must, like other nurses, have rest, Molly's ministering soul would have been sorely pinched and hampered; but when her aunt retired, she could do her part for the patient's peace. In a few days he had come to himself enough to know who were about him, and seemed to manifest a preference for Molly's nursing. To Aunt Ann this seemed very hard—and hard it would have been, but that, through all her kindness, Walter could not help foreseeing how she would treat him in the health to which she was doing her best to bring him back. He sorely dreaded the time when, strong enough to be tormented, but not able to lock his door against her, he would be at her mercy. But he cherished a hope that his father would interfere. If necessary he would appeal to him, and beg him to depose Aunt Ann, and put sweet Molly in her stead!

One morning—Molly had been sitting up the night with the invalid— she found Aunt Ann alone at the breakfast-table.

"His father is with him now," said Molly. "I think he is a little better; he slept more quietly."

"He'll do well enough!" grunted Aunt Ann. "There's no fear of him! he's not of the sort to die early! This is what comes of letting young people have their own way! My brother will be wiser now! and so, I hope, will Walter! It shall not be my fault if he's not made to understand! Old or young wouldn't listen to me! Now perhaps, while they are smarting from the rod, it may be of use to speak!"

"Aunt," said Molly, with her heart in her throat, but determined, "please do not say anything to him for a long time yet; you might make him ill again! You do not know how he hates being talked at!"

"Don't you be afraid! I won't talk at him! He shall be well talked to, and straight!"

"He won't stand it any more, auntie! He's a man now, you know! And when a mere boy, he used to complain that you were always finding fault with him!"

"Highty, tighty! What next! The gentleman has the choice, has he, when

138

to be found fault with, and when not!"

"I give you fair warning," said Molly, hurriedly, "that I will do what I can to prevent you!"

Aunt Ann was indignant.

"You dare to tell me, in my own"—she was going to say house, but corrected herself—"in my own home, where you live on the charity of—"

Molly interrupted her.

"I shall ask my father," she said, "whether he wishes me to have such words from you. If he does, you shall say what you please to me. But as to Walter, I will ask nobody. Till he is able to take care of himself, I shall not let you plague him. I will fight you first! There now!"

The flashing eyes and determined mouth of Molly, who had risen, and stood regarding her aunt in a flame of honest anger, cowed her. She shut her jaws close, and looked the picture of postponement.

That instant came the voice of Mr. Colman:

"Molly! Molly!"

"Yes, Richard!" answered Miss Hancock, rising.

But Molly was out of the door, almost before her aunt was out of her chair.

Walter had asked where she was, and wanted to see her. It was the first wish of any sort he had expressed!

CHAPTER XXIX. DREAM-MOLLY.

So far better as to be able to talk, Walter one day told Molly the strange dream which, as he looked back, seemed to fill the whole time almost from his leaving his lodging to his recognition of his father by his bedside.

It was a sweet day in the first of the spring. He lay with his head toward the window, and the sun shining into the room, with the tearful radiance of sorrows overlived and winter gone, when Molly entered. She was at once whelmed in the sunlight, so that she could see nothing, while Walter could almost have counted her eyelashes.

"Stand there, Molly," he cried, "one moment! I want to look at you!"

"It is not fair!" returned Molly. "The sun is in my eyes! I am as blind as a bat!"

"I won't ask you, if you mind, Molly!" returned Walter.

In these days he had grown very gentle. He seemed to dread the least appearance of exaction.

"I will stand where you like, and as long as you like, Walter! Have you not consented to live a little longer with us! Oh, Walter, you don't know what it was like when the doctor looked so grave!"

Molly stood in the sun, and Walter looked at her till his eyes were wearied with the brightness she reflected, and his heart made strong by the better brightness she radiated. For Molly was the very type of a creature born of the sun and ripened by his light and heat—a glowing fruit of the tree of life amid its healing foliage, all splendor, and color, and overflowing strength. Self-will is weakness; the will to do right is strength; Molly willed the right thing and held to it. Hence it was that she was so gentle. She walked lightly over the carpet, because she could run up a hill like a hare. When she caught selfishness in her, she was down upon it with the knee and grasp of a giant. Strong is man and woman whose eternal life subjects the individual liking to the perfect will. Such man, such woman, is free man, free woman.

Molly was in a daring dress of orange and red. Scarce a girl in London would have ventured to wear it; few girls would not have looked vulgar in it; yet Molly was right. Like a dark-colored sunflower, she caught and kept the sun.

Having gazed at her in silence for awhile, Walter said, "Come and sit by me, Molly. I want to tell the dream I have been having."

She came at once, glad to get out of the sun. But she sat where he could still see her, and waited.

"I think I remember reaching the railway, Molly, but I remember nothing after that until I thought I was in a coal-pit, with a great roaring everywhere about me. I was shut up forever by an explosion, and the tumbling subterranean waters were coming nearer and nearer! They never came, but they were always coming! Suddenly some one took me by the arm, and pulled me out of the pit. Then I was on the hill above the pit, and had to get to the top of it. But it was in the teeth of a snow-storm! My breath was very short, and I could hardly drag one foot up after the other. All at once there was an angel with wings by my side, and I knew it was Molly. I never wondered that she had wings. I only said to myself, 'How clever she must be to stow them away when she doesn't want them!' Up and up we toiled, and the way was very long. But when I got too tired, you stood before me, and I leaned against you, and you folded your wings about my head, and so I got breath to go on again. And I tried to say, 'How can you be so kind to me! I never was good to you!'"

"You dreamed quite wrong there, Walter!" interposed Molly. "You were always good to me—except, perhaps, when I asked you too many questions!"

"Your questions were too wise for me, Molly! If I had been able to answer them, this trouble would never have come upon me. But I do wish I could tell you how delightful the dream was, for all the wind and the snow! I remember exactly how I felt, standing shadowed by your wings, and leaning against you!"

Molly's face flushed, and a hazy look came into her eyes, but she did not turn them away.

He stopped, and lay brooding on his dream.

"But all at once," he resumed, "it went away in a chaos of coal-pits, and snow-storms, and eyes not like yours, Molly! I was tossed about for ages in heat and cold, in thirst and loathing, with now one now another horrid draught held to my lips, thirst telling me to drink, and disgust making me dash it on the ground—only to be back at my lips the next moment. Once I was a king sitting upon a great tarnished throne, dusty and worm-eaten, in a lofty room of state, the doors standing wide, and the spiders weaving webs across them, for nobody ever came in, and no sound shook the moat-filled air: on that throne I had to sit to all eternity, because I had said I was a poet and was not! I was a fellow that had stolen the poet-book of the universe, torn leaves from it, and pieced the words together so that only one could make sense of them—and she would not do it! This vanished—and I was lying under a heap of dead on a battle-field. All above me had died doing their duty, and I lay at the bottom of the heap and could not die, because I had fought, not for the right, but for the glory of a soldier. I was full of shame, for I was not worthy to die! I was not permitted to give my life for the great cause for which the rest were dead. But one of the dead woke, and turned, and clasped me; and then I woke, and it was your arms about me, Molly! and my head was leaning where it leaned! when your wings were about me!"

By this time Molly was quietly weeping.

"I wish I had wings, Walter, to flap from morning to night for you!" she said, laughing through her tears.

"You are always flapping them, Molly! only nobody can see them except in a dream. There are many true things that can not be seen with the naked eye! The eye must be clothed and in its right mind first!"

"Your poetry is beginning to come, Walter! I don't think it ever did before!" said Molly.

Walter gazed at her wonderingly: was little Molly going to turn out a sibyl? How grown she was! What a peace and strength shone from her countenance! She was woman, girl, and child, all in one! What a fire of life there was in this lady with the brown hands—so different from the white, wax-doll ends to Lufa's arms! She was of the cold and ice, of the white death and lies! Here was the warm, live, woman-truth! He would never more love woman as he had! Could that be a good thing which a creature like Lufa roused in him? Could that be true which had made him lie? If his love had been of the truth, would it not have known that she was not a live thing? True love would have known when it took in its arms a dead thing, a body without a soul, a material ghost!

Another time—it was a cold evening; the wind howled about the house; but the fire was burning bright, and Molly, having been reading to him, had stopped for a moment—Walter said,

"I could not have imagined I should ever feel at home as I do now! I wonder why it is!"

"I think I could tell you!" said Molly.

"Tell me then."

"It is because you are beginning to know your father!"

"Beginning to know my father, Moll!"

"You never came right in sight of him till now. He has been the same always, but you did not—could not see him!"

"Why couldn't I see him, wise woman?" said Walter.

"Because you were never your father's son till now," answered Molly. "Oh, Walter, if you had heard Jane tell what a cry he gave when he found his boy on the cold bench, in the gusty dark of the winter morning! Half your father's heart is with your mother, and the other half with you! I did not know how a man could love till I saw his face as he stood over you once when he thought no one was near!"

"Did he find me on the stone bench?" "Yes, indeed! Oh, Walter, I have

143

known God better, and loved him more, since I have seen how your father loves you!"

Walter fell a thinking. Ha had indeed, since he came to himself, loved his father as he had never loved him before; but he had not thought how he had been forgetting him. And herewith a gentle repentance began, which had a curing and healing effect on his spirit. Nor did the repentance leave him at his earthly father's door, but led him on to his father in heaven.

The next day he said,

"I know another thing that makes me feel more at home: Aunt Ann never scolds at me now. True, she seldom comes near me, and I can not say I want her to come! But just tell me, do you think she has been converted?"

"Not that I know of. The angels will have a bad time of it before they bring her to her knees—her real knees, I mean, not her church-knees! For Aunt Ann to say she was wrong, would imply a change I am incapable of imagining. Yet it must come, you know, else how is she to enter the kingdom of heaven?"

"What then makes her so considerate?"

"It's only that I've managed to make her afraid of me."

CHAPTER XXX. WORKADAY MOLLY.

The days passed; week after week went down the hill—or, is it not rather, up the hill?—and out of sight; the moon kept on changelessly changing; and at length Walter was well, though rather thin and white.

Molly saw that he was beginning to brood. She saw also, as clearly as if he had opened his mind to her, what troubled him: it needed no witch to divine that! he must work: what was his work to be?

Whatever he do, if he be not called to it, a man but takes it up "at his own hand, as the devil did sinning."

Molly was one of the wise women of the world—and thus: thoughts grew for her first out of things, and not things out of thoughts. God's things come out of His thoughts; our realities are God's thoughts made manifest in things; and out of them our thoughts must come; then the things that come out of our thoughts will be real. Neither our own fancies, nor the judgments of the world, must be the ground of our theories or behavior. This, at least, was Molly's working theory of life. She saw plainly that her business, every day, hour, moment, was to order her way as He who had sent her into being would have her order her way; doing God's things, God's thoughts would come to her; God's things were better than man's thoughts; man's best thoughts the discovery of the thoughts hidden in God's things? Obeying him, perhaps a day would come in which God would think directly into the mind of His child, without the intervention of things! [Footnote: It may interest some of my readers to be told that I had got thus far in preparation for this volume, when I took a book from the floor, shaken with hundreds beside from my shelves by an earthquake the same morning, and opening it—it was a life of Lavater which I had not known I possessed—found these words written by him on a card, for a friend to read after his death: "Act according to thy faith in Christ, and thy faith will soon become sight."]

For Molly had made the one rational, one practical discovery, that life is to be lived, not by helpless assent or aimless drifting, but by active co-operation with the Life that has said "Live." To her everything was part of a whole, which, with its parts, she was learning to know, was finding out, by obedience to what she already knew. There is nothing for developing even the common intellect like obedience, that is, duty done. Those who obey are soon wiser than all their lessons; while from those who do not, will be taken away even what knowledge they started with.

Molly was not prepared to attempt convincing Walter, who was so much more learned and clever than she, that the things that rose in men's minds even in their best moods were not necessarily a valuable commodity, but that their character depended on the soil whence they sprung. She believed, however, that she had it in her power to make him doubt his judgment in regard to the work of other people, and that might lead him to doubt his judgment of himself, and the thoughts he made so much of.

One lovely evening in July, they were sitting together in the twilight, after a burial of the sun that had left great heaps of golden rubbish on the sides of his grave, in which little cherubs were busy dyeing their wings.

"Walter," said Molly, "do you remember the little story—quite a little story, and not very clever—that I read when you were ill, called 'Bootless Betty'?"

"I should think I do! I thought it one of the prettiest stories I had ever read, or heard read. Its fearless directness, without the least affectation of boldness, enchanted me. How one—clearly a woman—whose grammar was nowise to be depended upon, should yet get so swiftly and unerringly at what she wanted to say, has remained ever since a worshipful wonder to me. But I have seen something like it before, probably by the same writer!"

"You may have seen the same review of it I saw; it was in your own paper."

"You don't mean you take in 'The Field Battery'?"

"We did. Your father went for it himself, every week regularly. But we could not always be sure which things you had written!"

Walter gave a sigh of distaste, but said nothing. The idea of that paper

146

representing his mind to his father and Molly was painful to him.

"I have it here: may I read it to you?"

"Well—I don't know!—if you like. I can't say I care about reviews."

"Of course not! Nobody should. They are only thoughts about thoughts about things. But I want you to hear this!" pleaded Molly, drawing the paper from her pocket.

The review was of the shortest—long enough, however, to express much humorous comment for the kind of thing of which it said this was a specimen. It showed no suspicion of the presence in it of the things Walter had just said he saw there. But as Molly read, he stopped her.

"There is nothing like that in the story! The statement is false!" he exclaimed.

"Not a doubt of it!" responded Molly, and went on. But arrested by a certain phrase, Walter presently stopped her again.

"Molly," he said, seizing her hand, "is it any wonder I can not bear the thought of touching that kind of work again? Have pity upon me, Molly! It was I, I myself, who wrote that review! I had forgotten all about it! I did not mean to lie, but I was not careful enough not to lie! I have been very unjust to some one!"

"You could learn her name, and how to find her, from the publisher of the little book!" suggested Molly.

"I will find her, and make a humble apology. The evil, alas! is done; but I could—and will write another notice quite different."

Molly burst into the merriest laugh.

"The apology is made, Walter, and the writer forgives you heartily! Oh, what fun! The story is mine! You needn't stare so—as if you thought I couldn't do it! Think of the bad grammar! It was not a strong point at Miss Talebury's! Yes, Walter," she continued, talking like a child to her doll, "it was little Molly's first! and her big brother cut it all up into weeny weeny pieces for her! Poor Molly! But then it was a great honor, you know—greater than ever she could have hoped for!"

Walter stared bewildered, hardly trusting his ears. Molly an authoress!—in a small way, it might be, but did God ever with anything begin it big? Here was he, home again defeated!—to find the little bird he had left in the nest beautifully successful!

The lords of creation have a curious way of patronizing the beings they profess to worship. Man was made a little lower than the angels; he calls woman an angel, and then looks down upon her! Certainly, however, he has done his best to make her worthy of his condescension! But Walter had begun to learn humility, and no longer sought the chief place at the feast.

"Molly!" he said, in a low, wondering voice.

"Yes?" answered Molly.

"Forgive me, Molly. I am unworthy."

"I forgive you with all my heart, and love you for thinking it worth while to ask me."

"I am full of admiration of your story!"

"Why? It was not difficult."

Walter took her little hand and kissed it as if she had been a princess. Molly blushed, but did not take her hand from him. Walter might do what he liked with her ugly little hand! It was only to herself she called it ugly, however, not to Walter! Anyhow she was wrong; her hand was a very pretty one. It was indeed a little spoiled with work, but it was gloved with honor! It were good for many a heart that its hands were so spoiled! Human feet get a little broadened with walking; human hands get a little roughened with labor; but what matter! There are others, after like pattern but better finished, making, and to be ready by the time these are worn out, for all who have not shirked work.

Walter rose and went up the stairs to his own room, a chamber in the roof, crowded with memories. There he sat down to think, and thinking led to something else. Molly sat still and cried; for though it made her very glad to see him take it so humbly, it made her sad to give him pain. But not once did she wish she had not told him.

CHAPTER XXXI. THIS PICTURE AND THIS.

After awhile, as he did not appear, Molly went up to find him: she was anxious he should know how heartily she valued his real opinion.

"I have got a little poem here—if you can call it a poem—a few lines I wrote last Christmas: would you mind looking at it, and telling me if it is anything?"

"So, my bird of paradise, you sing too?" said Walter.

"Very little. A friend to whom I sent it, took it, without asking me, to one of the magazines for children, but they wouldn't have it. Tell me if it is worth printing. Not that I want it printed—not a bit!"

"I begin to think, Molly, that anything you write must be worth printing! But I wonder you should ask one who has proved himself so incompetent to give a true opinion, that even what he has given he is unable to defend!"

"I shall always trust your opinion, Walter—only it must be an opinion: you gave a judgment then without having formed an opinion. Shall I read?"

"Yes, please, Molly. I never used to like having poetry read to me, but you can read poetry!"

"This is easy to read!" said Molly.

"See the countless angels hover!

See the mother bending over!

See the shepherds, kings and cow!

What is baby thinking now?

Oh, to think what baby thinks

Would be worth all holy inks!

But he smiles such lovingness,

That I will not fear to guess!—

'Father called; you would not come!

Here I am to take you home!

'For the father feels the dearth

Of his children round his hearth—

'Wants them round and on his knee—

That's his throne for you and me!'

Something lovely like to this

Surely lights that look of bliss!

Or if something else be there,

Then 'tis something yet more fair;

For within the father's breast

Lies the whole world in its nest,"

She ceased.

Walter said nothing. His heart was full. What verses were these beside Lufa's fire-works!

"You don't care for them!" said Molly, sadly, but with the sweetest smile. "It's not that I care so much about the poetry; but I do love what I thought the baby might be thinking: it seems so true! so fit to be true!"

"The poetry is lovely, anyhow!" said Walter. "And one thing I am sure of—the father will not take me on his knee, if I go on as I have been doing! You must let me see everything you write, or have written, Molly! Should you mind?"

"Surely not, Walter! We used to read everything we thought might be yours!"

"Oh, don't!" cried Walter. "I can't bear to think of the beastly business!—I beg your pardon, Molly; but I am ashamed of the thing. There was not one stroke of good in the whole affair!"

"I admit," said Molly, "the kind of thing is not real work, though it may well be hard enough! But all writing about books and authors is not of that kind. A good book, like a true man, is well worth writing about by any one who understands it. That is very different from making it one's business to sit in judgment on the work of others. The mental condition itself of habitual judgment is a false one. Such an attitude toward any book requiring thought, and worthy of thought, renders it impossible for the would-be judge to know what is in the book. If, on the other hand, the book is worth little or nothing, it is not worth writing about, and yet has a perfect claim to fair play. If we feel differently at different times about a book we know, how am I to know the right mood for doing justice to a new book?"

"I am afraid the object is to write, not to judge righteous judgment!"

"One whose object is to write, and with whom judgment is the mere pretext for writing, is a parasite, and very pitiful, because, being a man, he lives as a flea lives. You see, Walter, by becoming a critic, you have made us critical—your father and me! We have talked about these things ever since you took to the profession!"

"Trade, Molly!" said Walter, gruffly.

"A profession, at least, that is greater than its performance! But it has been to me an education. We got as many as we were able of the books you took pains with, and sometimes could not help doubting whether you had seen the object of the writer. In one you dwelt scornfully on the unscientific allusions, where the design of the book was perfectly served by those allusions, which were merely to illustrate what the author meant. Your social papers, too, were but criticism in another direction. We could not help fearing that your criticism would prove a quicksand, swallowing your faculty for original, individual work. Then there was one horrid book you reviewed!"

"Well, I did no harm there! I made it out horrid enough, surely!"

"I think you did harm. I, for one, should never have heard of the book, and nobody down here would, I believe, if you had not written about it! You advertised it! Let bad books lie as much unheard of as may be. There is no injustice in leaving them alone."

Walter was silent.

"I have no doubt," he said at length, "that you are out and out right, Molly! Where my work has not been useless, it has been bad!"

"I do not believe it has been always useless," returned Molly. "Do you know, for instance, what a difference there was between your notices of the first and second books of one author—a lady with an odd name—I forget it? I have not seen the books, but I have the reviews. You must have helped her to improve!"

Walter gave a groan.

"My sins are indeed finding me out!" he said. Then, after a pause— "Molly," he resumed, "you can't help yourself—you've got to be my confessor! I am going to tell you an ugly fact—an absolute dishonesty!"

From beginning to end he told her the story of his relations with Lufa and her books; how he had got the better of his conscience, persuading himself that he thought that which he did not think, and that a book was largely worthy, where at best it was worthy but in a low degree; how he had suffered and been punished; how he had loved her, and how his love came to a miserable and contemptible end. That it had indeed come to an end, Molly drew from the quiet way in which he spoke of it; and his account of the letter he had written to Lufa, confirmed her conclusion.

How delighted she was to be so thoroughly trusted by him!

"I'm so glad, Walter!" she said.

"What are you glad of, Molly?"

"That you know one sort of girl, and are not so likely to take the next upon trust."

"We must take some things on trust, Molly, else we should never have anything!"

"That is true, Walter; but we needn't without a question empty our pockets to the first beggar that comes! When you were at home last, I wondered whether the girl could be worthy of your love."

"What girl?" asked Walter, surprised.

"Why, that girl, of course!"

"But I never said anything!"

"Twenty times a day!"

"What then made you doubt her worth?"

"That you cared less for your father."

"I am a brute, Molly! Did he feel it very much?"

"He always spoke to God about it, not to me. He never finds it easy to talk to his fellow-man; but I always know when he is talking to God! May I tell your father what you have just told me Walter? But of course not! You will tell him yourself!"

"No, Molly! I would rather you should tell him. I want him to know, and would tell him myself, if you were not handy. Then, if he chooses, we can have a talk about it! But now, Molly, what am I to do?"

"You still feel as if you had a call to literature, Walter?"

"I have no pleasure in any other kind of work."

"Might not that be because you have not tried anything else?"

"I don't know. I am drawn to nothing else."

"Well, it seems to me that a man who would like to make a saddle, must first have some pig-skin to make it of! Have you any pig-skin, Walter?"

"I see well enough what you mean!"

"A man must want long leisure for thought before he can have any material for his literary faculty to work with.

"You could write a history, but could you write one now? Even for a biography, you would have to read and study for months—perhaps years. As to the social questions you have been treating, men generally change their opinions about such things when they know a little more; and who would utter his opinions, knowing he most by and by wish he had not uttered them!"

"No one; but unhappily every one is cock-sure of his opinion till he changes it—and then he is as sure as before till he changes it again!"

"Opinion is not sight, your father says," answered Molly; and again a little pause followed.

"Well, but, Molly," resumed Walter, "how is that precious thing, leisure for thought, to be come by? Write reviews I will not! Write a history, I can not. Write a poem I might, but they wouldn't buy copies enough of it to pay for the paper and printing. Write a novel I might, if I had time; but how to live, not to say how to think, while I was writing it? Perhaps I ought to be a tutor, or a school-master!"

"Do you feel drawn to that, Walter?"

"I do not."

"And you do feel drawn to write?"

"I dare not say I have thoughts which demand expression; and yet somehow I want to write."

"And you say that some begin by writing what is of no value, but come to write things that are precious?"

"It is true."

"Then perhaps you have served your apprenticeship in worthless things, and the inclination to write comes now of precious things on their way, which you do not yet see or suspect, not to say know!"

"But many men and women have the impulse to write, who never write anything of much worth!"

Molly thought awhile.

"What if they yielded to the impulse before they ought? What if their eagerness to write when they ought to have been doing something else, destroyed the call in them? That is perhaps the reason why there are so many dull preachers—that they begin to speak before they have anything to say!"

"Teaching would be favorable to learning!"

"It would tire your brain, and give you too much to do with books! You would learn chiefly from thoughts, and I stand up for things first. And where would be your leisure?"

"You have something in your mind, Molly! I will do whatever you would have me!"

"No, Walter," exclaimed Molly, with a flash, "I will take no such promise! You will, I know, do what I or any one else may propose, if it appears to you right! But don't you think that, for the best work, a man ought to be independent of the work?"

"You would have your poet a rich man!"

"Just the contrary, Walter! A rich man is the most dependent of all— at least most rich men are. Take his riches, and what could himself do for himself? He depends on his money. No; I would have the poet earn his bread by the sweat of his brow—with his hands feed his body, and with his heart and brain the hearts of his brothers and sisters. We have talked much about this, your father and I. That a man is not a gentleman who works with his hands, is the meanest, silliest article in the social creed of our country. He who would be a better gentleman than the Carpenter of Nazareth, is not worthy of Him. He gave up His working only to do better work for His brothers and sisters, and then He let the men and women, but mostly, I suspect, the women, that loved Him, support him! Thousands upon thousands of young men think it more gentlemanly to be clerks than to be carpenters, but, if I were a man, I would rather make anything, than add up figures and copy stupid letters all day long! If I had brothers, I would ten times rather see them masons, or carpenters, or book-binders, or shoe-makers, than have them doing what ought to be left for the weaker and more delicate!"

"Which do you want me to be, Molly—a carpenter or a shoe-maker?"

"Neither, Walter—but a farmer: you don't want to be a finer gentleman than your father! Stay at home and help him, and grow strong. Plow and cart, and do the work of a laboring man. Nature will be your mate in her own work-shop!"

Molly was right. If Burns had but kept to his plow and his fields, to the birds and the beasts, to the storms and the sunshine! He was a free man while he lived by his labor among his own people! Ambition makes of gentlemen time-servers and paltry politicians; of the plowman-poet it made an exciseman!

"What will then become of the leisure you want me to have, Molly?"

"Your father will see that you have it! In winter, which you say is the season for poetry, there will be plenty of time, and in summer there will be some. Not a stroke of your pen will have to go for a dinner or a pair of shoes! Thoughts born of the heaven and the earth and the fountains of water, will spring up in your soul, and have time to ripen. If you find you are not wanted for an author, you will thank God you are not an author. What songs you would write then, Walter!"

He sat motionless most of the time. Now and then he would lift his head as if to speak, but he did not speak; and when Molly was silent, he rose and again went to his room. What passed there, I need not say. Walter was a true man in that he was ready to become truer: what better thing could be said of any unfinished man!

CHAPTER XXXII. THE LAST, BUT NOT THE END.

It was the second spring, and Molly and Walter sat again in the twilighted garden. Walter had just come home from his day's work; he had been plowing. He was a broad-shouldered, lean, powerful, handsome fellow, with a rather slow step, but soldierly carriage. His hands were brown and mighty, and took a little more washing than before.

"My father does not seem quite himself!" he said to Molly.

"He has been a little depressed for a day or two," she answered.

"There's nothing wrong, is there, Molly?"

"No, nothing. It is only his spirits. They have never been good once your mother died. He declares himself the happiest man in the county, now you are at home with us."

Walter was up early the next morning, and again at his work. A new-born wind blew on his face, and sent the blood singing through his veins. If we could hear all finest sounds, we might, perhaps, gather not only the mood, but the character of a man, by listening to the music or the discord the river of his blood was making, as through countless channels it irrigated lungs and brain: Walter's that morning must have been weaving lovely harmonies! It was a fresh spring wind, the breath of the world reviving from its winter-swoon. His father had managed to pay his debts; his hopes were high, his imagination active; his horses were pulling strong; the plow was going free, turning over the furrow smooth and clean; he was one of the powers of nature at work for the harvest of the year; he was in obedient consent with the will that makes the world and all its summers and winters! He was a thinking, choosing, willing part of the living whole, its vital fountain issuing from the heart of the Father of men! Work lay all about him, and he was doing the work! And Molly was at home, singing about hers! At night, when the sun was set, and his day's work done, he would go home to her and his father, to his room and his books and his writing!

But as he labored, his thought this day was most of his father: he was trying to make something to cheer him. The eyes of the old man never lost their love, but when he forgot to smile, Molly looked grave, and Walter felt that a cloud was over the sun. They were a true family: when one member suffered, all the members suffered with it.

So throughout the morning, as his horses pulled, and the earth opened, and the plow folded the furrow back, Walter thought, and made, and remembered: he had a gift for remembering completions, and forgetting the chips and rejected rubbish of the process. In the evening he carried borne with him these verses:

> *How shall he sing who hath no song?*
>
> *He laugh who hath no mirth?*
>
> *Will strongest can not wake a song!*
>
> *It is no use to strive or long*
>
> *To sing with them that have a song,*
>
> *And mirthless laugh with mirth!*
>
> *Though sad, he must confront the wrong,*
>
> *And for the right face any throng,*
>
> *Waiting, with patience sweet and strong,*
>
> *Until God's glory fills the earth;*
>
> *Then shall he sing who had no song,*
>
> *He laugh who had no mirth!*
>
> *Yea, if like barren rock thou sit*
>
> *Upon a land of dearth,*
>
> *Round which but phantom waters flit,*
>
> *Of visionary birth—*

Yet be thou still, and wait, wait long;

There comes a sea to drown the wrong,

His glory shall o'erwhelm the earth,

And thou, no more a scathed rock,

Shall start alive with gladsome shock,

Shalt a hand-clapping billow be,

And shout with the eternal sea!

To righteousness and love belong

The dance, the jubilance, the song!

For, lo, the right hath quelled the wrong,

And truth hath stilled the lying tongue!

For, lo, the glad God fills the earth.

And Love sits down by every hearth!

Now must thou sing because of song,

Now laugh because of mirth!

Molly read the verses, and rose to run with them to her father. But Walter caught and held her.

"Remember, Molly," he said, "I wrote it for my father; it is not my own feeling at the moment. For me, God has sent a wave of his glory over the earth; it has come swelling out of the deep sea of his thought, has caught me up, and is making me joyful as the morning. That wave is my love for you, Molly—is you, my Molly!"

She turned and kissed him, then ran to his father. He read, turned, and kissed Molly.

In his heart he sung this song:

"Blessed art thou among women! for thou hast given me a son of consolation!"

And to Molly he said,

"Let us go to Walter!"

THE END.

THE ELECT LADY

CHAPTER I. LANDLORD'S DAUGHTER AND TENANT'S SON.

In a kitchen of moderate size, flagged with slate, humble in its appointments, yet looking scarcely that of a farmhouse—for there were utensils about it indicating necessities more artificial than usually grow upon a farm—with the corner of a white deal table between them, sat two young people evidently different in rank, and meeting upon no level of friendship. The young woman held in her hand a paper, which seemed the subject of their conversation. She was about four- or five-and-twenty, well grown and not ungraceful, with dark hair, dark hazel eyes, and rather large, handsome features, full of intelligence, but a little hard, and not a little regnant—as such features must be, except after prolonged influence of a heart potent in self-subjugation. As to her social expression, it was a mingling of the gentlewoman of education, and the farmer's daughter supreme over the household and its share in the labor of production.

As to the young man, it would have required a deeper-seeing eye than falls to the lot of most observers, not to take him for a weaker nature than the young woman; and the deference he showed her as the superior, would have enhanced the difficulty of a true judgment. He was tall and thin, but plainly in fine health; had a good forehead, and a clear hazel eye, not overlarge or prominent, but full of light; a firm mouth, with a curious smile; a sun-burned complexion; and a habit when perplexed of pinching his upper lip between his finger and thumb, which at the present moment he was unconsciously indulging. He was the son of a small farmer—in what part of Scotland is of little consequence—and his companion for the moment was the daughter of the laird.

"I have glanced over the poem," said the lady, "and it seems to me quite up to the average of what you see in print."

"Would that be reason for printing it, ma'am?" asked the man, with amused smile.

"It would be for the editor to determine," she answered, not perceiving the hinted objection.

"You will remember, ma'am, that I never suggested—indeed I never thought of such a thing!"

"I do not forget. It was your mother who drew my attention to the verses."

"I must speak to my mother!" he said, in a meditative way.

"You can not object to my seeing your work! She does not show it to everybody. It is most creditable to you, such an employment of your leisure."

"The poem was never meant for any eyes but my own—except my brother's."

"What was the good of writing it, if no one was to see it?"

"The writing of it, ma'am."

"For the exercise, you mean?"

"No; I hardly mean that."

"I am afraid then I do not understand you."

"Do you never write anything but what you publish?"

"Publish! I never publish! What made you think of such a thing?"

"That you know so much about it, ma'am."

"I know people connected with the papers, and thought it might encourage you to see something in print. The newspapers publish so many poems now!"

"I wish it hadn't been just that one my mother gave you!"

"Why?"

"For one thing, it is not finished—as you will see when you read it more carefully."

"I did see a line I thought hardly rhythmical, but—"

"Excuse me, ma'am; the want of rhythm there was intentional."

"I am sorry for that. Intention is the worst possible excuse for wrong! The accent should always be made to fall in the right place."

"Beyond a doubt—but might not the right place alter with the sense?"

"Never. The rule is strict"

"Is there no danger of making the verse monotonous?"

"Not that I know."

"I have an idea, ma'am, that our great poets owe much of their music to the liberties they take with the rhythm. They treat the rule as its masters, and break it when they see fit."

"You must be wrong there! But in any case you must not presume to take the liberties of a great poet."

"It is a poor reward for being a great poet to be allowed to take liberties. I should say that, doing their work to the best of their power, they were rewarded with the discovery of higher laws of verse. Every one must walk by the light given him. By the rules which others have laid down he may learn to walk; but once his heart is awake to truth, and his ear to measure, melody and harmony, he must walk by the light, and the music God gives him."

"That is dangerous doctrine, Andrew!" said the lady, with a superior smile. "But," she continued, "I will mark what faults I see, and point them out to you."

"Thank you, ma'am, but please do not send the verses anywhere."

"I will not, except I find them worthy. You need not be afraid. For my father's sake I will have an eye to your reputation."

"I am obliged to you, ma'am," returned Andrew, but with his curious smile, hard to describe. It had in it a wonderful mixing of sweetness and humor, and a something that seemed to sit miles above his amusement. A heavenly smile it was, knowing too much to be angry. It had in it neither offense nor scorn. In respect of his poetry he was shy like a girl, but he showed no rejection of the patronage forced upon him by the lady.

He rose and stood a moment.

"Well, Andrew, what is it?"

"When will you allow me to call for the verses?"

"In the course of a week or so. By that time I shall have made up my mind. If in doubt, I shall ask my father."

"I wouldn't like the laird to think I spend my time on poetry."

"You write poetry, Andrew! A man should not do what he would not have known."

"That is true, ma'am; I only feared an erroneous conclusion."

"I will take care of that. My father knows that you are a hard-working young man. There is not one of his farms in better order than yours. Were it otherwise, I should not be so interested in your poetry."

Andrew wished her less interested in it. To have his verses read was like having a finger poked in his eye. He had not known that his mother looked at his papers. But he showed little sign of his annoyance, bade the lady good-morning, and left the kitchen.

Miss Fordyce followed him to the door, and stood for a moment looking out. In front of her was a paved court, surrounded with low buildings, between two of which was visible, at the distance of a mile or so, a railway line where it approached a viaduct. She heard the sound of a coming train, and who in a country place will not stand to see one pass!

CHAPTER II. AN ACCIDENT.

While the two were talking, a long train, part carriages, part trucks, was rattling through a dreary country, where it could never have been were there not regions very different on both sides of it. For miles in any direction, nothing but humpy moorland was to be seen, a gathering of low hills, with now and then a higher one, its sides broken by occasional torrents, in poor likeness of a mountain. No smoke proclaimed the presence of human dwelling; but there were spots between the hills where the hand of man had helped the birth of a feeble fertility; and in front was a small but productive valley, on the edge of which stood the ancient house of Potlurg, with the heath behind it: over a narrow branch of this valley went the viaduct.

It was a slow train, with few passengers. Of these one was looking from his window with a vague, foolish sense of superiority, thinking what a forgotten, scarce created country it seemed. He was a well-dressed, good-looking fellow, with a keen but pale-gray eye, and a fine forehead, but a chin such as is held to indicate weakness. More than one, however, of the strongest women I have known, were defective in chin. The young man was in the only first-class carriage of the train, and alone in it. Dressed in a gray suit, he was a little too particular in the smaller points of his attire, and lacked in consequence something of the look of a gentleman. Every now and then he would take off his hard round hat, and pass a white left hand through his short-cut mousey hair, while his right caressed a far longer mustache, in which he seemed interested. A certain indescribable heaviness and lack of light characterized his pale face.

It was a lovely day in early June. The air was rather cold, but youth and health care little about temperature on a holiday, with the sun shining, and that sweetest sense—to such at least as are ordinarily bound by routine—of having nothing to do. To many men and women the greatest trouble is to choose, for self is the hardest of masters to please; but as yet George Crawford had not been troubled with much choosing.

A crowded town behind him, the loneliness he looked upon was a pleasure to him. Compelled to spend time in it, without the sense of being on the way out of it, his own company would soon have grown irksome to him; for however much men may be interested in themselves, there are few indeed who are interesting to themselves. Those only whose self is aware of a higher presence can escape becoming bores and disgusts to themselves. That every man is endlessly greater than what he calls himself, must seem a paradox to the ignorant and dull, but a universe would be impossible without it. George had not arrived at the discovery of this fact, and yet was for the present contented both with himself and with his circumstances.

The heather was not in bloom, and the few flowers of the heathy land made no show. Brown and darker brown predominated, with here and there a shadow of green; and, weary of his outlook, George was settling back to his book, when there came a great bang and a tearing sound. He started to his feet, and for hours knew nothing more. A truck had run off the line and turned over; the carriage in which he was had followed it, and one of the young man's legs was broken.

CHAPTER III. HELP.

"Papa! papa! there is an accident on the line!" cried Miss Fordyce, running into her father's study, where he sat surrounded with books. "I saw it from the door!"

"Hush!" returned the old man, and listened. "I hear the train going on," he said, after a moment.

"Part of it is come to grief, I am certain," answered his daughter. "I saw something fall."

"Well, my dear?"

"What shall we do?"

"What would you have us do?" rejoined her father, without a movement toward rising. "It is too far off for us to be of any use."

"We ought to go and see."

"I am not fond of such seeing, Alexa, and will not go out of my way for it. The misery I can not avoid is enough for me."

But Alexa was out of the room, and in a moment more was running, in as straight a line as she could keep, across the heath to the low embankment. Andrew caught sight of her running. He could not see the line, but convinced that something was the matter, turned and ran in the same direction.

It was a hard and long run for Alexa, over such ground. Troubled at her father's indifference, she ran the faster—too fast for thinking, but not too fast for the thoughts that came of themselves. What had come to her father? Their house was the nearest! She could not shut out the conviction that, since succeeding to the property, he had been growing less and less neighborly.

She had caught up a bottle of brandy, which impeded her running. Yet she made good speed, her dress gathered high in the other hand. Her long dark hair broken loose and flying in the wind, her assumed dignity forgotten, and only the woman awake, she ran like a deer over the heather, and in little more than a quarter of an hour, though it was a long moor-mile, reached the embankment, flushed and panting.

Some of the carriages had rolled down, and the rails were a wreck. But the engine and half the train had kept on: neither driver nor stoker was hurt, and they were hurrying to fetch help from the next station. At the foot of the bank lay George Crawford insensible, with the guard of the train doing what he could to bring him to consciousness. He was on his back, pale as death, with no motion and scare a sign of life.

Alexa tried to give him brandy, but she was so exhausted, and her hand shook so, that she had to yield the bottle to the guard, and, hale and strong as she was, could but drag herself a little apart before she fainted.

In the meantime, as the train approached the station, the driver, who belonged to the neighborhood, saw the doctor, slackened speed, and set his whistle shrieking wildly. The doctor set spurs to his horse, and came straight over everything to his side.

"You go on," he said, having heard what had happened; "I shall be there sooner than you could take me."

He came first upon Andrew trying to make Miss Fordyce swallow a little of the brandy.

"There's but one gentleman hurt, sir," said the guard. "The other's only a young lady that's run till she's dropped."

"To bring brandy," supplemented Andrew.

The doctor recognized Alexa, and wondered what reception her lather would give his patient, for to Potlurg he must go! Suddenly she came to herself, and sat up, gazing wildly around. "Out of breath, Miss Fordyce; nothing worse!" said the doctor, and she smiled.

He turned to the young man, and did for him what he could without splints or bandages; then, with the help of the guard and Andrew, constructed, from pieces of the broken carriages, a sort of litter on which to carry him to Potlurg.

"Is he dead?" asked Alexa.

"Not a bit of it. He's had a bad blow on the head, though. We must get him somewhere as fast as we can!"

"Do you know him?"

"Not I. But we must take him to your house. I don't know what else to do with him!"

"What else should you want to do with him?"

"I was afraid it might bother the laird."

"You scarcely know my father, Doctor Pratt!"

"It would bother most people to have a wounded man quartered on them for weeks!" returned the doctor. "Poor fellow! A good-looking fellow too!"

A countryman who had been in the next carriage, but had escaped almost unhurt, offering his service, Andrew and he took up the litter gently, and set out walking with care, the doctor on one side, leading his horse, and Miss Fordyce on the other.

It was a strange building to which, after no small anxiety, they drew near; nor did it look the less strange the nearer they came. It was unsheltered by a single tree; and but for a low wall and iron rail on one side, inclosing what had been a garden, but was now a grass-plot, it rose straight out of the heather. From this plot the ground sloped to the valley, and was under careful cultivation. The entrance to it was closed with a gate of wrought iron, of good workmanship, but so wasted with rust that it seemed on the point of vanishing. Here at one time had been the way into the house; but no door, and scarce a window, was now to be seen on this side of the building. It was very old, and consisted of three gables, a great half-round between two of them, and a low tower with a conical roof.

Crawford had begun to recover consciousness, but when he came to himself he was received by acute pain. The least attempt to move was torture, and again he fainted.

CHAPTER IV. THE LAIRD.

Conducted by the lady, they passed round the house to the court, and across the court to a door in one of the gables. It was a low, narrow door, but large enough for the man that stood there—a little man, with colorless face, and quiet, abstracted look. His eyes were cold and keen, his features small, delicate, and regular. He had an erect little back, and was dressed in a long-tailed coat, looking not much of a laird, and less of a farmer, as he stood framed in the gray stone wall, in which odd little windows, dotted here and there at all heights and distances, revealed a wonderful arrangement of floors and rooms inside.

"Good-morning, Mr. Fordyce!" said the doctor. "This is a bad business, but it might have been worse! Not a soul injured but one!"

"Souls don't commonly get injured by accident!" returned the laird, with a cold smile that was far from discourteous. "Stick to the body, doctor! There you know something!"

"It's a truth, laird!" answered the doctor—but added to himself—"Well! it's awful to hear the truth from some mouths!"

The laird spoke no word of objection or of welcome. They carried the poor fellow into the house, following its mistress to a room, where, with the help of her one domestic, and instructed by the doctor, she soon had a bed prepared for him. Then away rode the doctor at full speed to fetch the appliances necessary, leaving the laird standing by the bed, with a look of mild dissatisfaction, but not a whisper of opposition.

It was the guest-chamber to which George Crawford had been carried, a room far more comfortable than a stranger might, from the aspect of the house, have believed possible. Everything in it was old-fashioned, and, having been dismantled, it was not in apple-pie order; but it was rapidly and silently restored to its humble ideal; and when the doctor, after an incredibly brief absence, returned with his assistant, he seemed both surprised and pleased at the change.

"He must have some one to sit up with him, Miss Fordyce," he said, when all was done.

"I will myself," she answered. "But you must give me exact directions, for I have done no nursing."

"If you will walk a little way with me, I will tell you all you need know. He will sleep now, I think—at least till you get back: I shall not keep you beyond a few minutes. It is not a very awkward fracture," he continued, as they went. "It might have been much worse! We shall have him about in a few weeks. But he will want the greatest care while the bones are uniting."

The laird turned from the bed, and went to his study, where he walked up and down, lost and old and pale, the very Bibliad of the room with its ancient volumes all around. Whatever his eyes fell upon, he turned from, as if he had no longer any pleasure in it, and presently stole back to the room where the sufferer lay. On tiptoe, with a caution suggestive of a wild beast asleep, he crept to the bed, looked down on his unwelcome guest with an expression of sympathy crossed with dislike, and shook his head slowly and solemnly, like one injured but forgiving.

His eye fell on the young man's pocket-book. It had fallen from his coat as they undressed him, and was on a table by the bedside. He caught it up just ere Alexa reentered.

"How is he, father?" she asked.

"He is fast asleep," answered the laid. "How long does the doctor think he will have to be here?"

"I did not ask him," she replied.

"That was an oversight, my child," he returned. "It is of consequence we should know the moment of his removal."

"We shall know it in good time. The doctor called it an affair of weeks—or months—I forget. But you shall not be troubled, father. I will attend to him."

"But I am troubled, Alexa! You do not know how little money I have!"

Again he retired—slowly, shut his door, locked it, and began to search the pocket-book. He found certain banknotes, and made a discovery concerning its owner.

With the help of her old woman, and noiselessly, while Crawford lay in a half slumber, Alexa continued making the chamber more comfortable. Chintz curtains veiled the windows, which, for all their narrowness, had admitted too much light; and an old carpet deadened the sound of footsteps on the creaking boards—for the bones of a house do not grow silent with age; a fire burned in the antique grate, and was a soul to the chamber, which was chilly, looking to the north, with walls so thick that it took half the summer to warm them through. Old Meg, moving to and fro, kept shaking her head like her master, as if she also were in the secret of some house-misery; but she was only indulging the funereal temperament of an ancient woman. As Alexa ran through the heather in the morning, she looked not altogether unlike a peasant; her shoes were strong, her dress was short; but now she came and went in a soft-colored gown, neither ill-made nor unbecoming. She did not seem to belong to what is called society, but she looked dignified, at times almost stately, with an expression of superiority, not strong enough to make her handsome face unpleasing. It resembled her father's, but, for a woman's, was cast in a larger mold.

The day crept on. The invalid was feverish. His nurse obeyed the doctor minutely, to a single drop. She had her tea brought her, but when the supper hour arrived went to join her father in the kitchen.

CHAPTER V. AFTER SUPPER.

They always eat in the kitchen. Strange to say, there was no dining-room in the house, though there was a sweetly old-fashioned drawing-room. The servant was with the sufferer, but Alexa was too much in the sick-room, notwithstanding, to know that she was eating her porridge and milk. The laird partook but sparingly, on the ground that the fare tended to fatness, which affliction of age he congratulated himself on having hitherto escaped. They eat in silence, but not a glance of her father that might indicate a want escaped the daughter. When the meal was ended, and the old man had given thanks, Alexa put on the table a big black Bible, which her father took with solemn face and reverent gesture. In the course of his nightly reading of the New Testament, he had come to the twelfth chapter of St. Luke, with the Lord's parable of the rich man whose soul they required of him: he read it beautifully, with an expression that seemed to indicate a sense of the Lord's meaning what He said.

"We will omit the psalm this evening—for the sake of the sufferer," he said, having ended the chapter. "The Lord will have mercy and not sacrifice."

They rose from their chairs and knelt on the stone floor. The old man prayed with much tone and expression, and I think meant all he said, though none of it seemed to spring from fresh need or new thankfulness, for he used only the old stock phrases, which flowed freely from his lips. He dwelt much on the merits of the Saviour; he humbled himself as the chief of sinners, whom it must be a satisfaction to God to cut off, but a greater satisfaction to spare for the sake of one whom he loved. Plainly the man counted it a most important thing to stand well with Him who had created him. When they rose, Alexa looked formally solemn, but the wan face of her father shone: the Psyche, if not the Ego, had prayed—and felt comfortable. He sat down, and looked fixedly, as if into eternity, but perhaps it was into vacancy; they are much the same to most people.

"Come into the study for a moment, Lexy, if you please," he said, rising at length. His politeness to his daughter, and indeed to all that came near him, was one of the most notable points in his behavior.

Alexa followed the black, slender, erect little figure up the stair, which consisted of about a dozen steps, filling the entrance from wall to wall, a width of some twelve feet. Between it and the outer door there was but room for the door of the kitchen on the one hand, and that of a small closet on the other. At the top was a wide space, a sort of irregular hall, more like an out-of-door court, paved with large flat stones into which projected the other side of the rounded mass, bordered by the grassy inclosure.

The laird turned to the right, and through a door into a room which had but one small window hidden by bookcases. Naturally it smelled musty, of old books and decayed bindings, an odor not unpleasant to some nostrils. He closed the door behind him, placed a chair for his daughter, and set himself in another by a deal table, upon which were books and papers.

"This is a sore trial, Alexa!" he said with a sigh.

"It is indeed, father—for the poor young man!" she returned.

"True; but it would be selfish indeed to regard the greatness of his suffering as rendering our trial the less. It is to us a more serious matter than you seem to think. It will cost much more than, in the present state of my finances, I can afford to pay. You little think—"

"But, father," interrupted Alexa, "how could we help it?"

"He might have been carried elsewhere!"

"With me standing there! Surely not, father! Even Andrew Ingram offered to receive him."

"Why did he not take him then?"

"The doctor wouldn't hear of it. And I wouldn't hear of it either."

"It was ill-considered, Lexy. But what's done is done—though, alas! not paid for."

"We must take the luck as it comes, father!"

"Alexa," rejoined the laird with solemnity, "you ought never to mention luck. There is no such thing. It was either for the young man's sins, or to prevent worse, or for necessary discipline, that the train was overturned. The cause is known to Him. All are in His hands—and we must beware of attempting to take any out of His hands, for it can not be done."

"Then, father, if there be no chance, our part was ordered too. So there is the young man in our spare room, and we must receive our share of the trouble as from the hand of the Lord."

"Certainly, my dear! it was the expense I was thinking of. I was only lamenting—bear me witness, I was not opposing—the will of the Lord. A man's natural feelings remain."

"If the thing is not to be helped, let us think no more about it!"

"It is the expense, my dear! Will you not let your mind rest for a moment upon the fact? I am doing my utmost to impress it upon you. For other expenses there is always something to show; for this there will be nothing, positively nothing!"

"Not the mended leg, father?"

"The money will vanish, I tell you, as a tale that is told."

"It is our life that vanishes that way!"

"The simile suits either. So long as we do not use the words of Scripture irreverently, there is no harm in making a different application of them. There is no irreverence here: next to the grace of God, money is the thing hardest to get and hardest to keep. If we are not wise with it, the grace—I mean money—will not go far."

"Not so far as the next world, anyhow!" said Alexa, as if to herself.

"How dare you, child! The Redeemer tells us to make friends of the mammon of unrighteousness, that when we die it may receive us into everlasting habitations!"

"I read the passage this morning, father: it is they, not it, will receive you. And I have heard that it ought to be translated, 'make friends with, or by means of the mammon of unrighteousness.'"

"I will reconsider the passage. We must not lightly change even the translated word!"

The laird had never thought that it might be of consequence to him one day to have friends in the other world. Neither had he reflected that the Lord did not regard the obligation of gratitude as ceasing with this life.

Alexa had reason to fear that her father made a friend of, and never a friend with the mammon of unrighteousness. At the same time the half-penny he put in the plate every Sunday must go a long way if it was not estimated, like that of the poor widow, according to the amount he possessed, but according to the difficulty he found in parting with it.

"After weeks, perhaps months of nursing and food and doctor's stuff," resumed the laird, "he will walk away, and we shall see not a plack of the money he carries with him. The visible will become the invisible, the present the absent!"

"The little it will cost you, father—"

"Hold there, my child! If you call any cost little, I will not hear a word more: we should be but running a race from different points to different goals! It will cost—that is enough! How much it will cost me, you can not calculate, for you do not know what money stands for in my eyes. There are things before which money is insignificant!"

"Those dreary old books!" said Alexa to herself, casting a glance on the shelves that filled the room from floor to ceiling, and from wall to wall.

"What I was going to say, father," she returned, "was, that I have a little money of my own, and this affair shall cost you nothing. Leave me to contrive. Would you tell him his friends must pay his board, or take him away? It would be a nice anecdote in the annals of the Fordyces of Potlurg!"

"At the same time, what more natural?" rejoined her father. "His friends must in any case be applied to! I learn from his pocket-book—"

"Father!"

"Content yourself, Alexa. I have a right to know whom I receive under my roof. Besides, have I not learned thereby that the youth is a sort of connection!"

"You don't mean it, father?"

"I do mean it. His mother and yours were first cousins."

"That is not a connection; it's a close kinship!"

"Is it?" said the laird, dryly.

"Anyhow," pursued Alexa, "I give you my word you shall hear nothing more of the expense."

She bade her father good-night, and returning to the bedside of her patient, released Meg.

CHAPTER VI. ABOUT THE LAIRD.

Thomas Fordyce was a sucker from the root of a very old family tree, born in poverty, and, with great pinching of father and mother, brothers and sisters, educated for the Church. But from pleasure in scholarship, from archaeological tastes, a passion for the arcana of history, and a love of literature, strong, although not of the highest kind, he had settled down as a school-master, and in his calling had excelled. By all who knew him he was regarded as an accomplished, amiable, and worthy man.

When his years were verging on the undefined close of middle age he saw the lives between him and the family property, one by one wither at the touch of death, until at last there was no one but himself and his daughter to succeed. He was at the time the head of a flourishing school in a large manufacturing town; and it was not without some regret, though with more pleasure, that he yielded his profession and retired to Potlurg.

Greatly dwindled as he found the property, and much and long as it had been mismanaged, it was yet of considerable value, and worth a wise care. The result of the labor he spent upon it was such that it had now for years yielded him, if not a large rental, one far larger at least than his daughter imagined. But the sinking of the school-master in the laird seemed to work ill for the man, and good only for the land. I say seemed, because what we call degeneracy is often but the unveiling of what was there all the time; and the evil we could become, we are. If I have in me the tyrant or the miser, there he is, and such am I—as surely as if the tyrant or the miser were even now visible to the wondering dislike of my neighbors. I do not say the characteristic is so strong, or would be so hard to change as by the revealing development it must become; but it is there, alive, as an egg is alive; and by no means inoperative like a mere germ, but exercising real though occult influence on the rest of my character. Therefore, except the growing vitality be in process of killing these ova of death, it is for the good of the man that they should be so far developed as to show their existence. If the man do not then starve and slay them they will drag him to the judgment-seat of a fiery indignation.

For the laird, nature could ill replace the human influences that had surrounded the school-master; while enlargement both of means and leisure enabled him to develop by indulgence a passion for a peculiar kind of possession, which, however refined in its objects, was yet but a branch of the worship of Mammon. It suits the enemy just as well, I presume, that a man should give his soul for coins as for money. In consequence he was growing more and more withdrawn, ever filling less the part of a man—which is to be a hiding-place from the wind, a covert from the tempest. He was more and more for himself, and thereby losing his life. Dearly as he loved his daughter, he was, by slow fallings away, growing ever less of a companion, less of a comfort, less of a necessity to her, and requiring less and less of her for the good or ease of his existence. We wrong those near us in being independent of them. God himself would not be happy without His Son. We ought to lean on each other, giving and receiving—not as weaklings, but as lovers. Love is strength as well as need. Alexa was more able to live alone than most women; therefore it was the worse for her. Too satisfied with herself, too little uneasy when alone, she did not know that then she was not in good enough company. She was what most would call a strong nature, nor knew what weaknesses belong to, and grow out of, such strength as hers.

The remoter scions of a family tree are not seldom those who make most account of it; the school-master's daughter knew more about the Fordyces of Potlurg, and cared more for their traditions, than any who of later years had reaped its advantages or shared its honors. Interest in the channel down which one has slid into the world is reasonable, and may be elevating; with Alexa it passed beyond good, and wrought for evil. Proud of a family with a history, and occasionally noted in the annals of the country, she regarded herself as the superior of all with whom she had hitherto come into relation. To the poor, to whom she was invariably and essentially kind, she was less condescending than to such as came nearer her own imagined standing; she was constantly aware that she belonged to the elect of the land! Society took its revenge; the rich trades-people looked down upon her as the school-master's daughter. Against their arrogance her indignation buttressed her lineal with her mental superiority. At the last the pride of family is a personal arrogance. And now at length she was in her natural position as heiress of Potlurg!

She was religious—if one may be called religious who felt no immediate relation to the source of her being. She felt bound to defend, so far as she honestly could, the doctrines concerning God and His ways transmitted by the elders of her people; to this much, and little more, her religion toward God amounted. But she had a strong sense of obligation to do what was right.

Her father gave her so little money to spend that she had to be very careful with her housekeeping, and they lived in the humblest way. For her person she troubled him as little as she could, believing him, from the half statements and hints he gave, and his general carriage toward life, not a little oppressed by lack of money, nor suspecting his necessities created and his difficulties induced by himself. In this regard it had come to be understood between them that the produce of the poultry-yard was Alexa's own; and to some little store she had thus gathered she mainly trusted for the requirements of her invalid. To this her father could not object, though he did not like it; he felt what was hers to be his more than he felt what was his to be hers.

Alexa had not learned to place value on money beyond its use, but she was not therefore free from the service of Mammon; she looked to it as to a power essential, not derived; she did not see it as God's creation, but merely as an existence, thus making of a creature of God the mammon of unrighteousness. She did not, however, cling to it, but was ready to spend it. At the same time, had George Crawford looked less handsome or less of a gentleman, she would not have been so ready to devote the contents of her little secret drawer.

The discovery of her relationship to the young man waked a new feeling. She had never had a brother, never known a cousin, and had avoided the approach of such young men as, of inferior position in her eyes, had sought to be friendly with her; here was one thrown helpless on her care, with necessities enough to fill the gap between his real relation to her, and that of the brother after whom she had sighed in vain! It was a new and delightful sensation to have a family claim on a young man—a claim, the material advantage of which was all on his side, the devotion all on hers. She was invaded by a flood of tenderness toward the man. Was he not her cousin, a gentleman, and helpless as any new-born child? Nothing should be wanting that a strong woman could do for a powerless man.

CHAPTER VII. THE COUSINS.

George Crawford was in excellent health when the accident occurred, and so when he began to recover, his restoration was rapid. The process, however, was still long enough to compel the cousins to know more of each other than twelve months of ordinary circumstance would have made possible.

George, feeling neither the need, nor, therefore, the joy of the new relationship so much as Alexa, disappointed her by the coolness of his response to her communication of the fact; and as they were both formal, that is, less careful as to the reasonable than as to the conventional, they were not very ready to fall in love. Such people may learn all about each other, and not come near enough for love to be possible between them. Some people approximate at once, and at once decline to love, remaining friends the rest of their lives. Others love at once; and some take a whole married life to come near enough, and at last love. But the reactions of need and ministration can hardly fail to breed tenderness, and disclose the best points of character.

The cousins were both handsome, and—which was of more consequence—each thought the other handsome. They found their religious opinions closely coincident—nor any wonder, for they had gone for years to the same church every Sunday, had been regularly pumped upon from the same reservoir, and had drunk the same arguments concerning things true and untrue.

George found that Alexa had plenty of brains, a cultivated judgment, and some knowledge of literature; that there was no branch of science with which she had not some little acquaintance, in which she did not take some small interest. Her father's teaching was beyond any he could have procured for her, and what he taught she had learned; for she had a love of knowing, a tendency to growth, a capacity for seizing real points, though as yet perceiving next to nothing of their relation to human life and hope. She believed herself a judge of verse, but in truth her knowledge of poetry was limited to its outer forms, of which she had made good studies with her father. She had learned the how before the what, knew the body before the soul—could tell good binding but not bad leather—in a word, knew verse but not poetry.

She understood nothing of music, but George did not miss that; he was more sorry she did not know French—not for the sake of its literature, but because of showing herself an educated woman.

Diligent in business, not fervent in spirit, she was never idle. But there are other ways than idleness of wasting time. Alexa was continually "improving herself," but it was a big phrase for a small matter; she had not learned that to do the will of God is the only way to improve one's self. She would have scorned the narrowness of any one who told her so, not understanding what the will of God means.

She found that her guest and cousin was a man of some position, and wondered that her father should never have mentioned the relationship. The fact was that, in a time of poverty, the school-master had made to George's father the absurd request of a small loan without security, and the banker had behaved as a rich relation and a banker was pretty sure to behave.

George occupied a place of trust in the bank, and, though not yet admitted to a full knowledge of its more important transactions, hoped soon to be made a partner.

When his father came to Potlurg to see him the laird declined to appear, and the banker contented himself thereafter with Alexa's bulletins.

CHAPTER VIII. GEORGE AND THE LAIRD.

Alexa's money was nearly exhausted, and most of her chickens had been devoured by the flourishing convalescent, but not yet would the doctor allow him to return to business.

One night the electric condition of the atmosphere made it heavy, sultry and unrefreshing, and George could not sleep. There came a terrible burst of thunder; then a bannered spear of vividest lightning seemed to lap the house in its flashing folds, and the simultaneous thunder was mingled with the sound, as it seemed, of the fall of some part of the building. George sat up in bed and listened. All was still. He must rise and see what had happened, and whether any one was hurt. He might meet Alexa, and a talk with her would be a pleasant episode in his sleepless night. He got into his dressing-gown, and taking his stick, walked softly from the room.

His door opened immediately on the top of the stair. He stood and listened, but was aware of no sequel to the noise. Another flash came, and lighted up the space around him, with its walls of many angles. When the darkness was returned and the dazzling gone, and while the thunder yet bellowed, he caught the glimmer of a light under the door of the study, and made his way toward it over the worn slabs. He knocked, but there was no answer. He pushed the door, and saw that the light came from behind a projecting book-case. He hesitated a moment, and glanced about him.

A little clinking sound came from somewhere. He stole nearer the source of the light; a thief might be there. He peeped round the end of the book-case. With his back to him the laird was kneeling before an open chest. He had just counted a few pieces of gold, and was putting them away. He turned over his shoulder a face deathly pale, and his eyes for a moment stared blank. Then with a shivering smile he rose. He had a thin-worn dressing-gown over his night-shirt, and looked a thread of a man.

"You take me for a miser?" he said, trembling, and stood expecting an answer.

Crawford was bewildered: what business had he there?

"I am not a miser!" resumed the laird. "A man may count his money without being a miser!"

He stood and stared, still trembling, at his guest, either too much startled or too gentle to find fault with his intrusion.

"I beg your pardon, laird," said George. "I knocked, but receiving no answer, feared something was wrong."

"But why are you out of bed—and you an invalid?" returned Mr. Fordyce.

"I heard a heavy fall, and feared the lightning had done some damage."

"We shall see about that in the morning, and in the meantime you had better go to bed," said the laird.

They turned together toward the door.

"What a multitude of books, you have, Mr. Fordyce!" remarked George. "I had not a notion of such a library in the county!"

"I have been a lover of books all my life," returned the laird. "And they gather, they gather!" he added.

"Your love draws them," said George.

"The storm is over, I think," said the laird.

He did not tell his guest that there was scarcely a book on those shelves not sought after by book-buyers—not one that was not worth money in the book-market. Here and there the dulled gold of a fine antique binding returned the gleam of the candle, but any gathering of old law or worthless divinity would have looked much the same.

"I should like to glance over them," said George. "There must be some valuable volumes among so many!"

"Rubbish! rubbish!" rejoined the old man, testily, almost hustling him from the room. "I am ashamed to hear it called a library."

It seemed to Crawford, as again he lay awake in his bed, altogether a strange incident. A man may count his money when he pleases, but not the less must it seem odd that he should do so in the middle of the night, and with such a storm flashing and roaring around him, apparently unheeded. The next morning he got his cousin to talk about her father, but drew from her nothing to cast light on what he had seen.

CHAPTER IX. IN THE GARDEN.

Of the garden which had been the pride of many owners of the place, only a small portion remained. It was strangely antique, haunted with a beauty both old and wild, the sort of garden for the children of heaven to play in when men sleep.

In a little arbor constructed by an old man who had seen the garden grow less and less through successive generations, a tent of honeysuckle in a cloak of sweet pease, sat George and Alexa, two highly respectable young people, Scots of Scotland, like Jews of Judaea, well satisfied of their own worthiness. How they found their talk interesting, I can scarce think. I should have expected them to be driven by very dullness to love-making; but the one was too prudent to initiate it, the other too staid to entice it. Yet, people on the borders of love being on the borders of poetry, they had got talking about a certain new poem, concerning which George, having read several notices of it, had an opinion to give.

"You should tell my father about it, George," said Alexa; "he is the best judge I know."

She did not understand that it was a little more than the grammar of poetry the school-master had ever given himself to understand. His best criticism was to show phrase calling to phrase across gulfs of speech.

The little iron gate, whose hinges were almost gone with rust, creaked and gnarred as it slowly opened to admit the approach of a young countryman. He advanced with the long, slow, heavy step suggestive of nailed shoes; but his hazel eye had an outlook like that of an eagle from its eyrie, and seemed to dominate his being, originating rather than directing its motions. He had a russet-colored face, much freckled; hair so dark red as to be almost brown; a large, well-shaped nose; a strong chin; and a mouth of sweetness whose smile was peculiarly its own, having in it at once the mystery and the revelation of Andrew Ingram. He took off his bonnet as he drew near, and held it as low as his knee, while with something of the air of an old-fashioned courtier, he stood waiting. His clothes, all but his coat, which was of some blue stuff, and his Sunday one, were of a large-ribbed corduroy. For a moment no one spoke. He colored a little, but kept silent, his eyes on the lady.

"Good-morning, Andrew!" she said at length. "There was something, I forget what, you were to call about! Remind me—will you?"

"I did not come before, ma'am, because I knew you were occupied. And even now it does not greatly matter."

"Oh, I remember!—the poem! I am very sorry, but I had so much to think of that it went quite out of my mind."

An expression half amused, half shy, without trace of mortification, for an instant shadowed the young man's face.

"I wish you would let me have the lines again, ma'am! Indeed I should be obliged to you!" he said.

"Well, I confess they might first be improved! I read them one evening to my father, and he agreed with me that two or three of them were not quite rhythmical. But he said it was a fair attempt, and for a working-man very creditable."

What Andrew was thinking, it would have been hard to gather from his smile; but I believe it was that, if he had himself read the verses aloud, the laird would have found no fault with their rhythm. His carriage seemed more that of a patient, respectful amusement than anything else.

Alexa rose, but resumed her seat, saying:

"As the poem is a religious one, there can be no harm in handing it you on Sunday after church!—that is," she added, meaningly, "if you will be there!"

"Give it to Dawtie, if you please, ma'am," replied Andrew.

"Ah!" rebuked Miss Fordyce, in a tone almost of rebuke.

"I seldom go to church, ma'am," said Andrew, reddening a little, but losing no sweetness from his smile.

"I understand as much! It is very wrong! Why don't you?"

Andrew was silent.

"I wish you to tell me," persisted Alexa, with a peremptoriness which came of the school-master. She had known him too as a pupil of her father's!

"If you will have it, ma'am, I not only learn nothing from Mr. Smith, but I think much that he says is not true."

"Still you ought to go for the sake of example."

"Do wrong to make other people follow my example? Can that be to do right?"

"Wrong to go to church! What do you mean? Wrong to pray with your fellow-men?"

"Perhaps the hour may come, ma'am, when I shall be able to pray with my fellow-men, even though the words they use seem addressed to a tyrant, not to the Father of Jesus Christ. But at present I can not. I might endure to hear Mr. Smith say evil things concerning God, but the evil things he says to God make me quite unable to pray, and I feel like a hypocrite!"

"Whatever you may think of Mr. Smith's doctrines, it is presumptuous to set yourself up as too good to go to church."

"I most bear the reproach, ma'am. I can not consent to be a hypocrite in order to avoid being called one!"

Either Miss Fordyce had no answer to this, or did not choose to give any. She was not troubled that Andrew would not go to church, but offended at the unhesitating decision with which he set her counsel aside. Andrew made her a respectful bow, turned away, put on his bonnet, which he had held in his hand all the time, and passed through the garden gate.

"Who is the fellow?" asked George, partaking sympathetically of his companion's annoyance.

"He is Andrew Ingram, the son of a small farmer, one of my father's tenants. He and his brother work with their father on the farm. They are quite respectable people. Andrew is conceited, but has his good points. He imagines himself a poet, and indeed his work has merit. The worst of him is that he sets up for being better than other people."

"Not an unusual fault with the self-educated!"

"He does go on educating himself, I believe, but he had a good start to begin with. My father took much pains with him at school. He helped to carry you here after the accident—and would have taken you to his father's if I would have let him."

George cast on her a look of gratitude.

"Thank you for keeping me," he said. "But I wish I had taken some notice of his kindness!"

CHAPTER X. ANDREW INGRAM.

Of the persons in my narrative, Andrew Ingram is the simplest, therefore the hardest to be understood by an ordinary reader. I must take up his history from a certain point in his childhood.

One summer evening, he and his brother Sandy were playing together on a knoll in one of their father's fields. Andrew was ten years old, and Sandy a year younger. The two quarreled, and the spirit of ancestral borderers waking in them, they fell to blows. The younger was the stronger for his years, and they were punching each other with relentless vigor, when suddenly they heard a voice, and stopping their fight, saw before them an humble-looking man with a pack on his back. He was a peddler known in the neighborhood, and noted for his honesty and his silence, but the boys had never seen him. They stood abashed before him, dazed with the blows they had received, and not a little ashamed; for they were well brought up, their mother being an honest disciplinarian, and their father never interfering with what she judged right. The sun was near the setting, and shone with level rays full on the peddler; but when they thought of him afterward, they seemed to remember more light in his face than that of the sun. Their conscience bore him witness, and his look awed them. Involuntarily they turned from him, seeking refuge with each other: his eyes shone so! they said; but immediately they turned to him again.

Sandy knew the pictures in the "Pilgrim's Progress," and Andrew had read it through more than once: when they saw the man had a book in his hand, open, and heard him, standing there in the sun, begin to read from it, they thought it must be Christian, waiting for Evangelist to come to him. It is impossible to say how much is fact and how much imagination in what children recollect; the one must almost always supplement the other; but they were quite sure that the words he read were these: "And lo, I am with you always, even to the end of the world!" The next thing they remembered was their walking slowly down the hill in the red light, and all at once waking up to the fact that the man was gone, they did not know when or where. But their arms were round each other's necks, and they were full of a strange awe. Then Andrew saw something red on Sandy's face.

"Eh, Sandy!" he cried, "it's bluid!" and burst into tears.

It was his own blood, not Sandy's!—the discovery of which fact relieved Andrew, and did not so greatly discompose Sandy, who was less sensitive.

They began at length to speculate on what had happened. One thing was clear: it was because they were fighting that the man had come; but it was not so clear who the man was. He could not be Christian, because Christian went over the river! Andrew suggested it might have been Evangelist, for he seemed to be always about. Sandy added, as his contribution to the idea, that he might have picked up Christian's bundle and been carrying it home to his wife. They came, however, to the conclusion, by no ratiocination, I think, but by a conviction which the idea itself brought with it, that the stranger was the Lord himself, and that the pack on His back was their sins, which He was carrying away to throw out of the world.

"Eh, wasna it fearfu' He should come by jist when we was fechtin'!" said Sandy.

"Eh, na! it was a fine thing that! We micht hae been at it yet! But we winna noo!—will we ever, Sandy?"

"Na, that we winna!"

"For," continued Andrew, "He said 'Lo, I am with you always!' And suppose He werena, we daurna be that ahint His back we would na be afore His face!"

"Do you railly think it was Him, Andrew?"

"Weel," replied Andrew, "gien the deevil be goin' aboot like a roarin' lion, seekin' whom he may devour, as father says, it's no likely He would na be goin' aboot as weel, seekin' to haud him aff o' 's!"

"Ay!" said Sandy.

194

"And noo," said the elder, "what are we to do?"

For Andrew, whom both father and mother judged the dreamiest of mortals, was in reality the most practical being in the whole parish—so practical that by and by people mocked him for a poet and a heretic, because he did the things which they said they believed. Most unpractical must every man appear who genuinely believes in the things that are unseen. The man called practical by the men of this world is he who busies himself building his house on the sand, while he does not even bespeak a lodging in the inevitable beyond.

"What are we to do?" said Andrew. "If the Lord is going about like that, looking after us, we've surely got something to do looking after Him!"

There was no help in Sandy; and it was well that, with the reticence of children, neither thought of laying the case before their parents; the traditions of the elders would have ill agreed with the doctrine they were now under! Suddenly it came into Andrew's mind that the book they read at worship to which he had never listened, told all about Jesus.

He began at the beginning, and grew so interested in the stories that he forgot why he had begun to read it One day, however, as he was telling Sandy about Jacob—"What a shame!" said Sandy; and Andrew's mind suddenly opened to the fact that he had got nothing yet out of the book. He threw it from him, echoing Sandy's words, "What's a shame!"—not of Jacob's behavior, but of the Bible's, which had all this time told them nothing about the man that was going up and down the world, gathering up their sins, and carrying them away in His pack! But it dawned upon him that it was the New Testament that told about Jesus Christ, and they turned to that. Here also I say it was well they asked no advice, for they would probably have been directed to the Epistle to the Romans, with explanations yet more foreign to the heart of Paul than false to his Greek. They began to read the story of Jesus as told by his friend Matthew, and when they had ended it, went on to the gospel according to Mark. But they had not read far when Sandy cried out:

"Eh, Andrew, it's a' the same thing ower again!"

"No a'thegither," answered Andrew. "We'll gang on, and see!"

195

Andrew came to the conclusion that it was so far the same that he would rather go back and read the other again, for the sake of some particular things he wanted to make sure about So the second time they read St. Matthew, and came to these words:

"If two of you shall agree on earth as touching anything that they shall ask, it shall be done for them of My Father which is in heaven."

"There's twa o' 's here!" cried Andrew, laying down the book. "Lat's try 't!"

"Try what?" said Sandy.

His brother read the passage again.

"Lat the twa o' 's speir Him for something!" concluded Andrew. "What wull't be?"

"I won'er if it means only ance, or may be three times, like 'The Three Wishes!'" suggested Sandy, who, like most Christians, would rather have a talk about it than do what he was told.

"We might ask for what would not be good for us!" returned Andrew.

"And make fools of ourselves!" assented Sandy, with "The Three Wishes" in his mind.

"Do you think He would give it us then?"

"I don't know."

"But," pursued Andrew, "if we were so foolish as that old man and woman, it would be better to find it out, and begin to grow wise!—I'll tell you what we'll do: we'll make it our first wish to know what's best to ask for; and then we can go on asking!"

"Yes, yes; let us!"

"I fancy we'll have as many wishes as we like! Doon upo' yer knees, Sandy!"

They knelt together.

196

I fear there are not a few to say, "How ill-instructed the poor children were!—actually mingling the gospel and the fairy tales!" "Happy children," say I, "who could blunder into the very heart of the will of God concerning them, and do the thing at once that the Lord taught them, using the common sense which God had given and the fairy tale nourished!" The Lord of the promise is the Lord of all true parables and all good fairy tales.

Andrew prayed:

"Oh, Lord, tell Sandy and me what to ask for. We're unanimous."

They got up from their knees. They had said what they had to say: why say more!

They felt rather dull. Nothing came to them. The prayer was prayed, and they could not make the answer! There was no use in reading more! They put the Bible away in a rough box where they kept it among rose-leaves—ignorant priests of the lovely mystery of Him who was with them always—and without a word went each his own way, not happy, for were they not leaving Him under the elder-tree, lonely and shadowy, where it was their custom to meet! Alas for those who must go to church to find Him, or who can not pray unless in their closet!

They wandered about disconsolate, at school and at home, the rest of the day—at least Andrew did; Sandy had Andrew to lean upon! Andrew had Him who was with them always, but He seemed at the other end of the world. They had prayed, and there was no more of it!

In the evening, while yet it was light, Andrew went alone to the elder-tree, took the Bible from its humble shrine, and began turning over its leaves.

"And why call ye me, Lord, Lord, and do not the things which I say?" He read, and sunk deep in thought.

This is the way his thoughts went:

"What things? What had He been saying? Let me look and see what He says, that I may begin to do it!"

He read all the chapter, and found it full of tellings. When he read it before he had not thought of doing one of the things He said, for as plainly as He told him! He had not once thought He had any concern in the matter!

"I see!" he said; "we must begin at once to do what He tells us!"

He ran to find his brother.

"I've got it!" he cried: "I've got it!"

"What?"

"What we've got to do"

"And what is it?"

"Just what He tells us."

"We were doing that," said Sandy, "when we prayed Him to tell us what to pray for!"

"So we were! That's grand!"

"Then haven't we got to pray for anything more?"

"We'll soon find out; but first we must look for something to do!"

They began at once to search for things the Lord told them to do. And of all they found, the plainest and easiest was: "Whosoever shall smite thee on thy right cheek, turn to him the other also." This needed no explanation! it was as clear as the day to both of them!

The very next morning the school-master, who, though of a gentle disposition, was irritable, taking Andrew for the offender in a certain breach of discipline, gave him a smart box on the ear. Andrew, as readily as if it had been instinctively, turned to him the other cheek.

An angry man is an evil interpreter of holy things, and Mr. Fordyce took the action for one of rudest mockery, nor thought of the higher master therein mocked if it were mockery: he struck the offender a yet smarter blow. Andrew stood for a minute like one dazed; but the red on his face was not that of anger; he was perplexed as to whether he ought now to turn the former cheek again to the striker. Uncertain, he turned away, and went to his work.

Stops a reader here to say: "But do you really mean to tell us we ought to take the words literally as Andrew did?" I answer: "When you have earned the right to understand, you will not need to ask me. To explain what the Lord means to one who is not obedient, is the work of no man who knows his work."

It is but fair to say for the school-master that, when he found he had mistaken, he tried to make up to the boy for it—not by confessing himself wrong—who could expect that of only a school-master?—but by being kinder to him than before. Through this he came to like him, and would teach him things out of the usual way—such as how to make different kinds of verse.

By and by Andrew and Sandy had a quarrel. Suddenly Andrew came to himself, and cried:

"Sandy! Sandy! He says we're to agree!"

"Does He?"

"He says we're to love one another, and we canna do that if we dinna agree!"

There came a pause.

"Perhaps after all you were in the right, Sandy!" said Andrew.

"I was just going to say that; when I think about it, perhaps I wasn't so much in the right as I thought I was!"

"It can't matter much which was in the right, when we were both in the wrong!" said Andrew. "Let's ask Him to keep us from caring which is in the right, and make us both try to be in the right We don't often differ about what we are to ask for, Sandy!"

"No, we don't."

"It's me to take care of you, Sandy!"

"And me to take care of you, Andrew!"

Here was the nucleus of a church!—two stones laid on the foundation-stone.

"Luik here, Sandy!" said Andrew; "we maun hae anither, an' syne there'll be four o' 's!"

"How's that?" asked Sandy.

"I won'er 'at we never noticed it afore! Here's what He says: 'For where two or three are gathered together in My name, there am I in the midst of them.' In that way, wherever He micht be walkin' aboot, we could aye get Him! He likes twa, an' His Father 'ill hear the 'greed prayer, but He likes three better—an' that stan's to rizzon, for three maun be better 'n twa! First ane maun lo'e Him; an' syne twa can lo'e Him better, because ilk ane is helpit by the ither, an' lo'es Him the mair that He lo'es the ither ane! An' syne comes the third, and there's mair an' mair throwin' o' lichts, and there's the Lord himsel' i' the mids' o' them! Three maks a better mids' than twa!"

Sandy could not follow the reasoning quite, but he had his own way of understanding.

"It's jist like the story o' Shadrach, Meshach, and Abednego!" he said. "There was three o' them, an' sae He made four! Eh, jist think o' Him bein' wi' 's His verra sel'!"

Here now was a church indeed: the idea of a third was the very principle of growth! They would meet together and say: "Oh, Father of Jesus Christ, help us to be good like Jesus;" and then Jesus himself would make one of them, and worship the Father with them!

The next thing, as a matter of course, was to look about for a third.

"Dawtie!" cried both at once.

Dawtie was the child of a cotter pair, who had an acre or two of their father's farm, and helped him with it. Her real name has not reached me; Dawtie means darling, and is a common term of endearment—derived, Jamieson suggests, from the Gaelic dalt, signifying a foster-child. Dawtie was a dark-haired, laughing little darling, with shy, merry manners, and the whitest teeth, full of fun, but solemn in an instant. Her small feet were bare and black—except on Saturday nights and Sunday mornings—but full of expression, and perhaps really cleaner, from their familiarity with the sweet all-cleansing air, than such as hide the day-long in socks and shoes.

Dawtie's specialty was love of the creatures. She had an undoubting conviction that every one of them with which she came in contact understood and loved her. She was the champion of the oppressed, without knowing it. Every individual necessity stood on its own merits, and came to her fresh and sole, as if she had forgotten all that went before it. Like some boys she had her pockets as well as her hands at the service of live things; but unlike any boy, she had in her love no admixture of natural history; it was not interest in animals with her, but an individual love to the individual animal, whatever it might be, that presented itself to the love-power in her.

It may seem strange that there should be three such children together. But their fathers and mothers had for generations been poor—which was a great advantage, as may be seen in the world by him who has eyes to see, and heard in the parable of the rich man by him who has ears to hear. Also they were God-fearing, which was a far greater advantage, and made them honorable; for they would have scorned things that most Christians will do. Dawtie's father had a rarely keen instinct for what is mean, and that not in the way of abhorrence in others, but of avoidance in himself. To shades and nuances of selfishness, which men of high repute and comfortable conscience would neither be surprised to find in their neighbors nor annoyed to find in themselves, he would give no quarter. Along with Andrew's father, he had, in childhood and youth, been under the influence of a simple-hearted pastor, whom the wise and prudent laughed at as one who could not take care of himself, incapable of seeing that, like his master, he laid down his life that he might take it again. He left God to look after him, that he might be free to look after God.

Little Dawtie had learned her catechism, but, thank God, had never thought about it or attempted to understand it—good negative preparation for becoming, in a few years more, able to understand the New Testament with the heart of a babe.

The brothers had not long to search before they came upon her, where she sat on the ground at the door of the turf-built cottage, feeding a chicken with oatmeal paste.

"What are you doin', Dawtie?" they asked.

"I'm tryin'," she answered, without looking up, "to haud the life i' the chuckie."

"What's the matter wi' 't?"

"Naething but the want o' a mither."

"Is the mither o' 't deid?"

"Na, she's alive eneuch, but she has ower mony bairns to hap them a'; her wings winna cower them, and she drives this ane awa', and winna lat it come near her."

"Sic a cruel mither!"

"Na, she's no' cruel. She only wants to gar't come to me! She kenned I would tak it. Na, na; Flappy's a guid mither! I ken her weel; she's ane o' our ain! She kens me, or she would hae keepit the puir thing, and done her best wi' her."

"I ken somebody," said Andrew, "that would fain spread oot wings, like a great big hen, ower a' the bairns, you an' me an' a', Dawtie!"

"That's my mither!" cried Dawtie, looking up, and showing her white teeth.

"Na, it's a man," said Sandy.

"It's my father, than!"

"Na, it's no. Would ye like to see Him?"

"Na, I'm no carin'."

"Sandy and me's gaein' to see Him some day."

"I'll gang wi' ye. But I maun tak' my chuckie!"

202

She looked down where she had set the little bird on the ground; it had hobbled away and she could not see it!

"Eh," she cried, starting up, "ye made me forget my chuckie wi' yer questions! It's mither 'ill peck it!"

She darted off, and forsook the tale of the Son of Man to look after her chicken. But presently she returned with it in her hands.

"Tell awa'," she said, resuming her seat "What do they ca' Him?"

"They ca' Him the Father o' Jesus Christ."

"I'll gang wi' ye," she answered.

So the church was increased by a whole half, and the fraction of a chicken—type of the groaning creation, waiting for the sonship.

The three gathered to read and pray. And almost always there was some creature with them in the arms or hands of Dawtie. And if the Lord was not there, too, then are we Christians most miserable, for we see a glory beyond all that man could dream, and it is but a dream! Whose dream?

They went on at other times with the usual employments and games of children. But there was this difference between them and most grown Christians, that when anything roused thought or question they at once referred it to the word of Jesus, and having discovered His will, made haste to do it. It naturally followed that, seeing He gives the spirit to them that obey Him, they grew rapidly in the modes of their Master, learning to look at things as He looked at them, to think of them as He thought of them, to value what He valued, and despise what He despised—all in simplest order of divine development, in uttermost accord with highest reason, the whole turning on the primary and continuous effort to obey.

It was long before they came to have any regular time of meeting. Andrew always took the initiative in assembling the church. When he called they came together. Then he would read from the story, and communicate any discovery he had made concerning what Jesus would have them do. Next, they would consult and settle what they should ask for, and one of them, generally Andrew, but sometimes Sandy, would pray. They made no formal utterance, but simply asked for what they needed. Here are some specimens of their petitions:

"Oh, Lord, Sandy canna for the life o' 'im un'erstan' the rule o' three; please, Lord, help him."

"Oh, Lord, I dinna ken onything I want the day; please gi'e us what we need, an' what ye want us to hae, wi'oot our askin' it."

"Lord, help us; we're ill-natnr'd (bad-tempered) the day; an' ye wadna hae us that."

"Lord, Dawtie's mither has a sair heid (headache); mak her better, gien ye please."

When their prayers were ended Andrew would say: "Sandy, have you found anything He says?" and there-upon, if he had, Sandy would speak. Dawtie never said a word, but sat and listened with her big eyes, generally stroking some creature in her lap.

Surely the part of every superior is to help the life in the lower!

Once the question arose, in their assembly of three and a bird, whose leg Dawtie had put in splints, what became of the creatures when they died. They concluded that the sparrow that God cared for must be worth caring for; and they could not believe He had made it to last only such a little while as its life in this world. Thereupon they agreed to ask the Lord that, when they died, they might have again a certain dog, an ugly little white mongrel, of which they had been very fond. All their days thereafter they were, I believe, more or less consciously, looking forward to the fulfillment of this petition. For their hope strengthened with the growth of their ideal; and when they had to give up any belief it was to take a better in its place.

They yielded at length the notion that the peddler was Jesus Christ, but they never ceased to believe that He was God's messenger, or that the Lord was with them always. They would not insist that He was walking about on the earth, but to the end of their days they cherished the uncertain hope that they might, even without knowing it, look upon the face of the Lord in that of some stranger passing in the street, or mingling in a crowd, or seated in a church; for they knew that all the shapes of man belong to Him, and that, after He rose from the dead there were several occasions on which He did not at first look like Himself to those to whom He appeared.

The child-like, the essential, the divine notion of serving, with their every-day will and being, the will of the living One, who lived for them that they might live, as once He had died for them that they might die, ripened in them to a Christianity that saw God everywhere, saw that everything had to be done as God would have it done, and that nothing but injustice had to be forsaken to please Him. They were under no influence of what has been so well called other-worldliness, for they saw this world as much God's as that, saw that its work has to be done divinely, that it is the beginning of the world to come. It was to them all one world, with God in it, all in all; therefore the best work for the other world was the work of this world.

Such was the boyhood of that Andrew Ingram whom Miss Fordyce now reproved for not setting the good example of going to church.

The common sense of the children rapidly developed, for there is no teacher like obedience, and no obstruction like its postponement. When in after years their mothers came at length to understand that obedience had been so long the foundation of their life, it explained to them many things that had seemed strange, and brought them to reproach themselves that they should have seemed strange.

It ought not to be overlooked that the whole thing was wrought in the children without directed influence of kindred or any neighbor. They imitated none. The galvanism of imitation is not the life of the spirit; the use of form where love is not is killing. And if any one is desirous of spreading the truth let him apply himself, like these children, to the doing of it; not obeying the truth, he is doubly a liar pretending to teach it; if he obeys it already, let him obey it more. It is life that awakes life. All form of persuasion is empty except in vital association with regnant obedience. Talking and not doing is dry rot.

Cottage children are sometimes more fastidious about their food than children that have a greater variety; they have a more delicate perception and discrimination in the simple dishes on which they thrive; much choice, though little refusal. Andrew had a great dislike to lumps in his porridge; and one day the mother having been less careful than usual in cooking it, he made a wry face at the first spoonful.

"Andrew," said Sandy, "take no thought for what ye eat."

It was a wrong interpretation, but a righteous use of the word. Happy the soul that mistakes the letter only to get at the spirit!

Andrew's face smoothed itself, began to clear up, and broke at last into a sunny smile. He said nothing, but eat his full share of the porridge without a frown. This was practical religion; and if any one judge it not worth telling, I count his philosophy worthless beside it. Such a doer knows more than such a reader will ever know, except he take precisely the same way to learn. The children of God do what He would have them do, and are taught of Him.

A report at length reached the pastor, now an old man, of ripe heart and true insight, that certain children in his parish "played at the Lord's Supper." He was shocked, and went to their parents. They knew nothing of the matter. The three children were sought, and the pastor had a private interview with them. From it he reappeared with a solemn, pale face, and silent tongue. They asked him the result of his inquiry. He answered that he was not prepared to interfere: as he was talking with them, the warning came that there were necks and mill-stones. The next Sunday he preached a sermon from the text, "Out of the month of babes and sucklings Thou hast perfected praise."

The fathers and mothers made inquisition, and found no desire to conceal. Wisely or not, they forbade the observance. It cost Andrew much thought whether he was justified in obeying them; but he saw that right and wrong in itself was not concerned, and that the Lord would have them obey their parents.

It was necessary to tell so much of the previous history of Andrew, lest what remains to be told should perhaps be unintelligible or seem incredible without it. A character like his can not be formed in a day; it must early begin to grow.

The bond thus bound between the children, altering in form as they grew, was never severed; nor was the lower creation ever cut off from its share in the petitions of any one of them. When they ceased to assemble as a community, they continued to act on the same live principles.

Gladly as their parents would have sent them to college, Andrew and Sandy had to leave school only to work on the farm. But they carried their studies on from the point they had reached. When they could not get further without help, they sought and found it. For a year or two they went in the winter to an evening school; but it took so much time to go and come that they found they could make more progress by working at home. What help they sought went a long way, and what they learned, they knew.

When the day's work was over, and the evening meal, they went to the room their own hands had made convenient for study as well as sleep, and there resumed the labor they had dropped the night before. Together they read Greek and mathematics, but Andrew worked mainly in literature, Sandy in mechanics. On Saturdays, Sandy generally wrought at some model, while Andrew read to him. On Sundays, they always, for an hour or two, read the Bible together.

The brothers were not a little amused with Miss Fordyce's patronage of Andrew; but they had now been too long endeavoring to bring into subjection the sense of personal importance, to take offense at it.

Dawtie had gone into service, and they seldom saw her except when she came home for a day at the term. She was a grown woman now, but the same loving child as before. She counted the brothers her superiors, just as they counted the laird and his daughter their superiors. But whereas Alexa claimed the homage, Dawtie yielded where was no thought of claiming it. The brothers regarded her as their sister. That she was poorer than they, only made them the more watchful over her, and if possible the more respectful to her. So she had a rich return for her care of the chickens and kittens and puppies.

CHAPTER XI. GEORGE AND ANDREW.

George went home the next day; and the following week sent Andrew a note, explaining that when he saw him he did not know his obligation to him, and expressing the hope that, when next in town, he would call upon him. This was hardly well, being condescension to a superior. Perhaps the worst evil in the sense of social superiority is the vile fancy that it alters human relation. George did not feel bound to make the same acknowledgment of obligation to one in humble position as to one in the same golden rank with himself! It says ill for social distinction, if, for its preservation, such an immoral difference be essential. But Andrew was not one to dwell upon his rights. He thought it friendly of Mr. Crawford to ask him to call; therefore, although he had little desire to make his acquaintance, and grudged the loss of time, to no man so precious as to him who has a pursuit in addition to a calling, Andrew, far stronger in courtesy than the man who invited him, took the first Saturday afternoon to go and see him.

Mr. Crawford the elder lived in some style, and his door was opened by a servant whose blatant adornment filled Andrew with friendly pity: no man would submit to be dressed like that, he judged, except from necessity. The reflection sprung from no foolish and degrading contempt for household service. It is true Andrew thought no labor so manly as that in the earth, out of which grows everything that makes the loveliness or use of Nature; for by it he came in contact with the primaries of human life, and was God's fellow laborer, a helper in the work of the universe, knowing the ways of it and living in them; but not the less would he have done any service, and that cheerfully, which his own need or that of others might have required of him. The colors of a parrot, however, were not fit for a son of man, and hence his look of sympathy. His regard was met only by a glance of plain contempt, as the lackey, moved by the same spirit as his master, left him standing in the hall—to return presently, and show him into the library—a room of mahogany, red morocco, and yellow calf, where George sat. He rose, and shook hands with him.

"I am glad to see you, Mr. Ingram," he said. "When I wrote I had but just learned how much I was indebted to you."

"I understand what you must mean," returned Andrew, "but it was scarce worth alluding to. Miss Fordyce had the better claim to serve you!"

"You call it nothing to carry a man of my size over a mile of heather!"

"I had help," answered Andrew; "and but for the broken leg," he added, with a laugh, "I could have carried you well enough alone."

There came a pause, for George did not know what next to do with the farmer fellow. So the latter spoke again, being unembarrassed.

"You have a grand library, Mr. Crawford! It must be fine to sit among so many books! It's just like a wine-merchant's cellars—only here you can open and drink, and leave the bottles as full as before!"

"A good simile, Mr. Ingram!" replied George. "You must come and dine with me, and we'll open another sort of bottle!"

"You must excuse me there, sir! I have no time for that sort of bottle."

"I understand you read a great deal?"

"Weather permitting," returned Andrew.

"I should have thought if anything was independent of the weather, it must be reading!"

"Not a farmer's reading, sir. To him the weather is the Word of God, telling him whether to work or read."

George was silent. To him the Word of God was the Bible!

"But you must read a great deal yourself, sir!" resumed Andrew, casting a glance round the room.

"The books are my father's!" said George.

He did not mention that his own reading came all in the library-cart, except when he wanted some special information; for George was "a practical man!" He read his Bible to prepare for his class in the Sunday-school, and his Shakespeare when he was going to see one of his plays acted. He would make the best of both worlds by paying due attention to both! He was religious, but liberal.

His father was a banker, an elder of the kirk, well reputed in and beyond his circle. He gave to many charities, and largely to educational schemes. His religion was to hold by the traditions of the elders, and keep himself respectable in the eyes of money-dealers. He went to church regularly, and always asked God's blessing on his food, as if it were a kind of general sauce. He never prayed God to make him love his neighbor, or help him to be an honest man. He "had worship" every morning, no doubt; but only a Nonentity like his God could care for such prayers as his. George rejected his father's theology as false in logic and cruel in character: George knew just enough of God to be guilty of neglecting Him.

"When I am out all day, I can do with less reading; for then I have the 'book of knowledge fair,'" said Andrew, quoting Milton. "It does not take all one's attention to drive a straight furrow or keep the harrow on the edge of the last bout!"

"You don't mean you can read your Bible as you hold the plow!" said George.

"No, sir," answered Andrew, amused. "A body could not well manage a book between the stilts of the plow. The Bible will keep till you get home; a little of it goes a long way. But Paul counted the book of creation enough to make the heathen to blame for not minding it. Never a wind wakes of a sudden, but it talks to me about God. And is not the sunlight the same that came out of the body of Jesus at His transfiguration?"

"You seem to have some rather peculiar ideas of your own, Mr. Ingram!"

"Perhaps, sir! For a man to have no ideas of his own, is much the same as to have no ideas at all. A man can not have the ideas of another man, any more than he can have another man's soul, or another man's body!"

"That is dangerous doctrine."

"Perhaps we are not talking about the same thing! I mean by ideas, what a man orders his life by."

"Your ideas may be wrong!"

"The All-wise is my judge."

"So much the worse, if you are in the wrong!"

"It is the only good, whether I be in the right or the wrong. Would I have my mistakes overlooked? What judge would I desire but the Judge of all the earth! Shall He not do right? And will He not set me right?"

"That is a most dangerous confidence!"

"It would be if there were any other judge. But it will be neither the Church nor the world that will sit on the great white throne. He who sits there will not ask: 'Did you go to church?' or 'Did you believe in this or that?' but' Did you do what I told you?'"

"And what will you say to that, Mr. Ingram?"

"I will say: 'Lord, Thou knowest!'"

The answer checked George a little.

"Suppose He should say you did not, what would you answer?"

"I would say: 'Lord, send me where I may learn.'"

"And if He should say: 'That is what I sent you into the world for, and you have not done it!' what would you say then?"

"I should hold my peace."

"You do what He tells you then?"

"I try."

"Does He not say: 'Forsake not the assembling of yourselves together?'"

"No, sir."

"No?"

"Somebody says something like it in the Epistle to the Hebrews."

"And isn't that the same?"

"The Man who wrote it would be indignant at your saying so! Tell me, Mr. Crawford, what makes a gathering a Church?"

"It would take me some time to arrange my ideas before I could answer you."

"Is it not the presence of Christ that makes an assembly a Church?"

"Well?"

"Does He not say that where two or three are met in His name, there is He in the midst of them?"

"Yes."

"Then thus far I will justify myself to you, that, if I do not go to what you call church, I yet often make one of a company met in His name."

"He does not limit the company to two or three."

"Assuredly not. But if I find I get more help and strength with a certain few, why should I go with a multitude to get less? Will you draw another line than the Master's? Why should it be more sacred to worship with five hundred or five thousand than with three? If He is in the midst of them, they can not be wrong gathered!"

"It looks as if you thought yourselves better than everybody else!"

"If it were so, then certainly He would not be one of the gathering!"

"How are you to know that He is in the midst of you?"

"If we are not keeping His commandments, He is not. But His presence can not be proved; it can only be known. If He meets us, it is not necessary to the joy of His presence that we should be able to prove that He does meet us! If a man has the company of the Lord, he will care little whether another does or does not believe that he has."

212

"Your way is against the peace of the Church! It fosters division."

"Did the Lord come to send peace on the earth? My way, as you call it, would make division, but division between those who call themselves His and those who are His. It would bring together those that love Him. Company would merge with company that they might look on the Lord together. I don't believe Jesus cares much for what is called the visible Church; but He cares with His very Godhead for those that do as He tells them; they are His Father's friends; they are His elect by whom He will save the world. It is by those who obey, and by their obedience, that He will save those who do not obey, that is, will bring them to obey. It is one by one the world will pass to His side. There is no saving in the lump. If a thousand be converted at once, it is every single lonely man that is converted."

"You would make a slow process of it!"

"If slow, yet faster than any other. All God's processes are slow. How many years has the world existed, do you imagine, sir?"

"I don't know. Geologists say hundreds and hundreds of thousands."

"And how many is it since Christ came?"

"Toward two thousand."

"Then we are but in the morning of Christianity! There is plenty of time. The day is before us."

"Dangerous doctrine for the sinner!"

"Why? Time is plentiful for his misery, if he will not repent; plentiful for the mercy of God that would lead him to repentance. There is plenty of time for labor and hope; none for indifference and delay. God will have his creatures good. They can not escape Him."

"Then a man may put off repentance as long as he pleases!"

"Certainly he may—at least as long as he can—but it is a fearful thing to try issues with God."

"I can hardly say I understand you."

213

"Mr. Crawford, you have questioned me in the way of kindly anxiety and reproof; that has given me the right to question you. Tell me, do you admit we are bound to do what our Lord requires?"

"Of course. How could any Christian man do otherwise?"

"Yet a man may say: 'Lord, Lord,' and be cast out! It is one thing to say we are bound to do what the Lord tells us, and another to do what He tells us! He says: 'Seek ye first the kingdom of God and His righteousness:' Mr. Crawford, are you seeking the kingdom of God first, or are you seeking money first?"

"We are sent into the world to make our living."

"Sent into the world, we have to seek our living; we are not sent into the world to seek our living, but to seek the kingdom and righteousness of God. And to seek a living is very different from seeking a fortune!"

"If you, Mr. Ingram, had a little wholesome ambition, you would be less given to judging your neighbors."

Andrew held his peace, and George concluded he had had the best of the argument—which was all he wanted; of the truth concerned he did not see enough to care about it Andrew, perceiving no good was to be done, was willing to appear defeated; he did not value any victory but the victory of the truth, and George was not yet capable of being conquered by the truth.

"No!" resumed he, "we must avoid personalities. There are certain things all respectable people have agreed to regard as right: he is a presumptuous man who refuses to regard them. Reflect on it, Mr. Ingram."

The curious smile hovered about the lip of the plow-man; when things to say did not come to him, he went nowhere to fetch them. Almost in childhood he had learned that, when one is required to meet the lie, words are given him; when they are not, silence is better. A man who does not love the truth, but disputes for victory, is the swine before whom pearls must not be cast. Andrew's smile meant that it had been a waste of his time to call upon Mr. Crawford. But he did not blame himself, for he had come out of pure friendliness. He would have risen at once, but feared to seem offended. Crawford, therefore, with the rudeness of a superior, himself rose, saying:

"Is there anything I can do for you, Mr. Ingram?"

"The only thing one man can do for another is to be at one with him," answered Andrew, rising.

"Ah, you are a socialist! That accounts for much!" said George.

"Tell me this," returned Andrew, looking him in the eyes: "Did Jesus ever ask of His Father anything His Father would not give Him?"

"Not that I remember," answered George, fearing a theological trap.

"He said once: 'I pray for them which shall believe in Me, that they all may be one, as Thou Father art in Me, and I in Thee, that they also many be one in us.' No man can be one with another, who is not one with Christ."

As he left the house, a carriage drove up, in which was Mr. Crawford the elder, home from a meeting of directors, at which a dividend had been agreed upon—to be paid from the capital, in preparation for another issue of shares.

Andrew walked home a little bewildered. "How is it," he said to himself, "that so many who would be terrified at the idea of not being Christians, and are horrified at any man who does not believe there is a God, are yet absolutely indifferent to what their Lord tells them to do if they would be His disciples? But may not I be in like case without knowing it? Do I meet God in my geometry? When I so much enjoy my Euclid, is it always God geometrizing to me? Do I feel talking with God every time I dwell upon any fact of his world of lines and circles and angles? Is it God with me, every time that the joy of life, of a wind or a sky or a lovely phrase, flashes through me? Oh, my God," he broke out in speechless prayer as he walked—and those that passed said to themselves he was mad; how, in such a world, could any but a madman wear a face of joy! "Oh, my God, Thou art all in all, and I have everything! The world is mine because it is Thine! I thank Thee, my God, that Thou hast lifted me up to see whence I came, to know to whom I belong, to know who is my Father, and makes me His heir! I am Thine, infinitely more

215

than mine own; and Thou art mine as Thou art Christ's!"

He knew his Father in the same way that Jesus Christ knows His Father. He was at home in the universe, neither lonely, nor out-of-doors, nor afraid.

CHAPTER XII. THE CRAWFORDS.

Through strong striving to secure his life, Mr. Crawford lost it—both in God's sense of loss and his own. He narrowly escaped being put in prison, died instead, and was put into God's prison to pay the uttermost farthing. But he had been such a good Christian that his fellow-Christians mourned over his failure and his death, not over his dishonesty! For did they not know that if, by more dishonesty, he could have managed to recover his footing, he would have paid everything? One injunction only he obeyed—he provided for his own; of all the widows concerned in his bank, his widow alone was secured from want; and she, like a dutiful wife, took care that his righteous intention should be righteously carried out; not a penny would she give up to the paupers her husband had made.

The downfall of the house of cards took place a few months after George's return to its business. Not initiated to the mysteries of his father's transactions, ignorant of what had long been threatening, it was a terrible blow to him. But he was a man of action, and at once looked to America; at home he could not hold up his head.

He had often been to Potlurg, and had been advancing in intimacy with Alexa; but he would not show himself there until he could appear as a man of decision—until he was on the point of departure. She would be the more willing to believe his innocence of complicity in the deceptions that had led to his ruin! He would thus also manifest self-denial and avoid the charge of interested motives! he could not face the suspicion of being a suitor with nothing to offer! George had always taken the grand rôle—that of superior, benefactor, bestower. He was powerful in condescension!

Not, therefore, until the night before he sailed did he go to Potlurg.

Alexa received him with a shade of displeasure.

"I am going away," he said, abruptly, the moment they were seated.

Her heart gave a painful throb in her throat, but she did not lose her self-possession.

"Where are you going?" she asked.

"To New York," he replied. "I have got a situation there—in a not unimportant house. There at least I am taken for an honest man. From your heaven I have fallen."

"No one falls from any heaven but has himself to blame," rejoined Alexa.

"Where have I been to blame? I was not in my father's confidence. I knew nothing, positively nothing, of what was going on."

"Why then did you not come to see me?"

"A man who is neither beggar nor thief is not willing to look either."

"You would have come if you had trusted me," she said.

"You must pardon pride in a ruined man," he answered. "Now that I am starting to-morrow, I do not feel the same dread of being misunderstood!"

"It was not kind of you, George. Knowing yourself fit to be trusted, why did you not think me capable of trusting?"

"But, Alexa!—a man's own father!"

For a moment he showed signs of an emotion he had seldom had to repress.

"I beg your pardon, George!" cried Alexa. "I am both stupid and selfish! Are you really going so far?"

Her voice trembled.

"I am—but to return, I hope, in a very different position!"

"You would have me understand—"

"That I shall then be able to hold up my head."

"Why should an innocent man ever do otherwise?"

"He can not help seeing himself in other people's thoughts!"

"If we are in the right ought we to mind what people think of us?" said Alexa.

"Perhaps not. But I will make them think of me as I choose."

"How?"

"By compelling their respect."

"You mean to make a fortune?"

"Yes."

"Then it will be the fortune they respect! You will not be more worthy!"

"I shall not."

"Is such respect worth having?"

"Not in itself."

"In what then? Why lay yourself out for it?"

"Believe me, Alexa, even the real respect of such people would be worthless to me. I only want to bring them to their marrow-bones!"

The truth was, Alexa prized social position so dearly that she did not relish his regarding it as a thing at the command of money. Let George be as rich as a Jew or an American, Alexa would never regard him as her equal! George worshiped money; Alexa worshiped birth and land.

Our own way of being wrong is all right in our own eyes; our neighbor's way of being wrong is offensive to all that is good in us. We are anxious therefore, kindly anxious, to pull the mote out of his eye, never thinking of the big beam in the way of the operation. Jesus labored to show us that our immediate business is to be right ourselves. Until we are, even our righteous indignation is waste.

While he spoke, George's eyes were on the ground. His grand resolve did not give his innocence strength to look in the face of the woman he loved; he felt, without knowing why, that she was not satisfied with him. Of the paltriness of his ambition, he had no inward hint. The high resolves of a puny nature must be a laughter to the angels—the bad ones.

"If a man has no ambition," he resumed, feeling after her objection, "how is he to fulfill the end of his being! No sluggard ever made his mark! How would the world advance but for the men who have to make their fortunes! If a man find his father has not made money for him, what is he to do but make it for himself? You would not have me all my life a clerk! If I had but known, I should by this time have been well ahead!"

Alexa had nothing to answer; it all sounded very reasonable! Were not Scots boys everywhere taught it was the business of life to rise? In whatever position they were, was it not their part to get out of it? She did not see that it is in the kingdom of heaven only we are bound to rise. We are born into the world not to rise in the kingdom of Satan, but out of it And the only way to rise in the kingdom of heaven is to do the work given us to do. Whatever be intended for us, this is the only way to it We have not to promote ourselves, but to do our work. It is the master of the feast who says: "Go up." If a man go up of himself, he will find he has mistaken the head of the table.

More talk followed, but neither cast any light; neither saw the true question. George took his leave. Alexa said she would be glad to hear from him.

Alexa did not like the form of George's ambition—to gain money, and so compel the respect of persons he did not himself respect But was she clear of the money disease herself? Would she have married a poor man, to go on as hitherto? Would she not have been ashamed to have George know how she had supplied his needs while he lay in the house—that it was with the poor gains of her poultry-yard she fed him? Did it improve her moral position toward money that she regarded commerce with contempt—a rudiment of the time when nobles treated merchants as a cottager his bees?

George's situation was a subordinate one in a house of large dealings in Wall Street.

CHAPTER XIII. DAWTIE.

Is not the Church supposed to be made up of God's elect? and yet most of my readers find it hard to believe there should be three persons, so related, who agreed to ask of God, and to ask neither riches nor love, but that God should take His own way with them, that the Father should work His will in them, that He would teach them what He wanted of them, and help them to do it! The Church is God's elect, and yet you can not believe in three holy children! Do you say: "Because they are represented as beginning to obey so young?" "Then," I answer, "there can be no principle, only an occasional and arbitrary exercise of spiritual power, in the perfecting of praise out of the mouth of babes and sucklings, or in the preference of them to the wise and prudent as the recipients of divine revelation."

Dawtie never said much, but tried the more. With heartiness she accepted what conclusions the brothers came to, so far as she understood them—and what was practical she understood as well as they; for she had in her heart the spirit of that Son of Man who chose a child to represent Him and His Father. As to what they heard at church, their minds were so set on doing what they found in the Gospel, that it passed over them without even rousing their intellect, and so vanished without doing any hurt. Tuned to the truth by obedience, no falsehood they heard from the pulpit partisans of God could make a chord vibrate in response. Dawtie indeed heard nothing but the good that was mingled with the falsehood, and shone like a lantern through a thick fog.

She was little more than a child when, to the trouble of her parents, she had to go out to service. Every half year she came home for a day or so, and neither feared nor found any relation altered. At length after several closely following changes, occasioned by no fault of hers, she was without a place. Miss Fordyce heard of it, and proposed to her parents that, until she found another, she should help Meg, who was growing old and rather blind: she would thus, she said, go on learning, and not be idling at home.

Dawtie's mother was not a little amused at the idea of any one idling in her house, not to say Dawtie, whom idleness would have tried harder than any amount of work; but, if only that Miss Fordyce might see what sort of girl Dawtie was, she judged it right to accept her offer.

She had not been at Potlurg a week before Meg began to complain that she did not leave work enough to keep her warm. No doubt it gave her time for her book, but her eyes were not so good as they used to be, and she was apt to fall asleep over it, and catch cold! But when her mistress proposed to send her away, she would not hear of it So Alexa, who had begun to take an interest in her, set her to do things she had hitherto done herself, and began to teach her other things. Before three months were over, she was a necessity in the house, and to part with Dawtie seemed impossible. A place about that time turning up, Alexa at once offered her wages, and so Dawtie became an integral portion of the laird's modest household.

The laird himself at length began to trust her as he had never trusted servant, for he taught her to dust his precious books, which hitherto he had done himself, but of late had shrunk from, finding not a few of them worse than Pandora-boxes, liberating asthma at the merest unclosing.

Dawtie was now a grown woman, bright, gentle, playful, with loving eyes, and a constant overflow of tenderness upon any creature that could receive it. She had small but decided and regular features, whose prevailing expression was confidence—not in herself, for she was scarce conscious of herself even in the act of denying herself—but in the person upon whom her trusting eyes were turned. She was in the world to help—with no political economy beyond the idea that for help and nothing else did any one exist. To be as the sun and the rain and the wind, as the flowers that lived for her and not for themselves, as the river that flowed, and the heather that bloomed lovely on the bare moor in the autumn, such was her notion of being. That she had to take care of herself was a falsehood that never entered her brain. To do what she ought, and not do what she ought not, was enough on her part, and God would do the rest! I will not say she reasoned thus; to herself she was scarce a conscious object at all. Both bodily and spiritually she was in the finest health. If illness came, she would perhaps then discover a self with which she had to fight—I can not tell; but my impression is, that she had so long done the true thing, that illness would only develop unconscious victory, perfecting the devotion of her simple righteousness. It is because we are selfish, with that worst selfishness which is incapable of recognizing itself, not to say its own loathsomeness, that we have to be made ill. That they may leave the last remnants of their selfishness, are the saints themselves overtaken by age and death. Suffering does not cause the vile thing in us—that was there all the time; it comes to develop in us the knowledge of its presence, that it may be war to the knife between us and it. It was no wonder that Dawtie grew more and more of a favorite at Potlurg.

She did not read much, but would learn by heart anything that pleased her, and then go saying or singing it to herself. She had the voice of a lark, and her song prevented many a search for her. Against that "rain of melody," not the pride of the laird, or the orderliness of the ex-school-master ever put up the umbrella of rebuke. Her singing was so true, came so clear from the fountain of joy, and so plainly from no desire to be heard, that it gave no annoyance; while such was her sympathy, that, although she had never get suffered, you would, to hear her sing "My Nannie's awa'!" have thought her in truth mourning an absent lover, and familiar with every pang of heart-privation. Her cleanliness, clean even of its own show, was a heavenly purity; while so gently was all her spiriting done, that the very idea of fuss died in the presence of her labor. To the self-centered such a person soon becomes a nobody; the more dependent they are upon her unfailing ministration, the less they think of her; but they have another way of regarding such in "the high countries." Hardly any knew her real name; she was known but by her pet name Dawtie.

Alexa, who wondered at times that she could not interest her in things she made her read, little knew how superior the girl's choice was to her own! Not knowing much of literature, what she liked was always of the best in its kind, and nothing without some best element could interest her at all. But she was not left either to her "own sweet will" or to the prejudices of her well-meaning mistress; however long the intervals that parted them, Andrew continued to influence her reading as from the first. A word now and a word then, with the books he lent or gave her, was sufficient. That Andrew liked this or that, was enough to make Dawtie set herself to find in it what Andrew liked, and it was thus she became acquainted with most of what she learned by heart.

Above two years before the time to which I have now brought my narrative, Sandy had given up farming, to pursue the development of certain inventions of his which had met the approval of a man of means who, unable himself to devise, could yet understand a device: he saw that there was use, and consequently money in them, and wisely put it in Sandy's power to perfect them. He was in consequence but little at home, and when Dawtie went to see her parents, as she could much oftener now, Andrew and she generally met without a third. However many weeks might have passed, they always met as if they had parted only the night before. There was neither shyness nor forwardness in Dawtie. Perhaps a livelier rose might tinge her sweet round cheek when she saw Andrew; perhaps a brighter spark shone in the pupil of Andrew's eye; but they met as calmly as two prophets in the secret of the universe, neither anxious nor eager. The old relation between them was the more potent that it made so little outward show.

"Have you anything for me, Andrew?" Dawtie would say, in the strong dialect which her sweet voice made so pleasant to those that loved her; whereupon Andrew, perhaps without immediate answer more than a smile, would turn into his room, and reappear with what he had got ready for her to "chew upon" till they should meet again. Milton's sonnet, for instance, to the "virgin wise and pure," had long served her aspiration; equally wise and pure, Dawtie could understand it as well as she for whom it was written. To see the delight she took in it, would have been a joy to any loving student of humanity. It had cost her more effort to learn than almost any song, and perhaps therefore it was the more precious. Andrew seldom gave her a book to learn from; in general he copied, in his clearest handwriting, whatever poem or paragraph he thought fit for Dawtie; and when they met, she would not unfrequently, if there was time, repeat unasked what she had learned, and be rewarded with his unfailing look of satisfaction.

There was a secret between them—a secret proclaimed on the housetops, a secret hidden, the most precious of pearls, in their hearts—that the earth is the Lord's and the fullness thereof; that its work is the work of the Lord, whether the sowing of the field, the milking of the cow, the giving to the poor, the spending of wages, the reading of the Bible; that God is all in all, and every throb of gladness His gift; that their life came fresh every moment from His heart; that what was lacking to them would arrive the very moment He had got them ready for it. They were God's little ones in God's world— none the less their own that they did not desire to swallow it, or thrust it in their pockets.

Among poverty-stricken Christians, consumed with care to keep a hold of the world and save their souls, they were as two children of the house. By living in the presence of the living One, they had become themselves His presence—dim lanterns through which His light shone steady. Who obeys, shines.

CHAPTER XIV. SANDY AND GEORGE.

Sandy had found it expedient to go to America, and had now been there a twelvemonth; he had devised a machine of the value of which not even his patron could be convinced—that is, he could not see the prospect of its making money fast enough to constitute it a good thing. Sandy regarded it as a discovery, a revelation for the uplifting of a certain down-trodden portion of the community; and therefore, having saved a little money, had resolved to make it known in the States, where insight into probabilities is fresher. And now Andrew had a letter from him in which he mentioned that he had come across Mr. Crawford, already of high repute in Wall Street; that he had been kind to him, and having learned his object in visiting the country, and the approximate risk in bringing out his invention, had taken the thing into consideration. But the next mail brought another letter to the effect that, having learned the nature of the business done by Mr. Crawford, he found himself unable to distinguish between it and gambling, or worse; it seemed to him a vortex whose very emptiness drew money into it. He had therefore drawn back, and declined to put the thing in Crawford's hands. This letter Andrew gave Dawtie to read, that she might see that Sandy remained a true man. He had never been anxious on the point, but was very glad that ignorance had not drawn him into an evil connection.

Dawtie took the letter with her to read at her leisure. Unable, however, to understand something Sandy said concerning Mr. Crawford's business, she asked a question or two of her mistress, which led to questions on Alexa's part. Finding what was the subject of Sandy's letter, she wished to see it. Dawtie asked leave of Andrew, and gave it her.

Alexa was both distressed and indignant becoming at once George's partisan. Her distress diminished and her indignation increased as she reflected on the airt whence the unfavorable report reached her; the brothers were such peculiar men! She recalled the strange things she had heard of their childhood; doubtless the judgment was formed on an overstrained and quixotic idea of honesty! Besides, there had always been a strong socialistic tendency in them, which explained how Sandy could malign his benefactor! George was incapable of doing anything dishonorable! She would not trouble herself about it. But she would like to know how Andrew regarded the matter.

She asked him therefore what he thought of Sandy's procedure. Andrew replied that he did not know much about business; but that the only safety must lie in having nothing to do with what was doubtful; therefore Sandy had done right. Alexa said it was too bad of him to condemn where he confessed ignorance. Andrew replied:

"Ma'am, if Mr. Crawford is wrong he is condemned; if he is right my private doubt can not hurt him. Sandy must act by his own doubt, not by Mr. Crawford's confidence."

Alexa grew more distressed, for she began to recall things George had said which at the time she had not liked, but which she had succeeded in forgetting. If he had indeed gone astray, she hoped he would forget her; she could do without him! But the judgment of such a man as Sandy could settle nothing. Of humble origin and childish simplicity, he could not see the thing as a man of experience must. George might be all right notwithstanding. At the same time there was his father—whose reputation remained under a thick cloud, whose failed character rather than his ill-success had driven George to the other continent. Breed must go for something in a question of probabilities. It was the first time Alexa's thoughts had been turned into such a channel. She clung to the poor comfort that something must have passed at the interview so kindly sought by George to set the quixotical young farmer against him. She would not utter his name to Andrew ever again!

She was right in thinking that George cherished a sincere affection for her. It was one of the spurs which drove him too eagerly after money. I doubt if any man starts with a developed love of money for its own sake—except indeed he be born of generations of mammon worshipers. George had gone into speculation with the object of retrieving the position in which he had supposed himself born, and in the hope of winning the hand of his cousin— thinking too much of himself to offer what would not in the eyes of the world be worth her acceptance. When he stepped on the inclined plane of dishonesty he believed himself only engaging in "legitimate speculation;" but he was at once affected by the atmosphere about him. Wrapped in the breath of admiration and adulation surrounding men who cared for nothing but money-making, men who were not merely dishonest, but the very serpents of dishonesty, against whom pickpockets will "stick off" as angels of light; constantly under the softly persuasive influence of low morals and extravagant appreciation of cunning, he came by rapid degrees to think less and less of right and wrong. At first he called the doings of the place dishonest; then he called them sharp practice; then he called them a little shady; then, close sailing; then he said this or that transaction was deuced clever; then, the man was more rogue than fool; then he laughed at the success of a vile trick; then he touched the pitch, and thinking all the time it was but with one finger, was presently besmeared all over—as was natural, for he who will touch is already smeared.

While Alexa was fighting his battles with herself he had thrown down his arms in the only battle worth fighting. When he wrote to her, which he did regularly, he said no more about business than that his prospects were encouraging; how much his reticence may have had to do with a sense of her disapproval I can not tell.

CHAPTER XV. MOTHER AND DAUGHTER.

One lovely summer evening Dawtie, with a bundle in her hand, looked from the top of a grassy knoll down on her parents' turf cottage. The sun was setting behind her, and she looked as if she had stepped from it as it touched the ground on which she stood, rosy with the rosiness of the sun, but with a light in her countenance which came from a higher source, from the same nest as the sun himself. She paused but a moment, ran down the hill, and found her mother making the porridge. Mother and daughter neither embraced, nor kissed, nor even shook hands, but their faces glowed with delight, and words of joy and warmest welcome flowed between them.

"But ye haena lost yer place, hae ye, hinny?" said the mother.

"No, mother; there's no fear o' that, as lang's the laird or Miss Lexy's to the fore. They tret me—I winna say like ane o' themsel's, but as if they would hae likit me for ane o' themsel's, gien it had pleased the Lord to sen' me their way instead o' yours. They're that guid to me ye canna think!"

"Then what's broucht ye the day?"

"I beggit for a play-day. I wantit to see An'rew."

"Eh, lass! I'm feart for ye! Ye maunna set yer hert sae hie! An'rew's the best o' men, but a lass canna hae a man til hersel' jist 'cause he's the best man i' the warl'!"

"What mean ye by that, mother?" said Dawtie, looking a little scared. "Am I no' to lo'e An'rew, 'cause he's 'maist as guid's the Lord wad hae him? Wad ye hae me hate him for't? Has na he taught me to lo'e God—to lo'e Him better nor father, mither, An'rew, or onybody? I wull lo'e An'rew! What can ye mean, mother?"

"What I mean, Dawtie, is, that ye mamma think because ye lo'e him ye maun hae him; ye maunna think ye canna du wantin' An'rew!"

"It's true, mother, I kenna what I should do wantin' An'rew! Is na he aye shovin' the door o' the kingdom a wee wider to lat me see in the better? It's little ferly (marvel) I lo'e him! But as to wantin' him for my ain man, as ye hae my father!—mother, I wad be ashamet o' mysel' to think o' ony sic a thing!—clean affrontit wi' mysel' I wad be!"

"Weel, weel, bairn! Ye was aye a wise like lass, an' I maun lippen til ye! Only luik to yer hert."

"As for no' lo'ein' him, mither—me that canna luik at a blin' kittlin' ohn lo'ed it!—lo, mither! God made me sae, an didna mean me no' to lo'e An'rew!"

"Andrew!" she repeated, as if the word meant the perfection of earth's worthiest rendering the idea of appropriation too absurd.

Silence followed, but the mother was brooding.

"Ye maun bethink ye, lass, hoo far he's abune ye!" she said at length.

As the son of the farmer on whose land her husband was a cotter, Andrew seemed to her what the laird seemed to old John Ingram, and what the earl seemed to the laird, though the laird's family was ancient when the earl's had not been heard of. But Dawtie understood Andrew better than did her mother.

"You and me sees him far abune, mother, but Andrew himsel' never thinks o' nae sic things. He's sae used to luikin' up, he's forgotten to luik doon. He bauds his lan' frae a higher than the laird, or the yerl himsel'!"

The mother was silent. She was faithful and true, but, fed on the dried fish of logic and system and Roman legalism, she could not follow the simplicities of her daughter's religion, who trusted neither in notions about him, nor even in what he had done, but in the live Christ himself whom she loved and obeyed.

"If Andrew wanted to marry me," Dawtie went on, jealous for the divine liberty of her teacher, "which never cam intil's heid—na, no ance—the same bein' ta'en up wi' far ither things, it wouldna be because I was but a cotter lass that he wouldna tak his ain gait! But the morn's the Sabbath day, and we'll hae a walk thegither."

"I dinna a'thegither like thae walks upo' the Sabbath day," said the mother.

"Jesus walkit on the Sabbath the same as ony ither day, mother!"

"Weel, but He kenned what He was aboot!"

"And sae do I, mother! I ken His wull!"

"He had aye something on han' fit to be dune o' the Sabbath!"

"And so hae I the day, mother. If I was to du onything no fit i' this His warl', luikin' oot o' the e'en He gae me, wi' the han's an' feet He gae me, I wad jist deserve to be nippit oot at ance, or sent intil the ooter mirk (darkness)!"

"There's a mony maun fare ill then, lass!"

"I'm sayin' only for mysel'. I ken nane sae to blame as I would be mysel'."

"Is na that makin' yersel' oot better nor ither fowk, lass?"

"Gien I said I thoucht onything worth doin' but the wull o' God, I wad be a leear; gien I say man or woman has naething ither to do i' this warl' or the neist, I say it believin' ilkane o' them maun come til't at the lang last. Feow sees't yet, but the time's comin' when ilkabody will be as sure o' 't as I am. What won'er is't that I say't, wi' Jesus tellin' me the same frae mornin' to nicht!"

"Lass, lass, I fear me, ye'll gang oot o' yer min'!"

"It 'll be intil the mind o' Christ, then, mother! I dinna care for my ain min'. I hae nane o' my ain, an' will stick to His. Gien I dinna mak His mine, and stick til't, I'm lost! Noo, mother, I'll set the things, and run ower to the hoose, and lat An'rew ken I'm here!"

"As ye wull, lass! ye'r ayont me! I s' say naething anent a willfu' woman, for ye've been aye a guid dochter. I trust I hae risen to houp the Lord winna be disappointit in ye."

Dawtie found Andrew in the stable, suppering his horses, told him she had something to talk to him about, and asked if he would let her go with him in his walk the next day. Andrew was delighted to see her, but he did not say so; and she was back before her mother had taken the milk from the press. In a few minutes her father appeared, and welcomed her with a sober joy. As they eat their supper, he could not keep his eyes off her, she sat looking so well and nice and trim. He was a good-looking, work-worn man, his hands absolutely horny with labor. But inside many such horny husks are ripening beautiful kingdom hands, for the time when "dear welcome Death" will loose and let us go from the grave-clothes of the body that bind some of us even hand and foot. Rugged father and withered mother were beautiful in the eyes of Dawtie, and she and God saw them better than any other. Good, endless good was on the way to them all! It was so pleasant to be waiting for the best of all good things.

CHAPTER XVI. ANDREW AND DAWTIE.

Dawtie slept in peace and happy dreams till the next morning, when she was up almost with the sun, and out in his low clear light. For the sun was strong again; the red labor and weariness were gone from his shining face. Everything about her seemed to know God, or at least to have had a moment's gaze upon Him. How else could everything look so content, hopeful and happy. It is the man who will not fall in with the Father's bliss to whom the world seems soulless and dull. Dawtie was at peace because she desired nothing but what she knew He was best pleased to give her. Even had she cherished for Andrew the kind of love her mother feared, her Lord's will would have been her comfort and strength. If any one say: "Then she could not know what love is!" I answer: "That person does not know what the better love is that lifts the being into such a serene air that it can fast from many things and yet be blessed beyond what any other granted desire could make it." The scent of the sweet-pease growing against the turf wall entered Dawtie's soul like a breath from the fields of heaven, where the children made merry with the angels, the merriest of playfellows, and the winds and waters, and all the living things, and all the things half alive, all the flowers and all the creatures, were at their sportive call; where the little ones had babies to play with, and did not hurt them, and where dolls were neither loved nor missed, being never thought of. Suchlike were the girl's imaginings as her thoughts went straying, inventing, discovering. She did not fear the Father would be angry with her for being His child, and playing at creation. Who, indeed, but one that in loving heart can make, can rightly love the making of the Maker!

When they had had their breakfast, and the old people were ready for church—where they would listen a little, sleep a little, sing heartily, and hear nothing to wake hunger, joy or aspiration, Dawtie put a piece of oat-cake in her pocket, and went to join Andrew where they had made their tryst and where she found him waiting—at his length in a bush of heather, with Henry Vaughan's "Silex Scintillans," drawing from it "bright shoots of everlastingness" for his Sabbath day's delight. He read one or two of the poems to Dawtie, who was pleased but not astonished—she was never astonished at anything; she had nothing in her to make anything beautiful by contrast; her mind was of beauty itself, and anything beautiful was to her but in the order and law of things—what was to be expected. Nothing struck her because of its rarity; the rare was at home in her country, and she was at home with it. When, for instance, he read: "Father of lights, what sunny seeds," she took it up at once and understood it, felt that the good man had said the thing that was to be said, and loved him for it. She was not surprised to hear that the prayer was more than two hundred years old; were there not millions of years in front? why should it be wonderful that a few years behind men should have thought and felt as she did, and been able to say it as she never could! Had she not always loved the little cocks, and watched them learning to crow?

"But, An'rew," she said at length, "I want to tell ye something that's troublin' me; then ye can learn me what ye like."

"Tell on, Dawtie," said Andrew; and she began.

"Ae nicht aboot a fornight ago, I couldna sleep. I drave a' the sheep I could gether i' my brain, ower ae stile efter anither, but the sleep stack to the woo' o' them, an' ilk ane took o' 't awa' wi' him. I wadna hae tried, but that I had to be up ear', and I was feared I wad sleep in."

For the sake of my more polished readers—I do not say more refined, for polish and refinement may be worlds apart—I will give the rest in modern English.

"So I got up, and thought to sweep and dust the hall and the stairs; then if, when I lay down again, I should sleep too long, there would be a part of the day's work done! You know, Andrew, what the house is like; at the top of the stair that begins directly you enter the house, there is a big irregular place, bigger than the floor of your barn, laid with flags. It is just as if all the different parts of the house had been built at different times round about it, and then it was itself roofed in by an after-thought. That's what we call the hall. The spare room opens on the left at the top of the stair, and to the right, across the hall, beyond the swell of the short thick tower you see the half of outside, is the door of the study. It is all round with books—some of them,

234

mistress says, worth their weight in gold, they are so scarce. But the master trusts me to dust them. He used to do it himself; but now that he is getting old, he does not like the trouble, and it makes him asthmatic. He says books more need dusting than anything else, but are in more danger of being hurt by it, and it makes him nervous to see me touch them. I have known him stand an hour watching me while I dusted, looking all the time as if he had just taken a dose of medicine. So I often do a few books at a time, as I can, when he is not in the way to be worried with it. But he always knows where I have been with my duster and long-haired brush. And now it came across me that I had better dust some books first of all, as it was a good chance, he being sound asleep. So I lighted my lamp, went straight to the study, and began where I last left off.

"As I was dusting, one of the books I came to looked so new and different from the rest that I opened it to see what it was like inside. It was full of pictures of mugs, and gold and silver jugs and cups—some of them plain and some colored; and one of the colored ones was so beautiful that I stood and looked at it. It was a gold cup, I suppose, for it was yellow; and all round the edge, and on the sides, it was set with stones, like the stones in mistress's rings, only much bigger. They were blue and red and green and yellow, and more colors than I can remember. The book said it was made by somebody, but I forget his name. It was a long name. The first part of it began with a B, and the second with a C, I remember that much. It was like Benjamin, but it wasn't Benjamin. I put it back in its place, thinking I would ask the master whether there really were such beautiful things, and took down the next. Now whether that had been passed over between two batches I don't know, but it was so dusty that before I would touch another I gave the duster a shake, and the wind of it blew the lamp out I took it up to take it to the kitchen and kindle it again, when, to my astonishment, I saw a light under the door of a press which was always locked, and where master said he kept his most precious books. 'How strange!' I thought; 'a light inside a locked cupboard!' Then I remembered how in one place where I had been there was, in a room over the stable, a press whose door had no fastening except a bolt on the inside, which set me thinking, and some terrible things came to me that made me remember it. So now I said to myself: 'There's some one in there, after master's books!' It was not a likely thing, but the night is the time for fancies, and in the night you don't know what is likely and what is not. One thing, however, was clear—I ought to find out what the light meant. Fearful things darted one after the other through my head as I went to the door, but there was one thing I dared not do, and that was to leave it unopened. So I opened it as softly as I could, in terror lest the thief should hear my heart beating. When I could peep in what do you think I saw? I could not believe my eyes! There was a great big room! I rubbed my eyes, and stared; and rubbed them again and stared—thinking to rub it away; but there it was, a big odd-shaped room, part of it with round sides, and in the middle of the room a table, and on the table a lamp, burning as I had never seen lamp burn, and master at the table with his back to me. I was so astonished I forgot that I had no business there, and ought to go away. I stood like an idiot, mazed and lost. And you will not wonder when I tell you that the laird was holding up to the light, between his two hands, the very cup I had been looking at in the book, the stones of it flashing all the colors of the rainbow. I should think it a dream, if I did not know it was not. I do not believe I made any noise, for I could not move, but he started up with a cry to God to preserve him, set the cup on the table, threw something over it, caught up a wicked-looking knife, and turned round. His face was like that of a corpse, and I could see him tremble. I stood steady; it was no time then to turn away. I supposed he expected to see a robber, and would be glad when he discovered it was only me; but when he did his fear changed to anger, and he came at me. His eyes were flaming, and he looked as if he would kill me. I was not frightened—poor old man, I was able for him any day!—but I was afraid of hurting him. So I closed the door quickly, and went softly to my own room, where I stood a long time in the dark, listening, but heard nothing more. What am I to do, Andrew?"

"I don't know that you have to do anything. You have one thing not to do, that is—tell anybody what you have seen."

"I was forced to tell you because I did not know what to do. It makes me so sorry!"

"It was no fault of yours. You acted to the best of your knowledge, and could not help what came of it. Perhaps nothing more will come. Leave the thing alone, and if he say anything tell him how it happened."

"But, Andrew, I don't think you see what it is that troubles me. I am afraid my master is a miser. The mistress and he take their meals, like poor people, in the kitchen. That must be the dining-room of the house!—and though my eyes were tethered to the flashing cup, I could not help seeing it was full of strange and beautiful things. Among them, I knew, by pictures I had seen, the armor of knights, when they fought on their horses' backs. Before people had money they must have misered other things. Some girls miser their clothes, and never go decent!"

"Suppose him a miser," said Andrew, "what could you do? How are you to help it?"

"That's what I want to know. I love my master, and there must be a way to help it. It was terrible to see him, in the middle of the night, gazing at that cup as if he had found the most precious thing that can ever have existed on the earth."

"What was that?" asked Andrew.

He delighted in Dawtie's talk. It was like an angel's, he said, both in its ignorance and its wisdom.

"You can't have forgotten, Andrew. It's impossible!" she answered. "I heard you say yourself!"

Andrew smiled.

"I know," he said.

"Poor man!" resumed Dawtie; "he looked at the cup as you might at that manuscript! His soul was at it, feasting upon it! Now wasn't that miserly?"

"It was like it."

"And I love my master," repeated Dawtie, thus putting afresh the question what she was to do.

"Why do you love him, Dawtie?" asked Andrew.

"Because I'm set to love him. Besides, we're told to love our enemies—then surely we're to love our friends. He has always been a friend to me. He never said a hard word to me, even when I was handling his books. He trusts me with them! I can't help loving him—a good deal, Andrew! And it's what I've got to do!"

"There's not a doubt about it, Dawtie. You've got to love him, and you do love him!"

"But there's more than that, Andrew. To hear the laird talk you would think he cared more for the Bible than for the whole world—not to say gold cups. He talks of the merits of the Saviour, that you would think he loved Him with all his heart. But I can not get it out of my mind, ever since I saw that look on his face, that he loves that cup—that it's his graven image—his idol! How else should he get up in the middle of the night to—to—to—well, it was just like worshiping it."

"You're afraid then that he's a hypocrite, Dawtie!"

"No; I daren't think that—if it were only for fear I should stop loving him—and that would be as bad!"

"As bad as what, Dawtie?"

"I don't always know what I'm going to say," answered Dawtie, a little embarrassed, "and then when I've said it I have to look what it means. But isn't it as bad not to love a human being as it would be to love a thing?"

"Perhaps worse," said Andrew.

"Something must be done!" she went on. "He can't be left like that! But if he has any love to his Master, how is it that the love of that Master does not cast out the love of Mammon? I can't understand it."

"You have asked a hard question, Dawtie. But a cure may be going on, and take a thousand years or ages to work it out."

"What if it shouldn't be begun yet."

"That would be terrible."

"What then am I to do, Andrew? You always say we must do something! You say there is no faith but what does something!"

"The apostle James said so, a few years before I was born, Dawtie!"

"Don't make fun of me—please, Andrew! I like it, but I can't bear it to-day, my head is so full of the poor old laird!"

"Make fun of you, Dawtie! Never! But I don't know yet how to answer you."

"Well, then, what am I to do?" persisted Dawtie.

"Wait, of course, till you know what to do. When you don't know what to do, don't do anything—only keep asking the Thinker for wisdom. And until you know, don't let the laird see that you know anything."

With this answer Dawtie was content.

Business was over, and they turned to go home.

CHAPTER XVII. DAWTIE AND THE CUP.

The old man had a noteworthy mental fabric. Believing himself a true lover of literature, and especially of poetry, he would lecture for ten minutes on the right mode of reading a verse in Hilton or Dante; but as to Satan or Beatrice, would pin his faith to the majority of the commentators: Milton's Satan was too noble, and Beatrice was no woman, but Theology. He was discriminative to a degree altogether admirable as to the brightness or wrongness of a proposition with regard to conduct, but owed his respectability to good impulses without any effort of the will. He was almost as orthodox as Paul before his conversion, lacking only the heart and the courage to persecute. Whatever the eternal wisdom saw in him, the thing most present to his own consciousness was the love of rare historic relics. And this love was so mingled in warp and woof, that he did not know whether a thing was more precious to him for its rarity, its money value, or its historico-reliquary interest. All the time he was a school-master, he saved every possible half-penny to buy books, not because of their worth or human interest, but because of their literary interest, or the scarcity of the book or edition. In the holidays he would go about questing for the prey that his soul loved, hunting after precious things; but not even the precious things of the everlasting hills would be precious to him until they had received the stamp of curiosity. His life consisted in a continual search for something new that was known as known of old. It had hardly yet occurred to him that he must one day leave his things and exist without them, no longer to brood over them, take them in his hands, turn, and stroke, and admire them; yet, strange to say, he would at times anxiously seek to satisfy himself that he was safe for a better world, as he called it—to feel certain, that is, that his faith was of the sort he supposed intended by Paul—not that he had himself gathered anything from the apostle, but all from the traditions of his church concerning the teaching of the apostle. He was anxious, I say, as to his safety for the world to come, and yet, while his dearest joy lay treasured in that hidden room, he never thought of the hour when he must leave it all, and go houseless and pocketless, empty-handed if not armless, in the wide, closetless space, hearing ever in the winds and the rain and the sound of the sea-waves, the one question—"Whose shall those things be which thou hast provided?" Like the rich man to whom God said the words, he had gathered much goods for many years—hundreds and hundreds of things, every one of which he knew, and every one of which he loved. A new scratch on the bright steel of one of his suits of armor was a scratch on his heart; the moth and the rust troubled him sore, for he could not keep them away; and where his treasure was, there was his heart, devoured by the same moth, consumed by the same rust. He had much suffering from his possessions—was more exposed to misery than the miser of gold, for the hoarded coin of the latter may indeed be stolen, but he fears neither moth nor rust nor scratch nor decay. The laird cherished his things as no mother her little ones. Nearly sixty years he had been gathering them, and their money-worth was great, but he had no idea of its amount, for he could not have endured the exposure and handling of them which a valuation must involve.

His love for his books had somewhat declined in the growth of his love for things, and now, by degrees not very slow, his love for his things was graduating itself after what he supposed their money-value. His soul not only clave to the dust but was going deeper and deeper in the dust as it wallowed. All day long he was living in the past and growing old in it—it is one thing to grow old in the past, and another to grow old in the present! As he took his walk about his farms, or sat at his meals, or held a mild, soulless conversation with his daughter, his heart was growing old, not healthily in the present, which is to ripen, but unwholesomely in the past, which is to consume with a dry rot. While he read the Bible at prayers, trying hard to banish worldly things from his mind, his thoughts were not in the story or the argument he read, but hovering, like a bird over its nest, about the darlings of his heart. Yea, even while he prayed, his soul, instead of casting off the clay of the world, was loaded and dragged down with all the still-moldering, slow-changing things that lined the walls and filled the drawers and cabinets of his treasure-chamber. It was a place of whose existence not even his daughter knew; for before ever she entered the house, he had taken with him a mason from the town, and built up the entrance to it from the hall, ever afterward keeping the other door of it that opened from his study carefully locked, and leaving it to be regarded as the door of a closet.

It was as terrible as Dawtie felt it, that a live human soul should thus haunt the sepulcher of the past, and love the lifeless, turning a room hitherto devoted to hospitality and mirthful intercourse into the temple of his selfish idolatry. It was as one of the rooms carved for the dead in the Beban El Malook. Sure, if left to himself, the ghost that loved it would haunt the place! But he could not surely be permitted! for it might postpone a thousand years his discovery of the emptiness of a universe of such treasures. Now he was moldering into the world of spirits in the heart of an avalanche of the dust of ages, dust material from his hoards, dust moral and spiritual from his withering soul itself.

The next day he was ill, which, common as is illness to humanity, was strange, for it had never befallen him before. He was unable to leave his bed. But he never said a word to his daughter, who alone waited on him, as to what had happened in the night. He had passed it sleepless, and without the possibility of a dream on which to fall back; yet, when morning came, he was in much doubt whether what he had seen—the face, namely, of Dawtie, peeping in at the door—was a reality, or but a vision of the night. For when he opened the door which she had closed, all was dark, and not the slightest sound reached his quick ear from the swift foot of her retreat. He turned the key twice, and pushed two bolts, eager to regard the vision as a providential rebuke of his carelessness in leaving the door on the latch—for the first time, he imagined. Then he tottered back to his chair, and sunk on it in a cold sweat. For, although the confidence grew, that what he had seen was but

a false creation

Proceeding from the heat-oppressed brain,

it was far from comfortable to feel that he could no longer depend upon his brain to tell him only the thing that was true. What if he were going out of his mind, on the way to encounter a succession of visions—without reality, but possessed of its power! What if they should be such whose terror would compel him to disclose what most he desired to keep covered? How fearful to be no more his own master, but at the beck and call of a disordered brain, a maniac king in a cosmos acosmos! Better it had been Dawtie, and she had seen in his hands Benvenuto Cellini's chalice made for Pope Clement the Seventh to drink therefrom the holy wine—worth thousands of pounds! Perhaps she had seen it! No, surely she had not! He must be careful not to make her suspect! He would watch her and say nothing!

But Dawtie, conscious of no wrong, and full of love to the old man, showed an untroubled face when next she met him; and he made up his mind that he would rather have her ignorant. Thenceforward, naturally though childishly, he was even friendlier to her than before: it was so great a relief to find that he had not to fear her!

The next time Dawtie was dusting the books, she felt strongly drawn to look again at the picture of the cup: it seemed now to hold in it a human life! She took down the book, and began where she stood to read what it said about the chalice, referring as she read from letterpress to drawing. It was taken from an illumination in a missal, where the cup was known to have been copied; and it rendered the description in the letterpress unnecessary except in regard to the stones and dessins repoussés on the hidden side. She quickly learned the names of the gems, that she might see how many were in the high-priest's breast-plate and the gates of the new Jerusalem, then proceeded to the history of the chalice. She read that it had come into the possession of Cardinal York, the brother of Charles Edward Stuart, and had been by him intrusted to his sister-in-law, the Duchess of Albany, from whose house it disappeared, some said stolen, others said sold. It came next to the historic surface in the possession of a certain earl whose love of curiosities was well known; but from his collection again it vanished, this time beyond a doubt stolen, and probably years before it was missed.

A new train of thought was presently in motion in the mind of the girl: The beautiful cup was stolen! it was not where it ought to be! it was not at home! it was a captive, a slave! She lowered the book, half closed, with a finger between the leaves, and stood thinking. She did not for a moment believe her master had stolen it, though the fear did flash through her mind. It had been stolen and sold, and he had bought it at length of some one whose possession of it was nowise suspicious! But he must know now that it had been stolen, for here, with the cup, was the book which said so! That would be nothing if the rightful owner were not known, but he was known, and the thing ought to be his! The laird might not be bound, she was not sure, to restore it at his own loss, for when he bought it he was not aware that it was stolen; but he was bound to restore it at the price he had paid for it, if the former owner would give it! This was bare justice! mere righteousness! No theft could make the owner not the rightful owner, though other claims upon the thing might come in! One ought not to be enriched by another's misfortune! Dawtie was sure that a noble of the kingdom of heaven would not wait for the money, but would with delight send the cup where it ought to have been all the time! She knew better, however, than require magnificence in any shape from the poor wizened soul of her master—a man who knew all about everything, and whom yet she could not but fear to be nothing: as Dawtie had learned to understand life, the laird did not yet exist. But he well knew right from wrong, therefore the discovery she just made affected her duty toward him! It might be impossible to make impression on the miserliness of a miser, but upon the honesty in a miser it might be possible! The goblet was not his!

But the love of things dulls the conscience, and he might not be able, having bought and paid for it, to see that the thing was not therefore his! he might defend himself from seeing it! To Dawtie, this made the horror of his condition the darker. She was one of God's babes, who can not help seeing the true state of things. Logic was to her but the smoke that rose from the burning truth; she saw what is altogether above and beyond logic—the right thing, whose meanest servant, the hewer of its wood, not the drawer of its water, the merest scullion and sweeper away of lies from the pavement of its courts, is logic.

With a sigh she woke to the knowledge that she was not doing her work, and rousing herself, was about to put the book on its shelf. But, her finger being still in the place, she would have one more glance at the picture! To her dismay she saw that she had made a mark on the plate, and of the enormity of making a dirty mark on a book her master had made her well aware.

She was in great distress. What was to be done? She did not once think of putting it away and saying nothing. To have reasoned that her master would never know, would have been an argument, pressing and imperative, for informing him at once. She had done him an injury, and the injury must be confessed and lamented; it was all that was left to be done! "Sic a mischance!" she said, then bethought herself that there was no such thing as mischance, when immediately it flashed upon her that here was the door open for the doing of what was required of her. She was bound to confess the wrong, and that would lead in the disclosure of what she knew, rendering it comparatively easy to use some remonstrance with the laird, whom in her mind's eye she saw like a beggar man tottering down a steep road to a sudden precipice. Her duty was now so plain that she felt no desire to consult Andrew. She was not one to ask an opinion for the sake of talking opinion; she went to Andrew only when she wanted light to do the right thing; when the light was around her, she knew how to walk, and troubled no one.

At once she laid down book and duster, and went to find the laird. But he had slipped away to the town, to have a rummage in a certain little shop in a back street, which he had not rummaged for a long time enough, he thought, to have let something come in. It was no relief to Dawtie: the thing would be all the day before her instead of behind her! It burned within her, not like a sin, but like what it was, a confession unconfessed. Little wrong as she had done, Dawtie was yet familiar with the lovely potency of confession to annihilate it. She knew it was the turning from wrong that killed it, that confession gave the coup de grâce to offense. Still she dreaded not a little the displeasure of her master, and yet she dreaded more his distress.

She prepared the laird's supper with a strange mingling of hope and anxiety: she feared having to go to bed without telling him. But he came at last, almost merry, with a brown paper parcel under his arm, over which he was very careful. Poor man, he little knew there waited him at the moment a demand from the eternal justice almost as terrible as: "This night they require thy soul of thee!"—(What a they is that! Who are they?)—The torture of the moral rack was ready for him at the hands of his innocent house-maid! In no way can one torture another more than by waking conscience against love, passion, or pride.

He laid his little parcel carefully on the supper-table, said rather a shorter grace than usual, began to eat his porridge, praised it as very good, spoke of his journey and whom he had seen, and was more talkative than his wont He informed Alexa, almost with jubilation, that he had at length found an old book he had been long on the watch for—a book that treated, in ancient broad Scots, of the laws of verse, in full, even exhaustive manner. He pulled it from his pocket.

"It is worth at least ten times what I gave for it!" he said.

Dawtie wondered whether there ought not to have been some division of the difference; but she was aware of no call to speak. One thing was enough for one night!

Then came prayers. The old man read how David deceived the Philistines, telling them a falsehood as to his raids. He read the narrative with a solemnity of tone that would have graced the most righteous action: was it not the deed of a man according to God's own heart?—how could it be other than right! Casuist ten times a week, he made no question of the righteousness of David's wickedness! Then he prayed, giving thanks for the mercy that had surrounded them all the day, shielding them from the danger and death which lurked for them in every corner. What would he say when death did get him? Dawtie thought. Would he thank God then? And would he see, when she spoke to him, that God wanted to deliver him from a worse danger than any out-of-doors? Would he see that it was from much mercy he was made more uncomfortable than perhaps ever in his life before?

At length his offering was completed—how far accepted who can tell! He was God's, and He who gave him being would be his Father to the full possibility of God. They rose from their knees; the laird took up his parcel and book; his daughter went with him.

CHAPTER XVIII. DAWTIE AND THE LAIRD.

As soon as Dawtie heard her mistress's door close, she followed her master to the study, and arrived just as the door of the hidden room was shut behind him. There was not a moment to be lost! She went straight to it, and knocked rather loud. No answer came. She knocked again. Still there was no answer. She knocked a third time, and after a little fumbling with the lock, the door opened a chink, and a ghastly face, bedewed with drops of terror, peeped through. She was standing a little back, and the eyes did not at once find the object they sought; then suddenly they lighted on her, and the laird shook from head to foot.

"What is it, Dawtie?" he faltered out in a broken voice.

"Please, sir," answered Dawtie, "I have something to confess: would ye hearken to me?"

"No, no, Dawtie! I am sure you have nothing to confess!" returned the old man, eager to send her away, and to prevent her from seeing the importance of the room whose entrance she had discovered. "Or," he went on, finding she did not move, "if you have done anything, Dawtie, that you ought not to have done, confess it to God. It is to Him you must confess, not to a poor mortal like me! For my part, if it lies to me, I forgive you, and there is an end! Go to your bed, Dawtie."

"Please, sir, I canna. Gien ye winna hear til me, I'll sit doon at the door o' this room, and sit till—"

"What room, Dawtie? Call you this a room? It's a wee bit closet where I say my prayers before I go to bed."

But as he spoke his blood ran cold within him, for he had uttered a deliberate lie—two lies in one breath: the bit closet was the largest room in the house, and he had never prayed a prayer in it since first he entered it! He was unspeakably distressed at what he had done, for he had always cherished the idea that he was one who would not lie to save his life. And now in his old age he had lied who when a boy had honor enough to keep him from lying! Worst of all, now that he had lied, he must hold to the lie! He dared not confess it! He stood sick and trembling.

"I'll wait, sir," said Dawtie, distressed at his suffering, and more distressed that he could lie who never forgot his prayers! Alas, he was further down the wrong road than she had supposed!

Ashamed for his sake, and also for her own, to look him in the face—for did he not imagine she believed him, while she knew that he lied?—she turned her back on him. He caught at his advantage, glided out, and closed the door behind him. When Dawtie again turned, she saw him in her power.

Her trial was come; she had to speak for life or death! But she remembered that the Lord told His disciples to take no care how they should speak; for when the time came it would be given them to speak. So she began by simply laying down the thing that was in her hand.

"Sir," she said, "I am very sorry, but this morning I made a dirty mark in one of your books!"

Her words alarmed him a little, and made him forget for the instant his more important fears. But he took care to be gentle with her; it would not do to offend her! for was she not aware that where they stood was a door by which he went in and out?

"You make me uneasy, Dawtie!" he said. "What book was it? Let me see it."

"I will, sir."

She turned to take it down, but the laird followed her, saying:

"Point it out to me, Dawtie. I will get it."

She did so. It opened at the plate.

"There is the mark!" she said. "I am right sorry."

"So am I!" returned the laird. "But," he added, willing she should feel his clemency, and knowing the book was not a rare one, "it is a book still, and you will be more careful another time! For you must remember, Dawtie, that you don't come into this room to read the books, but to dust them. You can go to bed now with an easy mind, I hope!"

Dawtie was so touched by the kindness and forbearance of her master that the tears rose in her eyes, and she felt strengthened for her task. What would she not have encountered for his deliverance!

"Please, sir," she said, "let me show you a thing you never perhaps happened to read!" And taking the book from his hand—he was too much astonished to retain it—she turned over the engraving, and showed him the passage which stated that the cup had disappeared from the possession of its owner, and had certainly been stolen.

Finding he said not a word, she ventured to lift her eyes to his, and saw again the corpse-like face that had looked through the chink of the door.

"What do you mean?" he stammered. "I do not understand!"

His lips trembled: was it possible he had had to do with the stealing of it?

The truth was this: he had learned the existence of the cup from this very book; and had never rested until, after a search of more than ten years, he at length found it in the hands of a poor man who dared not offer it for sale. Once in his possession, the thought of giving it up, or of letting the owner redeem it, had never even occurred to him. Yet the treasure made him rejoice with a trembling which all his casuistry would have found it hard to explain; for he would not confess to himself its real cause—namely, that his God-born essence was uneasy with a vague knowledge that it lay in the bosom of a thief. "Don't you think, sir," said Dawtie, "that whoever has that cup ought to send it back to the place it was stolen from?"

Had the old man been a developed hypocrite, he would have replied at once: "He certainly ought." But by word of mouth to condemn himself would have been to acknowledge to himself that he ought to send the cup home, and this he dared not do. Men who will not do as they know, make strange confusion in themselves. The worst rancor in the vessel of peace is the consciousness of wrong in a not all-unrighteous soul. The laird was false to his own self, but to confess himself false would be to initiate a change which would render life worthless to him! What would all his fine things be without their heart of preciousness, the one jewel that now was nowhere in the world but in his house, in the secret chamber of his treasures, which would be a rifled case without it! As is natural to one who will not do right, he began to argue the moral question, treating it as a point of casuistry that troubled the mind of the girl.

"I don't know that, Dawtie!" he said. "It is not likely that the person that has the cup, whoever he may be—that is, if the cup be still in existence—is the same who stole it; and it would hardly be justice to punish the innocent for the guilty?—as would be the case, if, supposing I had bought the cup, I had to lose the money I paid for it. Should the man who had not taken care of his cup have his fault condoned at my expense? Did he not deserve, the many might say, to be so punished, placing huge temptation in the path of the needy, to the loss of their precious souls, and letting a priceless thing go loose in the world, to work ruin to whoever might innocently buy it?"

His logic did not serve to show him the falsehood of his reasoning, for his heart was in the lie. "Ought I or he," he went on, "to be punished because he kept the thing ill? And how far would the quixotic obligation descend? A score of righteous men may by this time have bought and sold the cup!—is it some demon-talisman, that the last must meet the penalty, when the original owner, or some descendant of the man who lost it, chooses to claim it? For anything we know, he may himself have pocketed the price of the rumored theft! Can you not see it would be a flagrant injustice?—fit indeed to put an end to all buying and selling! It would annihilate transfer of property! Possession would mean only strength to keep, and the world would fall into confusion."

"It would be hard, I grant," confessed Dawtie; "but the man who has it ought at least to give the head of the family in which it had been the chance of buying it back at the price it cost him. If he could not buy it back—then the thing would have to be thought over."

250

"I confess I don't see the thing," returned the laird. "But the question needs not keep you out of bed, Dawtie! It is not often a girl in your position takes an interest in the abstract! Besides," he resumed, another argument occurring to him, "a thing of such historical value and interest ought to be where it was cared for, not where it was in danger every moment."

"There might be something in that," allowed Dawtie, "if it were where everybody could see it. But where is the good if it be but for the eyes of one man?"

The eyes she meant fixed themselves upon her till their gaze grew to a stony stare. She must know that he had it! Or did she only suspect? He must not commit himself! He must set a watch on the door of his lips! What an uncomfortable girl to have in the house! Oh, those self-righteous Ingrams! What mischief they did! His impulse was to dart into his treasure-cave, lock himself in, and hug the radiant chalice. He dared not. He must endure instead the fastidious conscience and probing tongue of an intrusive maid-servant!

"But," he rejoined, with an attempt at a smile, "if the pleasure the one man took in it should, as is easy to imagine, exceed immeasurably the aggergate pleasure of the thousands that would look upon it and pass it by—what then?"

"The man would enjoy it the more that many saw it—except he loved it for greed, when he would be rejoicing in iniquity, for the cup would not be his. And anyhow, he could not take it with him when he died!"

The face of the miser grew grayer; his lip trembled; but he said nothing. He was beginning to hate Dawtie. She was an enemy! She sought his discomfiture, his misery! He had read strange things in certain old books, and half believed some of them: what if Dawtie was one of those evil powers that haunt a man in pleasant shape, learn the secrets of his heart, and gain influence over him that they may tempt him to yield his soul to the enemy! She was set on ruining him! Certainly she knew that cup was in his possession! He must temporize! He must seem to listen! But as soon as fit reason could be found, such as would neither compromise him nor offend her, she must be sent away! And of all things, she must not gain the means of proving what she now perhaps only suspected, and was seeking assurance of! He stood thinking. It was but for a moment; for the very next words from the lips of the girl that was to him little more than a house-broom, set him face to face with reality—the one terror of the unreal.

"Eh, maister, sir," said Dawtie, with the tears in her eyes, and now at last breaking down in her English, "dinna ye ken 'at ye hae to gie the man 'at aucht that gowden bicker, the chance o' buyin' 't back?"

The laird shivered. He dared not say: "How do you know?" for he dared not hear the thing proved to him. If she did know, he would not front her proof! He would not have her even suppose it an acknowledged fact!

"If I had the cup," he began—but she interrupted him: it was time they should have done with lying!

"Ye ken ye hae the cup, sir!" she said. "And I ken tu, for I saw 't i' yer han's!"

"You shameless, prying hussy!" he began, in a rage at last—but the eager, tearful earnestness of her face made him bethink himself: it would not do to make an enemy of her! "Tell me, Dawtie," he said, with sudden change of tone, "how it was you came to see it."

She told him all—how and when; and he knew that he had seen her see him.

He managed to give a poor little laugh.

"All is not gold that glitters, Dawtie!" he said. "The cup you saw was not the one in the book, but an imitation of it—mere gilded tin and colored glass—copied from the picture, as near as they could make it—just to see better what it must have been like. Why, my good girl, that cup would be worth thousands of pounds! So go to bed, and don't trouble yourself about gold cups. It is not likely any of them will come our way!"

Simple as Dawtie was, she did not believe him. But she saw no good to be done by disputing what he ought to know.

"It wasna aboot the gold cup I was troublin' mysel'!" she said, hesitatingly.

"You are right there!" he replied, with another deathly laugh, "it was not! But you have been troubling me about nothing half the night, and I am shivering with cold! We really must, both of us, go to bed! What would your mistress say!"

"No," persisted Dawtie, "it wasna aboot the cup, gowd or no gowd; it was and is aboot my maister I'm troubled! I'm terrible feart for ye, sir! Ye're a worshiper o' Mammon, sir!"

The laird laughed, for the danger was over!—to Dawtie's deep dismay he laughed!

"My poor girl," he said, "you take an innocent love of curious things for the worship of Mammon! Don't imagine me jesting. How could you believe an old man like me, an elder of the kirk, a dispenser of her sacred things, guilty of the awful crime of Mammon worship?"

He imagined her ignorantly associating the idea of some idolatrous ritual with what to him was but a phrase—the worship of Mammon. "Do you not remember," he continued, "the words of Christ, that a man can not serve God and Mammon? If I be a Christian, as you will hardly doubt, it follows that I am not a worshiper of Mammon, for the two can not go together."

"But that's just the question, sir! A man who worships God, worships Him with his whole heart and soul and strength and mind. If he wakes at night, it is to worship God; if he is glad in his heart, it is because God is, and one day he shall behold His face in brightness. If a man worships God, he loves Him so that no love can come between him and God; if the earth were removed, and the mountains cast into the midst of the sea, it would be all one to him, for God would be all the same. Is it not so, sir?"

"You are a good girl, Dawtie, and I approve of every word you say. It would more than savor of presumption to profess that I loved God up to the point you speak of; but I deserve to love Him. Doubtless a man ought to love God so, and we are all sinners just because we do not love God so. But we have the atonement!"

"But, sir," answered Dawtie, the silent tears running down her face, "I love God that way! I don't care a dust for anything without Him! When I go to bed, I don't care if I never wake again in this world; I shall be where He would have me!"

"You presume, Dawtie! I fear me much you presume! What if that should be in hell?"

"If it be, it will be the best. It will be to set me right. Oh, sir, He is so good! Tell me one thing, sir: when you die—"

"Tut, tut, lass! we're not come to that yet! There's no occasion to think about that yet awhile! We're in the hands of a reconciled God."

"What I want to know," pursued Dawtie, "is how you will feel, how you will get on when you haven't got anything!"

"Not got anything, girl! Are you losing your senses? Of course we shall want nothing then! I shall have to talk to the doctor about you! We shall have you killing us in our beds to know how we like it!"

He laughed; but it was a rather scared laugh.

"What I mean," she persisted, "is—when you have no body, and no hands to take hold of your cap, what will you do without it?"

"What if I leave it to you, Dawtie!" returned the laird, with a stupid mixture of joke and avarice in his cold eye.

"Please, sir, I didn't say what you would do with it, but what would you do without it when it will neither come out of your heart nor into your hands! It must be misery to a miser to have nothing!"

"A miser, hussy!"

"A lover of things, more than a lover of God!"

"Well, perhaps you have the better of me!" he said, after a cowed pause; for he perceived there was no compromise possible with Dawtie: she knew perfectly what she meant; and he could neither escape her logic, nor change her determination, whatever that might be. "I dare say you are right! I will think what ought to be done about that cup!"

He stopped, self amazed: he had committed himself!—as much as confessed the cup genuine! But Dawtie had not been deceived, and had not been thinking about the cup. Only it was plain that, if he would consent to part with it for its money-worth, that would be a grand beginning toward the renouncing of dead things altogether, toward the turning to the living One the love that now gathered, clinging and haunting, about gold cups and graved armor, and suchlike vapors and vanishings, that pass with the sunsets and the snows. She fell on her knees, and, in the spirit of a child and of the apostle of the Gentiles, cried, laying her little red hands together and uplifting them to her master in purest entreaty.

"Oh, laird, laird, ye've been gude and kin' to me, and I lo'e ye, the Lord kens! I pray ye for Christ's sake be reconciled to God, for ye hae been servin' Mammon and no Him, and ye hae jist said we canna serve the twa, and what 'ill come o' 't God only can tell, but it maun be misery!"

Words failed her. She rose, and left the room, with her apron to her eyes.

The laird stood a moment or two like one lost, then went hurriedly into his "closet," and shut the door. Whether he went on his knees to God as did Dawtie to Him, or began again to gloat over his Cellini goblet, I do not know.

Dawtie cried herself to sleep, and came down in the morning very pale. Her duty had left her exhausted, and with a kind of nausea toward all the ornaments and books in the house. A cock crew loud under the window of the kitchen. She dropped on her knees, said "Father of lights!" not a word beside, rose and began to rouse the fire.

When breakfast-time came, and the laird appeared, he looked much as usual, only a little weary, which his daughter set down to his journey the day before. He revived, however, as soon as he had succeeded in satisfying himself that Alexa knew nothing of what had passed. How staid, discreet, and compact of common sense Alexa seemed to him beside Dawtie, whose want of education left her mind a waste swamp for the vagaries of whatever will-o'-the-wisp an overstrained religious fantasy might generate! But however much the laird might look the same as before, he could never, knowing that Dawtie knew what she knew, be again as he had been.

"You'll do a few of the books to-day, won't you, Dawtie," he said, "when you have time? I never thought I should trust any one! I would sooner have old Meg shave me than let her dust an Elzevir! Ha! ha! ha!"

Dawtie was glad that at least he left the door open between them. She said she would do a little dusting in the afternoon, and would be very careful. Then the laird rose and went out, and Dawtie perceived, with a shoot of compassion mingled with mild remorse, that he had left his breakfast almost untasted.

But after that, so far from ever beginning any sort of conversation with her, he seemed uncomfortable the moment they happened to be alone together. If he caught her eye, he would say—hurriedly, and as if acknowledging a secret between them, "By and by, Dawtie;" or, "I'm thinking about the business, Dawtie;" or, "I'm making up my mind, Dawtie!" and so leave her. On one occasion he said, "Perhaps you will be surprised some day, Dawtie!"

On her part Dawtie never felt that she had anything more to say to him. She feared at times that she had done him evil rather than good by pressing upon him a duty she had not persuaded him to perform. She spoke of this fear to Andrew, but he answered decisively:

"If you believed you ought to speak to him, and have discovered in yourself no wrong motive, you must not trouble yourself about the result. That may be a thousand years off yet. You may have sent him into a hotter purgatory, and at the same time made it shorter for him. We know nothing but that God is righteous."

Dawtie was comforted, and things went on as before. Where people know their work and do it, life has few blank spaces for ennui, and they are seldom to be pitied. Where people have not yet found their work, they may be more to be pitied than those that beg their bread. When a man knows his work and will not do it, pity him more than one who is to be hanged to-morrow.

256

CHAPTER XIX. ANDREW AND ALEXA.

Andrew had occasion to call on the laird to pay his father's rent, and Alexa, who had not seen him for some time, thought him improved both in carriage and speech, and wondered. She did not take into account his intercourse with God, as with highest human minds, and his constant wakefulness to carry into action what things he learned. Thus trained in noblest fashions of freedom, it was small wonder that his bearing and manners, the natural outcome and expression of his habits of being, should grow in liberty. There was in them the change only of development. By the side of such education as this, dealing with reality and inborn dignity, what mattered any amount of ignorance as to social custom! Society may judge its own; this man was not of it, and as much surpassed its most accomplished pupils in all the essentials of breeding, as the apostle Paul was a better gentleman than Mr. Nash or Mr. Brummel. The training may be slow, but it is perfect. To him who has yielded self, all things are possible. Andrew was aware of no difference. He seemed to himself the same as when a boy.

Alexa had not again alluded to his brother's letter concerning George Crawford, fearing he might say what she would find unpleasant. But now she wanted to get a definite opinion from him in regard to certain modes of money-making, which had naturally of late occupied a good deal of her thought.

"What is your notion concerning money-lending—I mean at interest, Mr. Ingram?" she said. "I hear it is objected to nowadays by some that set up for teachers!"

"It is by no means the first time in the world's history," answered Andrew.

"I want to know what you think of it, Mr. Ingram?"

"I know little," replied Andrew, "of any matter with which I have not had to deal practically."

"But ought not one to have his ideas ready for the time when we will have to deal practically?" said Alexa.

"Mine would be pretty sure to be wrong," answered Andrew; "and there is no time to spend in gathering wrong ideas and then changing them!"

"On the contrary, they would be less warped by personal interest."

"Could circumstances arise in which it would not be my first interest to be honest?" said Andrew. "Would not my judgment be quickened by the compulsion and the danger? In no danger myself, might I not judge too leniently of things from which I should myself recoil? Selfishly smoother with regard to others, because less anxious about their honesty than my own, might I not yield them what, were I in the case, I should see at once I dared not allow to myself? I can perceive no use in making up my mind how to act in circumstances in which I am not—probably will never be. I have enough to occupy me where I find myself, and should certainly be oftener in doubt how to act, if I had bothered my brains how to think in circumstances foreign to me. In such thinking, duty is of necessity a comparatively feeble factor, being only duty imagined, not live duty, and the result is the more questionable. The Lord instructed His apostles not to be anxious what they should say when they were brought before rulers and kings: I will leave the question of duty alone until action is demanded of me. In the meantime I will do the duty now required of me, which is the only preparation for the duty that is to come."

Although Alexa had not begun to understand Andrew, she had sense enough and righteousness enough to feel that he was somehow ahead of her, and that it was not likely he and George Crawford would be of one mind in the matter that occupied her, so different were their ways of looking at things—so different indeed the things themselves they thought worth looking at.

She was silent for a moment, then said:

"You can at least tell me what you think of gambling!"

"I think it is the meanest mode of gaining or losing money a man could find."

"Why do you think so?"

"Because he desires only to gain, and can gain only by his neighbor's loss. One of the two must be the worse for his transaction with the other. Each must wish ill to his neighbor!"

"But the risk was agreed upon between them."

"True—but in what hope? Was it not, on the part of each, that he would be the gainer and the other the loser? There is no common cause, nothing but pure opposition of interest."

"Are there not many things in which one must gain and the other lose?"

"There are many things in which one gains and the other loses; but if it is essential to any transaction that only one side shall gain, the thing is not of God."

"What do you think of trading in stocks?"

"I do not know enough about it to have a right to speak."

"You can give your impression!"

"I will not give what I do not value."

"Suppose, then, you heard of a man who had made his money so, how would you behave to him?"

"I would not seek his acquaintance."

"If he sought yours?"

"It would be time to ask how he had made his money. Then it would be my business."

"What would make it your business?"

"That he sought my acquaintance. It would then be necessary to know something about him, and the readiest question would be—how he had made his money!"

Alexa was silent for some time.

"Do you think God cares about everything?" she said at length.

259

"Everything," answered Andrew, and she said no more.

Andrew avoided the discussion of moral questions. He regarded the thing as vermiculate, and ready to corrupt the obedience. "When you have a thing to do," he would say, "you will do it right in proportion to your love of right. But do the right, and you will love the right; for by doing it you will see it in a measure as it is, and no one can see the truth as it is without loving it. The more you talk about what is right, or even about the doing of it, the more you are in danger of exemplifying how loosely theory may be allied to practice. Talk without action saps the very will. Something you have to do is waiting undone all the time, and getting more and more undone. The only refuge is to do." To know the thing he ought to do was a matter of import, to do the thing he knew he ought to do was a matter of life and death to Andrew. He never allowed even a cognate question to force itself upon him until he had attended to the thing that demanded doing: it was merest common sense!

Alexa had in a manner got over her uneasiness at the report of how George was making his money, and their correspondence was not interrupted. But something, perhaps a movement from the world of spirit coming like the wind, had given her one of those motions to betterment, which, however occasioned, are the throb of the divine pulse in our life, the call of the Father, the pull of home, and the guide thither to such as will obey them. She had in consequence again become doubtful about Crawford, and as to whether she was right in corresponding with him. This led to her talk with Andrew, which, while it made her think less of his intellect, influenced her in a way she neither understood nor even recognized. There are two ways in which one nature may influence another for betterment—the one by strengthening the will, the other by heightening the ideal. Andrew, without even her suspicion of the fact, wrought in the latter way upon Alexa. She grew more uneasy. George was coming home: how was she to receive him? Nowise bound, they were on terms of intimacy: was she to encourage the procession of that intimacy, or to ward attempt at nearer approach?

CHAPTER XX. GEORGE AND ANDREW.

George returned, and made an early appearance at Potlurg. Dawtie met him in the court. She did not know him, but involuntarily shrunk from him. He frowned. There was a natural repugnance between them; the one was simple, the other double; the one was pure, the other selfish; the one loved her neighbor, the other preyed upon his.

George was a little louder, and his manners were more studied. Alexa felt him overblown. He was floridly at his ease. What little "atmosphere" there had been about him was gone, and its place taken by a colored fog. His dress was unobjectionable, and yet attracted notice; perhaps it was only too considered. Alexa was disappointed, and a little relieved. He looked older, yet not more manly—and rather fat. He had more of the confidence women dislike to see a man without, than was quite pleasant even to the confident Alexa. His speech was not a little infected with the nasality—as easy to catch as hard to get rid of—which I presume the Puritans carried from England to America. On the whole, George was less interesting than Alexa had expected.

He came to her as if he would embrace her, but an instinctive movement on her part sufficed to check him. She threw an additional heartiness into her welcome, and kept him at arm's-length. She felt as if she had lost an old friend, and not gained a new one. He made himself very agreeable, but that he made himself so, made him less so.

There was more than these changes at work in her; there was still the underlying doubt concerning him. Although not yet a live soul, she had strong if vague ideas about right and wrong; and although she sought many things a good deal more than righteousness, I do not see what temptation would at once have turned her from its known paths. At the same time I do not see what she had yet, more than hundreds of thousands of well-meaning women, to secure her from slow decay and final ruin.

They laughed and talked together very like the way they used, but "every like is not the same," and they knew there was a difference. George was stung by the sense of it—too much to show that he was vexed. He laid himself out to be the more pleasing, as if determined to make her feel what he was worth—as the man, namely, whom he imagined himself, and valued himself on being.

It is an argument for God, to see what fools those make of themselves who, believing there is a God, do not believe in Him—children who do not know the Father. Such make up the mass of church and chapel goers. Let an earthquake or the small-pox break loose among them, and they will show what sort their religion is. George had got rid of the folly of believing in the existence of a God, either interested in human affairs or careless of them, and naturally found himself more comfortable in consequence; for he never had believed in God, and it is awkward to believe and not believe at the same moment. What he had called his beliefs were as worthy of the name as those of most people, but whether he was better or worse without them hardly interests me, and my philanthropy will scarce serve to make me glad that he was more comfortable.

As they talked, old times came up, and they drew a little nearer, until at last a gentle spring of rose-colored interest began a feeble flow in Alexa's mind. When George took his leave, which he did soon, with the wisdom of one who feared to bore, she went with him to the court, where the gardener was holding his horse. Beside them stood Andrew, talking to the old man, and admiring the beautiful animal in his charge.

"The life of the Creator has run free through every channel up to this creature!" he was saying as they came near.

"What rot!" said George to himself, but to Alexa he said: "Here's my old friend, the farmer, I declare!" then to Andrew: "How do you do, Mr. Ingram?"

George never forgot a man's name, and went in consequence for a better fellow than he was. One may remember for reasons that have little to do with good-fellowship. He spoke as if they were old friends. "You seem to like the look of the beast!" he said: "you ought to know what's what in horses!"

262

"He is one of the finest horses I ever saw," answered Andrew. "The man who owns him is fortunate."

"He ought to be a good one!" said George. "I gave a hundred and fifty guineas for him yesterday."

Andrew could not help vaguely reflecting what kind of money had bought him, if Sandy was right.

Alexa was pleased to see Andrew. He made her feel more comfortable. His presence seemed to protect her a little.

"May I ask you, Mr. Ingram," she said, "to repeat what you were saying about the horse as we came up?"

"I was saying," answered Andrew, "that, to any one who understands a horse it is clear that the power of God must have flowed unobstructed through many generations to fashion such a perfection."

"Oh! you indorse the development theory—do you?" said George. "I should hardly have expected that of you."

"I do not think it has anything to do with what I said; no one disputes that this horse comes of many generations of horses. The development theory, if I understand aright, concerns itself with how his first ancestor in his own kind came to be a horse."

"And about that there can be no doubt in the mind of any one who believes in the Bible!" said George.

"God makes beautiful horses," returned Andrew; "whether He takes the one way or the other to make them, I am sure He takes the right way."

"You imply it is of little consequence what you believe about it."

"If I had to make them it would be of consequence. But what I think of consequence to us is—that He makes them, not out of nothing, but out of Himself. Why should my poor notion of God's how be of importance, so long as, when I see a horse like yours, Mr. Crawford, I say, God be praised? It is of eternal importance to love the animal, and see in him the beauty of the

Lord; it is of none to fancy I know which way God took to make him. Not having in me the power or the stuff to make a horse, I can not know how God made the horse; I can know him to be beautiful."

"But," said George, "the first horse was a very common-looking domestic animal, which they kept to eat—nothing like this one."

"Then you think God made the first horse, and after that the horses made themselves," said Andrew.

Alexa laughed; George said nothing; Andrew went on.

"But," he said, "if we have come up from the lower animals, through a million of kinds, perhaps—against which theory I have nothing to urge— then I am more than prepared to believe that the man who does not do the part of a man will have to go down again, through all the stages of his being, to a position beyond the lowest forms of the powers he has misused, and there begin to rise once more, haunted perhaps with dim hints of the world of humanity left so far above him."

"Bah! What's the use of bothering! Rubbish!" cried George, with rude jollity. "You know as well as I do, Mr. Ingram, it's all bosh! Things will go on as they're doing, and as they have been doing, till now from all eternity—so far as we know, and that's enough for us."

"They will not go on so for long in our sight, Mr. Crawford. The worms will have a word to say with us."

Alexa turned away.

"You've not given up preaching and taken to the practical yet, Mr. Ingram, I see," said George.

Andrew laughed.

"I flatter myself I have not ceased to be practical, Mr. Crawford. You are busy with what you see, and I am busy as well with what I don't see; but all the time I believe my farm is in as good a state as your books."

George gave a start, and stole a look at the young farmer, but was satisfied he "meant nothing." The self-seeker will walk into the very abyss protesting himself a practical man, and counting him unpractical who will not with him "jump the life to come." Himself, he neither measures the width nor questions his muscle.

CHAPTER XXI. WHAT IS IT WORTH?

Andrew, with all his hard work, harder since Sandy went, continued able to write, for he neither sought company nor drank strong drink, and was the sport of no passion. From threatened inroad he appealed to Him who created to lift His child above the torrent, and make impulse the slave of conscience and manhood. There were no demons riding the whirlwinds of his soul. It is not wonderful then that he should be able to write a book, or that the book should be of genuine and original worth. It had the fortune to be "favorably" reviewed, scarce one of those who reviewed it understanding it, while all of them seemed to themselves to understand it perfectly. I mention the thing because, had the book not been thus reviewed, Alexa would not have bought a copy, or been able to admire it.

The review she read was in a paper whose editor would not have admitted it had he suspected the drift which the reviewer had failed to see; and the passages quoted appealed to Alexa in virtue, partly, of her not seeing half they involved, or anything whatever of the said drift. But because he had got a book published, and because she approved of certain lines, phrases and passages in it; but chiefly because it had been praised by more than one influential paper, Andrew rose immensely in Alexa's opinion. Although he was the son of a tenant, was even a laborer on his farm, and had covered a birth no higher than that of Jesus Christ with the gown of no university, she began, against her own sense of what was fit, to look up to the plow-man. The plow-man was not aware of this, and would have been careless had he been. He respected his landlord's daughter, not ever questioned her superiority as a lady where he made no claim to being a gentleman, but he recognized in her no power either to help or to hurt.

When they next met, Alexa was no longer indifferent to his presence, and even made a movement in the direction of being agreeable to him. She dropped in a measure, without knowing she had ever used it, her patronizing carriage, but had the assurance to compliment him not merely on the poem he had written, but on the way it had been received; she could not have credited, had he told her, that he was as indifferent to the praise or blame of what is called the public, as if that public were indeed—what it is most like—a boy just learning to read. Yet it is the consent of such a public that makes the very essence of what is called fame. How should a man care for it who knows that he is on his way to join his peers, to be a child with the great ones of the earth, the lovers of the truth, the Doers of the Will. What to him will be the wind of the world he has left behind, a wind that can not arouse the dead, that can only blow about the grave-clothes of the dead as they bury their dead.

"Live, Dawtie," said Andrew to the girl, "and ane day ye'll hae yer hert's desire; for 'Blessed are they that hunger and thirst after righteousness.'"

Andrew was neither annoyed nor gratified with the compliments Alexa paid him, for she did not know the informing power of the book—what he cared for in it—the thing that made him write it. But her gentleness and kindness did please him; he was glad to feel a little at home with her, glad to draw a little nearer to one who had never been other than good to him. And then was she not more than kind, even loving to Dawtie?

"So, Andrew, you are a poet at last," she said, holding out her hand to him, which Andrew received in a palm that wrote the better verse that it was horny. "Please to remember I was the first that found you out!" she added.

"I think it was my mother," answered Andrew.

"And I would have helped you if you would have let me."

"It is not well, ma'am, to push the bird off because he can't sit safe on the edge of the nest."

"Perhaps you are right A failure then would have stood in the way of your coming fame."

"Oh, for that, ma'am, believe me, I do not care a short straw."

"What do you not care for?"

"For fame."

"That is wrong, Andrew. We ought to care what our neighbors think of us."

"My neighbors did not set me to do the work, and I did not seek their praise in doing it. Their friendship I prize dearly—more than tongue can tell."

"You can not surely be so conceited, Andrew, as to think nobody capable of judging your work."

"Far from it, ma'am. But you were speaking of fame, and that does not come from any wise judgment."

"Then what do you write for, if you care nothing for fame? I thought that was what all poets wrote for."

"So the world thinks; and those that do sometimes have their reward."

"Tell me then what you write for?"

"I write because I want to tell something that makes me glad and strong. I want to say it, and so try to say it. Things come to me in gleams and flashes, sometimes in words themselves, and I want to weave them into a melodious, harmonious whole. I was once at an oratorio, and that taught me the shape of a poem. In a pause of the music, I seemed all at once to see Handel's heavy countenance looking out of his great wig, as he sat putting together his notes, ordering about in his mind, and fixing in their places with his pen, his drums, and pipes, and fiddles, and roaring bass, and flageolets, and hautboys—all to open the door for the thing that was plaguing him with the confusion of its beauty. For I suppose even Handel did not hear it all clear and plain at first, but had to build his orchestra into a mental organ for his mind to let itself out by, through the many music holes, lest it should burst with its repressed harmonic delights. He must have felt an agonized need to set the haunting angels of sound in obedient order and range, responsive to the soul of the thing, its one ruling idea! I saw him with his white rapt face, looking like a prophet of the living God sent to speak out of the heart of the mystery of truth! I saw him as he sat staring at the paper before him, scratched all over as with the fury of a holy anger at his own impotence, and his soul communed with heavenliest harmonies! Ma'am, will any man persuade me that Handel at such a moment was athirst for fame? or that the desire to please a house full or world full of such as heard his oratorios, gave him the power to write his music? No, ma'am! he was filled, not with the longing for sympathy, and not even with the good desire to give delight, but with the music itself. It was crying in him to get out, and he heard it crying, and could not rest till he had let it out; and every note that dropped from his pen was a chip struck from the granite wall between the song-birds in their prison-nest, and the air of their liberty. Creation is God's self-wrought freedom. No, ma'am, I do not despise my fellows, but neither do I prize the judgment of more than a few of them. I prize and love themselves, but not their opinion."

Alexa was silent, and Andrew took his leave. She sat still for awhile thinking. If she did not understand, at least she remembered Andrew's face as he talked: could presumption make his face shine so? could presumption make him so forget himself?

CHAPTER XXII. THE GAMBLER AND THE COLLECTOR.

Things went swimmingly with George. He had weathered a crisis, and was now full of confidence, as well as the show of it. That he held himself a man who could do what he pleased, was plain to every one. His prosperity leaned upon that of certain princes of the power of money in America: gleaning after them he found his fortune.

But he did not find much increase of favor with Alexa. Her spiritual tastes were growing more refined. There was something about the man, and that not new, which she could no longer contemplate without dissatisfaction. It cost her tears at night to think that, although her lover had degenerated, he had remained true to her, for she saw plainly that it was only lack of encouragement that prevented him from asking her to be his wife. She must appear changeable, but this was not the man she had been ready to love! the plant had put forth a flower that was not in sequence with the leaf. The cause of his appearing different might lie in herself, but in any case he was not the gentleman she had thought! Had she loved him, she would have stood by him bravely, but now she could not help recalling the disgrace of the father, and shrunk from sharing it with the son. Would it be any wonder if the son himself proved less than honorable? She would have broken with him quite but for one thing: he had become intimate with her father, and the laird enjoyed his company.

George had a large straggling acquaintance with things, and could readily appear to know more than he did. He was, besides, that most agreeable person to a man with a hobby, a good listener—when he saw reason. He made himself so pleasant that the laird was not only always glad to see him, but would often ask him to stay to supper, when he would fish up from the wine-cellar he had inherited a bottle with a history and a character, and the two would pass the evening together, Alexa trying not to wish him away, for was not her poor old father happy with him! Though without much pleasure of his own in such things, George, moved by the reflection of the laird's interest, even began to collect a little, mainly in the hope of picking up what might gratify the laird; nor, if he came upon a thing he must covet, would hesitate to spend on it a good sum. Naturally the old man grew to regard him as a son of the best sort, one who would do anything to please his father and indulge his tastes.

It may seem surprising that such a man as George should have remained so true; but he had a bull-dog tenacity of purpose, as indeed his money-making indicated. Then there was good in him to the measure of admiring a woman like Alexa, though not of admiring a far better. He saw himself in danger of losing her; concluded influences at work to the frustration of his own; surmised that she doubted the character of his business; feared the clownish farmer-poet might have dazzled with his new reputation her womanly judgment; and felt himself called upon to make good his position against any and every prejudice she might have conceived against him! He would yield nothing! If he was foiled he was foiled, but it should not be his fault! His own phrase was, that he would not throw up the sponge so long as he could come up grinning. He had occasional twinges of discomfort, for his conscience, although seared indeed, was not seared as with the hottest iron, seeing he had never looked straight at any truth: it would ease those twinges, he vaguely imagined, so to satisfy a good woman like Alexa, that she made common cause with him, accepting not merely himself, but the money of which he had at such times a slight loathing. Then Alexa was handsome—he thought her very handsome, and, true to Mammon, he would gladly be true also to something better. There might be another camp, and it would be well to have friends in that too!

So unlike Andrew, how could he but dislike him! and his dislike jealousy fostered into hatred. Cowed before him, like Macbeth before Banquo, because he was an honest man, how could he but hate him! He called him, and thought him a canting, sneaking fellow—which he was, if canting consist in giving God His own, and sneaking consist in fearing no man—in fearing nothing, indeed, but doing wrong. How could George consent even to the far-off existence of such a man!

The laird also had taken a dislike to him.

271

From the night when Dawtie made her appeal, he had not known an hour's peace. It was not that it had waked his conscience, though it had made it sleep a little less soundly; it was only that he feared she might take further action in regard to the cup. She seemed to him to be taking part with the owner of the cup against him; he could not see that she was taking part with himself against the devil; that it was not the cup she was anxious about, but the life of her master. What if she should acquaint the earl's lawyer with all she knew! He would be dragged into public daylight! He could not pretend ignorance concerning the identity of the chalice! that would be to be no antiquarian, while Dawtie would bear witness that he had in his possession a book telling all about it! But the girl would never of herself have turned against him! It was all that fellow Ingram, with his overstrained and absurd notions as to what God required of His poor sinful creatures! He did not believe in the atonement! He did not believe that Christ had given satisfaction to the Father for our sins! He demanded in the name of religion more than any properly educated and authorized minister would! and in his meddlesomeness had worried Dawtie into doing as she did! The girl was a good and modest girl, and would never of herself have so acted! Andrew was righteous overmuch, therefore eaten up with self-conceit, and the notion of pleasing God more than other men! He cherished old grudges against him, and would be delighted to bring his old school-master to shame! He was not a bad boy at school; he had always liked him; the change in him witnessed to the peril of extremes! Here they had led to spiritual pride, which was the worst of all the sins! The favorite of heaven could have no respect for the opinion of his betters! The man was bent on returning evil for all the good he had done the boy! It was a happy thing young Crawford understood him! He would be his friend, and defeat the machinations of his enemy! If only the fellow's lease were out, that he might get rid of him!

Moved by George's sympathy with his tastes, he drew nearer and nearer to disclosing the possession which was the pride of his life. The enjoyment, of connoisseur or collector rests much on the glory of possession—of having what another has not, or, better still, what no other can possibly have.

From what he had long ago seen on the night of the storm, and now from the way the old man hinted, and talked, and broke off; also from the uneasiness he sometimes manifested, George had guessed that there was something over whose possession he gloated, but for whose presence among his treasures he could not comfortably account He therefore set himself, without asking a single question, to make the laird unbosom. A hold on the father would be a hold on the daughter!

One day, in a pawnbroker's shop, he lighted upon a rarity indeed, which might or might not have a history attributed to it, but was in itself more than interesting for the beauty of both material and workmanship. The sum asked for it was large, but with the chance of pleasing the laird, it seemed to George but a trifle. It was also, he judged, of intrinsic value to a great part of the price. Had he been then aware of the passion of the old man for jewels in especial, he would have been yet more eager to secure it for him. It was a watch, not very small, and by no means thin—a repeater, whose bell was dulled by the stones of the mine in which it lay buried. The case was one mass of gems of considerable size, and of every color. Ruby, sapphire, and emerald were judiciously parted by diamonds of utmost purity, while yellow diamonds took the golden place for which the topaz had not been counted of sufficient value. They were all crusted together as close as they could lie, the setting of them hardly showing. The face was of fine opals, across which moved the two larger hands radiant with rubies, while the second-hand flitted flashing around, covered with tiny diamonds. The numerals were in sapphires, within a bordering ring of emeralds and black pearls. The jewel was a splendor of color and light.

George, without preface, took it from his pocket, held it a moment in the sunlight, and handed it to the laird. He glowered at it. He saw an angel from heaven in a thing compact of earth-chips! As near as any thing can be loved of a live soul, the laird loved a fine stone; what in it he loved most, the color, the light, the shape, the value, the mystery, he could not have told!— and here was a jewel of many fine stones! With both hands he pressed it to his bosom. Then he looked at it in the sun, then went into the shadow of the house, for they were in the open air, and looked at it again. Suddenly he thrust it into his pocket, and hurried, followed by George, to his study. There

273

he closed the shutters, lighted a lamp, and gazed at the marvel, turning it in all directions. At length he laid it on the table, and sunk with a sigh into a chair. George understood the sigh, and dug its source deeper by telling him, as he had heard it, the story of the jewel.

"It may be true," he said as he ended. "I remember seeing some time ago a description of the toy. I think I could lay my hand on it!"

"Would you mind leaving it with me till you come again?" faltered the laird.

He knew he could not buy it: he had not the money; but he would gladly dally with the notion of being its possessor. To part with it, the moment after having held it in his hand and gloated over it for the first time, would be too keen a pain! It was unreasonable to have to part with it at all! He ought to be its owner! Who could be such an owner to a thing like that as he! It was a wrong to him that it was not his! Next to his cup, it was the most precious thing he had ever wished to possess!—a thing for a man to take to the grave with him! Was there no way of carrying any treasure to the other world? He would have sold of his land to secure the miracle, but, alas, it was all entailed! For a moment the Cellini chalice seemed of less account, and he felt ready to throw open the window of his treasure-room and pitch everything out. The demon of having is as imperious and as capricious as that of drink, and there is no refuge from it but with the Father. "This kind goeth not out by prayer."

The poor slave uttered, not a sigh now, but a groan. "You'll tell the man," he said, thinking George had borrowed the thing to show him, "that I did not even ask the price: I know I can not buy it!"

"Perhaps he would give you credit!" suggested George, with a smile.

"No! I will have nothing to do with credit! I should not be able to call it my own!"—Money-honesty was strong in the laird. "But," he continued, "do try and persuade him to let me have it for a day or two—that I may get its beauty by heart, and think of it all the days, and dream of it all the nights of my life after!"

"There will be no difficulty about that," answered George. "The owner will be delighted to let you keep it as long as you wish!"

"I would it were so!"

"It is so!"

"You don't mean to say, George, that that queen of jewels is yours, and you will lend it me?"

"The thing is mine, but I will not lend it—not even to you, sir!"

"I don't wonder!—I don't wonder! But it is a great disappointment! I was beginning to hope I—I—might have the loan of it for a week or two even!"

"You should indeed if the thing were mine!" said George, playing him; "but—"

"Oh, I beg your pardon! I thought you said it was yours!"

"So it was when I brought it, but it is mine no longer. It is yours. I purchased it for you this morning."

The old man was speechless. He rose, and seizing George by both hands, stood staring at him. Something very like tears gathered within the reddened rims of his eyes. He had grown paler and feebler of late, ever in vain devising to secure possession of the cup—possession moral as well as legal. But this entrancing gift brought with it strength and hope in regard to the chalice! "To him that hath shall be given!" quoted the Mammon within him.

"George!" he said, with a moan of ecstasy, "you are my good angel!" and sat down exhausted. The watch was the key to his "closet," as he persisted in calling his treasury.

In old times not a few houses in Scotland held a certain tiny room, built for the head of the family, to be his closet for prayer: it was, I believe, with the notion of such a room in his head, that the laird had called his museum his closet; and he was more right than he meant to be; for in that chamber he did his truest worship—truest as to the love in it, falsest as to its object; for there he worshiped the god vilest bred of all the gods, bred namely of man's distrust in the Life of the universe.

And now here also were two met together to worship; for from this time the laird, disclosing his secret, made George free of his sanctuary.

George was by this time able to take a genuine interest in the collection. But he was much amused, sometimes annoyed, with the behavior of the laird in his closet: he was more nervous and touchy over his things than a she-bear over her cubs.

Of all dangers to his darlings he thought a woman the worst, and had therefore seized with avidity the chance of making that room a hidden one, the possibility of which he had spied almost the moment he first entered it.

He became, if possible, fonder of his things than ever, and flattered himself he had found in George a fellow-worshiper: George's exaggerated or pretended appreciation enhanced his sense of their value.

CHAPTER XXIII. ON THE MOOR.

Alexa had a strong shaggy pony, which she rode the oftener that George came so often; taking care to be well gone before he arrived on his beautiful horse.

One lovely summer evening she had been across the moor a long way, and was returning as the sun went down. A glory of red molten gold was shining in her face, so that she could see nothing in front of her, and was a little startled by a voice greeting her with a respectful good-evening. The same moment she was alongside of the speaker in the blinding veil of the sun. It was Andrew walking home from a village on the other side of the moor. She drew rein, and they went together.

"What has come to you, Mr. Ingram?" she said; "I hear you were at church last Sunday evening!"

"Why should I not be, ma'am?" asked Andrew.

"For the reason that you are not in the way of going."

"There might be good reason for going once, or for going many times, and yet not for going always!"

"We won't begin with quarreling! There are things we shall not agree about!"

"Yes; one or two—for a time, I believe!" returned Andrew.

"What did you think of Mr. Rackstraw's sermon? I suppose you went to hear him.'"

"Yes, ma'am—at least partly."

"Well?"

"Will you tell me first whether you were satisfied with Mr. Rackstraw's teaching? I know you were there."

"I was quite satisfied."

"Then I don't see reason for saying anything about it."

"If I am wrong, you ought to try to set me right!"

"The prophet Elisha would have done no good by throwing his salt into the running stream. He cast it, you will remember, into the spring!"

"I do not understand you."

"There is no use in persuading a person to change an opinion."

"Why not?"

"Because the man is neither the better nor the worse for it. If you had told me you were distressed to hear a man in authority speak as Mr. Rackstraw spoke concerning a being you loved, I would have tried to comfort you by pointing out how false it was. But if you are content to hear God so represented, why should I seek to convince you of what is valueless to you? Why offer you to drink what your heart is not thirsting after? Would you love God more because you found He was not what you were quite satisfied He should be?"

"Do tell me more plainly what you mean?"

"You must excuse me. I have said all I will. I can not reason in defense of God. It seems blasphemy to argue that His nature is not such as no honorable man could love in another man."

"But if the Bible says so?"

"If the Bible said so, the Bible would be false. But the Bible does not say so."

"How is it then that it seems to say so?"

"Because you were taught falsely about Him before you desired to know Him."

"But I am capable of judging now!"

Andrew was silent.

"Am I not?" insisted Alexa.

"Do you desire to know God?" said Andrew.

"I think I do know Him."

"And you think those things true?"

"Yes."

"Then we are where we were, and I say no more."

"You are not polite."

"I can not help it. I must let you alone to believe about God what you can. You will not be blamed for not believing what you can not."

"Do you mean that God never punishes any one for what He can not help?"

"Assuredly."

"How do you prove that?"

"I will not attempt to prove it. If you are content to think He does, if it do not trouble you that your God should be unjust, go on thinking so until you are made miserable by it, then I will pour out my heart to deliver you."

She was struck, not with any truth in what he said, but with the evident truthfulness of the man himself. Right or wrong, there was that about him—a certain radiance of conviction—which certainly was not about Mr. Rackstraw.

"The things that can be shaken," said Andrew, as if thinking with himself, "may last for a time, but they will at length be shaken to pieces, that the things which can not be shaken may show what they are. Whatever we call religion will vanish when we see God face to face."

For awhile they went brushing through the heather in silence.

"May I ask you one question, Mr. Ingram?" said Alexa.

"Surely, ma'am! Ask me anything you like."

"And you will answer me?"

"If I am at liberty to answer you I will."

"What do you mean by being at liberty? Are you under any vow?"

"I am under the law of love. I am bound to do nothing to hurt. An answer that would do you no good I will not give."

"How do you know what will or will not do me good?"

"I must use what judgment I have."

"Is it true, then, that you believe God gives you whatever you ask?"

"I have never asked anything of Him that He did not give me."

"Would you mind telling me anything you have asked of Him?"

"I have never yet required to ask anything not included in the prayer, 'Thy will be done.'"

"That will be done without your praying for it."

"Pardon me; I do not believe it will be done, to all eternity, without my praying for it. Where first am I accountable that His will should be done? Is it not in myself? How is His will to be done in me without my willing it? Does He not want me to love what He loves?—to be like Himself?—to do His will with the glad effort of my will?—in a word, to will what He wills? And when I find I can not, what am I to do but pray for help? I pray, and He helps me."

"There is nothing strange in that!"

"Surely not It seems to me the simplest common sense. It is my business, the business of every man, that God's will be done by his obedience to that will, the moment he knows it."

"I fancy you are not so different from other people as you think yourself. But they say you want to die."

"I want nothing but what God wants. I desire righteousness."

"Then you accept the righteousness of Christ?"

"Accept it! I long for it."

"You know that it is not what I mean!"

"I seek first the kingdom of God and God's righteousness."

"You avoid my question. Do you accept the righteousness of Christ instead of your own?"

"I have no righteousness of my own to put it instead of. The only righteousness there is God's, and He will make me righteous like Himself. He is not content that His one Son only should be righteous; He wants all His children to be righteous as He is righteous. The thing is plain; I will not argue about it."

"You do not believe in the atonement."

"I believe in Jesus Christ. He is the atonement. What strength God has given me I will spend in knowing Him and doing what He tells me. To interpret His plans before we know Himself is to mistake both Him and His plans. I know this, that he has given His life for what multitudes who call themselves by His name would not rise from their seats to share in."

"You think me incapable of understanding the gospel?"

"I think if you did understand the gospel of Christ you would be incapable of believing the things about His Father that you say you do believe. But I will not say a word more. When you are able to see the truth, you will see it; and when you desire the truth you will be able."

Alexa touched her pony with her whip. But by and by she pulled him up, and made him walk till Andrew overtook her.

The sun was by this time far out of sight, the glow of the west was over, and twilight lay upon the world. Its ethereal dimness had sunk into her soul.

"Does the gloaming make you sad, Mr. Ingram?" she asked.

"It makes me very quiet," he answered—"as if all my people were asleep, and waiting for me."

"Do you mean as if they were all dead? How can you talk of it so quietly?"

"Because I do not believe in death."

"What do you mean?"

"I am a Christian!"

"I hope you are, Mr. Ingram, though, to be honest with you, some things make me doubt it Perhaps you would say I am not a Christian."

"It is enough that God knows whether you are a Christian or not. Why should I say you are or you are not?"

"But I want to know what you meant when you said you were a Christian. How should that make you indifferent to the death of your friends? Death is a dreadful thing, look at it how you like."

"The Lord says, 'He that liveth and believeth in Me shall never die.' If my friends are not dead, but living and waiting for me, why should I wait for them in a fierce, stormy night, or a black frost, instead of the calm of such a sleeping day as this—a day with the son hid, Shakespeare calls it."

"How you do mix up things! Shakespeare and Jesus Christ!"

"God mixed them first, and will mix them a good deal more yet," said Andrew.

But for the smile which would hover like a heavenly Psyche about his mouth, his way of answering would sometimes have seemed curt to those who did not understand him. Instead of holding aloof in his superiority, however, as some thought he did when he would not answer, or answered abruptly, Andrew's soul would be hovering, watching and hoping for a chance of lighting, and giving of the best he had. He was like a great bird changing parts with a child—the child afraid of the bird, and the bird enticing the child to be friends. He had learned that if he poured out his treasure recklessly it might be received with dishonor, and but choke the way of the chariot of approaching truth.

"Perhaps you will say next there is no such thing as suffering," resumed Alexa.

"No; the Lord said that in the world His friends should have tribulation."

"What tribulation have you, who are so specially His friend?"

"Not much yet It is a little, however, sometimes, to know such strong, and beautiful, and happy-making things, and all the time my people, my beloved humans, born of my Father in heaven, with the same heart for joy and sorrow, will not listen and be comforted, I think that was what made our Lord sorriest of all."

"Mr. Ingram, I have no patience with you. How dare you liken your trouble to that of our Lord—making yourself equal with Him!"

"Is it making myself equal with Him to say that I understand a little how He felt toward His fellow-men? I am always trying to understand Him; would it be a wonder if I did sometimes a little? How is a man to do as He did, without understanding Him?"

"Are you going to work miracles next?"

"Jesus was always doing what God wanted Him to do. That was what He came for, not to work miracles. He could have worked a great many more if He had pleased, but He did no more than God wanted of Him. Am I not to try to do the will of God, because He who died that I might, always succeeded however hard it was, and I am always failing and having to try again?"

"And you think you will come to it in this life?"

"I never think about that; I only think about doing His will now—not about doing it then—that is, to-morrow or next day or next world. I know only one life—the life that is hid with Christ in God; and that is the life by which I live here and now. I do not make schemes of life; I live. Life will teach me God's plans; I will take no trouble about them; I will only obey, and receive the bliss He sends me. And of all things I will not make theories of God's plans for other people to accept. I will only do my best to destroy such theories as I find coming between some poor glooming heart, and the sun shining in his strength. Those who love the shade of lies, let them walk in it until the shiver of the eternal cold drive them to seek the face of Jesus Christ. To appeal to their intellect would be but to drive them the deeper into the shade to justify their being in it. And if by argument you did persuade them out of it, they would but run into a deeper and worse darkness."

"How could that be?"

"They would at once think that, by an intellectual stride they had advanced in the spiritual life, whereas they would be neither the better nor the worse. I know a man, once among the foremost in denouncing the old theology, who is now no better than a swindler."

"You mean—"

"No one you know, ma'am. His intellectual freedom seems only to have served his spiritual subjugation. Right opinion, except it spring from obedience to the truth, is but so much rubbish on the golden floor of the temple."

The peace of the night and its luminous earnestness were gleaming on Andrew's face, and Alexa, glancing up as he ceased, felt again the inroad of a sense of something in the man that was not in the other men she knew—the spiritual shadow of a dweller in regions beyond her ken. The man was before her, yet out of her sight!

The whole thing was too simple for her, only a child could understand it Instead of listening to the elders and priests to learn how to save his soul, he cast away all care of himself, left that to God, and gave himself to do the will of Him from whose heart he came, even as the eternal Life, the Son of God, required of him; in the mighty hope of becoming one mind, heart, soul, one eternal being, with Him, with the Father, with every good man, with the universe which was his inheritance—walking in the world as Enoch walked with God, held by his hand. This is what man was and is meant to be, what man must become; thither the wheels of time are roaring; thither work all the silent potencies of the eternal world; and they that will not awake and arise from the dead must be flung from their graves by the throes of a shivering world.

When he had done speaking Andrew stood and looked up. A few stars were looking down through the limpid air. Alexa rode on. Andrew let her go, and walked after her alone, sure that her mind must one day open to the eternal fact that God is all in all, the perfect friend of His children; yea, that He would cease to be God sooner than fail His child in his battle with death.

CHAPTER XXIV. THE WOOER.

Alexa kept hoping that George would be satisfied she was not inclined toward him as she had been; and that, instead of bringing the matter to open issue, he would continue to come and go as the friend of her father. But George came to the conclusion that he ought to remain in doubt no longer, and one afternoon followed her into the garden. She had gone there with a certain half-scientific, half-religious book in her hand, from which she was storing her mind with arguments against what she supposed the opinions of Andrew. She had, however, little hope of his condescending to front them with counter-argument. His voice returned ever to the ear of her mind in words like these: "If you are content to think so, you are in no condition to receive what I have to communicate. Why should I press water on a soul that is not thirsty? Let us wait for the drought of the desert, when life is a low fever, and the heart is dry; when the earth is like iron, and the heavens above it are as brass."

She started at the sound of George's voice.

"What lovely weather!" he said.

Even lovers betake themselves to the weather as a medium—the side of nature which all understand. It was a good, old-fashioned, hot, heavy summer afternoon, one ill-chosen for love-making.

"Yes?" answered Alexa, with a point of interrogation subaudible, and held her book so that he might feel it on the point of being lifted again to eager eyes. But he was not more sensitive than sentimental.

"Please put your book down for a moment. I have not of late asked too much of your attention, Alexa!"

"You have been very kind, George!" she answered.

"Kind is not asking much of your attention?"

"Yea—that, and giving my father so much of yours."

"I certainly have seen more of him than of you!" returned George, hoping her words meant reproach. "But he has always been kind to me, and pleased to see me! You have not given me much encouragement!"

To begin love-making with complaint is not wise, and George felt that he had got into the wrong track; but Alexa took care that he should not get out of it easily. Not being simple, he always settled the best course to pursue, and often went wrong. The man who cares only for what is true and right is saved much thinking and planning. He generally sees but one way of doing a thing!

"I am glad to hear you say so, George! You have not mistaken me!"

"You were not so sharp with me when I went away, Alexa!"

"No; then you were going away!"

"Should you not show a fellow some kindness when he is come back?"

"Not when he does not seem content with having come back!"

"I do not understand!"

But Alexa gave no explanation.

"You would be kind to me again if I were going away again?"

"Perhaps."

"That is, if you were sure I was not coming back."

"I did not say so."

"I can't make it out, Alexa! I used to think there could never be any misunderstanding between you and me! But something has crept in between us, and for the life of me I do not know what it is!"

"There is one thing for which I am more obliged to you than I can tell, George—that you did not say anything before you went."

"I am awfully sorry for it now; but I thought you understood!"

"I did; and I am very glad, for I should have repented it long ago!"

This was hardly logical, but George seemed to understand.

"You are cruel!" he said. "I should have made it the business of my life that you never did!"

Yet George knew of things he dared not tell that had taken place almost as soon as he was relieved from the sustaining and restraining human pressure in which he had grown up!

"I am certain I should," persisted Alexa.

"Why are you so certain?"

"Because I am so glad now to think I am free."

"Some one has been maligning me, Alexa! It is very hard not to know where the stab comes from!"

"The testimony against you is from your own lips, George. I heard you talking to my father, and was aware of a tone I did not like. I listened more attentively, and became convinced that your ways of thinking had deteriorated. There seemed not a remnant left of the honor I then thought characterized you!"

"Why, certainly, as an honest man, I can not talk religion like your friend the farmer!"

"Do you mean that Andrew Ingram is not an honest man?" rejoined Alexa, with some heat.

"I mean that I am an honest man."

"I am doubtful of you."

"I can tell the quarter whence that doubt was blown!"

"It would be of greater consequence to blow it away! George Crawford, do you believe yourself an honest man?"

"As men go, yes."

"But not as men go, George? As you would like to appear to the world

288

when hearts are as open as faces?"

He was silent.

"Would the way you have made your money stand the scrutiny of—"

She had Andrew in her mind, and was on the point of saying "Jesus Christ," but felt she had no right, and hesitated.

"—Of our friend Andrew?" supplemented George, with a spiteful laugh. "The only honest mode of making money he knows is the strain of his muscles—the farmer-way! He wouldn't keep up his corn for a better market—not he!"

"It so happens that I know he would not; for he and my father had a dispute on that very point, and I heard them. He said poor people were not to go hungry that he might get rich. He was not sent into the world to make money, he said, but to grow corn. The corn was grown, and he could get enough for it now to live by, and had no right, and no desire to get more— and would not keep it up! The land was God's, not his, and the poor were God's children, and had their rights from him! He was sent to grow corn for them!"

"And what did your father say to that wisdom?"

"That is no matter. Nor do I profess to understand Mr. Ingram. I only know," added Alexa, with a little laugh, "that he is consistent, for he has puzzled me all my life. I can, however, see a certain nobility in him that sets him apart from other men!"

"And I can see that when I left I was needlessly modest! I thought my position too humble!"

"What am I to understand by that?"

"What you think I mean."

"I wish you a good-afternoon, Mr. Crawford!"

Alexa rose and left him.

George had indeed grown coarser! He turned where he stood with his hands in his pockets, and looked after her; then smiled to himself a nasty smile, and said: "At least I have made her angry, and that's something! What has a fellow like that to give her? Poet, indeed! What's that! He's not even the rustic gentleman! He's downright vulgar!—a clod-hopper born and bred! But the lease, I understand, will soon be out, and Potlurg will never let him have it! I will see to that! The laird hates the canting scoundrel! I would rather pay him double the rent myself!"

His behavior now did not put Andrew's manners in the shade! Though he never said a word to flatter Alexa, spoke often in a way she did not at all like, persistently refused to enter into argument with her when most she desired it, yet his every tone, every movement toward her was full of respect And however she strove against the idea, she felt him her superior, and had indeed begun to wish that she had never shown herself at a disadvantage by the assumption of superiority. It would be pleasant to know that it pained him to disapprove of her! For she began to feel that, as she disapproved of George, and could not like him, so the young farmer disapproved of her, and could not like her. It was a new and by no means agreeable thought. Andrew delighted in beautiful things: he did not see anything beautiful in her! Alexa was not conceited, but she knew she was handsome, and knew also that Andrew would never feel one heart-throb more because of any such beauty as hers. Had he not as good as told her she was one of the dead who would not come alive! It would be something to be loved by a man like that! But Alexa was too maidenly to think of making any man love her—and even if he loved her she could not marry a man in Andrew's position! She might stretch a point or two were the lack but a point or two, but there was no stretching points to the marrying of a peasant, without education, who worked on his father's farm! The thing was ridiculous!—of course she knew that!—the very idea too absurd to pass through her idlest thoughts! But she was not going to marry George! That was well settled! In a year or two he would be quite fat! And he always had his hands in his pockets! There was something about him not like a gentleman! He suggested an auctioneer or a cheap-jack!

She took her pony and went for a ride. When she came back, the pony looked elf-ridden.

But George had no intention of forsaking the house—yet, at least. He was bent on humbling his cousin, therefore continued his relations with her father, while he hurried on, as fast as consisted with good masonry, the building of a house on a small estate he had bought in the neighborhood, intending it to be such as must be an enticement to any lady. So long had he regarded everything through the veil of money, that he could not think of Alexa even without thinking of Mammon as well. By this time also he was so much infected with the old man's passion for things curious and valuable, that the idea of one day calling the laird's wonderful collection his own, had a real part in his desire to become his daughter's husband. He would not accept her dismissal as final!

CHAPTER XXV. THE HEART OF THE HEART.

The laird had been poorly for some weeks, and Alexa began to fear that he was failing. Nothing more had passed between him and Dawtie, but he knew that anxious eyes were often watching him, and the thought worried him not a little. If he would but take a start, thought Dawtie, and not lose all the good of this life! It was too late for him to rise very high; he could not now be a saint, but he might at least set a foot on the eternal stair that leads to the fullness of bliss! He would have a sore fight with all those imps of things, before he ceased to love that which was not lovely, and to covet that which was not good! But the man gained a precious benefit from this world, who but began to repent before he left it! If only the laird would start up the hill before his body got quite to the bottom! Was there any way to approach him again with her petition that he would be good to himself, good to God, good to the universe, that he would love what was worth loving, and cast away what was not? She had no light, and could do nothing!

Suddenly the old man failed quite—apparently from no cause but weakness. The unease of his mind, the haunting of the dread thought of having to part with the chalice, had induced it. He was in his closet one night late into the morning, and the next day did not get up to breakfast He wanted a little rest, he said. In a day he would be well! But the hour to rise again, much anticipated, never came. He seemed very troubled at times, and very desirous of getting up, but never was able. It became necessary to sit with him at night. In fits of delirium he would make fierce endeavor to rise, insisting that he must go to his study. His closet he never mentioned: even in dreams was his secrecy dominant. Dawtie, who had her share in nursing him, kept hoping her opportunity would come. He did not seem to cherish any resentment against her. His illness would protect him, he thought, from further intrusion of her conscience upon his! She must know better than irritate a sick man with overofficiousness! Everybody could not be a saint! It was enough to be a Christian like other good and salvable Christians! It was enough for him if through the merits of his Saviour he gained admission to the heavenly kingdom at last! He never thought now, once in, he could bear to stay in; never thought how heaven could be to him other than the dullest place in the universe of God, more wearisome than the kingdom of darkness itself! And all the time the young woman with the savior-heart was watching by his bedside, ready to speak; but the Spirit gave her no utterance, and her silence soothed his fear of her.

One night he was more restless than usual. Waking from his troubled slumber, he called her—in the tone of one who had something important to communicate.

"Dawtie," he said, with feeble voice but glittering eye, "there is no one I can trust like you. I have been thinking of what you said that night ever since. Go to my closet and bring me the cup."

Dawtie held a moment's debate whether it would be right; but she reflected that it made little difference whether the object of his passion was in his hand or in his chest, while it was all the same deep in his heart. Then his words seemed to imply that he wanted to take his farewell of it; and to refuse his request might only fan the evil love, and turn him from the good motion in his mind. She said: "Yes, sir," and stood waiting. He did not speak.

"I do not know where to find it," she said.

"I am going to tell you," he replied, but seemed to hesitate.

"I will not touch a single thing beside," said Dawtie.

He believed her, and at once proceeded:

"Take my bunch of keys from the hook behind me. There is the key of the closet door!—and there, the key of all the bunch that looks the commonest, but is in reality the most cunningly devised, is the key of the cabinet in which I keep it!"

Then he told her where, behind a little book-case, which moved from the wall on hinges, she would find the cabinet, and in what part of it the cup, wrapped in a piece of silk that had once been a sleeve, worn by Mme. de Genlis—which did not make Dawtie much wiser.

She went, found the chalice, and brought it where the laird lay straining his ears, and waiting for it as a man at the point of death might await the sacramental cup from absolving priest.

His hands trembled as he took it; for they were the hands of a lover—strange as that love was, which not merely looked for no return, but desired to give neither pleasure nor good to the thing loved! It was no love of the merely dead, but a love of the unliving! He pressed the thing to his bosom; then, as if rebuked by the presence of Dawtie, put it a little from him, and began to pore over every stone, every repoussé figure between, and every engraved ornament around the gems, each of which he knew, by shape, order, quality of color, better than ever face of wife or child. But soon his hands sunk on the counterpane of silk patchwork, and he lay still, grasping tight the precious thing.

He woke with a start and a cry, to find it safe in both his hands.

"Ugh!" he said; "I thought some one had me by the throat! You didn't try to take the cup from me—did you, Dawtie?"

"No, sir," answered Dawtie; "I would not care to take it out of your hand, but I should be glad to take it out of your heart!"

"If they would only bury it with me!" he murmured, heedless of her words.

"Oh, sir! Would you have it burning your heart to all eternity? Give it up, sir, and take the treasure thief never stole."

"Yes, Dawtie, yes! That is the true treasure!"

"And to get it we must sell all that we have!"

"He gives and withholds as He sees fit."

"Then, when you go down into the blackness, longing for the cup you will never see more, you will complain of God that he would not give you strength to fling it from you?"

He hugged the chalice.

"Fling it from me!" he cried, fiercely. "Girl, who are you to torment me before my time!"

"Tell me, sir," persisted Dawtie, "why does the apostle cry, 'Awake thou that sleepest!' if they couldn't move?"

"No one can move without God."

"Therefore, seeing every one can move, it must be God giving him the power to do what he requires of him; and we are fearfully to blame not using the strength God gives us!"

"I can not bear the strain of thinking!" gasped the laird.

"Then give up thinking, and do the thing! Shall I take it for you?"

She put out her hand as she spoke.

"No! no!" he cried, grasping the cup tighter. "You shall not touch it! You would give it to the earl! I know you! Saints hate what is beautiful!"

"I like better to look at things in my Father's hand than in my own!"

"You want to see my cup—it is my cup!—in the hands of that spendthrift fool, Lord Borland!"

"It is in the Father's hand, whoever has it!"

"Hold your tongue, Dawtie, or I will cry out and wake the house!"

"They will think you out of your mind, and come and take the cup from you! Do let me put it away; then you will go to sleep."

"I will not; I can not trust you with it! You have destroyed my confidence in you! I may fall asleep, but if your hand come within a foot of the cup, it will wake me! I know it will! I shall sleep with my heart in the cup, and the least touch will wake me!"

"I wish you would let Andrew Ingram come and see you, sir!"

"What's the matter with him?"

"Nothing's the matter with him, sir; but he helps everybody to do what

295

is right."

"Conceited rascal! Do you take me for a maniac that you talk such foolery?"

His look was so wild, his old blue faded eyes gleamed with such a light of mingled fear and determination, that Dawtie was almost sorry she had spoken. With trembling hands he drew the cup within the bed-clothes, and lay still. If the morning would but come, and bring George Crawford! He would restore the cup to its place, or hide it where he should know it safe and not far from him!

Dawtie sat motionless, and the old man fell into another feverish doze. She dared not stir lest he should start away to defend his idol. She sat like an image, moving only her eyes.

"What are you about, Dawtie?" he said at length. "You are after some mischief, you are so quiet!"

"I was telling God how good you would be if he could get you to give up your odds and ends, and take Him instead."

"How dared you say such a thing, sitting there by my side! Are you to say to Him that any sinner would be good, if He would only do so and so with him! Tremble, girl, at the vengeance of the Almighty!"

"We are told to make prayers and intercessions for all men, and I was saying what I could for you." The laird was silent, and the rest of the night passed quietly.

His first words in the morning were:

"Go and tell your mistress I want her."

When his daughter came, he told her to send for George Crawford. He was worse, he said, and wanted to see him.

Alexa thought it best to send Dawtie with the message by the next train. Dawtie did not relish the mission, for she had no faith in Crawford, and did not like his influence on her master. Not the less when she reached his hotel, she insisted on seeing him and giving her message in person; which done, she made haste for the first train back: they could not do well without her! When she arrived, there was Mr. Crawford already on the platform! She set out as fast as she could, but she had not got further than half-way when he overtook her in a fly, and insisted she should get in.

CHAPTER XXVI. GEORGE CRAWFORD AND DAWTIE.

"What is the matter with your master?" he asked.

"God knows, sir."

"What is the use of telling me that? I want you to tell me what you know."

"I don't know anything, sir."

"What do you think then?"

"I should think old age had something to do with it, sir."

"Likely enough, but you know more than that!"

"I shouldn't wonder, sir, if he were troubled in his mind."

"What makes you think so?"

"It is reasonable to think so, sir. He knows he must die before long, and it is dreadful to leave everything you care for, and go where there is nothing you care for!"

"How do you know there is nothing he would care for?"

"What is there, sir, he would be likely to care for?"

"There is his wife. He was fond of her, I suppose, and you pious people fancy you will see each other again."

"The thought of seeing her would give him little comfort, I am afraid, in parting with the things he has here. He believes a little somehow—I can't understand how."

"What does he believe?"

"He believes a little—he is not sure—that what a man soweth he shall also reap."

"How do you know what he is or is not sure of? It can't be a matter of interest to you?"

"Those that come of one Father must have interest in one another."

"How am I to tell we come of one Father—as you call Him? I like to have a thing proved before I believe it. I know neither where I came from, nor where I am going; how then can I know that we come from the same father?"

"I don't know how you're to know it, sir. I take it for granted, and find it good. But there is one thing I am sure of."

"What is that?"

"That if you were my master's friend you would not rest till you got him to do what was right before he died."

"I will not be father-confessor to any man. I have enough to do with myself. A good worthy old man like the laird must know better than any other what he ought to do."

"There is no doubt of that, sir."

"What do you want then?"

"To get him to do it. That he knows, is what makes it so miserable. If he did not know he would not be to blame. He knows what it is and won't do it, and that makes him wretched—as it ought, thank God!"

"You're a nice Christian. Thanking God for making a man miserable. Well."

"Yes," answered Dawtie.

George thought a little.

"What would you have me persuade him to?" he asked, for he might hear something it would be useful to know. But Dawtie had no right and no inclination to tell him what she knew.

"I only wish you would persuade him to do what he knows he ought to do," she replied.

CHAPTER XXVII. THE WATCH.

George stayed with the laird a good while, and held a long, broken talk with him. When he went Alexa came. She thought her father seemed happier. George had put the cup away for him. Alexa sat with him that night. She knew nothing of such a precious thing being in the house—in the room with them.

In the middle of the night, as she was arranging his pillows, the laird drew from under the bed-clothes, and held up to her, flashing in the light of the one candle, the jeweled watch. She stared. The old man was pleased at her surprise and evident admiration. She held out her hand for it. He gave it her.

"That watch," he said, "is believed to have belonged to Ninon de l'Enclos. It may, but I doubt it myself. It is well known she never took presents from her admirers, and she was too poor to have bought such a thing. Mme. de Maintenon, however, or some one of her lady-friends, might have given it her. It will be yours one day—that is, if you marry the man I should like you to marry."

"Dear father, do not talk of marrying. I have enough with you," cried Alexa, and felt as if she hated George.

"Unfortunately, you can not have me always," returned her father. "I will say nothing more now, but I desire you to consider what I have said."

Alexa put the watch in his hand.

"I trust you do not suppose," she said, "that a house full of things like that would make any difference."

He looked up at her sharply. A house full—what did she know? It silenced him, and he lay thinking. Surely the delight of lovely things must be in every woman's heart. Was not the passion, developed or undeveloped, universal? Could a child of his not care for such things?

"Ah," he said to himself, "she takes after her mother."

A wall seemed to rise between him and his daughter. Alas! alas! the things he loved and must one day yield would not be cherished by her. No tender regard would hover around them when he was gone. She would be no protecting divinity to them. God in heaven! she might—she would—he was sure she would sell them.

It seems the sole possible comfort of avarice, as it passes empty and hungry into the empty regions—that the things it can no more see with eyes or handle with hands will yet be together somewhere. Hence the rich leave to the rich, avoiding the man who most needs, or would best use their money. Is there a lurking notion in the man of much goods, I wonder, that, in the still watches of the night, when men sleep, he will return to look on what he leaves behind him? Does he forget the torture of seeing it at the command, in the enjoyment of another—his will concerning this thing or that but a mockery? Does he know that he who then holds them will not be able to conceive of their having been or ever being another's as now they are his?

As Alexa sat in the dim light by her brooding father she loathed the shining thing he had again drawn under the bed-clothes—shrunk from it as from a manacle the devil had tried to slip on her wrist. The judicial assumption of society suddenly appeared in the emptiness of its arrogance. Marriage for the sake of things. Was she not a live soul, made for better than that She was ashamed of the innocent pleasure the glittering toy had given her.

The laird cast now and then a glance at her face, and sighed. He gathered from it the conviction that she would be a cruel step-mother to his children, her mercy that of a loveless non-collector. It should not be. He would do better for them than that. He loved his daughter, but needed not therefore sacrifice his last hopes where the sacrifice would meet with no acceptance. House and land should be hers, but not his jewels; not the contents of his closet.

CHAPTER XXVIII. THE WILL.

George came again to see him the next day, and had again a long conference with him. The laird told him that he had fully resolved to leave everything to his daughter, personal as well as real, on the one condition that she should marry her cousin; if she would not, then the contents of his closet, with his library, and certain articles specified, should pass to Crawford.

"And you must take care," he said, "if my death should come suddenly, that anything valuable in this room be carried into the closet before it is sealed up."

Shrinking as he did from the idea of death, the old man was yet able, in the interest of his possessions, to talk of it! It was as if he thought the sole consolation that, in the loss of their owner, his things could have, was the continuance of their intercourse with each other in the heaven of his Mammon-besotted imagination.

George responded heartily, showing a gratitude more genuine than fine: every virtue partakes of the ground in which it is grown. He assured the laird that, valuable as was in itself his contingent gift, which no man could appreciate more than he, it would be far more valuable to him if it sealed his adoption as his son-in-law. He would rather owe the possession of the wonderful collection to the daughter than to the father! In either case the precious property would be held as for him, each thing as carefully tended as by the laird's own eye and hand!

Whether it would at the moment have comforted the dying man to be assured, as George might have him, that there would be nothing left of him to grieve at the loss of his idols—nothing left of him but a memory, to last so long as George and Alexa and one or two more should remain unburied, I can not tell. It was in any case a dreary outlook for him. Hope and faith and almost love had been sucked from his life by "the hindering knot-grass" which had spread its white bloodless roots in all directions through soul and heart and mind, exhausting and choking in them everything of divinest origin. The weeds in George's heart were of another kind, and better nor worse in themselves; the misery was that neither of them was endeavoring to root them out. The thief who is trying to be better is ages ahead of the most honorable man who is making no such effort. The one is alive; the other is dead and on the way to corruption.

They treated themselves to a gaze together on the cup and the watch; then George went to give directions to the laird's lawyer for the drawing up of his new will.

The next day it was brought, read, signed by the laird, and his signature duly witnessed.

Dawtie being on the spot was made one of the witnesses. The laird trembled lest her fanaticism should break out in appeal to the lawyer concerning the cup; he could not understand that the cup was nothing to her; that she did not imagine herself a setter right of wrongs, but knew herself her neighbor's keeper, one that had to deliver his soul from death! Had the cup come into her possession, she would have sent it back to the owner, but it was not worth her care that the Earl of Borland should cast his eyes when he would upon a jewel in a cabinet!

Dawtie was very white as he signed his name. Where the others saw but a legal ceremony, she feared her loved master was assigning his soul to the devil, as she had read of Dr. Faustus in the old ballad. He was gliding away into the dark, and no one to whom he had done a good turn with the Mammon of unrighteousness, was waiting to receive him into an everlasting habitation! She had and she needed no special cause to love her master, any more than to love the chickens and the calves; she loved because something that could be loved was there present to her; but he had always spoken kindly to her, and been pleased with her endeavor to serve him; and now he was going where she could do nothing for him!—except pray, as her heart and Andrew had taught her, knowing that "all live unto Him!" But alas! what were prayers where the man would not take the things prayed for! Nevertheless all things were possible with God, and she would pray for him!

It was also with white face, and it was with trembling hand that she signed her own name, for she felt as if giving him a push down the icy slope into the abyss.

But when the thing was done, the old man went quietly to sleep, and dreamed of a radiant jewel, glorious as he had never seen jewel, ever within yet ever eluding his grasp.

CHAPTER XXIX. THE SANGREAL.

The next day he seemed better, and Alexa began to hope again. But in the afternoon his pulse began to sink, and when Crawford came he could welcome him only with a smile and a vain effort to put out his hand. George bent down to him. The others, at a sign from his eyes, left the room.

"I can't find it, George!" he whispered.

"I put it away for you last night, you remember!" answered George.

"Oh, no, you didn't! I had it in my hand a minute ago! But I fell into a doze, and it is gone! George, get it!—get it for me, or I shall go mad!" George went and brought it him.

"Thank you! thank you! Now I remember! I thought I was in hell, and they took it from me!"

"Don't you be afraid, sir! Fall asleep when you feel inclined. I will keep my eye on the cup."

"You will not go away?"

"No; I will stay as long as you like; there is nothing to take me away. If I had thought you would be worse, I would not have gone last night."

"I'm not worse! What put that in your head? Don't you hear me speaking better? I've thought about it, George, and am convinced the cup is a talisman! I am better all the time I hold it! It was because I let you put it away that I was worse last night—for no other reason. If it were not a talisman, how else could it have so nestled itself into my heart! I feel better, always, the moment I take it in my hand! There is something more than common about that chalice! George, what if it should be the Holy Grail!"

He said it with bated breath, and a great white awe upon his countenance. His eyes were shining; his breath came and went fast. Slowly his aged cheeks flushed with two bright spots. He looked as if the joy of his life was come.

"What if it should be the Holy Grail!" he repeated, and fell asleep with the words on his lips.

As the evening deepened into night, he woke. Crawford was sitting beside him. A change had come over him. He stared at George as if he could not make him out, closed his eyes, opened them, stared, and again closed them. He seemed to think he was there for no good.

"Would you like me to call Alexa?" said George.

"Call Dawtie; call Dawtie!" he replied.

George rose to go and call her.

"Beware of her!" said the laird, with glazy eyes, "Beware of Dawtie!"

"How?" asked George.

"Beware of her," he repeated. "If she can get the cup, she will! She would take it from me now, if she dared! She will steal it yet! Call Dawtie; call Dawtie!"

Alexa was in the drawing-room, on the other side of the hall. George went and told her that her father wanted Dawtie.

"I will find her," she said, and rose, but turned and asked:

"How does he seem now?"

"Rather worse," George answered.

"Are you going to be with him through the night?"

"I am; he insists on my staying with him," replied George, almost apologetically.

"Then," she returned, "you must have some supper. We will go down, and send up Dawtie."

He followed her to the kitchen. Dawtie was not there, but her mistress found her.

When she entered her master's room, he lay motionless, "and white with

306

the whiteness of what is dead."

She got brandy, and made him swallow some. As soon as he recovered a little, he began to talk wildly.

"Oh, Agnes!" he cried, "do not leave me. I'm not a bad man! I'm not what Dawtie calls me. I believe in the atonement; I put no trust in myself; my righteousness is as filthy rags. Take me with you. I will go with you. There! Slip that under your white robe—washed in the blood of the Lamb. That will hide it—with the rest of my sins! The unbelieving husband is sanctified by the believing wife. Take it; take it; I should be lost in heaven without it! I can't see what I've got on, but it must be the robe of His righteousness, for I have none of my own! What should I be without it! It's all I've got! I couldn't bring away a single thing besides—and it's so cold to have but one thing on—I mean one thing in your hands! Do you say they will make me sell it? That would be worse than coming without it!"

He was talking to his wife!—persuading her to smuggle the cup into heaven! Dawtie went on her knees behind the curtain, and began to pray for him all she could. But something seemed stopping her, and making her prayer come only from her lips.

"Ah," said the voice of her master, "I thought so! How could I go up, and you praying against me like that! Cup or no cup, the thing was impossible!"

Dawtie opened her eyes—and there he was, holding back the curtain and looking round the edge of it with a face of eagerness, effort, and hate, as of one struggling to go, and unable to break away.

She rose to her feet.

"You are a fiend!" he cried. "I will go with Agnes!" He gave a cry, and ceased, and all was still. They heard the cry in the kitchen, and came running up.

They found Dawtie bending over her master, with a scared face. He seemed to have struck her, for one cheek was marked with red streaks across its whiteness.

"The Grail! the Holy Grail!" he cried. "I found it! I was bringing it home! She took it from me! She wants it to—"

His jaw fell, and he was dead. Alexa threw herself beside the body. George would have raised her, but she resisted, and lay motionless. He stood then behind her, watching an opportunity to get the cup from under the bed-clothes, that he might put it in the closet.

He ordered Dawtie to fetch water for her mistress; but Alexa told her she did not want any. Once and again George tried to raise her, and get his hand under the bed-clothes to feel for the cup.

"He is not dead!" cried Alexa; "he moved!"

"Get some brandy," said George.

She rose, and went to the table for the brandy. George, with the pretense of feeling the dead man's heart, threw back the clothes. He could find no cup. It had got further down! He would wait!

Alexa lifted her father's head on her arm, but it was plain that brandy could not help. She went and sat on a chair away from the bed, hopeless and exhausted.

George lifted the clothes from the foot of the bed, then from the further side, and then from the nearer, without attracting her attention. The cup was nowhere to be seen! He put his hand under the body, but the cup was not there! He had to leave the room that Dawtie and Meg might prepare it for burial. Alexa went to her chamber.

A moment after, George returned, called Meg to the door, and said:

"There must be a brass cup in the bed somewhere! I brought it to amuse him. He was fond of odd things, you know! If you should find it—"

"I will take care of it," answered Meg, and turned from him curtly.

George felt he had not a friend in the house, and that he must leave things as they were! The door of the closet was locked, and he could not go again to the death-chamber to take the laird's keys from the head of the bed! He knew that the two women would not let him. It had been an oversight not to secure them! He was glad the watch was safe: that he had put in the closet before!—but it mattered little when the cup was missing! He went to the stable, got out his horse, and rode home in the still gray of a midsummer night.

The stillness and the night seemed thinking to each other. George had little imagination, but what he had woke in him now as he rode slowly along. Step by step the old man seemed following him, on silent church-yard feet, through the eerie whiteness of the night. There was neither cloud nor moon, only stars above and around, and a great cold crack in the north-east. He was crying after him, in a voice he could not make him hear! Was he not straggling to warn him not to come into like condemnation? The voice seemed trying to say, "I know! I know now! I would not believe, but I know now! Give back the cup; give it back!"

George did not allow to himself that there was "anything" there. It was but a vague movement in that commonplace, unmysterious region, his mind! He heard nothing, positively nothing, with his ears—therefore there was nothing! It was indeed somehow as if one were saying the words, but in reality they came only as a thought rising, continually rising, in his mind! It was but a thought-sound, and no speech: "I know now! I know now! Give it back; give the cup back!" He did not ask himself how the thought came; he cast it away as only that insignificant thing, a thought—cast it away none the less that he found himself answering it—"I can't give it back; I can't find it! Where did you put it? You must have taken it with you!"

"What rubbish!" he said to himself ten times, waking up; "of course Dawtie took it! Didn't the poor old fellow warn me to beware of her! Nobody but her was in the room when we ran in, and found him at the point of death! Where did you put it? I can't find it! I can't give it back!"

He went over in his mind all that had taken place. The laird had the cup when he left him to call Dawtie; and when they came, it was nowhere! He was convinced the girl had secured it—in obedience, doubtless, to the instruction of her director, ambitious to do justice, and curry favor by restoring it! But he could do nothing till the will was read! Was it possible Lexy had put it away? No; she had not had the opportunity!

CHAPTER XXX. GEORGE AND THE GOLDEN GOBLET.

With slow-pacing shadows, the hot hours crept athwart the heath, and the house, and the dead, and carried the living with them in their invisible current. There is no tide in time; it is a steady current, not returning. Happy they whom it bears inward to the center of things! Alas, for those whom it carries outward to "the flaming walls of creation!" The poor old laird who, with all his refinement, all his education, all his interest in philology, prosody, history, and reliquial humanity, had become the slave of a goblet, had left it behind him, had faced the empty universe empty-handed, and vanished with a shadow-goblet in his heart; the eyes that gloated over the gems had gone to help the grass to grow. But the will of the dead remained to trouble for a time the living, for it put his daughter in a painful predicament: until Crawford's property was removed from the house, it would give him constant opportunity of prosecuting the suit which Aleza had reason to think he intended to resume, and the thought of which had become to her insupportable.

Great was her astonishment when she learned to what the door in the study led, and what a multitude of curious and valuable things were there of whose presence in the house she had never dreamed. She would gladly have had them for herself; and it pained her to the heart to think of the disappointment of the poor ghost when he saw, if he could see, his treasured hoard emptied out of its hidden and safe abode. For, even if George should magnanimously protest that he did not care for the things enough to claim them, and beg that they might remain where they were, she could not grant his request, for it would be to accept them from him. Had her father left them to her, she would have kept them as carefully as even he could desire— with this difference only, that she would not have shut them up from giving pleasure to others.

She was growing to care more about the truth—gradually coming to see that much she had taken for a more liberal creed, was but the same falsehoods in weaker forms, less repulsive only to a mind indifferent to the paramount claims of God on His child. She saw something of the falseness and folly of attempting to recommend religion as not so difficult, so exclusive, so full of prohibition as our ancestors believed it. She saw that, although Andrew might regard some things as freely given which others thought God forbade, yet he insisted on what was infinitely higher and more than the abandonment of everything pleasant—the abnegation, namely, of the very self, and the reception of God instead. She had hitherto been, with all her supposed progress, only a recipient of the traditions of the elders! There must be a deeper something—the real religion! She did not yet see that the will of God lay in another direction altogether than the heartiest reception of dogma!—that God was too great and too generous to care about anything except righteousness, and only wanted us to be good children!—that even honesty was but the path toward righteousness, a condition so pure that honesty itself would never more be an object of thought!

She pondered much about her father, and would find herself praying for him, careless of what she had been taught. She could not blind herself to what she knew. He had not been a bad man, as men count badness, but could she in common sense think him a glorified saint, shining in white robes? The polite, kind old man! her own father!—could she, on the other hand, believe him in flames forever? If so, what a religion was that which required her to believe it, and at the same time to rejoice in the Lord always!

She longed for something positive to believe, something into accordance with which she might work her feelings. She was still on the outlook for definite intellectual formulae to hold. Her intercourse with Andrew had as yet failed to open her eyes to the fact that the faith required of us is faith in a person, and not in the truest of statements concerning anything, even concerning him; or to the fact, that faith in the living One, the very essence of it, consists in obedience to Him. A man can obey before he is sure, and except he obey the command he knows to be right, wherever it may come from, he will never be sure. To find the truth, man or woman must be true.

But she much desired another talk with Andrew.

Persuading himself that Alexa's former feeling toward him must in her trouble reassert itself, and confident that he would find her loath to part with her father's wonderful collection, George waited the effect of the will. After the reading of it he had gone away directly, that his presence might not add to the irritation which he concluded, not without reason, it must, even in the midst of her sorrow, cause in her; but at the end of a week he wrote, saying that he felt it his duty, if only in gratitude to his friend, to inform himself as to the attention the valuable things he had left him might require. He assured Alexa that he had done nothing to influence her father in the matter, and much regretted the awkward position in which his will had placed both her and him. At the same time it was not unnatural that he should wish such precious objects to be possessed by one who would care for them as he had himself cared for them. He hoped, therefore, that she would allow him access to her father's rooms. He would not, she might rest assured, intrude himself upon her sorrow, though he would be compelled to ask her before long whether he might hope that her father's wish would have any influence in reviving the favor which had once been the joy of his life.

Alexa saw that if she consented to see him he would take it as a permission to press his claim, and the idea was not to be borne. She wrote him therefore a stiff letter, telling him the house was at his service, but he must excuse herself.

The next morning brought him early to Potlurg. The cause of his haste was his uneasiness about the chalice.

Old Meg opened the door to him, and he followed her straight into the drawing-room. Alexa was there, and far from expecting him. But, annoyed at his appearance as she was, she found his manner and behavior less unpleasant than at any time since his return. He was gentle and self-restrained, assuming no familiarity beyond that of a distant relative, and gave the impression of having come against his will, and only from a sense of duty.

"Did you not have my note?" she asked.

He had hoped, he said, to save her the trouble of writing.

She handed him her father's bunch of keys, and left the room.

George went to the laird's closet, and having spent an hour in it, again sought Alexa. The wonderful watch was in his hand.

"I feel the more pleasure, Alexa," he said, "in begging you to accept this trinket, that it was the last addition to your dear father's collection. I had myself the good fortune to please him with it a few days before his death."

"No, thank you, George," returned Alexa. "It is a beautiful thing—my father showed it me—but I can not take it."

"It was more of you than him I thought when I purchased it, Alexa. You know why I could not offer it you."

"The same reason exists now."

"I am sorry to have to force myself on your attention, but—"

"Dawtie!" cried Alexa.

Dawtie came running.

"Wait a minute, Dawtie. I will speak to you presently," said her mistress.

George rose. He had laid the watch on the table, and seemed to have forgotten it.

"Please take the watch with you," said Alexa.

"Certainly, if you wish it!" he answered.

"And my father's keys, too," she added.

"Will you not be kind enough to take charge of them?"

"I would rather not be accountable for anything under them. No; you must take the keys."

"I can not help regretting," said George, "that your honored father should have thought fit to lay this burden of possession upon me."

Alexa made no answer.

"I comforted myself with the hope that you would feel them as much your own as ever!" he resumed, in a tone of disappointment and dejection.

"I did not know of their existence before I knew they were never to be mine."

"Never, Alexa?"

"Never."

George walked to the door, but there turned, and said:

"By the way, you know that cup your father was so fond of?"

"No."

"Not that gold cup, set with stones?"

"I saw something in his hands once, in bed, that might have been a cup."

"It is a thing of great value—of pure gold, and every stone in it a gem."

"Indeed!" returned Alexa, with marked indifference.

"Yes; it was the work of the famous Benvenuto Cellini, made for Pope Clement the Seventh, for his own communion-chalice. Your father priced it at three thousand pounds. In his last moments, when his mind was wandering, he fancied it the Holy Grail He had it in the bed with him when he died; that I know."

"And it is missing?"

"Perhaps Dawtie could tell us what has become of it. She was with the laird at the last."

Dawtie, who had stood aside to let him pass to the open door, looked up with a flash in her eyes, but said nothing.

"Have you seen the cup, Dawtie?" asked her mistress.

"No, ma'am."

"Do you know it?"

"Very well, ma'am."

"Then you don't know what has become of it?"

"No, ma'am; I know nothing about it."

"Take care, Dawtie," said George. "This is a matter that will have to be searched into."

"When did you last see it, Dawtie?" inquired Alexa.

"The very day my master died, ma'am. He was looking at it, but when he saw I saw him he took it inside the bed-clothes."

"And you have not seen it since?"

"No, ma'am."

"And you do not know where it is?" said George.

"No, sir. How should I?"

"You never touched it?"

"I can not say that, sir; I brought it him from his closet; he sent me for it."

"What do you think may have become of it?"

"I don't know, sir."

"Would you allow me to make a thorough search in the place where it was last seen?" asked George, turning to his cousin.

"By all means. Dawtie, go and help Mr. Crawford to look."

"Please, ma'am, it can't be there. We've had the carpet up, and the floor scrubbed. There's not a hole or a corner we haven't been into—and that yesterday."

"We must find it," said George. "It must be in the house."

"It must, sir," said Dawtie.

But George more than doubted it

"I do believe," he said, "the laird would rather have lost his whole

315

collection."

"Indeed, sir, I think he would."

"Then you have talked to him about it?"

"Yes, I have, sir," answered Dawtie, sorry she had brought out the question.

"And you know the worth of the thing?"

"Yes, sir; that is, I don't know how much it was worth, but I should say pounds and pounds."

"Then, Dawtie, I must ask you again, where is it?"

"I know nothing about it, sir. I wish I did!"

"Why do you wish you did?"

"Because—" began Dawtie, and stopped short; she shrunk from impugning the honesty of the dead man—and in the presence of his daughter.

"It looks a little fishy, don't it, Dawtie? Why not speak straight out? Perhaps you would not mind searching Meg's trunk for me. She may have taken it for a bit of old brass, you know."

"I will answer for my servants, Mr. Crawford," said Alexa. "I will not have old Meg's box searched."

"It is desirable to get rid of any suspicion," replied George.

"I have none," returned Alexa.

George was silent

"I will ask Meg, if you like, sir," said Dawtie; "but I am sure it will be no use. A servant in this house soon learns not to go by the look of things. We don't treat anything here as if we knew all about it."

"When did you see the goblet first?" persisted George.

"Goblet, sir? I thought you were speaking of the gold cup."

316

By goblet Dawtie understood a small iron pot.

"Goblet, or cup, or chalice—whatever you like to call it—I ask how you came to know about it."

"I know very little about it."

"It is plain you know more than you care to tell. If you will not answer me you will have to answer a magistrate."

"Then I will answer a magistrate," said Dawtie, beginning to grow angry.

"You had better answer me, Dawtie. It will be easier for you. What do you know about the cup?"

"I know it was not master's, and is not yours—really and truly."

"What can have put such a lie in your head?"

"If it be a lie, sir, it is told in plain print."

"Where?"

But Dawtie judged it time to stop. She bethought herself that she would not have said so much had she not been angry.

"Sir," she answered, "you have been asking me questions all this time, and I have been answering them; it is your turn to answer me one."

"If I see proper."

"Did my old master tell you the history of that cup?"

"I do not choose to answer the question."

"Very well, sir."

Dawtie turned to leave the room.

"Stop! stop!" cried Crawford; "I have not done with you yet, my girl. You have not told me what you meant when you said the cup did not belong to the laird."

"I do not choose to answer the question," said Dawtie.

"Then you shall answer it to a magistrate."

"I will, sir," she replied, and stood.

Crawford left the room.

He rode home in a rage. Dawtie went about her work with a bright spot on each cheek, indignant at the man's rudeness, but praying God to take her heart in His hand, and cool the fever of it.

The words rose in her mind:

"It must needs be that offenses come, but woe onto that man by whom they come."

She was at once filled with pity for the man who could side with the wrong, and want everything his own way, for, sooner or later, confusion must be his portion; the Lord had said: "There is nothing covered that shall not be revealed, neither hid that shall not be known."

"He needs to be shamed," she said, "but he is thy child; care for him, too."

George felt that he had not borne a dignified part, and knew that his last chance with Alexa was gone. Then he too felt the situation unendurable, and set about removing his property. He wrote to Alexa that he could no longer doubt it her wish to be rid of the collection, and able to use the room. It was desirable also, he said, that a thorough search should be made in those rooms before he placed the matter of the missing cup in the hands of the magistrates.

Dawtie's last words had sufficed to remove any lingering doubt as to what had become of the chalice. It did not occur to him that one so anxious to do the justice of restoration would hardly be capable of telling lies, of defiling her soul that a bit of property might be recovered; he took it for granted that she meant to be liberally rewarded by the earl.

George would have ill understood the distinction Dawtie made—that the body of the cup might belong to him, but the soul of the cup did belong to another; or her assertion that where the soul was there the body ought to be; or her argument that He who had the soul had the right to ransom the body—a reasoning possible to a child-like nature only; she had pondered to find the true law of the case, and this was her conclusion.

George suspected, and grew convinced that Alexa was a party to the abstraction of the cup. She had, he said, begun to share in the extravagant notions of a group of pietists whose leader was that detestable fellow, Ingram. Alexa was attached to Dawtie, and Dawtie was one of them. He believed Alexa would do anything to spite him. To bring trouble on Dawtie would be to punish her mistress, and the pious farmer, too.

CHAPTER XXXI. THE PROSECUTION.

As soon as Crawford had his things away from Potlurg, satisfied the cup was nowhere among them, he made a statement of the case to a magistrate he knew; and so represented it, as the outcome of the hypocrisy of pietism, that the magistrate, hating everything called fanatical, at once granted him a warrant to apprehend Dawtie on the charge of theft.

It was a terrible shock. Alexa cried out with indignation. Dawtie turned white and then red, but uttered never a word.

"Dawtie," said her mistress, "tell me what you know about the cup. You do know something that you have not told me!"

"I do, ma'am, but I will not tell it except I am forced."

"That you are going to be, my poor girl! I am very sorry, for I am perfectly sure you have done nothing you know to be wrong!"

"I have done nothing you or anybody would think wrong, ma'am."

She put on her Sunday frock, and went down to go with the policeman. To her joy she found her mistress at the door, ready to accompany her. They had two miles or more to walk, but that was nothing to either.

Questioned by the magistrate, not unkindly, for her mistress was there, Dawtie told everything—how first she came upon the likeness and history of the cup, and then saw the cup itself in her master's hands.

Crawford told how the laird had warned him against Dawtie, giving him to understand that she had been seized with a passion for the goblet such that she would peril her soul to possess it, and that he dared not let her know where it was.

"Sir," said Dawtie, "he could na hae distrusted me like that, for he gae me his keys, and sent me to fetch the cup when he was ower ill to gang till't."

"If that be true, your worship," said Crawford, "it does not affect the fact that the cup was in the hands of the old man when I left him and she went to him, and from that moment it has not been seen."

"Did he have it when you went to him?" asked the magistrate.

"I didna see't, sir. He was in a kind o' faint when I got up."

Crawford said that, hearing a cry, he ran up again, and found the old man at the point of death, with just strength to cry out before he died, that Dawtie had taken the cup from him. Dawtie was leaning over him, but he had not imagined the accusation more than the delirious fancy of a dying man, till it appeared that the cup was not to be found.

The magistrate made out Dawtie's commitment for trial. He remarked that she might have been misled by a false notion of duty: he had been informed that she belonged to a sect claiming the right to think for themselves on the profoundest mysteries—and here was the result! There was not a man in Scotland less capable of knowing what any woman was thinking, or more incapable of doubting his own insight.

Doubtless, he went on, she had superstitiously regarded the cup as exercising a Satanic influence on the mind of her master; but even if she confessed it now, he must make an example of one whose fanaticism would set wrong right after the notions of an illiterate sect, and not according to the laws of the land. He just send the case to be tried by a jury! If she convinced the twelve men composing that jury, of the innocence she protested, she would then be a free woman.

Dawtie stood very white all the time he was speaking, and her lips every now and then quivered as if she were going to cry, but she did not. Alexa offered bail, but his worship would not accept it: his righteous soul was too indignant. She went to Dawtie and kissed her, and together they followed the policeman to the door, where Dawtie was to get into a spring-cart with him, and be driven to the county town, there to lie waiting the assizes.

The bad news had spread so fast that as they came out, up came Andrew. At sight of him Dawtie gently laughed, like a pleased child. The policeman, who, like many present, had been prejudiced by her looks in her favor, dropped behind, and she walked between her mistress and Andrew to the cart.

"Dawtie!" said Andrew.

"Oh, Andrew! has God forgotten me?" she returned, stopping short.

"For God to forget," answered Andrew, "would be not to be God any longer!"

"But here I am on my road til a prison, Andrew! I didna think He would hae latten them do't!"

"A bairn micht jist as weel say, whan its nurse lays't intil its cradle, and says: 'Noo, lie still!' 'Mammy, I didna think ye would hae latten her do't!' He's a' aboot ye and in ye, Dawtie, and this is come to ye jist to lat ye ken 'at He is. He raised ye up jist to spen' His glory upo'! I say, Dawtie, did Jesus Christ deserve what He got?"

"No ae bit, Andrew! What for should ye speir sic a thing?"

"Then do ye think God hae forgotten Him?"

"May be He thoucht it jist for a minute!"

"Well, ye hae thoucht jist for a minute, and ye maun think it nae mair."

"But God couldna forget Him, An'rew: He got it a' for doin' His will!"

"Evil may come upon as from other causes than doing the will of God; but from whatever cause it comes, the thing we have to see to is, that through it all we do the will of God!"

"What's His will noo, An'rew?"

"That ye tak it quaietly. Shall not the Father do wi' His ain child what He will! Can He no shift it frae the tae airm to the tither, but the bairn maun girn? He has ye, Dawtie! It's a' richt!"

"Though He slay me, yet will I trust in Him!" said Dawtie.

She raised her head. The color had come back to her face; her lips had ceased to tremble; she stepped on steadily to where, a few yards from the door, the spring-cart was waiting her. She bade her mistress good-bye, then turned to Andrew and said:

"Good-bye, An'rew! I am not afraid."

"I am going with you, Dawtie," said Andrew.

"No, sir, you can't do that!" said the policeman; "at least you can't go in the trap!"

"No, no, Andrew!" cried Dawtie. "I would rather go alone. I am quite happy now. God will do with me as He pleases!"

"I am going with you," said Alexa, "if the policeman will let me."

"Oh, yes, ma'am! A lady's different!—I've got to account for the prisoner you see, sir!"

"I don't think you should, ma'am," said Dawtie. "It's a long way!"

"I am going," returned her mistress, decisively.

"God bless you, ma'am!" said Andrew.

Alexa had heard what he said to Dawtie. A new light had broken upon her. "God is like that, is He?" she said to herself. "You can go close up to Him whenever you like?"

CHAPTER XXXII. A TALK AT POTLURG.

It would be three weeks before the assizes came. The house of Potlurg was searched by the police from garret to cellar, but in vain; the cup was not found.

As soon as they gave up searching, Alexa had the old door of the laird's closet, discernible enough on the inside, reopened, and the room cleaned. Almost unfurnished as it was, she made of it her sitting-parlor. But often her work or her book would lie on her lap, and she would find herself praying for the dear father for whom she could do nothing else now, but for whom she might have done so much, had she been like Dawtie. Her servant had cared for her father more than she!

As she sat there one morning alone, brooding a little, thinking a little, reading a little, and praying through it all, Meg appeared, and said Maister Andrew wanted to see her.

He had called more than once to inquire after Dawtie, but had not before asked to see her mistress.

Alexa felt herself unaccountably agitated. When he walked into the room, however, she was able to receive him quietly. He came, he said, to ask when she had seen Dawtie. He would have gone himself to see her, but his father was ailing, and he had double work to do. Besides, she did not seem willing to see him! Alexa told him she had been with her the day before, and had found her a little pale, and, she feared, rather troubled in her mind. She said she would trust God to the last, but confessed herself assailed by doubts.

"I said to her," continued Alexa, "'Be sure, Dawtie, God will make your innocence known one day!' She answered: 'Of course, ma'am, there is nothing hidden that shall not be known; but I am not impatient about that. The Jews to this day think Jesus an impostor!' 'But surely,' said I, 'you care that people should understand you are no thief, Dawtie!' 'Yes, I do,' she answered; 'all I say is, that is does not trouble me. I want only to be downright sure that God is looking after me all the time. I am willing to sit in prison till I die, if He pleases.' 'God can't please that!' I said. 'If He does not care to take me out, I do not care to go out,' said Dawtie. 'It's not that I'm good; it's only that I don't care for anything He doesn't care for. What would it be that all men acquitted me, if God did not trouble Himself about His children!'"

"You see, ma'am, it comes to this," said Andrew: "it is God Dawtie cares about, not herself! If God is all right, Dawtie is all right. The if sometimes takes one shape, sometimes another, but the fear is the same—and the very fear is faith. Sometimes the fear is that there may be no God, and that you might call a fear for herself; but when Dawtie fears lest God should not be caring for her, that is a fear for God; for if God did not care for His creature, He would be no true God!"

"Then He could not exist!"

"True; and so you are back on the other fear!"

"What would you have said to her, Mr. Ingram?"

"I would have reminded her that Jesus was perfectly content with His Father; that He knew what was coming on Himself, and never doubted Him—just gloried that His Father was what He knew Him to be."

"I see! But what did you mean when you said that Dawtie's very fear was faith?"

"Think, ma'am: people that only care to be saved, that is, not to be punished for their sins, are anxious only about themselves, not about God and His glory at all. They talk about the glory of God, but they make it consist in pure selfishness! According to them, He seeks everything for Himself; which is dead against the truth of God, a diabolic slander of God. It does not trouble them to believe such things about God; they do not even desire that God should not be like that; they only want to escape Him. They dare not say God will not do this or that, however clear it be that it would not be fair; they are in terror of contradicting the Bible. They make more of the Bible than of God, and so fail to find the truth of the Bible, and accept things concerning God which are not in the Bible, and are the greatest of insults to Him! Dawtie never thinks about saving her soul; she has no fear about her soul; she is only anxious about God and His glory. How the doubts come, God knows; but if she did not love God, they would not be there. Jesus says God will speedily avenge His elect—those that cry day and night to Him—which I take to mean that He will soon save them from all such miseries. Free Dawtie from unsureness about God, and she has no fear left. All is well, in the prison or on the throne of God, if He only be what she thinks He is. If any one say that doubt can not coexist with faith, I answer, it can with love, and love is the greater of the two, yea, is the very heart of faith itself. God's children are not yet God's men and women. The God that many people believe in, claiming to be the religious because they believe in Him, is a God not worth believing in, a God that ought not to be believed in. The life given by such a God would be a life not worth living, even if He made His votaries as happy as they would choose to be. A God like that could not make a woman like Dawtie anxious about Him! If God be not each as Jesus, what good would the proving of her innocence be to Dawtie! A mighty thing indeed that the world should confess she was not a thief! But to know that there is a perfect God, one for us to love with all the power of love of which we feel we are capable, is worth going out of existence for; while to know that God himself, must make every throb of consciousness a divine ecstasy!"

Andrew's heart was full, and out of its fullness he spoke. Never before had he been able in the presence of Alexa to speak as he felt. Never before had he had any impulse to speak as now. As soon would he have gone to sow seed on a bare rock, as words of spirit and life in her ears!

"I am beginning to understand you," she said. "Will you forgive me? I have been very self-confident and conceited! What a mercy things are not as I thought they were—thought they ought to be!"

"And the glory of the Lord shall cover the earth as the waters cover the sea!" said Andrew. "And men's hearts shall be full of bliss, because they have found their Father, and He is what He is, and they are going home to Him."

He rose.

"You will come and see me again soon—will you not?" she said.

326

"As often as you please, ma'am; I am your servant."

"Then come to-morrow."

He went on the morrow, and the next day, and the day after—almost every day while Dawtie was waiting her trial.

Almost every morning Alexa went by train to see Dawtie; and the news she brought, Andrew would carry to the girl's parents. Dawtie continued unwilling to see Andrew: he had had trouble enough with her already, she said; but Andrew could not quite understand her refusal.

CHAPTER XXXIII. A GREAT OFFERING.

Two days before the assizes, Andrew was with Alexa in her parlor. It was a cool autumn evening, and she proposed they should go on the heath, which came close up to the back of the house.

When they reached the top of the hill, a cold wind was blowing, and Andrew, full of care for old and young, man and woman, made Alexa draw her shawl closer about her throat, where, with his rough, plow-man hands, he pinned it for her. She saw, felt, and noted his hands; a pitying admiration, of which only the pity was foolish, woke in her; and ere she knew, she was looking up in his face with such a light in her eyes that Andrew found himself embarrassed, and let his fall. Moved by that sense of class-superiority which has no place in the kingdom of heaven, she attributed his modesty to self-depreciation, and the conviction rose in her, which has often risen in such as she, that there is a magnanimity demanding the sacrifice, not merely of conventional dignity, but of conventional propriety. She felt that a great lady, to be more than great, must stoop; that it was her part to make the approach which, between equals, was the part of the man; the patroness must do what the woman might not. This man was worthy of any woman; and he should not, because of the humility that dared not presume, fail of what he deserved!

"Andrew," she said, "I am going to do an unusual thing, but you are not like other men, and will not misunderstand! I know you now—know you as far above other men as the clouds are above this heath!"

"Oh, no, no, ma'am!" protested Andrew.

"Hear me out, Andrew," she interrupted—then paused a little.

"Tell me," she resumed, "ought we not to love best the best we know?"

"Surely, ma'am!" he answered, uncomfortable, but not anticipating what was on the way.

"Andrew, you are the best I know! I have said it! I do not care what the world thinks; you are more to me than all the worlds! If you will take me, I am yours."

She looked him in the face with the feeling that she had done a brave and a right thing.

Andrew stood stock-still.

"Me, ma'am!" he gasped, and grew pale—then red as a foggy sun. But he made scarcely a moment's pause.

"It's a God-like thing you have done, ma'am!" he said. "But I can not make the return it deserves. From the heart of my heart I thank you. I can say no more."

His voice trembled. She heard a stifled sob. He had turned away to conceal his emotion.

And now came greatness indeed to the front. Instead of drawing herself up with the bitter pride of a woman whose best is scorned, Alexa behaved divinely. She went close to Andrew, laid her hand on his arm, and said:

"Forgive me, Andrew. I made a mistake. I had no right to make it. Do not be grieved, I beg; you are nowise to blame. Let us continue friends!"

"Thank you, ma'am!" said Andrew, in a tone of deepest gratitude; and neither said a word more. They walked side by side back to the house.

Said Alexa to herself:

"I have at least been refused by a man worthy of the honor I did him! I made no mistake in him!"

When they reached the door, she stopped. Andrew took off his hat, and said, holding it in his hand as he spoke:

"Good-night, ma'am! You will send for me if you want me?"

"I will. Good-night!" said Alexa, and went in with a strange weight on her heart.

Shut in her room, she wept sorely, but not bitterly; and the next day old

Meg, at least, saw no change in her.

Said Andrew to himself:

"I will be her servant always."

He was humbled, not uplifted.

CHAPTER XXXIV. ANOTHER OFFERING.

The next evening, that before the trial, Andrew presented himself at the prison, and was admitted. Dawtie came to meet him, held out her hand, and said:

"Thank you, Andrew!"

"How are you, Dawtie?"

"Well enough, Andrew!"

"God is with us, Dawtie."

"Are you sure, Andrew?"

"Dawtie, I can not see God's eyes looking at me, but I am ready to do what He wants me to do, and so I feel He is with me."

"Oh, Andrew, I wish I could be sure!"

"Let us take the risk together, Dawtie!"

"What risk, Andrew?"

"The risk that makes you not sure, Dawtie—the risk that is at once the worst and the least—the risk that our hope should be in vain, and there is no God. But, Dawtie, there is that in my heart that cries Christ did die, and did rise again, and God is doing His best. His perfect love is our perfect safety. It is hard upon Him that His own children will not trust Him!"

"If He would but show Himself!"

"The sight of Him now would make us believe in Him without knowing Him; and what kind of faith would that be for Him or for us! We should be bad children, taking Him for a weak parent! We must know Him! When we do, there will be no fear, no doubt. We shall run straight home! Dawtie, shall we go together?"

"Yes, surely, Andrew! God knows I try. I'm ready to do whatever you tell me, Andrew!"

"No, Dawtie! You must never do what I tell you, except you think it right."

"Yes, I know that. But I am sure I should think it right!"

"We've been of one mind for a long time now, Dawtie!"

"Sin' lang afore I had ony min' o' my ain!" responded Dawtie, turning to her vernacular.

"Then let us be of one heart too, Dawtie!"

She was so accustomed to hear Andrew speak in figures, that sometimes she looked through and beyond his words.

She did so now, and seeing nothing, stood perplexed.

"Winna ye, Dawtie?" said Andrew, holding out his hands.

"I dinna freely un'erstan' ye, An'rew."

"Ye h'avenly idiot," cried Andrew. "Wull ye be my wife, or wull ye no?"

Dawtie threw her shapely arms above her head—straight up, her head fell back, and she seemed to gaze into the unseen. Then she gave a gasp, her arms dropped to her sides, and she would have fallen had not Andrew taken her.

"Andrew! Andrew!" she sighed, and was still in his arms.

"Winna ye, Dawtie?" he whispered.

"Wait," she murmured; "wait."

"I winna wait, Dawtie."

"Wait till ye hear what they'll say the morn."

"Dawtie, I'm ashamed o' ye. What care I, an' what daur ye care what they say. Are ye no the Lord's clean yowie? Gien ye care for what ony man

332

thinks o' ye but the Lord himsel', ye're no a' His. Gien ye care for what I think o' ye, ither-like nor what He thinks, ye're no sae His as I maun hae ye afore we pairt company—which, please God, 'ill be on the ither side o' eternity."

"But, An'rew, it winna do to say o' yer father's son 'at he took his wife frae the jail."

"'Deed they s' say naething ither! What ither cam I for? Would ye hae me ashamed o' ane o' God's elec'—a lady o' the Lord's ain coort?"

"Eh, but I'm feart it's a' the compassion o' yer hert, sir. Ye wad fain mak' up to me for the disgrace. Ye could weel do wantin' me."

"I winna say," returned Andrew, "that I couldna live wantin' ye, for that wad be to say I wasna worth offerin' ye, and it would be to deny Him 'at made you and me for ane anither, but I wad have a some sair time! I'll jist speak to the minister to be ready the minute the Lord opens yer prison-door."

The same moment in came the governor with his wife; they were much interested in Dawtie.

"Sir, and ma'am," said Andrew, "will you please witness that this woman is my wife?"

"It's Maister Andrew Ingram o' the Knowe," said Dawtie. "He wants me to merry him."

"I want her to go before the court as my wife," said Andrew. "She would have me wait till the jury said this or that. The jury give me my wife. As if I didn't know her."

"You won't have him, I see," said Mrs. Innes, turning to Dawtie.

"Hae him!" cried Dawtie, "I wad hae him gien there war but the heid o' him."

"Then you are husband and wife," said the governor; "only you should have the thing done properly by the minister—afterward."

"I'll see to that, sir," answered Andrew.

"Come, wife," said the governor, "we must let them have a few minutes alone together."

"There," said Andrew, when the door closed, "ye're my wife, noo, Dawtie. Lat them acquit ye or condemn ye, it's you an' me, noo, whatever come!"

Dawtie broke into a flood of tears—an experience all but new to her—and found it did her good. She smiled as she wiped her eyes, and said:

"Weel, An'rew, gien the Lord hasna appeart in His ain likeness to deliver me, He's done the next best thing."

"Dawtie," answered Andrew, "the Lord never does the next best. The thing He does is always better than the thing He does not."

"Lat me think, an' I'll try to un'erstan'," said Dawtie, but Andrew went on.

"The best thing, whan a body's no ready for 't, would be the warst to gie him—or ony gait no the thing for the Father o' lichts to gie. Shortbreid micht be waur for a half hungert bairn nor a stane. But the minute it's fit we should look upo' the face o' the Son o' Man, oor ain God-born brither, we'll see him, Dawtie; we'll see him. Hert canna think what it'll be like. And noo, Dawtie, wull ye tell me what for ye wouldna lat me come and see ye afore?"

"I wull, An'rew; I was nae suner left to mysel' i' the prison than I faun' mysel' thinkin' aboot you—you first, and no the Lord. I said to mysel', 'This is awfu'. I'm leanin' upo' An'rew, and no upo' the First and the Last.' I saw that that was to brak awa' frae Him that was nearest me, and trust ane that was farther awa'—which wasna i' the holy rizzon o' things. Sae I said to mysel' I would meet my fate wi' the Lord alane, and wouldna hae you come 'atween Him and me. Noo ye hae 't, An'rew."

Andrew took her in his arms and said:

"Thank ye, Dawtie. Eh, but I am content And she thought she hadna faith. Good-night, Dawtie. Ye maun gane to yer bed, an' grow stoot in hert for the morn."

334

CHAPTER XXXV. AFTER THE VERDICT.

Through the governor of the jail Andrew obtained permission to stand near the prisoner at the trial. The counsel for the prosecution did all he could, and the counsel for the defense not much—at least Dawtie's friends thought so—and the judge summed up with the greatest impartiality. Dawtie's simplicity and calmness, her confidence devoid of self-assertion, had its influence on the jury, and they gave the uncomfortable verdict of "Not Proven," so that Dawtie was discharged.

Alexa had a carriage ready to take her home. As Dawtie went to it she whispered to her husband:

"Ye hae to tak me wantin' a character, Andrew."

"Jesus went home without a character, and was well received," said Andrew, with a smile. "You'll be over to-night to see the old folk?"

"Yes, Andrew; I'm sure the mistress will let me."

"Don't say a word to her of our marriage, except she has heard, and mentions it. I want to tell her myself. You will find me at the croft when you come, and I will go back with you."

In the evening Dawtie came, and brought the message that her mistress would like to see him.

When he entered the room Alexa rose to meet him. He stopped short.

"I thank you, ma'am," he said, "for your great kindness to Dawtie. We were married in the prison. She is my wife now."

"Married! Your wife?" echoed Alexa, flushing, and drawing back a step.

"I had loved her long, ma'am; and when trouble came her the time came for me to stand by her side."

"You had not spoken to her then—till—"

"Not till last night. I said before the governor of the prison and Mrs. Innes that we were husband and wife. If you please, ma'am, we shall have the proper ceremony as soon as possible."

"I wish I had known," said Alexa—almost to herself, with a troubled smile.

"I wish you had, ma'am," responded Andrew. She raised her face with a look of confidence.

"Will you please to forget, Andrew?"

Nobility had carried the day. She had not one mean thought either of him or the girl.

"To forget is not in man's power, ma'am; but I shall never think a thought you would wish unthought."

She held out her hand to him. They were friends forever.

"Will you be married here, Andrew? The house is at your service," she said.

"Don't you think it ought to be at her father's, ma'am?"

"You are right," said Alexa; and she sat down.

Andrew stood in silence, for he saw she was meditating something. At length she raised her head, and spoke.

"You have been compelled to take the step sooner than you intended—have you not?"

"Yes, ma'am."

"Then you can hardly be so well prepared as you would like to be!"

"We shall manage."

"It will hardly be convenient for your mother, I fear! You have nowhere else to take her—have you?"

"No, ma'am; but my mother loves us both. And," he added, simply,

336

"where there's room for me, there's room for her now!"

"Would you mind if I asked you how your parents take it?"

"They don't say much. You see, ma'am, we are all proud until we learn that we have one Master, and we all are brethren. But they will soon get over it."

When I see a man lifting up those that are beneath him, not pulling down those that are above him, I will believe in his communism. Those who most resent being looked down upon, are in general the readiest to look down upon others. It is not principle, it is not truth, it is themselves they regard. Of all false divinities, Self is the most illogical.

"If God had been the mighty monarch they represent Him," continued Andrew, "He would never have let us come near Him!"

"Did you hear Mr. Rackstraw's sermon on the condescension of God?" asked Alexa.

"The condescension of God, ma'am! There is no such thing. God never condescended, with one Jove-like nod, all his mighty, eternal life! God condescend to His children—their spirits born of His spirit, their hearts the children of His heart! No, ma'am! there never was a falser, uglier word in any lying sermon!"

His eyes flashed and his face shone. Alexa thought she had never seen him look so grand.

"I see!" she answered. "I will never use the word about God again!"

"Thank you, ma'am."

"Why should you thank me?"

"I beg your pardon; I had no right to thank you. But I am so tried with the wicked things said about God by people who think they are speaking to His pleasure and not in his despite, that I am apt to talk foolishly. I don't wonder at God's patience with the wicked, but I do wonder at His patience with the pious!"

"They don't know better!"

"How are they to know better while they are so sure about everything! I would infinitely rather believe in no God at all, than in such a God as they would have me believe in!"

"Oh, but Andrew, I had not a glimmer of what you meant—of what you really objected to, or what you loved! Now, I can not even recall what it was I did not like in your teaching. I think it was that, instead of listening to know what you meant, I was always thinking how to oppose you, or trying to find out by what name you were to be called. One time I thought you were an Arminian, another time a Socinian, then a Swedenborgian, then an Arian! I read a history of the sects of the middle ages, just to see where I could set you down. I told people you did not believe this, and did not believe that, when I knew neither what you believed, nor what you did not believe. I thought I did, but it was all mistake and imagination. When you would not discuss things with me, I thought you were afraid of losing the argument. Now I see that, instead of disputing about opinions, I should have been saying: 'God be merciful to me a sinner!'"

"God be praised!" said Andrew. "Ma'am, you are a free woman! The Father has called you, and you have said: 'Here I am.'"

"I hope so, Andrew, thanks to God by you! But I am forgetting what I wanted to say! Would it not be better—after you are married, I mean—to let Dawtie stay with me awhile?—I will promise you not to work her too hard," she added, with a little laugh.

"I see, ma'am! It is just like you! You want people to know that you believe in her!"

"Yes; but I want also to do what I can to keep such good tenants. Therefore I must add a room or two to your house, that there may be good accommodation for you all."

"You make thanks impossible, ma'am! I will speak to Dawtie about it. I know she will be glad not to leave you! I will take care not to trouble the house."

338

"You shall do just as Dawtie and you please. Where Dawtie is, there will be room for you!"

Already Alexa's pain had grown quite bearable.

Dawtie needed no persuading. She was so rich in the possession of Andrew that she could go a hundred years without seeing him, she said. It was only that he would come and see her, instead of her going to see him!

In ten days they were married at her father's cottage. Her father and mother then accompanied her and Andrew to the Knowe, to dine with Andrew's father and mother. In the evening the new pair went out for a walk in the old fields.

"It seems, Dawtie, as if God was here!" said Andrew.

"I would fain see him, Andrew! I would rather you went out than God!"

"Suppose he was nowhere, Dawtie?"

"If God werena in you, ye wadna be what ye are to yer ignorant Dawtie, Andrew! She needs her Father in h'aven sairer nor her Andrew! But I'm sayin' things sae true 'at it's jist silly to say them! Eh, it's like h'aven itsel' to be oot o' that prison, an' walkin' aboot wi' you! God has gien me a' thing!—jist a' thing, Andrew!"

"God was wi' ye i' the prison, Dawtie!"

"Ay! But I like better to be wi' Him here!"

"An' ye may be sure He likes better to ha'e ye here!" rejoined Andrew.

CHAPTER XXXVI. AGAIN THE GOBLET.

The next day Alexa set Dawtie to search the house yet again for the missing goblet.

"It must be somewhere!" she said. "We are beset with an absolute contradiction: the thing can't be in the house! and it must be in the house!"

"If we do find it," returned Dawtie, "folk'll say them 'at could hide could weel seek! I s' luik naegait wantin' you, mem!"

The study was bare of books, and the empty shelves gave no hint of concealment They stood in its dreariness looking vaguely round them.

"Did it ever come to ye, mem," said Dawtie, "that a minute or twa passed between Mr. Crawford comin' doon the stair wi' you, and me gaein' up to the maister? When I gaed intil the room, he lay pantin' i' the bed; but as I broodit upo' ilka thing alane i' the prison, he cam afore me, there i' the bed, as gien he had gotten oot o' 't, and hidden awa' the cup, and was jist gotten intil't again, the same moment I cam in."

"Dying people will do strange things!" rejoined her mistress. "But it brings us no nearer the cup!"

"The surer we are, the better we'll seek!" said Dawtie.

They began, and went over the room thoroughly—looking everywhere they could think of. They had all but given it up to go on elsewhere, when Dawtie, standing again in the middle and looking about in a sort of unconscious hopelessness, found her eyes on the mantel-shelf, and went and laid her hand upon it. It was of wood, and she fancied it a little loose, but she could not move it.

"When Andrew comes we'll get him to examine it!" said Alexa.

He came in the evening, and Alexa told him what they had been doing. She begged him to get tools, and see whether there was not a space under the mantel-shelf. But Andrew, accustomed to ponder contrivances with Sandy, would have a good look at it first He came presently upon a clever little spring, pressing which he could lift the shelf: there under it, sure enough, in rich response to the candle he held, flashed the gems of the curiously wrought chalice of gold! Alexa gave a cry, Andrew drew a deep breath, Dawtie laughed like a child. How they gazed on it, passed it from one to the other, pored over the gems, and over the raised work that inclosed them, I need not tell. They began to talk about what was to be done with it.

"We will send it to the earl!" said Alexa.

"No," said Andrew; "that would be to make ourselves judges in the case! Your father must have paid money for it; he gave it to Mr. Crawford, and Mr. Crawford must not be robbed!"

"Stop, Andrew!" said Alexa. "Everything in the next room was left to my cousin, with the library in this; whatever else was left him was individually described. The cup was not in the next room, and was not mentioned. Providence has left us to do with it as we may judge right. I think it ought to be taken to Borland Hall—and by Dawtie."

"Well! She will mention that your father bought it?"

"I will not take a shilling for it!"

"Is not that because you are not quite sure you have the right to dispose of it?"

"I would not take the price of it if my father had left the cup expressly to me!"

"Had he done so, you would have a right to what he paid for it. To give the earl the choice of securing it, would be a service rendered him. If he were too poor to buy it, the thing would have to be considered."

"Nothing could make me touch money for it. George would never doubt we had concealed it in order to trick him out of it!"

"He will think so all the same. It will satisfy him, and not a few beside, that Dawtie ought to have been convicted. The thing is certainly Mr. Crawford's—that is, his as not yours. Your father undoubtedly meant him to have the cup; and God would not have you, even to serve the right, take advantage of an accident. Whatever ought to be done with the cup, Mr. Crawford ought to do it; it is his business to do right in regard to it; and whatever advantage may be gained by doing right, Mr. Crawford ought to have the chance of gaining it. Would you deprive him of the opportunity, to which at least he has a right, of doing justice, and delivering his soul?"

"You would have us tell the earl that his cup is found, but Mr. Crawford claims it?" said Alexa.

"Andrew would have us take it to Mr. Crawford," said Dawtie, "and tell him that the earl has a claim to it."

"Tell him also," said Andrew, "where it was found, showing he has no legal right to it; and tell him he has no more moral right to it than the laird could give him. Tell him, ma'am," continued Andrew, "that you expect him to take it to the earl, that he may buy it if he will; and say that if, after a fortnight, you find it is not in the earl's possession, you will yourself ascertain from him whether the offer has been made him."

"That is just right," said Alexa.

And so the thing was done. The cup is now in the earl's collection, and without any further interference on her part.

A few days after she and Dawtie carried the cup to Crawford, a parcel arrived at Potlurg, containing a beautiful silver case, and inside the case the jeweled watch—with a letter from George, begging Alexa to accept his present, and assuring her of his conviction that the moment he annoyed her with any further petition, she would return it. He expressed his regret that he had brought such suffering upon Dawtie, and said he was ready to make whatever amends her husband might think fit.

Alexa accepted the watch, and wore it. She thought her father would like her to do so.

342

CHAPTER XXXVII. THE HOUR BEFORE DAWN.

The friendship of the three was never broken. I will not say that, as she lay awake in the dark, the eyes of Alexa never renewed the tears of that autumn night on which she turned her back upon the pride of self, but her tears were never those of bitterness, of self-scorn, or of self-pity.

"If I am to be pitied," she would say to herself, "let the Lord pity me! I am not ashamed, and will not be sorry. I have nothing to resent; no one has wronged me."

Andrew died in middle age. His wife said the Master wanted him for something nobody else could do, or He would not have taken him from her. She wept and took comfort, for she lived in expectation.

One night when she and Alexa were sitting together at Potlurg, about a month after his burial, speaking of many things with the freedom of a long and tried love, Alexa said, after a pause of some duration:

"Were you not very angry with me then, Dawtie?"

"When, ma'am?"

"When Andrew told you."

"Told me what, ma'am? I must be stupid to-night, for I can't think what you mean."

"When he told you I wanted him, not knowing he was yours."

"I ken naething o' what ye're mintin' at, mem," persisted Dawtie, in a tone of bewilderment.

"Oh! I thought you had no secrets from one another."

"I don't know that we ever had—except things in his books that he said were God's secrets, which I should understand some day, for God was telling them as fast as He could get his children to understand them."

"I see," sighed Alexa; "you were made for each other. But this is my secret, and I have the right to tell it. He kept it for me to tell you. I thought all the time you knew it."

"I don't want to know anything Andrew would not tell me."

"He thought it was my secret, you see, not his, and that was why he did not tell you."

"Of coarse, ma'am. Andrew always did what was right."

"Well, then, Dawtie—I offered to be his wife if he would have me."

"And what did he say?" asked Dawtie, with the composure of one listening to a story learned from a book.

"He told me he couldn't. But I'm not sure what he said. The words went away."

"When was it he asked you?" said Dawtie, sunk in thought.

"The night but one before the trial," answered Alexa.

"He micht hae ta'en you, then, i'stead o' me—a lady an' a'. Oh, mem! do you think he took me 'cause I was in trouble? He micht hae been laird himsel'."

"Dawtie! Dawtie!" cried Alexa. "If you think that would have weighed with Andrew, I ought to have been his wife, for I know him better than you."

Dawtie smiled at that.

"But I do know, mem," she said, "that Andrew was fit to cast the lairdship frae him to comfort ony puir lassie. I would ha' lo'ed him a' the same."

"As I have done, Dawtie," said Alexa, solemnly. "But he wouldn't have thrown me away for you, if he hadn't loved you, Dawtie. Be sure of that. He might have made nothing of the lairdship, but he wouldn't have made nothing of me."

"That's true, mem. I dinna doobt it."

344

"I love him still—and you mustn't mind me saying it, Dawtie. There are ways of loving that are good, though there be some pain in them. Thank God, we have our children to look after. You will let me say our children, won't you, Dawtie?"

Some thought Alexa hard, some thought her cold, but the few that knew her knew she was neither; and some of my readers will grant that such a friend as Andrew was better than such a husband as George.

THE END.

About Author

Elizabeth Yates wrote of Sir Gibbie, "It moved me the way books did when, as a child, the great gates of literature began to open and first encounters with noble thoughts and utterances were unspeakably thrilling."

Even Mark Twain, who initially disliked MacDonald, became friends with him, and there is some evidence that Twain was influenced by him. The Christian author Oswald Chambers wrote in his "Christian Disciplines" that "it is a striking indication of the trend and shallowness of the modern reading public that George MacDonald's books have been so neglected".

Early life

George MacDonald was born on 10 December 1824 at Huntly, Aberdeenshire, Scotland. His father, a farmer, was one of the MacDonalds of Glen Coe and a direct descendant of one of the families that suffered in the massacre of 1692.

MacDonald grew up in an unusually literate environment: one of his maternal uncles was a notable Celtic scholar, editor of the Gaelic Highland Dictionary and collector of fairy tales and Celtic poetry. His paternal grandfather had supported the publication of an Ossian edition, the controversial Celtic text believed by some to have contributed to the starting of European Romanticism. MacDonald's step-uncle was a Shakespeare scholar, and his paternal cousin another Celtic academic. Both his parents were readers, his father harbouring predilections for Newton, Burns, Cowper, Chalmers, Coleridge, and Darwin, to quote a few, while his mother had received a classical education which included multiple languages.

An account cited how the young George suffered lapses in health in his early years and was subject to problems with his lungs such as asthma, bronchitis and even a bout of tuberculosis. This last illness was considered a family disease and two of MacDonald's brothers, his mother, and later three of his own children actually died from the ailment. Even in his adult life, he was constantly travelling in search of purer air for his lungs.

MacDonald grew up in the Congregational Church, with an atmosphere of Calvinism. However, his family was atypical, with his paternal grandfather a Catholic-born, fiddle-playing, Presbyterian elder; his paternal grandmother an Independent church rebel; his mother was a sister to the Gallic-speaking radical who became moderator of the disrupting Free Church, while his step-mother, to whom he was also very close, was the daughter of a Scottish Episcopalian priest.

MacDonald graduated from the University of Aberdeen in 1845 with a master's degree in chemistry and physics. He spent the next several years struggling with matters of faith and deciding what to do with his life. His son, biographer Greville MacDonald stated that his father could have pursued a career in the medical field but he speculated that lack of money put an end to this prospect. It was only in 1848 when MacDonald began theological training at Highbury College for the Congregational ministry.

Early career

MacDonald was appointed minister of Trinity Congregational Church, Arundel, in 1850, after briefly serving as a locum minister in Ireland. However, his sermons—which preached God's universal love and that everyone was capable of redemption —met with little favour and his salary was cut in half. In May 1853, MacDonald tendered his resignation from his pastoral duties at Arundel. Later he was engaged in ministerial work in Manchester, leaving that because of poor health. An account cited the role of Lady Byron in convincing MacDonald to travel to Algiers in 1856 with the hope that the sojourn would help turn his health around. When he got back, he settled in London and taught for some time at the University of London. MacDonald was also for a time editor of Good Words for the Young.

Writing Career

MacDonald's first novel David Elginbrod was published in 1863.

George MacDonald is often regarded as the founding father of modern fantasy writing. George MacDonald's best-known works are Phantastes, The Princess and the Goblin, At the Back of the North Wind, and Lilith (1895), all fantasy novels, and fairy tales such as "The Light Princess", "The Golden Key", and "The Wise Woman". "I write, not for children," he wrote, "but for the child-like, whether they be of five, or fifty, or seventy-five." MacDonald also published some volumes of sermons, the pulpit not having proved an unreservedly successful venue.

After his literary success, MacDonald went on to do a lecture tour in the United States in 1872–1873, after being invited to do so by a lecture company, the Boston Lyceum Bureau. On the tour, MacDonald lectured about other poets such as Robert Burns, Shakespeare, and Tom Hood. He performed this lecture to great acclaim, speaking in Boston to crowds in the neighborhood of three thousand people.

MacDonald served as a mentor to Lewis Carroll (the pen-name of Charles Lutwidge Dodgson); it was MacDonald's advice, and the enthusiastic reception of Alice by MacDonald's many sons and daughters, that convinced Carroll to submit Alice for publication. Carroll, one of the finest Victorian photographers, also created photographic portraits of several of the MacDonald children. MacDonald was also friends with John Ruskin, and served as a go-between in Ruskin's long courtship with Rose La Touche. While in America he was befriended by Longfellow and Walt Whitman.

MacDonald's use of fantasy as a literary medium for exploring the human condition greatly influenced a generation of notable authors, including C. S. Lewis, who featured him as a character in his The Great Divorce. In his introduction to his MacDonald anthology, Lewis speaks highly of MacDonald's views:

This collection, as I have said, was designed not to revive MacDonald's literary reputation but to spread his religious teaching. Hence most of my extracts are taken from the three volumes of Unspoken Sermons. My own debt to this book is almost as great as one man can owe to another: and nearly all serious inquirers to whom I have introduced it acknowledge that it has given them great help—sometimes indispensable help toward the very acceptance of the Christian faith. ...

I know hardly any other writer who seems to be closer, or more continually close, to the Spirit of Christ Himself. Hence his Christ-like union of tenderness and severity. Nowhere else outside the New Testament have I found terror and comfort so intertwined. ...

In making this collection I was discharging a debt of justice. I have never concealed the fact that I regarded him as my master; indeed I fancy I have never written a book in which I did not quote from him. But it has not seemed to me that those who have received my books kindly take even now sufficient notice of the affiliation. Honesty drives me to emphasize it.

Others he influenced include J. R. R. Tolkien and Madeleine L'Engle. MacDonald's non-fantasy novels, such as Alec Forbes, had their influence as well; they were among the first realistic Scottish novels, and as such MacDonald has been credited with founding the "kailyard school" of Scottish writing.

Chesterton cited The Princess and the Goblin as a book that had "made a difference to my whole existence", in showing "how near both the best and the worst things are to us from the first... and making all the ordinary staircases and doors and windows into magical things."

Later life

In 1877 he was given a civil list pension. From 1879 he and his family moved to Bordighera, in a place much loved by British expatriates, the Riviera dei Fiori in Liguria, Italy, almost on the French border. In that locality there also was an Anglican church, All Saints, which he attended. Deeply enamoured of the Riviera, he spent 20 years there, writing almost half of his whole literary production, especially the fantasy work. MacDonald founded a literary studio in that Ligurian town, naming it Casa Coraggio (Bravery House). It soon became one of the most renowned cultural centres of that period, well attended by British and Italian travellers, and by locals, with presentations of classic plays and readings of Dante and Shakespeare often being held.

In 1900 he moved into St George's Wood, Haslemere, a house designed for him by his son, Robert, its building overseen by his eldest son, Greville.

George MacDonald died on 18 September 1905 in Ashtead, Surrey, England. He was cremated in Woking, Surrey, England and his ashes were buried in Bordighera, in the English cemetery, along with his wife Louisa and daughters Lilia and Grace.

Personal life

MacDonald married Louisa Powell in Hackney in 1851, with whom he raised a family of eleven children: Lilia Scott (1852), Mary Josephine (1853-1878), Caroline Grace (1854), Greville Matheson (1856-1944), Irene (1857), Winifred Louise (1858), Ronald (1860–1933), Robert Falconer (1862–1913), Maurice (1864), Bernard Powell (1865–1928), and George Mackay (1867–1909?).

His son Greville became a noted medical specialist, a pioneer of the Peasant Arts movement, wrote numerous fairy tales for children, and ensured that new editions of his father's works were published. Another son, Ronald, became a novelist. His daughter Mary was engaged to the artist Edward Robert Hughes until her death in 1878. Ronald's son, Philip MacDonald (George MacDonald's grandson), became a Hollywood screenwriter.

Tuberculosis caused the death of several family members, including Lilia, Mary Josephine, Grace, Maurice as well as one granddaughter and a daughter-in-law. MacDonald was said to have been particularly affected by the death of Lilia, her eldest.

Theology

According to biographer William Raeper, MacDonald's theology "celebrated the rediscovery of God as Father, and sought to encourage an intuitive response to God and Christ through quickening his readers' spirits in their reading of the Bible and their perception of nature."

MacDonald's oft-mentioned universalism is not the idea that everyone will automatically be saved, but is closer to Gregory of Nyssa in the view that all will ultimately repent and be restored to God.

MacDonald appears to have never felt comfortable with some aspects of Calvinist doctrine, feeling that its principles were inherently "unfair"; when the doctrine of predestination was first explained to him, he burst into tears (although assured that he was one of the elect). Later novels, such as Robert Falconer and Lilith, show a distaste for the idea that God's electing love is limited to some and denied to others.

Chesterton noted that only a man who had "escaped" Calvinism could say that God is easy to please and hard to satisfy.

MacDonald rejected the doctrine of penal substitutionary atonement as developed by John Calvin, which argues that Christ has taken the place of sinners and is punished by the wrath of God in their place, believing that in turn it raised serious questions about the character and nature of God. Instead, he taught that Christ had come to save people from their sins, and not from a Divine penalty for their sins: the problem was not the need to appease a wrathful God, but the disease of cosmic evil itself. MacDonald frequently described the atonement in terms similar to the Christus Victor theory. MacDonald posed the rhetorical question, "Did he not foil and slay evil by letting all the waves and billows of its horrid sea break upon him, go over him, and die without rebound—spend their rage, fall defeated, and cease? Verily, he made atonement!"

MacDonald was convinced that God does not punish except to amend, and that the sole end of His greatest anger is the amelioration of the guilty. As the doctor uses fire and steel in certain deep-seated diseases, so God may use hell-fire if necessary to heal the hardened sinner. MacDonald declared, "I believe that no hell will be lacking which would help the just mercy of God to redeem his children." MacDonald posed the rhetorical question, "When we say that God is Love, do we teach men that their fear of Him is groundless?" He replied, "No. As much as they were will come upon them, possibly far more. ... The wrath will consume what they call themselves; so that the selves God made shall appear."

However, true repentance, in the sense of freely chosen moral growth, is essential to this process, and, in MacDonald's optimistic view, inevitable for all beings (see universal reconciliation).

MacDonald states his theological views most distinctly in the sermon "Justice", found in the third volume of Unspoken Sermons. (Source: Wikipedia)

CPSIA information can be obtained
at www.ICGtesting.com
Printed in the USA
LVHW090831211019
634812LV00003B/310/P